He glared at me, like I was an itch he couldn't quite get at to scratch.

"Just so you know where you stand," he said. "My niece reckons you saved her life, so we owe you. But the less I see of you the better, and the same goes for the rest of us. When we want you, we'll send the boy for you. The rest of the time, be somewhere else. Got that?"

"Loud and clear," I said.

"Grand. Never sit with us at prayers or meals or anything ever again."

"Understood."

"And polish your shoes occasionally, for crying out loud. We aren't forking out for new ones."

I nodded.

"That's all right, then. What did you say your name was?"

"Felix. It's Robur for lucky."

He grinned. "Good name for you," he said. "Now piss off."

BY K. J. PARKER

The Fencer Trilogy
Colours in the Steel
The Belly of the Bow
The Proof House

The Scavenger Trilogy
Shadow
Pattern
Memory

The Engineer Trilogy
Devices and Desires
Evil for Evil
The Escapement

The Company

The Folding Knife

The Hammer

Sharps

The Two of Swords:
Volume One

The Two of Swords:
Volume Two

The Two of Swords:
Volume Three

Sixteen Ways to Defend
a Walled City

How to Rule an Empire
and Get Away With It

A Practical Guide to
Conquering the World

BY TOM HOLT

Expecting
Someone Taller

Who's Afraid
of Beowulf?

Flying Dutch

Ye Gods!

Overtime

Here Comes the Sun

Grailblazers

Faust Among Equals

Odds and Gods

Djinn Rummy

My Hero

Paint Your Dragon

Open Sesame

Wish You Were Here

Only Human

Snow White and the
Seven Samurai

Valhalla

Nothing But Blue Skies

Falling Sideways

Little People

The Portable Door

In Your Dreams

Earth, Air, Fire
and Custard

You Don't Have to Be
Evil to Work Here,
But It Helps

Someone Like Me

Barking

The Better Mousetrap

May Contain
Traces of Magic

Blonde Bombshell

Life, Liberty, and the
Pursuit of Sausages

Doughnut

When It's A Jar

The Outsorcerer's
Apprentice

The Good, the Bad
and the Smug

The Management Style
of the Supreme Beings

An Orc on
the Wild Side

Dead
Funny: Omnibus 1

Mightier Than the
Sword: Omnibus 2

The Divine
Comedies: Omnibus 3

For Two Nights
Only: Omnibus 4

Tall Stories: Omnibus 5

Saints and
Sinners: Omnibus 6

Fishy
Wishes: Omnibus 7

The Walled Orchard

Alexander at the
World's End

Olympiad

A Song for Nero

Meadowland

I, Margaret

Lucia Triumphant

Lucia in Wartime

A PRACTICAL GUIDE TO CONQUERING THE WORLD

K. J. PARKER

orbitbooks.net

Copyright © 2022 by One Reluctant Lemming Company Ltd.
Excerpt from *Brother Red* copyright © 2021 by Adrian Selby
Excerpt from *Engines of Empire* copyright © 2022 by R. S. Ford

Cover design by Lauren Panepinto
Cover images by Shutterstock
Cover copyright © 2022 by Hachette Book Group, Inc.

Orbit
Hachette Book Group
1290 Avenue of the Americas
New York, NY 10104
orbitbooks.net

First Edition: January 2022
Simultaneously published in Great Britain by Orbit

Orbit is an imprint of Hachette Book Group.
The Orbit name and logo are trademarks of Little, Brown Book Group Limited.

The publisher is not responsible for websites (or their content) that are not owned by the publisher.

The Hachette Speakers Bureau provides a wide range of authors for speaking events. To find out more, go to www.hachettespeakersbureau.com or call (866) 376-6591.

Library of Congress Control Number: 2021940496

ISBNs: 9780316498616 (trade paperback), 9780316498647 (ebook)

Printed in the United States of America

LSC-C

1 3 5 7 9 10 8 6 4 2

Constantiae constanter

1

My name is Felix. It means lucky: there's irony for you. This is the true history of the intended and unintended consequences of my life, the bad stuff I did on purpose, the good stuff that happened in spite of me.

It's unfortunate that I'm the main character in this story. I can see why everybody would want to hear about what I'm going to tell you – the most amazing thing that's happened in our lifetimes, quite possibly ever, the greatest story ever told – but me? I don't think so. I've found that people quite like me at first and can put up with me for a little while after that, but it's like they say in medicine, the dose makes the poison. Unfortunately, I come with the story. You want one, you're going to have to put up with the other. Sorry about that.

I was dreaming about – well, that stuff – when someone shook me and I woke up.

I'm not at my best when I've just been dragged out of sleep. I saw three soldiers, in armour and uniform. I thought, oh

God, they've come to arrest me, for my crime. Then I remembered, that was years ago and a very long way away, in another jurisdiction.

"You the translator?"

The sergeant spoke in barbarous Robur; in case he'd got the wrong man, presumably. "Yes, that's me," I replied in Echmen.

"Sorry to disturb you, sir," he lied, "but you're needed."

Someone had lit the lamp. I glanced over the sergeant's head at the window. "It's the middle of the night," I said. "Can't it wait?"

"No, sir."

The Echmen invented diplomatic immunity, so I guessed they probably wouldn't kill me if I refused. Nor, I suspected, would they go away. "Fine," I said. "Just give me a few minutes to get dressed, would you?"

"Sorry, sir. Our orders are, fetch you straight away."

I felt that little twist in my stomach. "Yes, all right, but would you please wait outside?"

"Sorry, sir."

I suppose he was used to arresting people, rather than escorting diplomats. I told myself it didn't matter, then threw back the sheets and hopped out of bed. I thought I'd managed to keep my back to him as I hauled myself into my trousers, but a sharp intake of breath told me I hadn't. I pulled on my shirt and turned to face him.

"What the hell happened to you?" he asked.

"Ready when you are," I said.

The Echmen are a remarkable people, and one of the areas in which they excel is architecture. Everything they build is as big, complicated and ornate as they can possibly manage, and the Imperial palace is, quite properly, the supreme expression of Echmen aesthetics. They say that they build to impress the gods; seen from the Portals of the Sunrise, therefore, a hundred miles over our heads, the palace is a dazzling fusion of geometry and art. At ground level, it's a rabbit warren. I know for a fact that from my garret in the lower west wing to the offices of the diplomatic service where I did most of my work was a hundred yards in a straight line, as measured by the divine dividers, but one thousand, eight hundred and forty-odd yards actual distance travelled; up stairs, along passages, down stairs, along more passages, through galleries, across cloisters, and every inch of the way decorated with the most bewilderingly lovely examples of abstract art. From my quarters to the cells underneath the Justice department is even shorter on paper and about twice as far on foot. Which gave me plenty of time to talk to my new friend the sergeant, something I really didn't want to do.

"Are you a—?" he asked. "You know."

Yes, I knew. But I deliberately misunderstood him. "Translator," I said. "Yes. Who am I going to see?"

"Sorry, sir, classified."

"I'm only asking," I said, "because if it's a language I don't know, we're all wasting our time."

"Dejauzi, sir."

Fine; I know Dejauzi, God only knows why. As far as anyone knows, Dejauzi speakers occupy about a third of the surface of the world, but since they're peaceful, they don't have anything anyone wants and they're too fast moving, fly and vicious to be harvestable as manpower, they're of very little interest to any of the three major governments. Actually, none of those three statements is true, but that's what everybody believes. I learned Dejauzi when I was convalescing, because there happened to be a Dejauzi grammar lying about. It's one of the easiest spoken languages in the world, with practically no irregular verbs.

Please note that I didn't use the word *dungeon*. That would be utterly misleading. The cells, which I'd never been to before, turned out to be characteristically Echmen: graceful, symmetrical, exquisitely proportioned rooms which happened to be used for storing criminals. I think the only difference between the cell I was shown into and my own apartment was the steel door and the fact that only the ceiling was decorated, with stunningly lovely mosaic.

Inside the cell, an Echmen official, standing holding a document, and a teenage female in Echmen court dress but with the unmistakeable Dejauzi hair and makeup, sitting on a sort of stone bench. The official scowled at my sergeant. "You took your time," he said.

"Sorry, sir." He apologised a lot, that sergeant, though I don't think he meant it.

"This him?"

"Sir."

The official nodded, and the sergeant retreated, standing in front of the door.

"Sorry to drag you out of bed," the official said. "But our man's sick. You know Dejauzi."

"Yes," I said.

"Good man. Right, read this to her in Dejauzi, and then you can go."

He handed me the document. It was written in that horrible Echmen law style they insist on using for official stuff, even though the characters are obsolete for everyday use; in effect, you have to know an additional eight thousand characters in order to make sense of it. Fortunately, I do.

I looked at the girl, who wasn't looking at me. Then I read her the document, which was her death warrant. When I'd finished, she looked up and scowled at me.

"Ask her if she's understood," the official said.

"Do you understand?" I asked her.

"Fuck off."

"She understands."

The official nodded. "Ask her if she wishes to make any legal representations."

So I did that. "Go fuck yourself," she said.

"Not at this time," I translated.

"And tell him to go fuck himself, too," she added.

"But she reserves the right to make representations at a later date."

The official grunted. "She'd better get a move on, then. Her head's coming off at dawn."

I turned back to her. "The arsehole says you're—"

"Yes, I know. I heard him."

"You can talk Echmen?"

"Better than you can, blueskin."

"Do you want me to get you a lawyer?"

"Go fuck yourself."

"Ah," I said, "would that that were possible. I'm sorry. I hope—" I tried to remember what little I knew about Dejauzida religion. "May the Great-Great watch over you," I said.

"Fuck the Great-Great. I'm Hus."

I bowed politely, then turned back to the official. "Can I have a word with you outside?" I said.

He looked surprised, but nodded. The sergeant stood aside to let us pass.

"What did she do?" I asked.

"Nothing. She's a hostage."

Ah. Hostage for good behaviour. The daughter of some chieftain, deposited with the Echmen as a guarantee on the signing of a treaty. If the treaty is broken, the hostage is killed.

"So the Hus have broken—"

"The Dejauzida."

"She's not Dejauzida, she's Hus."

He stared at me. "Are you sure?"

"That's what she says," I told him. "Also, she's got a blue lifelock in her hair, and the Dejauzida lifelock is green, and the tattoos on her face are the double peacock, which is Hus."

"You're sure about that."

"Yes," I said. "No Dejauzi would have the double peacock, it's taboo."

"Oh, for crying out loud. You're *sure*."

"I've got a book you can borrow, if it'd help."

He didn't tell me what I could do with my book. He didn't have to. "You're coming with me," he said. "We've got to get this sorted out."

"Just a moment," I said. "I'm not an expert on tribal nomads, and I don't think my ambassador would want me getting involved in Echmen foreign affairs."

"Maybe you should have thought about that before you opened your big mouth," he replied, reasonably enough. "Come on, we've got a lot of work to do."

It was a long night. Half a dozen officials of escalating importance had to be hauled out of their beds, explained to and induced to sign and seal things, and all of them wanted to know what the blueskin had to do with anything; with just under an hour to go, the permanent assistant deputy something-or-other pulled a sad face and said it was a terrible shame but too late to do anything about it now; whereupon one of the other officials (by now we were trailing along a small army of sleep-deprived government officers, like someone driving geese to market) pointed out that if they executed a friendly hostage, they'd all be in the shit, and it turned out that there was just enough time after all. A stay of execution was drawn up and sealed, and they needed a translator to translate it . . .

"You again," she said.

"It's all right. There's been a mistake. You're not going to die after all."

She gave me a look I'll never forget. "Are you serious?"

"They thought you were the Dejauzi hostage. I explained that you're Hus. You are Hus, aren't you?"

"They made a *mistake*."

"Yes, but it's all sorted out now. You are Hus, aren't you?"

"Of course I'm bloody Hus, what do you think these are, pimples? They threw me in here and told me they were going to kill me, and it's all a *mistake*. Oh for—"

"But it's all right now," I said. "It's all been—"

"No, it fucking isn't all right. I've been scared shitless. I've been sitting here all night thinking this is it, I'm going to die, and all because some *idiot*—"

Tears had cut deep channels in her chalk-white makeup. "I'm sorry," I said. "But it's all been sorted out, they're going to let you go. But first I've got to read this to you, or it won't be legal."

"You what?"

"Shut up," I said, "and let me read you this. Then you can go."

She took a long, deep breath. "Get on with it, then."

So I read her the document. "Do you understand?" I said.

"Of course I understand, what do you think I am, simple?"

"I need you to say you understand, it's a required formality."

"Go fuck yourself."

"You keep saying that," I said. "Thank you for your patience. Goodbye."

I turned to leave. "By the way," I told the official – the first one, who'd shared the whole wonderful experience with me, "she can understand Echmen perfectly, so you didn't need me after all."

He looked mildly stunned. "She didn't say."

"Did you ask?" I replied, and walked out of the cell.

Needless to say I got hopelessly lost trying to find my way back to my room, so my grand gesture turned round and bit me, the way grand gestures generally do. Even so.

Easy mistake to make. The Dejauzida and the Hus look identical, speak the same language and come from the same ethnic stock, but otherwise they're completely different. The Dejauzida worship the Great-Great, the Hus are fire-worshippers, like the Echmen (though I gather it's sort of a different fire). They hate each other like poison, as do the other twenty or so entirely distinct and separate nations that look just like the Dejauzida and speak the same language. Which is just as well for us, according to the monumental *Concerning the Savages*, our standard reference in the diplomatic service; because if they didn't, and they all got along like one big happy family instead of ripping each other's throats out at the slightest provocation, they'd be unstoppable and a real and present danger to civilisation.

There are a hell of a lot of them, that's for sure. Nobody knows quite how many; they certainly don't. They live in the badlands that run across the northern top end of all the three great empires, an area so vast that you can't really get your head around it. They don't read or write – don't rather than can't, please note; there's all sorts of things we do and they don't, which is why we tend to write them off as half-human savages. But, according to them, they don't do them because they don't want to, and they point to us and say, look what reading and writing and living in cities have turned you into, and we want no part of that. Well, it's a point of view.

But the practical upshot of that is, if you want to find out anything about them, you're entirely reliant on the testimony of outsiders, most of whom have agendas of their own. The Dejauzida don't come and visit us if they can possibly help it, so such evidence as there is derives from diplomatic missions – invariably unsuccessful – and the few half-witted traders who thought against all the evidence that it might be possible to sell things to them. Failure doesn't tend to make people well disposed towards those who thwarted them, and it's easy to explain your lack of success by saying that the people who didn't want to know are ignorant barbarians.

Some people can manage perfectly well on next to no sleep; not me. Also, like money, sleep is something I find hard to come by. By the time I eventually got back to my garret (up no less than eighty-seven winding stone stairs) I knew it was pointless going back to bed. I only had a couple of hours before I was due back on duty (the Echmen have these wonderful water clocks), and a night spent trudging up and down had left me sweaty and undiplomatically bedraggled. I plodded down the stairs to the cistern, washed off the worst of the sweat, then back up again to put on some respectable clothes and drag a comb through my hair.

Since I had a bit of time in hand, I made a detour to the clerks' office. It's a huge place. Once upon a time, the north wing of the palace was a monastery, staffed by a thousand monks, all praying for the souls of dead emperors. What's now the clerks' room used to be the monks' dormitory, and even so the clerks are cramped for space. The Echmen invented writing, and they're very fond of written records.

One of the thousand-odd clerks working there – only one – was a Lystragonian, and how he came to end up working for the Imperial secretariat must be a fascinating story, though I've never been able to drag it out of him. But he and I were the only Robur-speakers, below senior administrative level, in the whole of that vast complex, so we'd got into the habit of talking to each other.

The work ethic in the clerks' office isn't unbearably intense, so nobody minds if friends drop in and share a bowl of tea. My friend was happy to see me, since none of the Echmen clerks was prepared to talk to him. I told him about the amusing mix-up that nearly cost an innocent woman her life. Just to be on the safe side, I asked him could he possibly check the records and confirm that there was a Hus hostage on the books? Because if not, I'd just caused a monumental bog-up, and I'd need to explain myself to my ambassador before he heard all about it from the Echmen.

My friend pulled a face. "What's her name?"

"You know better than that."

"No, I don't. And I can't pull the file if I don't know the name."

I explained. The Dejauzida (including, in this instance, the Hus) have all sorts of weird taboos about names. You can't, for example, say the name of someone who's died; you have to use an elaborate periphrasis. Nor can you ask someone their name; nor can you tell someone yours. If you really want to know, you have to ask a member of the family (and not just any member; there's a rigid protocol, governed by family status and the name owner's position in the family hierarchy). Asking a princess her name would constitute an insult that could only be avenged in blood. "So I didn't ask."

"Fine," said my friend. "Only, like I said, that could make it difficult."

"Do you really think there's more than one Hus hostage in here at the moment?"

He scowled at me. "The list isn't cross-referenced by nationality," he said. "No name, I can't help you. Sorry."

Another apology for my collection. I shrugged. "Never mind," I said. "If I got it wrong, I'll find out soon enough when they throw me out of the service. Of course, I'll have to walk home, because they'll revoke my pass for the mail, but it's only a couple of thousand miles, and there's plenty of wear left in these sandals."

He rolled his eyes. "I'll see what I can do," he said.

"Just as well you don't have any real work to do."

"Drop dead, blueskin."

I glanced up at the water clock; I was on duty. I gave him my big smile and hurried up to our department, on the fifth floor of the North tower.

Our department consisted of the ambassador, his airhead

nephew, someone else's airhead nephew and me; just as well there was never anything for us to do, or it wouldn't have got done. Usually the ambassador didn't put in an appearance until the middle of the afternoon, so I was a bit taken aback to find him sitting behind the desk (we only had one) with a roll of parchment in his hands.

"Sorry I'm late," I said, and started telling him about my recent adventure. He wasn't listening. "Read this," he said, and handed me the parchment.

It was in Sashan; later, the ambassador told me his Sashan opposite number had given it to him to read, although strictly speaking it was classified, et cetera. It was a copy of a report from the Sashan embassy in Aelia – one of the milkface republics on the bottom edge of the Middle Sea that we never got round to conquering. It described how an army, so far unidentified, had lured the City garrison out into some forest and annihilated it, leaving the City itself completely defenceless; by the time you read this, the report said, the City will have fallen. Furthermore, the Sashan ambassador had heard reports, so far unconfirmed but from absolutely reliable sources, of an unknown but extremely powerful and well-equipped confederacy against the Robur, which was conquering and absorbing the provinces of our overseas empire at an extraordinary rate. Their declared intention was to exterminate the Robur down to the last man. If they continued their progress, said the report, it could only be a matter of weeks before the Robur empire and incidentally the Robur nation ceased to exist.

I glanced at the date on the top. The report was two months old.

I looked at the ambassador. His face was expressionless.

"It can't be true," I said.

He looked up at me. "When was the last time we heard from home?" he said.

"About two months. But that doesn't mean anything."

"I get a despatch every week," he said. "Or I'm supposed to. I've been writing home every day for the last month, asking what the hell's going on."

"The City can't fall," I said.

"It can if there's no one to defend it."

I looked at the report, but I couldn't make out the words; something in my eye. "It can't be true."

"You already said that."

"What are we going to do?"

He laughed. "I'm claiming political asylum," he said. "If that thing's true, I don't suppose I'll get it. If I were you, I'd make myself scarce. Get as far away as you can, and stay there." He jerked his head towards the door that connected the outer office to the cubbyhole where the nephews worked. "They're long gone," he said. "Don't tell me where you're going, I told them, that way I can't tell anyone else."

I stared at him. "Who are these people?"

He shrugged. "You know as much as I do," he said. "The Sashan don't know anything either. But they believe it. That's their man's idea of sportsmanship. Giving us a head start."

I put the parchment on the desk. "Who hates us that much?"

That got me a big grin. "Everybody," he said. "Don't you follow current affairs?"

I ran down the stairs and along the passages to the clerks' room. My friend the Lystragonian was at his desk, with his feet up, reading *The Mirror of Earthly Passion*.

"Her name," he yawned, "is She Stamps Them Flat. And, yes, she's Hus all right. You owe me."

I told him what I'd just heard. He stared at me. "That's not possible," he said.

"You haven't heard anything?"

He closed the book and put it down. "No, but I wouldn't have."

"Can you ask around?"

"Nobody talks to me, you know that. Still," he added, looking at me, "I'll see what I can do. Where will you be?"

Good question. Like I said, the Echmen are red hot on diplomatic immunity. Query, though; if a nation no longer exists, can it have diplomats? "The White Garden," I said. "They like me there."

So I went to the White Garden, though I didn't sit at my usual table. I chose a dark corner, next to the fire. There I spent possibly the worst hour of my life. And then the soldiers came for me.

"Nothing personal," the sergeant said, as he tied my hands behind my back. Not the same sergeant, probably just as well. "Try and hold still, we don't want any broken bones."

The Echmen have this wooden collar for putting round prisoners' necks. It's about the size of an infantry shield, with a hole in the middle for your neck, and hinges, and a padlock. It presses directly on your collarbone, and when you're wearing it you can't see your own feet. Wonderfully practical design, like everything the Echmen make. The sergeant wasn't inclined to chat, for which I was grateful.

The Echmen official I eventually got to see was an elderly man with a sad face. Yes, he said, as far as anyone knew the report was true. An Echmen agent had personally seen the ruins of five Robur cities on the east coast of the Friendly Sea, which was as far west as the Echmen were prepared to go, and his sources confirmed the Sashan account in every detail. As far as the Echmen were concerned, the Robur no longer existed.

"Apart from you," he added.

I looked at him.

"Your ambassador," he said, "applied for political asylum, which we felt unable to grant. He took his own life. Your two colleagues in the Robur mission are also dead. They made the mistake of letting themselves be seen in the streets. I gather that news of what happened has reached the public at large, and the Robur—" He gave me a sad smile. "They were never very popular with our people at the best of times."

I opened my mouth but nothing came out.

"I have received," he went on, "an official application from one of the other embassies, asking for you to be transferred to their staff as a translator. If you accept the post, you will of course enjoy full diplomatic privileges. I have absolutely no idea why they would want to do this. However, I should point out that if your diplomatic status lapses, you will class as an unregistered alien, and you will no longer enjoy the protection of the law." He paused and gave me the sort of look you really don't want, ever. "Do you want the job or not?"

"Yes."

He nodded to the sergeant, who came forward and unlocked that horrible collar and untied my hands. "In that case," he said, "I suggest you report to your new masters, before they change their minds."

"Of course," I said. "Who —?"

He told me. One damn thing after another.

*

"We have this really stupid tradition," she told me. "If someone saves your life, your soul belongs to them for nine consecutive reincarnations, unless you can save them back. Personally I think it's bullshit, but I guess you never know."

At least I knew her name, though it was more than my life was worth to say it. "Thank you," I said.

"Don't mention it. I think I'll give you to my uncle," she went on, "he collects rare and unique objects. Right now, from what I gather, a Robur's about as rare and unique as it's possible to get."

Rather than live in a world without Robur, my ambassador had killed himself – by drinking poison, I later found out; not just any poison, real connoisseur stuff. It's distilled from some incredibly scarce and valuable exotic flower, and you die entranced with the most gorgeous and wonderful visions, so that you feel yourself ascending bodily to heaven to the sound of harps and trumpets. On a translator's salary, however, it'd take me ten years saving up to buy enough to kill a chicken.

"I thought you wanted me as a translator," I said.

She nodded. "How many languages do you know?"

"I'm fluent in twelve," I said, "and I can get by in nine more."

Her eyes widened. "How many are there, for God's sake?"

"The official figure is seventy-six," I said, "but I think there's a lot more than that."

"And you know twenty-one of them. That's—"

"Twenty now, of course. I don't suppose Robur counts any more."

That just sort of slipped out. It got me a scowl.

She was short, even by Dejauzi standards; not fat exactly, more squat and stocky, with a square face and a flat, wide nose. She had big hands, almost like a man's. Like all Dejauzi, she'd plastered every square inch of exposed skin with brilliant white stuff (basically chalk dust and lard, with other bits and pieces in it to keep it from cracking and flaking); she wore her hair in a bun on top of her head, and it was dyed a purply blue, almost lavender. The peacocks reached from just under her eyes down to the line of her jaw; we call them tattoos but really they're scars, carved with a flake of sharp flint around the age of twelve. The scar tissue is picked out in five different colours of greasepaint and has to be done from scratch every morning, using a basin of water as a mirror. Incidentally, there are fourteen synonyms for handsome in Dejauzi, but no word meaning pretty. She was somewhere between twelve and fifteen; I'm hopeless at women's ages.

"We're a bit pushed for space," she said, "so you'll have to sleep in here. You won't mind that." Statement of fact, not a query. "I know it's not what you're used to, but I can't help that."

No chair in the room; nomads sit on the ground. The floor was covered in stupendous Echmen tiles, all the colours of the rainbow and harder than granite. "It'll be fine," I said.

I didn't sleep much that night. Partly because Her Majesty was in the room next door and she snored like someone killing pigs; partly because I had things on my mind. There was no window in the room, and just one little clay lamp, which soon burned out. It stank to high heaven of some kind of fat, so I didn't mind that.

I'll spare you a report of my mental turmoil and emotional anguish, though to be honest with you I was still in that just-been-kicked-in-the-head phase when you can't feel anything at all. I tried to make a list of all the things I'd been planning to do when I finished my tour of duty and went home, which I wouldn't be doing now – some bad, some good, I'll never do that or see them again versus I won't have to do that or see them, at any rate. I remember getting up off the floor and standing upright, shoulders back, head up, chin in, like the drill sergeant taught us; I thought, I'm still the same but from now on everything else is going to be completely different. It occurred to me that this universal-except-for-me change was bound to cause me problems; the logical thing, therefore, would be for me to change, too. How, exactly? Insufficient data for an informed decision. The ambassador had killed himself rather than face the humiliation of being someone else, and I could see a certain degree of merit in that approach. On the other hand, death isn't like the last ship east in autumn; if you miss it, you're stuck where you are for at least three months until the weather improves. Death is prepared to wait. It's always there for you, like your mother.

I am by nature a relatively cheerful person. I'm inherently frivolous. I like to find the humour in everything, like a mine-owner grinding up a whole mountain to extract one ounce of pure copper. In Blemya, so they tell me, there are little tiny birds which make their living picking fibres of meat out of the yawning jaws of crocodiles, and I think I'm probably one of them; the crocodiles being Life. I'm prepared to engage with the world – at any moment my head might get bitten off by it, but that's the risk you have to take – in order to extract a minuscule shred of something worth having. The alternative would be to curl up in a ball and never speak. That has its attractions, believe me, but I'm not quite ready for it yet. Tomorrow, maybe.

And what a laugh, what an absolute blast, life is, to be sure. Which is to say, life is a rock in which the veins of humour run deep. I'm talking about the sort of humour where somebody falls over or gets hit by something or finds a scorpion in his dish of noodles, the kind of stuff we all find hilarious. The humour-bearing quartz is the bedrock of our experience, on which we build our houses and cities, knowing full well that the ground beneath our feet is shot through with side-splitting possibilities for other people's mirth, like a ship's hull riddled with teredo worms. Comedy to observers, tragedy to participants; I consider myself an observer. I fly over my life like a migrating bird, and I only ever play for beans or counters, never for real money. I'm an accredited diplomat assigned to my own country, reporting back to Infinity; my embassy is a tiny patch of home soil in the middle of the alien nation where I happen to have been born and spent my entire life.

The hell with it. They can't hurt you unless you care, and I don't.

Fine words, which according to my mother butter no parsnips. In one pan of the scale, everything I'd ever known had been lost and destroyed, and I was quite possibly the only brown-skinned human being left on the face of the earth. In the other pan, a new life, scintillating new opportunities, a job (nobody had said anything about pay, but let's not push our luck) and a powerful friend at the royal court of what would presumably henceforth be my country. If you can meet with triumph and disaster, says Saloninus in the *Ballads*, and treat those two imposters just the same – disaster in one pan, triumph in the other, and the bit of cord from which the scale dangles is gripped between the podgy fingers of a fourteen-year-old with peacocks tattooed all over her face. Enough, surely, to make a cat laugh.

I don't say what I think. I translate what other people say. That's my job. Just as well, sometimes.

2

The Echmen, bless them, are a nation of early risers. They start the day off with the cheerful hammering of gongs and the raucous laughter of enormous bells, calling the faithful to prayer. At least, that's what they do in the cities. In the rural districts, I guess it's probably different; the head of the family staggers out of bed in the pitch dark and feebly rattles a cowbell or whacks a tin plate, I don't know. But anywhere with more than a dozen houses, the day starts with the most appalling racket, enough to make your teeth hurt.

Foreign diplomats aren't required to attend morning service, in the same way as there's no law explicitly forbidding you to fart when you're saying grace at a state banquet. Every quite-some-time-before-dawn for three years, I'd dragged myself into my clothes and stumbled out of the door towards the chapel. The ambassador, rest his soul, was always in his pew when I got there, immaculately turned out, sitting bolt upright and fast asleep with his eyes open. I could never quite summon up that much class. The nephews, on the other hand, slumped in their seats like piles of dirty washing from which someone had neglected to remove the contents. I nearly headed for what used to be our pew, and then I remembered. It also occurred to me that I didn't know where the Hus pew was. Still, I figured, a row of people with chalk-white faces tattooed with peacocks would be hard to miss. I was right.

There were nine of them, all sitting perfectly still with their eyes tight shut. Later I discovered that this was to avoid spiritual contamination. If they couldn't see the disgusting idols and the abominable priests in their loathsome vestments, they couldn't be defiled by them. I dropped in at the end of the row, next to a fat man. If he knew I was there, he gave no sign of it.

I rather like the Echmen liturgy. The music is slow and soothing. The chanted prayers are actually rather fine if you stop and listen to the words, and the actual theology is so mild and wishy-washy that you'd be hard put to it to be offended, even if you were a raving zealot. You don't join in except to mutter "So be it" at the ends of paragraphs. The artwork on the walls is, of course, bewilderingly beautiful. Morning prayers last two and a bit hours. If you have nothing urgent you ought to be doing, and no low-level diplomatic attaché ever has, it's a pleasant enough way to pass the time.

My neighbours (my new fellow countrymen, God help me) didn't seem to be enjoying it at all. It's really bad manners to look round during the service – you're supposed to sit there with your eyes fixed on either the altar flame or the priest's face from the moment you arrive until it's time to go – so I couldn't see what they were doing, but as soon as the priest started to recite the introductory prayer, the fat man next to me began to hum. I don't think it was a tune or even an attempt at one. It was just a noise designed to stop him hearing what the priest was saying. When there was a pause in the service, he stopped. When the priest started again, so did he.

Not good, I thought. The Echmen are refined, artistic, intellectual, spiritual, courteous to a fault and a whole bunch of other good things. Easy-going they are not. Yes, diplomatic immunity, they invented it and they abide by the spirit as well as the letter whenever conveniently possible, but there are limits. A fat, chalk-faced foreigner deliberately blotting out the Divine Word with off-key bee imitations had to be pretty close to those limits, and I was sitting next to him. For two pins I'd have got up and sat somewhere else, if not for the uncomfortable knowledge that these people – these *clowns* – were all that stood between me and death in a hail of stones and half-bricks. I got hit on the head by a stone once, as it happens. I was walking down the street and a carriage horse happened to flick up a loose cobble with its hooves, right between my eyes. I remember the pain to this day, an intolerable ache deep in the bone. Death by stoning would probably be even worse than that. I stayed where I was and tried to be invisible.

Two of the principal tenets of the Echmen faith are: love your neighbour and forgive your enemy. They're realistic enough to admit that these are things you should aspire to rather than actually do, but it's a noble ambition and one which, at that precise moment, I found absolutely impossible. I had no idea who my enemy was, only that he'd wiped out my entire race and left me dependent on the charity of my neighbour, who nobody could possibly love, not ever. I tried thinking about other things – summer meadows, horse racing, the Nine Basic Assumptions in Saloninus' *Ethics*, sheep jumping over a low wall – but I couldn't. My mind was completely occupied with the weird hybrid of Echmen plainsong and the fat man's humming. It was worse than barley straw down the back of your neck, and all I could do was sit there and suffer.

Finally, quite some time after I could tolerate no more, the priest recited the grace and led the minor clergy in procession into the nave, and we were free to go. I jumped up. A hand grabbed my wrist and dragged me down again as though I was gossamer. The fat man had opened his eyes and was looking at me.

I don't think he liked what he saw. "You the translator?"

"Yes."

"Oh, for crying out loud."

He carried on scowling at me, and his grip on my wrist was turning my fingers numb. I opened my mouth, then closed it again.

"Come on," he said. "I haven't got all day."

I call him the fat man because he was fat. Seriously fat. Huge.

The enlightened, sophisticated societies of the far north, where they seem to spend all their time writing snotty commentaries on each other's books, have recently started taking the view that if someone's fat, you shouldn't say so. Most definitely, you shouldn't frame any reference to a person's fatness in terms that might be construed as critical or disapproving. I have no quarrel with that. Sneering at people and making fun of the way they look may be a fundamental human instinct, but so are lust and smashing bones. We should aspire to be better than we were made. Fine.

The fat man, though, would've been livid if I were to try and play down his immense bulk. Among the Dejauzi, a race who often don't have quite enough to eat, being fat marks you out as superior. If so and so looks like a sixty-gallon barrel, he clearly knows where his next meal is coming from, therefore he must be rich and powerful, so be sure to do as he says and not piss him off. You can tell at a glance, and so unfortunate mistakes are pre-empted and don't happen. Affluent Dejauzi accordingly stuff themselves like geese in autumn, and those who aspire but lack the necessary means wear padded clothes and wrap sacking round their stomachs under their coats. Lots of the women and some of the men stuff their cheeks with pads of felt to get that pigs' chaps look, and they have these artfully designed collars worn under a scarf that give you an instant double chin. The doorposts of Dejauzi tents are set much wider apart than they need to be, to create a subliminal impression of the owner's girth, and their chairs are massive, to support their owners' notional weight. Like the supercilious northerners, like all of us, the Dejauzi aspire to be better than they were made. In their case, quality is directly equated with quantity. There's a sort of logic, I suppose.

As a translator, I don't make judgements. They get in the way of the translation, leading to inaccuracy and error. For me, it's a matter of equivalences of meaning. If, in their mental language, the word for beautiful is fat, that's not something to pass judgement on. I just take note of it for future reference. My own opinion on the matter, if I have one, is of no use to anyone, particularly me, so screw it.

"My niece," said the fat man, "has given you to me."

"Ah."

He scowled at me. "Eat much?"

"Excuse me?"

"Do you eat much?"

"No, not really."

He nodded. I'd given the correct answer. He peered at me. "Those clothes ought to last a good while longer, if you take care of them. What do you do, hang them up at night?"

"Actually, I put them under the mattress."

He was staring at my shoes. "Years of wear left in those," he said. "Show me the soles."

I showed him. "Excuse me," I said.

"We don't use coined money," he said, ignoring me, "so you won't get paid. Daily allowance is a bowl of rice, two wheat flatbreads, two ounces of cheese and either grapes or an apple." He hesitated. "There's beer if you want it, but I don't think you'd like it. Probably not to your taste. You can sleep on the floor in the little round room we don't use. Got a blanket?"

"Yes."

He nodded again, more slowly this time. "We all speak Echmen," he said. "I speak Sashan and Rosinholet, and one of the others knows Vesani, so we don't actually need you for anything."

"I see."

He frowned. "But," he said, "we think it's not a bad idea to pretend we can't understand what the fuckers are saying, even though we can, so we'll have you along to sit in on meetings and do your stuff. At the moment, they provide the translators, so we can say we don't trust their translators any more, so we've got one of our own. Scores a point, you see. It's all about scoring points with these arseholes."

"Got you."

He sighed. "I never did like the Robur much," he said, "and now you're all dead it doesn't bother me at all. The world's a better place without you, in my opinion."

"Noted," I said.

He glared at me, like I was an itch he couldn't quite get at to scratch. "Just so you know where you stand," he said. "My niece reckons you saved her life, so we owe you. But the less I see of you the better, and the same goes for the rest of us. When we want you, we'll send the boy for you. The rest of the time, be somewhere else. Got that?"

"Loud and clear," I said.

"Grand. Never sit with us at prayers or meals or anything ever again."

"Understood."

"And polish your shoes occasionally, for crying out loud. We aren't forking out for new ones."

I nodded.

"That's all right, then. What did you say your name was?"

"Felix. It's Robur for lucky."

He grinned. "Good name for you," he said. "Now piss off."

I went back to my room – my old room – and found it empty.

A bit upsetting. All my books had been there, not to mention my clothes and the few but precious bits and pieces I'd brought from home, including the thing I loved most in all the world, my bow.

I could understand the logic; Echmen logic, the finest in the world, naturally. Since the Robur nation no longer existed, it couldn't have diplomatic representatives, just as you can't have a shadow of something that isn't there. Accordingly, the room I used to occupy was an unoccupied room, and anything it contained belonged to nobody. All ownerless property in the empire belongs to the emperor. In practice, since his divine majesty can only cope with so much stuff, surplus property is sold at auction and the proceeds accrue to the Treasury. I went to see Oio, my Lystragonian pal, who wasn't pleased to see me.

"Go away," he said.

"As soon as you've told me something."

He pulled a face. "You just don't get it, do you? You're a non-person. I really don't need to be seen with you."

"Fine," I said. "The sooner you get rid of me the better."

I felt sorry for him. "What?" he said.

"All my stuff's gone into the next auction," I said. "If you get it back for me, I'll never speak to you again."

"I can't do that."

"Fine," I said. "In that case, tell me when the auction's going to be, and I'll go and buy it back. Only I haven't got any money, so you'll have to lend me some."

He closed his eyes. He hadn't done anything wrong, and everything was turning out to be his fault. "I know where they keep the list of confiscated property," he said. "I'll see what I can do. But that's it. If you show up here ever again, I'll call the guards."

I smiled at him. "It was a pleasure knowing you," I said.

"Piss off and die."

The bow was worth it, though. I don't suppose you're remotely interested, so I won't bore you with the details. No, actually, I will. However, I won't be offended if you skip the next inch or so. Cast your eye down the page and start reading again at *after that I went* below . . .

My bow is a one hundred and fifteen-pound draw weight composite with a maple core, gazelle-horn belly and wild ass backstrap sinew back. The ears are sharply reflexed sugar maple, with bone bridges. The string is twenty plies of silk, pre-stretched, with linen serving at the nock and loops. At fifty-six inches nock to nock it's longer than is strictly fashionable these days, but I like the extra length for accuracy, stability and docility of release; it sends a six hundred grain arrow two hundred yards plus, but without shaking you to bits in the process, and I can actually hit things with it. It'll draw thirty-one inches without complaining, and once you've got the knack it's no bother to string. If you haven't got the knack it'll jump up and knock your eye out, but that means people aren't keen to borrow it, which in my opinion is a bonus. Unstrung, it bends back so much the other way that the ears touch – practically a perfect circle. I had it made for me by the third best bowyer in the City, after I got an unexpected legacy when I was nineteen. He told me when I went to pick it up that he'd never had a more demanding, irritating, nit-picking customer in thirty years in the trade. I took that as a compliment.

I could tell you loads more about it if I wanted to – the smoothness of its draw, the complete absence of stack, its superior cast, which I attribute to the ear geometry – but I won't. Why should I? You've never done me any harm. Suffice to say, it's the only nice thing I've ever owned, my only encounter with Perfection. My family were furious with me for spending all that money on what was basically a toy, but I didn't care. As far as I was concerned, they'd missed the point. I caused that utterly perfect object to be brought into existence, it was joined to me by a love that can't be crammed into mere words, and I wanted it back. Enough, I think, said.

After that, I went and found the room the fat man had told me about, where I'd be sleeping. I knew what to look for and where I'd find it as soon as he told me the room was round and they didn't use it. The Hus had their quarters at the far end of the North wing of the palace, just underneath the watchtower, so the floor above their room would inevitably be round. And they didn't use it because it's the garderobe. In case you're not familiar with Echmen military architecture, a garderobe is where you go to pee. There's a channel in the floor that leads to a pipe through the wall.

The first thing I saw was my bow. It was on the garderobe floor, in a silk bag, with a note pinned to it; a release docket from the Treasurer's Office, explaining that the enclosed item had been confiscated in error by the Treasurer's bailiff under the impression that it was the personal property of a member of the now disaccredited Robur delegation. The truth having emerged – that it had been intended as a diplomatic gift from the Robur emperor to the Hus, but had subsequently been misappropriated by a junior member of the Robur mission – the Treasurer was pleased to return it to its intended recipients, with apologies for any inconvenience. The docket was beautifully inscribed in authentic civil service calligraphy and sealed with what was almost certainly the Treasury seal, except that some fool had pressed it into the hot wax twice, so some of the details were a bit smudged. The rest of my stuff was nowhere to be seen, but you can't have everything. Having just one thing is enough, if it's something perfect.

Oio is short for Oionoisi de'Pasi. I believe the de'Pasi clan are a big noise in southern Lystragonia. If so, it was unfortunate for Oio, since the Lystragonians are firm believers in noblesse oblige. Lystragonia is a horrible place where it's always blisteringly hot. The humidity is murder. For a third of the year it rains incessantly, and for two-thirds it doesn't rain at all.

Lystragonia is mostly heavily forested mountains. In most of the country you can't grow crops or herd animals, so the Lystragonians live by trade. They have only two exports. One of them is the tailfeathers of certain huge, incredibly colourful birds, once plentiful but now for some reason getting scarce and fiendishly hard to catch. The other export of Lystragonia is Lystragonians. Twice a year, they round up about a thousand of their best and brightest young men and women and exchange them for seven thousand fifty-gallon jars of barley flour. This, as far as they're concerned, is a good deal, since the alternative is mass starvation. They've been doing it for quite some time and they've got it organised down to the last detail. There's no dodging the draft, no matter how noble and influential your clan happens to be; but better-off families educate their first-born so they'll end up as clerks and scribes rather than fieldhands or coalminers. An educated Lystragonian is therefore very educated indeed, and Oio was smart and erudite, even for a Lystragonian. As a result, he ended up at the Echmen Imperial court, where he's spent the last five years making himself indispensable. He's a year younger than me; a big man, almost as tall and broad as a Robur, with sand-coloured skin, curly red hair, blue eyes and freckles.

Oio is my friend. He didn't want to be. He doesn't like my name – Felix, meaning lucky.

Lystragonians have strong views about luck. They figure that lucky people crash through a basically unlucky world like the bows of a ship, drenching bystanders with a wake of corrosive misfortune, and are therefore best shunned as sources of danger and grief. I point out that I'm incredibly unlucky; if I wasn't, I wouldn't be here in this mess. He says that in order to have encountered all the bad luck I've run into and sliced through and still be alive, I must be the luckiest man going, and therefore a clear and present danger to all those around me. Accordingly, he'd have preferred to avoid me like the plague. Circumstances conspired, however, to make us true friends, grappled to each other's souls with hoops of steel, whether either of us liked it or not (tell you about that some time). *Circumstances conspired* is, of course, just another way of saying luck, so I guess he and the Lystragonians are probably right. Like it matters.

"You promised me," he said. "You promised me I'd never see you again, in this world or the next. You lied to me."

I like Oio. "Just one little favour," I said, "and then I'll leave you alone. Really."

"What?"

"I need a library pass."

He gazed at me with something approaching awe. "I'll say this for you," he said, "you're no piker. You're sure you wouldn't settle for the crown jewels instead. Or the hand of the Princess Royal in marriage."

The Echmen palace library is the biggest and best in the world. Access to it, however, is rigidly controlled. To get a pass – a jade badge in the shape of a heron, so intricately carved it's impossible to fake, why a heron I have no idea – you have to show your credentials, from the precentor of your home monastery or university, to the Chief Proctor of the Imperial chapel, who decides whether or not to forward your application to the supreme conclave of the House of Cardinals, who meet twice a year to issue passes; generally speaking, about one application in fifty actually gets approved. Alternatively, you can have a friend in the clerks' office who'll steal you one.

"Please?" I said.

"All right," Oio said wearily, "let's just suppose for one minute that I owe you some incredible debt of gratitude, because you saved me from being eaten by bears or rescued my entire family from headhunters. What makes you think I could get my paws on one of those things, even if I was minded to? I don't even work in the same *building*—"

"Because you're wonderfully intelligent and resourceful and everybody likes you."

The look he gave me was designed to shrivel my skin and strip the enamel off my teeth, but I'm used to people looking at me like that. "What in God's name do you want it for, anyway?"

"I'd like something to read."

He considered me as though I was one of those riddles in fairy stories; get me right and he'd win the princess, get me wrong and they'd throw him in the snake pit. "You're something else, you know that?"

"Thank you."

"No promises," he said. "Now go away. *Please.*"

Something to read; some way of passing the time. Being alive is clearly the most important thing, but it's not everything. I was alive, thanks to the Hus, but they had absolutely no use for me, except as an accessory for their long-standing practical joke. Once every ten days or so, the boy – seven years old, at a guess, disturbingly thin and whip-scarred – would materialise out of nowhere and beckon me to follow. Then I'd sit in a stunningly elegant anteroom and do my job, translating Echmen and Sashan and Rosinholet into Dejauzi for the benefit of men who knew those languages just as well as I did. Then the foreigners would stand up, bow and leave. The Hus would wait for a count of twelve and then leave, too, never once having looked at me or acknowledged that I was there.

The promised food rations never materialised, but that didn't matter. Inside the palace, food isn't a problem. There's mountains of it, at all times of the day and night. Someone's always holding a banquet or a reception, and even when they aren't, you just hang around the corridors and someone will come along with food, on silver trays, in baskets, on their way to gorge some treble-chinned diplomat who can't be bothered to waddle to the dining hall. The leftovers go to the Imperial pigs, who live short but amazingly decadent lives in surgically clean glazed brick sties out the back of the New Wing. Position yourself by the kitchen gate and you can help yourself from the wheelbarrows as they go past; a thousand rich and rare delicacies from fifty different countries, together costing more than a master stonemason gets paid in a lifetime, all jumbled in on top of each other in a coagulating heap. You could die of obesity or a surfeit of truffles in the corridors of the Imperial palace, but not starvation. So I wasn't costing my new masters anything. Maybe if I had, they'd have noticed me.

Now, you could spend a long lifetime in the palace, sleeping four hours a night and skipping lunch, and still not have time to see all the world-class works of art and masterpieces of architecture, but only if you had all the necessary passes, and a wheelbarrow to move them around in. I had no passes at all, and the bits of the palace I was authorised to see were all very well in their way but not really enough to substitute for a life. But the library – just the one pass, and using up my time would no longer be a problem. Furthermore (a small but nevertheless valid consideration), I was pretty sure the starved, brutalised boy couldn't get inside the library, so I'd never have to set eyes on the Hus ever again, nor they – I like to spread happiness and joy wherever I go – on me. Being a ghost is a pretty miserable existence, but a ghost with the Echmen Imperial library at his disposal would probably resent the time he'd wasted on being alive.

Oio got me my pass. It appeared one night on the floor of my toilet home, wrapped in the inevitable silk bag, and it changed my view of the world completely. A few moments before, the world was a lonely, hostile place and life was sour wine in a leaky jar, slowly but surely dripping away, but I didn't really care because it was horrible. One little jade heron changed all that.

It was a beautiful object, the sort of thing the Echmen do exquisitely. If I close my eyes I can picture it. The stance, the way it was poised a split second before striking down with its beak, was so real it was practically alive, but the shape, the lines and proportions, were nature corrected and improved by impeccable Echmen taste. It was no heron that ever hatched from anything as crude as an egg. It was the original blueprint for a heron that formed in the mind of God, but which His subordinates were too ignorant to interpret correctly when they tried to put it into flesh, bone and feather. The workshop that makes the things for the government has been in business for three hundred years. They make a hundred and twenty of them a year, all identical to within ten-thousandths of an inch and a tenth of a grain, all marked with a security code and a serial number in characters so small you need a magnifying lens (there are ten in the whole of the empire) to read them.

The hell with how it looked. What mattered was that, with my little green heron on a ribbon round my neck, I could walk straight past the two seven-foot-tall eunuchs who guard the library door as though they weren't there and take down any book I liked and read it, and nobody would take any notice.

Oh, come on, you're saying. Sitting in a library all day reading; this is your idea of a life? Really?

Well, yes. Not perhaps the perfect life, everything I could possibly wish for, but close enough for government work, in the circumstances.

My father was easy-going and rarely there, but my mother was a strong-minded woman with traditional views, and she maintained that too much reading damaged your eyesight. So, like other things reputed to make you go blind, I wasn't supposed to do it. My tutor objected that if I didn't read books I wouldn't get educated. My mother pointed out that he could read the stupid books to me out loud – since he was a servant his eyesight was of no value, going blind was what he was paid for, and other things in a similar vein. My tutor was, in hindsight, a good, wise man, but he had a voice like an orphan lamb bleating for its dead mother, and even the Precepts of Saloninus lose their bite when read out in an unwavering monotone by a voice like that. In consequence, I read alone, furtively and insatiably.

Lots of things, according to my mother, ruined your health. Staying indoors gave you consumption, the fresh air gave you pneumonia. Wearing too many clothes stunted your growth, too few and you'd catch a chill and die. Carrots, she maintained to her dying day, addle your brains, and pork causes rabies. If you went barefoot, worms would get inside you through the soles of your feet, wrap themselves round your spine and paralyse you; tight-fitting shoes restricted the flow of blood and made you stupid. Music, even hymns, inflamed the passions and was responsible for most murders and all rapes. Writing gave you rheumatism, archery warped your bones and would turn you into a shambling, knuckle-dragging ape by the age of thirty. Country walks involved fresh air (see above) and you shouldn't go out in the city streets without a scarf over your face in case you breathed in a demon and went mad. Wheat flour was just a synonym for poison, running on a full stomach was so inherently lethal that nobody had ever done it and lived to tell the tale, toothache was almost certainly imaginary, the result of a guilty conscience, and washing your hands more than once a day leached all the protective oils out of your skin and left you prey to malaria and leprosy. It wasn't all negative, though. If you coated yourself with sheep's wool grease morning and evening you were safe from nearly everything, and eating beetroot until your pee goes the colour of blood would guarantee that you live practically for ever.

My mother died when I was fifteen of a particularly horrible disease that shrivelled her up like a leaf but didn't kill her for a very long time. Her voice – loud, clear as a bell and a better curdler of milk than any rennet – went quiet, so I had to lean very close to hear her, and being close to that horrible withered skin made me feel sick. She never once complained about the pain, which the doctors assured me was constant and excruciating, but she complained about everything else, the servants, my father and me in particular. I could see what a terrible effort it was for her to speak, like lifting an impossibly heavy weight, but she simply wouldn't shut up; words of advice, admonishment and reproof ground out in a rasping whisper, hour after hour. I stayed by her bedside for seven months, and when she died I felt like a bird let out of a cage.

Her death broke my father's heart, but he hadn't been there. He was on active service, fighting the Nunes Mai on the north-east frontier. On the day she died, he sacked a castle he'd been besieging for the best part of a year and gave orders for every living thing in it, human and animal, to be killed. That was, of course, government policy; if they'd surrendered, they'd have been allowed to go wherever they wanted and take everything they could carry with them, but, no, they had to be stubborn, and we can't have that. The sight of the emaciated garrison dangling from gibbets didn't bother him much, he told me later, but when he saw a heap of slaughtered chickens he burst into tears.

He missed the funeral, so I was chief mourner, but he got back shortly after, and we had a week together before it was time for me to go and join my regiment. He'd called in all his favours and secured me a commission in the Lancers, a really plum first posting for a kid just shy of his sixteenth birthday. We spent nearly the whole week in the home paddock, shooting at the mark, the popinjay and the long sheet. My father had been a champion archer, won the Divisional three years in a row; it was the thing he was proudest of. When you're older, he'd promised me for as long as I could remember, I'll show you how to use a bow; but, of course, he was never there, so I started without him, every moment I could scrounge when my mother wasn't looking. It came as a shock to both of us, I think, when it turned out that I was better than him, significantly better. His first six at thirty yards were all in the gold, but mine were in there and touching. I remember the astonished look on his face. Fluke, he didn't say. Do it again, he said, and I did, because as far as I was concerned it was no big deal, I could put six in at thirty with my eyes shut. He had a go and he was trying way too hard, so he dropped one into the inner, which made him livid. We moved back to fifty yards. I'm better at fifty than thirty; in fact, the further back I go, the better I get. He, on the other hand, rarely shot beyond fifty because his form went all to pieces at the longer ranges. After an hour or so I had a very bad feeling. Any minute, he was going to explode and he'd probably never talk to me again. Screw this, he said, let's set up the popinjay, I'm good at that. And so he was, but not as good as me. Of course, it never occurred to me to miss deliberately. I'm not sure I could, actually. I know I've never tried.

After my sixteenth consecutive hit on the popinjay, he turned and looked at me. "You're good at this," he said.

"Am I?"

"Yes."

That thought had never occurred to me, either. "It's a fact of life," he went on. "Everyone, everybody in the world, is good at *something*. I'm guessing this is your something."

I was lost for words. Nobody had ever even suggested I might be good at anything before. Up till then, all people had ever done was urge me to try and do better at everything, with the implication that the room for improvement was a vast desert or steppe, stretching away into the distance as far as the eye could see.

After that, my father and I got on like a house on fire. He accepted that although he was very, very good, I was *even better*; this, furthermore, was a good thing. He'd never imagined, all the time he'd known me, that he'd ever be in a position to be proud of me, so after the initial shock it came as a pleasant surprise. "Your technique is all wrong," he told me. "You know that?"

"Sorry."

"Actually, I wouldn't worry about it," he said with a grin. "You really figured it all out for yourself?"

"I read a book," I confessed.

"You figured it out from a book. On your own."

"Yes."

He shrugged. "There's a saying in our family," he said, "the self-taught man has a fool for a tutor. Only goes to show. What book?"

"It's called *The Archer's Mirror.* I've got it indoors." Under a floorboard, I didn't tell him.

"Oh, that. It's rubbish. Tell you what," he said, "don't bother with books, or lessons. Just carry on as you are. You'll be fine."

"Really?"

He rolled his eyes. "Really."

The last day of the week we shot on the long sheet; flight shooting, in which the object isn't to hit anything in particular, just to send the arrow as far as it'll go. He was much better than me at that, because he was stronger and his bow drew a hundred and twenty pounds, as against my seventy-five. When you're older, he promised me, I'll teach you how to shoot flight. And then he went back to the frontier, and I joined my regiment at Scoira Limen. I never saw him again.

Is there a point to all this, you're asking? Not really. I'm just trying to explain why reading books and teaching myself things from them is more of a pleasure to me than you might think.

3

One day I was in the library –

(One day; I think it was Saloninus who came up with the idea of the Eternal Recurrence; that time isn't linear, with a beginning and an end, bracketed by some sort of impossible nothing, but in fact circular; stuff happens, and then it happens all over again, no beginning, no ending, no Creation or Day of Judgement, just a process ... I don't recall Saloninus ever being mentioned as having visited the Echmen Imperial palace, but that theory of his only makes sense if he did. And in the palace, a circular understanding of time isn't just a neat hypothesis, it's a basic survival mechanism. If you truly believed that time is linear and you only had one lifetime between the dark bookends, you'd slash your wrists just to get it over and done with. Put it another way; one day is very much like another, until you lose track. I looked up and three years had gone by, but everyone else apart from me was looking the other way when it happened.)

One day I was in the library, reading an Echmen translation

of Saloninus' *Principles of Alchemy*, when a shadow fell across
the page and I looked up.

"Thought it was you," she said.

Nobody, not even the emperor, is allowed to talk in the
Imperial library. I stared at her in horror and made shush-
ing gestures.

I hadn't seen her for two years, maybe three. She'd grown a
bit, but apart from that she didn't seem to have changed much;
hard to tell, behind all those scars and under all that makeup.
She gave me a shove to make me slide up the bench, and sat
next to me. There's no law that says women aren't allowed
in the library, but I'd never seen one in there. She wasn't, I
noticed, wearing a heron.

I took the scrap of paper I'd been making notes on and
wrote: *how did you get in here?* Then it occurred to me that
maybe she couldn't read; why should she, after all? But she
snatched the pen out of my hand, stabbed it in the ink so it
dribbled, and wrote, *come outside and I'll tell you* in beautiful, classical Echmen calligraphy. The hell with it, I thought.
Saloninus and the secret of the elixir of eternal life would still
be there tomorrow, and quite possibly the day after that.

"Piece of piss," she told me, as we walked down the long
cloister from the library court to the Peach Garden. "You go
down to the laundry, where there's an old corridor they don't
use any more. It's directly underneath the library stacks. Then
all you've got to do is climb up the disused well shaft that was
there before they built the library – it's got steps cut in the
wall, so that's no bother – and there you are in Modern Sashan
Literature. There's a sort of hinged wooden hatch you've got to
push open with your head, but that's nothing to worry about.
I thought everybody knew that."

I shook my head. "How did you find out about it?"

"Asked one of the servants."

"He told you?"

"She." She grinned. "Soon as I stopped hitting her she was only too pleased to help. What were you doing in a *library*?"

"Reading books. What about you?"

She scowled at me. "I'm not a savage," she said.

"Does your uncle know you do this sort of thing?"

"He'd have a fit." Her scowl deepened. "If you tell him I'll cut your throat."

"Why would I do something like that?"

"What sort of books?"

A priest turned his head and stared at us. I did a quick bit of mental arithmetic, calculating the number of rules of Echmen polite society we were violating. I made it seven. "What?" she said.

"We shouldn't be talking to each other. And specially not here."

"Fuck you, then."

That sounded like a stomping-off-in-a-huff line, but no such luck. Instead, she glared at me. Two clerks and a junior administrator up from the country had joined the priest in looking at us. Hardly surprising. She had a voice that carried, just like my mother. Also, to people who don't know the language, anything said in Dejauzi does sound a bit like a violent quarrel.

"Let's go into the garden," I said. "Nobody goes there at this time of day."

She did a lot-of-fuss-about-nothing shrug. I started walking quickly. She followed.

The Peach Garden is called that because once, about two hundred years ago, there were peach trees espaliered on the south wall. These days it's all wisteria, and nobody goes there when the wind's from the east because of the perfume from a nearby cesspool. There's a stone bench and a fountain. Court ladies go there to be seen feeding the birds, but not in the early afternoon. She sat on the bench. I stood.

"What sort of books?" she said.

"Interesting ones."

She sighed. "I asked you a civil question."

True; she had. "History, mostly," I said. "And geography. I like reading about people. What they do and where they live."

She made no comment.

"And useful ones," I went on. "Books about how to do things."

"Saloninus on alchemy."

Observant. "Very useful book," I said.

"You want to live for ever."

"Perish the thought. But one day I might want to know how to test something to see if it's pure gold, or burn through an iron bar, or blast a hole in a wall."

She looked at me. "Really?"

"You never know."

She shook her head. "You'll never own any gold, so you won't need to test its purity. And burning through steel and blowing up buildings aren't much in your line either, I wouldn't have thought."

"No," I conceded, "probably not."

"My favourite," she went on, "is the bit about how to do silver plating using aqua saeva and lacrimae draconis. Now that's something that might come in useful some day."

"You've read Saloninus on alchemy?"

"If you were faking silver coins, for instance. Make the

forgery out of copper, which is cheap, and then plate it to look like silver. You could make a lot of money that way."

"Literally," I said. "Except, do you know how much aqua saeva and lacrimae draconis cost? You'd be lucky to break even."

She was impressed. "You're smart," she said. "Or at any rate, you're not stupid."

"Thank you."

Still no sign of her going away. She bit a fingernail and spat out the harvest. "My father's got lots of books," she said.

"Is that so?"

She nodded. "Trophies of war. He took them off the Ai Chauzida, who took them off the Agna, who sacked a monastery near the Sashan border."

"I remember hearing about that."

"He's got them in big boxes. He doesn't know I've read them." She frowned. "There's a couple that can't have come from a monastery, because they're all about—" She scowled. "That. With pictures."

"*The Garden of Earthly Delight?*"

"Yes, how did you—?"

"Lucky guess."

She gave me a look. "I might have guessed you'd know all about books like that."

"Academic interest," I told her. "Some of the artwork reflects clear Mannerist influences, particularly in the treatment of light and shade."

She made a rude noise. "Is that the sort of book you go to the library for?"

"No. Besides, there's a waiting list as long as your arm. I prefer military and economic history."

I shuffled my feet. I had nowhere in particular to go, but her company made me anxious to go there. But you know how it is with long silences. "What sort of books do you like?" I asked.

"Not sure," she replied. "I've only just got used to the idea of there being more than twelve."

"But you like reading?"

She shrugged. "It's something I'm not supposed to do."

"So's murder."

She gave me a grin I didn't like. "Where you come from, maybe," she said, and for the first time I realised that the Dejauzi word for murder is a loan word from Sashan; not a concept native to Dejauzi society. "Sometimes I like doing what I'm not supposed to."

Like talking to a social inferior of the opposite sex in a public place off limits except to Echmen citizens and accredited diplomats. "Not me," I said. "If you do that, you get in trouble."

"So?"

"I've had a lot of trouble in my life. It'd be greedy and selfish to want any more. It might mean someone else having to go without."

She laughed, a noise like a big dog barking. "You?" she said. "You don't know anything about trouble. I bet your life's been all feather beds and goose-liver pâté."

My mother spent the last seven months of her life in a feather bed. "You're probably right," I said. "Having my entire nation wiped out was a bit of a nuisance, but I ought to be man enough to take it in my stride."

"You escaped, didn't you?"

"True."

"Well, then."

I really wanted one or the other of us to leave. She pulled off one of her shoes and looked at her toes. "You've got a bow in that room where you sleep."

I felt uneasy, as if I'd noticed someone I didn't know watching me. "That's right."

"But no arrows."

"No."

"Not much use for anything, a bow with no arrows."

I didn't answer.

"It's pretty," she said. "I want it."

"You can't have it. Sorry."

"If I asked my uncle, he'd take it off you."

"Yes, I suppose he would."

"Why do you want it, if it's no use?"

"Because it's all I've got."

She pulled a face. "That's a silly answer."

"Yes."

"You can keep it. I don't want it. It's too heavy for me to draw."

Dejauzi noblewomen are supposed to learn archery, though not many of them actually do. "Probably," I said.

"I tried stringing it. It jumped up and hit me in the face."

I loved it even more, which I wouldn't have thought possible. "There's a knack to it," I said.

"Teach me."

"Some time, maybe."

"Now."

I saw a rabbit in a snare once. The more it pulled, the tighter the snare drew. "I'd rather not, if that's all right."

"If you show me how you string it, I'll get you some arrows."

There was a whole world of things wrong with that proposition. Not the least of them was the idea of me, illegally practising archery inside the palace grounds using stolen arrows. "My uncle practises every day in the meadow next to the stable yard." She wasn't looking at me; I saw her in profile. It's harder to read someone's expression from that angle. "Some of the Sashan guards got permission to set up a target, and my uncle asked if he could join." She pulled a face. "Actually, he paid them. He gave them a mountain."

"A—"

"On the border. They wanted it to build a castle on. But actually it's not in our territory, it belongs to the Agna. Their maps are all wrong. They haven't found out yet."

The Agna are some of the touchiest and most warlike people on earth. "Your uncle's got an interesting way of doing diplomacy."

"He says, if they can't be bothered to draw proper maps, fuck them. Anyway, he's got permission to shoot in the meadow. If I asked him, he'd let you go, too. He's not really a diplomat," she added. "He's my dad's brother. But my dad can't stand him, so it was have him killed or send him a long way away."

That sounded odd to me. "You're all right with that," I said. "Being far from home with your father's mortal enemy."

She laughed. "You don't know the first thing about us, or you wouldn't ask something like that. Do you want the arrows and the shooting practice or not?"

"Your uncle can't stand the sight of me."

"He doesn't like the Sashan much, but he spends an hour a day with them. Anyway, that's your problem. Yes or no."

I looked at her. Very hard to read under all that hostility and powdered chalk. A tiny voice in the back of my mind said something about having been here before.

My own actions and decisions have shaped my history the way volcanoes and the impact of falling stars shape a landscape. Volcanoes are explosions of built-up pressure; falling stars are the weapons of a by and large just god. "No," I said. "Sorry."

If she'd had a knife handy, I know for sure she'd have stuck it in me. "Fine," she said. "Piss off and die." She shot up and swept past me across the short grass of the lawn, only realising when she reached the paved cloister that she was wearing only one shoe. I picked up the other one and brought it to her. She snatched it out of my hand and went on her majestic way, hobbling slightly.

Two or three days later – time spent in the Echmen court isn't a straight line, more a sort of squiggle – I came back to my toilet dwelling to find the fat man, her uncle, sitting in the middle of the floor. Across his knees was my bow, unstrung. He had the string in his left hand. His lip was swollen and he had a slight nosebleed.

"I can't string this fucker," he said.

My great-grandfather came home unexpectedly one day to find my great-grandmother in bed with the butler. He killed them both. I sort of understood how he must have felt. "There's a knack to it," I said.

"Show me."

"No."

He looked at me without speaking for what felt like a very long time. "My niece says you like shooting."

"That's right."

"You haven't got any arrows."

"No."

He sighed. "Suppose you'd better borrow some of mine," he said. "Just take care of them, that's all. I hate people messing up my things."

I started practising at the stable-meadow butts with the fat man and the Sashan guards. The Sashan don't draw the string with their fingers. They use a horn ring, worn on the thumb, which you hook the string onto. I never could see the point of doing it that way. Their bows were like mine but shorter and weaker, and they aimed, using the tip of the arrowhead as a sight, rather than shooting instinctively, like we do.

The fat man was good, better than the Sashan; not as good as me. I didn't think much of his bow, just a plain piece of wood, what we call a self bow, without sinew or horn. It was slightly taller than he was, and to be fair you could get accurate with it quite quickly. Its length made it stable, and there was practically no hand shock when you loosed. But the cast was pathetic. Not that cast matters when all you're doing is punching a blunt tip into a heap of turf at thirty yards, but I like to get some sort of return on my effort. His bow was the same draw weight as mine – actually, it felt more, because it got harder to draw the further you drew it, unlike mine, which eases up as you go – but his arrows didn't go into the bank nearly as deep as mine did. I didn't like his arrows much either; too light, so unless I was careful they drifted to the left.

"Thank you," I said to him, the first day. "This really means a lot to me."

He looked at me as though he'd just found me on the sole of his shoe. "Wasn't my idea," he said. Subject closed.

Even so; you can't shoot regularly with the same people without becoming sort of friends. I got on well with the

Sashan, once they'd forgiven me for being a better shot than they were. The Sashan express affection the same way cats do, by scratching; snide and inappropriate remarks, finding your weak spot and never letting it alone. In Sashan society, insults must be avenged instantly in blood; therefore, if someone insults you deliberately, plainly not expecting you to stab him to death on the spot, it must be because you're friends and it's all in fun. My role was to take it in good part but not to dish it out. If a Sashan does it to a foreigner it's good-natured ribbing. If the foreigner does it back, knives flash and the crows get lucky. Just as well I knew all that, having read it in a book in the library.

The fat man still didn't like me very much, but I guess he'd decided I was now his fault, therefore to be tolerated in the same way that one tolerates one's own shortcomings. I knew he was dying to ask me how I did it, why I could hit the inner gold six times in six and he couldn't, even though, as far as he could judge, he did everything exactly the same way I did. Out of the corner of my eye I could see him watching me constantly, but of course he never said a word. I noticed him copying my mannerisms, which are nothing to do with technique, and getting annoyed when they didn't translate into extra points scored. I could see that I was upsetting his fundamental view of how the cosmos works; the superior man can do everything better than the inferior man, except for this one bizarre anomaly. It itched him like mad, but the superior man never scratches in public. To do so would be to admit to having an itch.

An hour each day at the butts, reading in the best library in the world, the sort of food ninety-nine per cent of the world's population never even get to sniff, and the hard floor of a toilet all to myself to sleep on. Actually, the food's not a bad metaphor for my time in the Echmen palace. Wonderful ingredients, rich, rare and wholesome, but jumbled together into garbage. The fact that I look back on it with nostalgia – go figure. Personally, I think it's the sort of life I was born and equipped to lead, but that would involve concepts of destiny and predestination, which may just be too hot to handle.

I was sleeping peacefully, on my side, with my ear in the piss-channel, when someone woke me up. I opened my eyes and saw Oio looking down at me. I'd been good and kept my promise; hadn't seen him for about three years.

"Trouble," he said.

I'm not at my absolute razor-sharp best when I've just woken up. "What?"

He knelt down beside me. "Big trouble," he said. "You know these Hus you've been hanging out with?"

I nodded.

"I don't know all the facts," Oio said, "but something bad's happening with them. Very bad. You might want to find somewhere else to be."

I shook my head. "Got nowhere else to go," I told him. "What's going on?"

My stupidity was annoying him. "The Echmen have just sent five squadrons of Imperial heavy dragoons into Hus territory," he said. "I'm guessing they aren't there to pick flowers."

"I don't understand. Why would they—?"

"You don't need to understand," Oio hissed at me. "You need to hide." He shoved something at me. It was the silk bag I kept my bow and arrows in; my only possession. "Go and camp out in the library," he said. "Ten minutes before closing time, make your way down into the stacks and stay there.

Don't ask me what you're going to do about food. Catch mice or something." He stood up. "You didn't hear this from me, I was never here, I don't know you. Capisce?"

He left so quickly and quietly that I wondered if I'd been dreaming. But there was the bow case in my arms, so presumably not.

My brain slowly started working. I couldn't very well take the bow case in past the library guards, nor did I know anywhere safe I could stash it. But I knew a back way into the library stacks. I'd even explored it for myself, out of curiosity and a vague feeling that the knowledge might be useful one day. A man could make a comfortable, peaceful nest for himself in the dry, dark void behind Comparative Theology, then venture up into the library proper, proudly wearing his heron, as though he'd come in righteously past the guards and through the gates. Not much use if anyone was actively searching for me, but I was inclined to doubt that that would happen, given that I was a mere diplomatic accessory, hard to notice even if you were looking. Not a bad plan, therefore. I got up, tiptoed down the horrible narrow spiral staircase and headed for the laundry.

I spent the next day in the library, as usual, and slept behind Comparative Theology with a stack of commentaries on the Rosinholet *Book of the Dead* for a pillow. Next morning I got up early, crept up into the library proper, went to my usual seat and got arrested.

Two guardsmen in gilded scale armour grabbed my elbows and hustled me out into the corridor, where a short, bald man in a dark green silk gown with a jewelled gold belt was sitting on an ivory stool. "You the translator?" he asked me.

"Yes, that's me."

"You speak Dejauzi?"

"Yes."

He looked over my shoulder and nodded. I heard the boot-stamp noise Echmen guards make when they salute, then footsteps. He stood up. "You're with me," he said. "Bring the stool."

For a short man, he walked very fast. "You belong to the Hus delegation," he told me. "I've heard about you. Sort of like a pet."

"Yes, that's right."

"Well," he said, and all I could see of him was the back of his head, "there's been developments. For reasons I won't go into, we had to intervene in the Hus royal house. A bit of judicious pruning. Don't worry," he added, "you're all right. Just do as I tell you and you'll be fine."

For some reason I thought about my bow, hidden under twenty volumes of pre-Restoration Vesani homilies. I hoped I'd get to see it again, but I wasn't confident. "What's happened?" I asked.

"A series of unfortunate accidents. Try and keep up, will you?"

"What about my friends? Are they all right?"

"They were no friends of yours, son. I wouldn't worry about that."

As a translator, I'm keenly aware of tenses. *Were*. Here we go again, I thought. The bald man was walking even faster. I shifted the stool from my right hand to my left (it was surprisingly heavy) and followed him, breathing hard.

As I believe I said earlier, you shouldn't think of them as dungeons. The corridor that leads from the iron gate with two permanent guards down to the terrifyingly narrow spiral staircase is decorated with a marble frieze of intertwined dragons, the most amazing thing you ever saw. Helpfully they're picked out in different colours of paint, so you can follow where the red dragon weaves in and out of the coils of the green dragon and the blue dragon and the gold dragon; there's undoubtedly a complex symbolism to it, but I never found the book that explains it. They're the cardinal virtues or the points of the compass or the four bodily humours or something like that. The mustn't-call-them-dungeons were purpose-built, so all this art and sensibility was put there for the edification of enemies of the state and the people paid to guard them; that's the Echmen for you. I read somewhere that the Echmen consider art to be the marrow in the bones of a building. I'm not entirely sure what that means, but it sounds great.

The staircase is red granite. It spirals down like a screw thread, and then you're into the cells. Been there before, as you know. So had she. She looked up as the door opened and scowled at me.

"Your Majesty," said the bald man.

There was a pause. I realised I was supposed to be translating. "I don't know what's going on," I said to her in Dejauzi. "Do you?"

"They came in the middle of the night and took my uncle and my cousins," she said. "And they put me in here."

"Her Majesty wishes to lodge an official complaint concerning her treatment," I said. "She also wishes to know the reason for her confinement, and demands to speak to her uncle immediately."

The bald man said: "Her uncle is dead. So is her father and all her relatives. They were found to be plotting against the security of the empire. Break it to her gently if you can."

She, of course, understood every word. Somehow, she kept

her face perfectly straight. I had to say something, to keep up the pretence of translating, so I said: "I'm so very sorry. I didn't know your uncle very well but he was kind to me, in his way."

"No, he wasn't, and I didn't like him very much. And they weren't plotting anything. I'd have known if they were."

"Her Majesty wishes to know what you intend to do to her," I said.

"Tell her that she is now the queen of the Hus, and naturally the empire wants to continue the peaceful and mutually beneficial relationship that prevailed before her father's unfortunate lapse of judgement. Accordingly, she has nothing to fear from us, and as soon as the situation is stable, she will be released and permitted to communicate with her government."

"He's saving you for later," I said. "This is very bad. You need to get away from here. If I can get loose, I'll talk to my friend Oio. Would the other Dejauzi take you in, or should I try the Sashan? Or maybe the Blemyans. They hate the Echmen, and they're a very long way away."

"Not the Dejauzi," she said. "And if I made a run for it, how far do you think I'd get? Talk sense."

"Her Majesty wishes me to state that she is firmly committed to good relations with the empire," I said.

"And tell him he's an arsehole and a motherfucker, and first chance I get I will personally slit him open and wind his guts out on a stick."

"But she regards her imprisonment as an affront to the entire Hus nation. Kindly release her immediately."

"She has my personal undertaking that her release will be expedited as soon as the situation is stable."

"I'll talk to Oio," I said. "Don't trust these people any further than you can spit."

"Don't bother," she said. "If you try anything, you'll fuck it up and get caught and then we'll both be in the shit."

"She thanks you for your courtesy in informing her of the position and awaits further developments," I translated.

The bald man bowed low, then turned and marched out. I only just made it after him before the door shut.

"Savages," the bald man said. "Personally I'd slaughter the lot of them." He sighed. "Stay where I can find you," he said. "I'll have plenty for you to do in the next few weeks."

"Thank you," I said. "Were they really plotting against the empire?"

"I expect so," he said. He frowned, weighing up whether it was worth telling me anything. "The fact is, we need labour, for various building projects. So the Hus will be brought here and put to work. It only goes to show, everything can be useful, even garbage. You can translate for me. I think she'll be happier with a familiar face."

"I'll be in the library," I said.

He peered at me, as if he knew I was in there somewhere. "Is that a real heron?"

"Yes."

"How the hell did you get one? I've been applying for seven years, but they keep telling me there's a waiting list."

I forget what I told him, but it must have been convincing.

4

I went to the library. Luckily, *Concerning the Savages* is on the open shelves; also the authoritative Echmen reference, *Ways to Defeat the Barbarians*, the Sashan diplomatic bible *On the Inferiority of the Lesser Races*, the Fremden *Mirror of Geography* and Saloninus' *Geographical Speculations* and *On the Genealogy of Morals*. The last one doesn't have much about geography in it, but an idea was tapping its shell in the back of my mind.

On a corner of the flyleaf of Erzen's *Humans and Semi-Humans Beyond the Frontier* I scribbled a brief note. The punishment for defacing a library book is death, but fortunately no one was looking. I tore it off and tucked it in my sleeve; then, after the library closed, I sneaked down a lot of lesser used corridors and passageways and slipped the note under Oio's door.

"It's pretty straightforward," he told me the next day, after he'd called me names for disturbing him yet again. "The Echmen are going to build a wall, from Mount Gana to the sea, to keep the savages out. They need the Hus to build it for them. The Hus and a lot of other people, naturally."

That made sense. It was an old idea. The Sapphire emperor gave orders for it to be done when the empire was first founded, but it had to go through committee first. "Slave labour," I said.

He gave me a pained look. "The technical term, I believe, is corvée," he said. "Blemyan word for a Blemyan idea. Basically, the people remain legally free but they're treated as slaves until the job's done. In this case, I should imagine, around a thousand years. You can see why you wouldn't want to conscript your own people for something like that. They wouldn't be paying any taxes, and you'd have to feed them."

"Is it true," I said, "about the royal family?"

"The Hus? It's standard Imperial operating procedure, so I imagine it is, yes. No great loss, from what I've heard." He paused and looked at me. "So now you want me to get you out, presumably."

"Yes."

He nodded slowly. "Thought you might. Listen, I can get you out of the palace. After that, you're on your own."

"Maybe not quite yet."

He raised an eyebrow. "Are you mad?"

"I've been offered translating work by a senior official."

He whistled. "Jammy sod," he said. "You know how many exams an Echmen's got to take to get a job like that? Plus about fifteen thousand in sweeteners."

"I don't think I get paid," I said mildly. "Anyway, that's not the point."

Frown. "Are you taking the job or aren't you?"

"I don't know," I said. "It's not like I've got anywhere else to go."

"True. But staying here would probably be a bad idea, once

you're no longer needed. Of course you might be able to worm your way in, show them how useful and reliable you are. But you're the wrong colour entirely, so if I were you I wouldn't bank on it. The Echmen are wonderfully open-minded, but you know how the entire human race feels about your lot."

I was wrong. I did get paid. The Echmen are punctilious about that sort of thing. When I got to my usual desk in the library, there was a little paper packet waiting for me, containing a warrant for seventy-six *dael* for an hour's work and a docket for temporary accommodation; West Building, Block 3, Room 2117. When the library closed I went and looked at it. Slightly bigger than a barn back home, the walls done in eggshell-blue plaster with moulded cornices and a fresco of leopards and pheasants; a plain plank bed with ropes instead of a mattress; one chair, slightly broken. Oio, and about ten million people in other parts of the world, would reckon I'd fallen on my feet. I had a job with the Echmen government.

I cashed in the warrant and slept in the bed but left my bow where it was. Luck, according to Saloninus, is like a cart full of diamonds perched on the very edge of a cliff. Best if you don't push it.

Ask most people to tell you precisely when and where their life went down the toilet and they'd have to think about it, weighing one event against another, tracing chains of consequence down through the spiralling years. I can answer that question easily, without notes or hesitation; the upper room of a house in Scoira Limen on the afternoon of the fifth Monday after Ascension, auc 2173. It's something I prefer not to dwell on so we'll leave it for now. But she could answer the same question just as promptly. Something we have in common, I guess.

It was about ten days before I saw her again. A different official this time: a nondescript man in a sky-blue gown, wearing an elaborate black lacquer sort-of-hat that presumably went with the profoundly exalted job, whatever it was. He had me fetched from the library. "This way," he said. I didn't have to carry anything, which was nice.

"Tell her she'll be pleased to hear that the situation in her country is vastly improved," he said. "Law and order have been re-established, and the criminals responsible have been firmly dealt with."

I turned to her. "They've enslaved the Hus to build a wall," I said. "Oio reckons the first batch of deportees will be arriving soon, but he hasn't found out anything definite. It's not the department he works in."

"What wall?" she said.

"She thanks you for your government's efforts on her behalf," I said.

He nodded. "Tell her that because of the rebels' mismanagement of the economy and the damage to agriculture and trade resulting from the suppression of the attempted coup, her people are in grave danger of famine if they stay where they are. Accordingly, in consideration of the long and friendly relationship between our two great nations, the emperor has graciously agreed to allow the Hus people to relocate to Imperial territory until conditions improve."

"A wall to keep your lot out, I gather. Savages in general, anyway. It's a very big project, so I'm guessing this is meant to be long-term, probably permanent. Why they're doing it now I couldn't tell you. I don't think they need a reason, it's just something that's gradually worked its way up their to-do list."

She looked at me for a moment. "Why didn't they kill me, too?"

"Her Majesty is eternally grateful," I said.

He smiled. "The empire looks after its friends," he said.

"Because they need a puppet ruler, and you're a girl, so you won't be a nuisance," I translated.

"Can you get me some poison? Or a knife?"

"Her Majesty will be delighted to help in any way she can."

He made a stately bow. "Tell her her co-operation is appreciated."

"Don't do anything stupid," I told her. "I've got an idea."

Another hour's work, another seventy-six *dael*. Outside the palace, a hundred and fifty-two *dael* would pay my rent and feed me for a month, but I wasn't outside, I was inside. Getting into the palace requires either diplomatic credentials or a letter of introduction from a level six official or above (countersigned by a magistrate, commissioned military officer or chief of regional police), a considerable amount of money, persistence and a soupçon of dumb luck. To get out again, you need either a warrant of absence or a warrant of departure, sealed by the Grand Domestic. The third way (in Echmen there's always a third way for everything) involves a door negligently left unbolted at a specified time by a junior member of the domestic staff caught out in some minor scam. I knew Oio could arrange that for me; but, as I'd told him, where would I go?

There's a story about a young palace clerk who'd had word that his childhood sweetheart back in his home village was being courted by the local tanner. He couldn't afford the bribe for a warrant of absence, so he forged despatches from military intelligence, which misled the joint chiefs of the defence staff into thinking the Hasrut were planning to invade. The joint chiefs went to the emperor and persuaded him to levy the biggest conscript army the empire had ever seen, in order to deal with the Hasrut once and for all. The young clerk wangled a posting as a deputy assistant quartermaster with the expeditionary force, which he accompanied just as far as the turning off the Great Military Road that led to his village, two miles away. The army, meanwhile, continued on into Hasrut territory, was ambushed at the Two Horns and wiped out to the last man, leading in turn to the fall of the Nineteenth Dynasty and thirty years of civil war. Moral: even the humblest of us can make a difference, and it's love that makes the world go round, or at least wobble horribly.

Two days later, they let her go. At least, they unlocked her cell and took her upstairs to a spacious, beautifully furnished apartment overlooking the river, where two maids and an Imperial hairdresser were waiting to transform her from a hideous mess into the living image of authority and power as perceived by the Hus. You'll want to look your best, they told me to tell her, when you give your first audience to your new ministers of state.

Say what you like about the Echmen, but they know how to throw a party. Picture a chamber with a tad under half an acre of floorspace, said floor being tiled in a chequerboard pattern with alternating plain white and blue and white geometric-patterned glazed tiles. The chamber is perfectly circular, and the walls swoop up, like a tent caught by the wind, into the cupola of a colossal dome, the inside of which blazes with a gold-leaf background, across which silver hounds at full stretch snap perpetually at the heels of fleeing milk-white unicorns. Light enters this space through long, narrow floor-to-ceiling slits, the sunbeams slicing into the thin fog of incense from over two hundred free-standing brass burners.

The walls are plain white, and up them grow a riot of painted vines, twisting in and out of each other in intricate but distinct patterns and exploding at mathematically ordained intervals into red and blue flowers more gloriously exquisite than anything that ever came up out of the ground. In the dead centre of the chamber is a single chair, ivory, that looks like it was carved with scenes of idealised country life by a million incredibly talented and artistic termites; tiny detail, utterly perfect, as you'd confirm if you got down on your hands and knees and pressed your nose against it. No other furniture, but facing the chair a semicircle of plump silk cushions, that being what nomads prefer to sit on.

In the chair, dressed in a new floor-length Echmen gown of white silk embroidered with perfectly rendered Hus peacocks facing the wrong way, sits the unhappiest seventeen-year-old in the world. Awkwardly on the cushions – most Dejauzi are nomads; the Hus aren't – squat a dozen men in dirty brown robes with mud-encrusted hems. They look almost as sad as she does, but not quite. Behind the throne stand three Echmen officials in sky-blue silk gowns. Behind them but towering self-consciously over them is a single shabbily dressed Robur, trying to pretend he isn't there. He mutters a running translation into the ear of the shortest and most important official, who neither moves nor makes a sound.

The left-hand official nods to one of the bedraggled men, who stands up, then bows low to the girl in the chair. It's not a very good bow, because Hus don't. But the Echmen think they should, so he's been having bowing lessons. The girl in the chair stares at him as if he's got three ears.

The bedraggled man starts by pledging his undying loyalty, and that of the whole Hus nation, to their rightful queen, who carries on staring. Then he expresses his sincere sympathy for the loss of her entire family, regretting that she should have been caused so much distress by their reckless and selfish ingratitude. But never mind; ninety-seven thousand Hus families are now on their way to the Echmen border fort at Red River Ford and will soon be tucked up safe and sound in a string of labour camps on the scarp side of the river valley. The Echmen have graciously permitted them to bring with them their flocks and herds, which they're at perfect liberty to graze anywhere on the Echmen side of the valley, and all the valuable portable items in the kingdom, which the Echmen have very generously agreed to place in safekeeping in the provincial governor's treasury at Tin Chirra. If it pleases Her Majesty, the bedraggled man says, looking at his shoes, he is prepared to carry on as acting temporary grand vizier until further notice, ably assisted by his eleven department heads, representing between them the twelve clans. He pauses and waits. If it pleases Her Majesty, he repeats.

Dead silence. After what feels like a very long time, the shortest official digs me in the rib with his elbow. "She needs to say yes," he whispers.

I walk round the back of the three officials, across a long stretch of very loud floor, and stand directly behind the throne. "You need to say yes," I whisper.

"Tell them to go fuck themselves."

"Don't scowl," I say. "It spoils the effect. We're pleased and happy to co-operate, remember?

"Fuck you. What's this idea of yours? I insist you tell me, right now."

"Later. There isn't time now and they're staring. Smile happily and say something."

She smiles, rather beautifully. "Stick it up your arse," she says.

I nod and report back. "Her Majesty must first receive a sign from the spirits of her ancestors," I improvise. "Would you happen to have such a thing as a white dove anywhere?" Silly question. Within minutes, someone's fetched a white dove, scrambled up on a ladder and shooed the wretched thing in through one of the narrow windows, nearly breaking its wings in the process. It flutters round in a circle three times. To my lasting regret, it doesn't shit on anyone's head. Then it pitches on the floor and tries to peck the diamond-hard tiles.

The chief bedraggled man looks at the shortest official, who nods. The ancestors are deemed to have spoken. The chief bedraggled man must be either well-informed or naturally quite bright, because white doves don't figure at all in Hus mythology, not being native to the region. But they're a big deal to the Echmen, and that's all that matters. The chief bedraggled man reprises his painful bow, the other eleven bedraggled men stand up, and they file out of the room, looking very pleased to be getting out of there alive.

The shortest official elbows me again. "Tell her it all went very well," he says.

Possibly the easiest seventy-six *dael* I've ever earned, in terms of work done and energy expended, but I had my misgivings. As far as I could tell, as far as the Echmen were concerned, the ceremony was sufficient to transfer executive power from the queen to the council of ministers. That done, did they need the queen any more? An interesting point of Hus constitutional law, which my studies in the library failed to resolve, since there aren't any books about it.

Around this time, I started thinking a lot about home.

*

Define home; where you live, obviously. Now let's try and apply that to the history of my life. We'll go backwards, because it'll be easier that way.

For six years out of the twenty-six, home has been the Echmen Imperial palace. Before that, for four years, the army base at Scoira Limen. That leaves sixteen years growing up in a smallish manor house a few miles outside Ennea Crounoe, which you won't have heard of; it's a minor provincial town about eighty miles north-east of the City, to which I've never been.

The Sashan report about the annihilation of the Robur didn't mention Ennea Crounoe but it did refer to Stratopedon, the provincial capital, which is twelve miles further down the Southern Trunk Road. To get to Stratopedon from practically anywhere, you pass within a mile or so of Ennea Crounoe. Stratopedon, according to the Sashan intelligence corps, had been so comprehensively flattened that you'd never know it had ever been there. Without being unduly pessimistic, therefore, I could probably assume that my old home no longer existed. Scoira Limen had probably gone the same way, being a military installation, not that I minded its loss one little bit. The palace – the palace is many wonderful things, homely it isn't. Therefore, I had no home; unless, because I'm Robur, you count the City.

Which is where we all mean when we use the H word. Partly it's a religious thing. In theory at least, the temple of the Invincible Sun in Hill Street is the only place on earth where He can hear you when you pray. All Robur are supposed to go there once a year to confess their sins and receive absolution. We get round that by means of what we call embassy theory; an embassy is supposed to be the native soil of its country, even though it patently isn't. Very well, then. Robur who can't get to the City pray in a building containing a bit of the City temple – a roof tile, a scrap of plaster from the last redecoration, a splinter of obsolete floorboard; every time they have the builders in, there's a waiting list for the trash. The principle, however, is clearly understood by all Robur. There's only one temple, and it's in the City.

Likewise the ward system. We all belong to a City ward, even if we were born a thousand miles away and have never been there. It's built into our names, even; X son of Y of Z ward. I'm Old Gate, and from that you know everything you need to know about me; a minor offshoot or sucker of a subordinate branch of a noble house, titles but no money, therefore almost certainly a military family, therefore a soldier's son and probably a soldier myself. All that, from the fact that my lot were originally registered in what used to be the garrison quarter, about six hundred years ago.

And then there's the themes. They started off as packs of fans at the chariot races in the Hippodrome; four teams, each with its own colour. Over the course of time two colours dropped out, leaving the Blues and the Greens. Gradually, which colour you were didn't just signify who you wanted to win the Spring Crown. It governed and decided where you lived, what job you did, which gang boss you took orders from, which theme treasury you paid your dues to and received your dole money from when you were sick or out of a job. Posh people like me aren't supposed to be in themes, but in the army you can't help it. I joined a Blue regiment, so I'm Blue, till I die.

Home, therefore, must be the City, by default. The last anyone heard it was still standing, but an army of a quarter of a million savages was on its way to storm it. Now then, what happens to cities when they're taken by an enemy? As with so many things, it depends on geography. The Sashan, who've taken more cities than any other race in the world, invariably reduce the places they capture to ashes and dust, then build new cities on top of the ruins. The Echmen, by contrast, generally only take a city when they actually want it for something, and they go to great lengths to minimise damage to the actual bricks and mortar; they deport the inhabitants and resettle them somewhere a thousand miles away, but the buildings are sacrosanct, and if they get knocked around in the course of the assault, they're lovingly restored to the way they were. The Rosinholet and the Aram no Vei tend to set fire to anything that'll burn and leave it at that. The Vesani prefer to capture cities by bribing someone to leave a gate open; what they want is a going concern with the goodwill uncompromised. The Robur are, sorry, *were* smashers and burners, but unlike the Sashan they didn't tend to rebuild, preferring to sow the levelled site with brambles so that even the subsoil would never be any good to anyone ever again. You can see why people didn't like us very much.

As for these milkfaces who'd banded together to exterminate my nation, what would they do with the City? Nobody knew anything about them, so it was anybody's guess. Either they'd given us a taste of our own medicine and raised the world's most expensive thistle nursery, or they'd taken one look at the magnificent, gorgeous City, compared it with what they'd got at home, and moved in.

By this time, I said to myself, someone must know what's happened. Unless you're in the direct stream, so to speak, news of events in distant lands percolates through the Echmen Imperial court like water through limestone; even so. After three years snooping round the place, I now had certain resources. I decided I'd quite like to find out.

Another meeting of the Hus council of ministers; in a different room this time, much smaller but floored, walled and roofed in polished, figured porphyry; no windows, so lit to dazzling brightness by seventy-seven gilded bronze lamps in the form of lotus flowers. Just one official, a man I hadn't seen before in a saffron yellow silk gown and the weirdest hat of office you ever set eyes on. He wasn't that much older than me, but smoother and harder than marble.

"You want to be careful," he hissed in my ear as the councillors, no longer bedraggled but just as sad looking as last time, filed in and sat down on the uncomfortable cushions.

"I'm sorry," I said. "I don't know what you mean."

"You and the queen," he said. "Naturally, we don't give a damn what you get up to. But these people—" The tiniest possible nod in the direction of the councillors. "Death by crucifixion, isn't it, a commoner screwing a royal?"

"You're thinking of the Maudit," I told him. "With the Hus, it's being buried alive."

"I stand corrected," he said graciously. "Anyway, be careful."

"There's nothing like that," I said.

"Of course not. She asks for you specifically when we offer her an Echmen translator because she admires your sibilants." The tiniest possible shrug. "No skin off our noses what they do to you, but we'd really rather avoid bloodshed inside the palace precincts. So probably better all round if you give it up completely."

Here we go again, I thought, and then she came in and the meeting started. She was wearing the same outfit and the same look on her face. The new grand vizier waited for the nod from the official, then did his bow (he'd been practising) and cleared his throat.

His loyalty to the royal house, he said, was as true as steel and would last until the sun itself went cold and all the stars went out. However, certain facts had been brought to his attention, and he regretted to have to announce that Her Majesty was not, in fact, her father's daughter. The perpetrator, her real father, had been found and had confessed. Accordingly, though it broke his heart to say this, he had no alternative but to declare Her Majesty deposed forthwith. Since the royal line was now completely extinct, he had asked the Echmen emperor to accept the role of emergency acting regent until the council was in a position to call a general assembly of the entire Hus nation and elect a new king. He was overjoyed to be able to announce that the emperor had graciously agreed to shoulder this burden. From now on, therefore, all the royal powers, privileges, estates, herds and property would vest in the emperor, who he sincerely wished would live forever. Then, knowing a good exit line when he saw one, he sat down again.

"Now just a—" she said. The official cleared his throat.

"Tell them," he told me, "that since the female She Stamps Them Flat is not a member of the royal house she has no official standing to address the council, and must therefore stay silent or be removed from the chamber."

I started to translate. She stood up and walked out.

It was a long time before I was able to get away, and then I had to find Oio; but the selfish, inconsiderate bastard was out of his office, doing the work he was supposed to be doing instead of being there to bend the rules for me. When eventually he showed up I was so angry with him I could barely speak. I need to know which room she's in, I shouted.

"I don't know, do I?"

"Find out."

He stared at me. "What's got into you?"

"*Now*," I said. "It's important."

It took him several hours. I ran halfway across the palace and arrived sweating and gasping for breath, to find half a dozen maids cleaning an empty room.

I should have known. Since she was no longer the queen, she was no longer an accredited diplomat, therefore she didn't qualify for accommodation. "Where is she?" I yelled at those poor inoffensive women. "Where did you take her stuff?"

They didn't know, and couldn't suggest anyone I could ask. The furious energy drained out of me, like wine from a punctured skin. I thanked them as politely as I could and left them alone.

I went back to my room. On the chair was a warrant for seventy-six *dael*. I went to the paymaster's office and cashed it. All of a sudden it was raining money.

I realised that, with no conscious decision on my part, I was heading for the library. I stopped dead in my tracks. Idiot, I thought. I started walking again. Somehow I managed not to run.

5

The world, according to Adzo Silanicus' *Principles of Advanced Geography*, is a very big place, reaching from one side of the sky to the other, and although we know about lots of places, there are lots of places we don't know about. Take Borabo, for example. Most people who've studied the subject in any depth will tell you it doesn't exist; it's simply not there, isn't, wasn't, never will be. Others, mostly madmen, will tell you about various ship's captains across the ages who were blown far off course by terrible storms, and who swore blind that as they were being churned by spire-high waves, they caught sight of a huge land mass on the western horizon; but of course they didn't stop and investigate because at the time they were somewhat preoccupied with other things. What you might call the middle path of received opinion, or only a little bit delusional, cites the voyage of Archias of Beloisa, who set sail for Blemya with a cargo of lemons, disappeared in a freak typhoon, was declared legally dead and reappeared six years later in the same ship, laden perilously low in the water with tin ingots, bales of silk, gold bullion and jars of truly weird aromatics and spices, the like of which had never been seen before or since. Having disposed of his cargo and become thereby the third richest man in the Vesani Republic, he bought a country estate, retired there and refused to say a single word about his adventures. There were, however, rumours based on the testimony of his crew, who'd been sworn to silence; he'd arrived at a strange land where they had every good thing you could possibly imagine in ridiculous abundance, apart from lemons. This strange land, argues the middle path of scholarly opinion, must have been Borabo, although apparently it's not actually called that; it exists and it's out there somewhere, or at least it was three hundred years ago when Archias made his voyage.

A number of people have set out to find Borabo. A few of them even came back, to say that they'd failed and Borabo was just a myth. These days, received academic opinion is that Borabo is not so much a place as a state of mind. It's the elusive, illusory, indispensable Somewhere Else we all need to believe in, whether we call it Borabo, Paradise or the Afterlife. There's got to be something better, we tell ourselves, and if only we had a boat and a lucky wind we could go there and be happy. We don't try, needless to say, but knowing we could keeps us from opening a vein and drifting away.

The idea that you can make life bearable merely by living it in a different place has always struck me as bizarre. I base this view on experience. Wherever I've gone, I've always still been me, and some obstacles are too much even for geography to overcome. Fortunately, I'm in the minority. Most people don't seem to be able to tell the difference between movement and amelioration. They believe in the Promised Land. They also can't get past the misconception that if you move away from something bad, inevitably you're moving towards something better. This is just bad geometry, a total failure to understand the properties of a straight line, but never mind. Simply because something is factually wrong doesn't make it untrue.

Please take note of that last word, *untrue*, because much of what follows concerns the way, the truth and the better life. I thought it up mostly in the library, or lying awake in my dark room staring at the ceiling, or in corridors. It should go without saying that I'm not proud of it. Big deal.

Of course I found her in the library stacks. She was curled up behind a shelf of forgotten periodicals, and when she saw me she produced a penknife and waved it under my nose.

"Fuck you," she said. "I'm not going to the slave camps. You'll have to kill me instead."

I spread my arms wide, to convey peaceful intentions, and took a step back. "I'm on your side, you stupid bitch," I said. "Put that thing away before you do me an injury."

"What did you just call me?"

I was in the army for several years before I screwed up my life, so I knew all about what to do next. I stepped smartly forward and carried out a basic disarming move, which very nearly worked perfectly. "For God's sake," I yelled at her, clamping my hand tight onto the cut. "Now look what you've done."

It turned out to be far less bad than it looked, but even so. I have a certain amount of history with cutting edges. They make me go all to pieces.

"Oh, for crying out loud," she said, knocking my hand away. "Keep still."

It was little more than a scratch, from my left eye socket halfway to my mouth. She spat on her handkerchief and dabbed away the blood. "You clown," she said.

"I came to see if you're all right."

"I was fine before you turned up."

"Shut up and listen to me," I said. "Things are very bad. They're almost certainly going to kill you."

"I'd sort of figured that out for myself. What's it got to do with you?"

"I can get us out of here," I said, "but we need somewhere to go. I've thought of somewhere. But you need to do exactly what I tell you. Or you can stay here and starve until they catch you and cut your throat."

She looked at me. "You can't even take a knife off a girl," she said. "What makes you think—?"

"Listen," I said. And I told her about my idea. Some of it, anyway.

"That," she said, "is the most stupid idea I've ever heard. You're crazy. Leave me alone."

I'd have been disappointed by anything less. "Fine," I said. "Clearly you're very intelligent, and I expect you're highly resourceful and resilient, too, so I'll let you get on with it. I'll go back to my secure and well-paid job, and I'll never bother you again. Here's your knife back."

She took it. I didn't move. She sighed.

"Can you really get me out of the palace?"

"Yes."

"Fat lot of good that'll do."

"Not," I said, "if we do as I say."

"Go to the slave camp. *Voluntarily*."

I nodded. "Exactly. For a start, it's the last place they'd ever think of looking for you."

"No, it's not."

"It's the only place you can go. I explained all that."

She sighed. "People will recognise me," she said. "Too many people will know me, men I've known all my life. They'll turn me in to the soldiers, and I'll die."

"Yes, they'll recognise you. No, they won't turn you in. Not if we do what I—"

"Piss off," she reasoned. "If I'm going to die, I might as well do it here. Save myself a long walk."

The Hus don't like walking, under any circumstances. Walking is something horses do, with people sitting on them. "I've got money," I said. "I'll buy a horse. Well, a donkey."

"You buy what you like. Now go away."

I told myself, I need her, or it won't happen. "Suit yourself," I said. "I saved your life once, I don't see why I should make a habit of it. You're nothing to do with me, after all."

This time I walked away. She let me go. Damn, I thought.

I went to my usual desk in the library and sat down, but I wasn't in the mood for reading. No point, now that the plan I'd been researching for so long wasn't going to happen. Probably just as well, I told myself. It was a crazy idea anyway, just like she'd said. I sat there for an hour, then went back down to the stacks. She was where I'd left her.

"Last chance," I said. "Then I wash my hands of you."

She looked at me. "I don't like being on my own," she said.

"It's never bothered me," I told her.

"I'm not used to it."

"When they catch you," I said, "they'll put you in a cell, on your own, and leave you there. They may take you out and kill you, they may not. You could be in a cell on your own for years before they get round to killing you. Twenty years. Thirty."

"Shut up."

"The Echmen believe in efficiency and caution," I said. "Efficiency means getting rid of people they don't need who might be dangerous. Caution means waiting to see if an asset might be needed before disposing of it. They're very patient people. Or they might just forget you're there for twenty years. It's been known."

Being cruel doesn't come naturally to me. Neither does playing the flute, but I forced myself to practise regularly and now I'm quite good at it. "Why are you picking on me?" she said. "I never did you any harm."

"I feel responsible for you," I said. "God knows why, but I do."

She closed her eyes, sighed and stood up. "How would it be," she said, "if I pretended to agree, you got us both out of the palace, then I stabbed you in the back when you're not looking and ran away?"

"If you're going to talk like that, let's forget the whole thing. I've tried to help. That lets me off the hook, as far as I'm concerned."

"I don't want to go to the slave camp."

"Nobody in her right mind would. But it's necessary." I stood up. "You've insulted me, you've stuck me with a knife, and when I try and help, you make difficulties. The hell with you. I've had enough."

I walked away. She called me back. What've I got myself into, I asked myself, but there was nobody available to tell me.

Oio wasn't there to see us off. Somehow from somewhere he'd managed to scrape together six hundred *dael*, which I hadn't even asked for. I have absolutely no idea why he liked me, but evidently he did.

The door that had been negligently left open for us led to a tunnel, a very long one; pitch dark, and there was no time to go back for a lamp, even if I knew where to steal one from without getting caught. I'm not at my absolute best in confined spaces in the dark. After we'd been walking for what seemed like my entire life, I got the horrors, crouched down on the floor and refused to go any further. But she yelled at me and kicked me and yelled at me some more, telling me I was pathetic and useless and I deserved to be left there to die of starvation and be eaten by rats, until eventually I dragged myself to my feet and stumbled forward into the darkness just to get away from her voice and her very hard left foot. What Oio had neglected to mention was that the tunnel had been built to connect the office of the duty watch commander with the House of Enduring Fragrance, which nestles by special dispensation of the military authorities against the flank of the palace wall. Eyebrows were raised as we stumbled through the door at the end into the unbearably dazzling light, but they didn't ask us who we were or what we were up to, no doubt preferring to draw their own conclusions.

We left. She gave me a confused look. "What was that place?"

"A brothel."

"What's a brothel?"

Oh boy. "It's somewhere you buy broth." I stopped. "You're talking in Echmen."

"Well, yes. If I started talking Hus, people would think we're having a row or something."

"Smart."

She shrugged. "Where are we going?"

"I haven't got the faintest idea."

The look on her face.

I hadn't been able to find a map, but I did come across an album of watercolours painted by some long-dead emperor's aunt, including a view of the palace grounds from the nearest hilltop. I'd memorised every detail of it, to the point where I could see it plain as day every time I closed my eyes. From it I knew the basic geography; river, bridge, main north/south road. Good reconnaissance is never wasted.

Two problems, however. The picture was painted when it was all orchards and open fields, before they built the town. Also, by now it was too dark to see the hill. So I had no way of getting my bearings. All I could see was the dark mouths of alleys, waiting to gobble me up.

"I can't believe you didn't figure out a plan before we left," she said. "How could you have been so stupid?"

"Of course I've got a plan," I said. "This is just a minor hiccup."

She called me something; literally inaccurate but metaphorically quite apt. "We need to find the Southern Military Road," I said. "That takes us straight to where we're going, more or less. Also, we need to buy a cart and a donkey. Or a mule."

"How far is it to the slave camp?"

"About three hundred and fifty miles."

"Three hundred and—"

"It's all right," I said. "We've got best part of a thousand *dael*. Allow two-fifty for the donkey and cart, that still leaves plenty for food. On the military road, say thirty miles a day, twelve days. I was in the army, and you come from a long line of sedentarised nomads. Piece of cake."

"You idiot."

I was starting to think the same thing myself. Would they come looking for her? Would they even realise she'd gone? The Echmen, yes; a place for everyone and everyone in his place, lest the heavens fall. And if I was the officer given the job of finding a stray Hus princess, the first place I'd look would be the Hus labour camps, and the road leading to them. And she would never pass for Echmen with those peacocks carved all over her face, and I'm Robur, so blending inconspicuously into the travelling population was probably out. "I've got it all figured out," I told her. "I had Oio get me a set of credentials for a translator assigned to the labour camp commandant, so I'm covered. You—" I hesitated. "I thought you could hide in the back of the cart, or something. Under a tarpaulin."

You know the look you get when there are no words to express the depth of feeling. She grabbed my sleeve and towed me into the shadows of the nearest alley. "All right," she said. "Obviously we can't go back, we'd never get inside again. How much money did you say we've got?"

"Over nine hundred *dael*."

"Is that a lot?"

"No, not really. Enough for a donkey, a cart and food for three weeks."

"And we're heading south, on the military road. That's the one I came up on when I first came here."

"That's right."

She nodded. "Fine," she said. "What do you know about the Imperial mail?"

Oh boy.

The Imperial mail, which carries government documents

all around the empire, is the most incredible thing in the world. State-of-the-art mail coaches, sleek and fast and each one costing about as much as a warship to build, cover a hundred and twenty miles a day over dead straight, immaculately maintained military roads. Every thirty miles there's a way station; they're all identical, same floor plan, same colour plaster on the walls, and a stable full of fresh thoroughbreds ready for a quick change any hour of the day or night. A mail coachman gets paid more than a cavalry officer, and earns every penny. Other nations have tried to copy the Echmen mail, but their very best efforts are pale imitations of the sublime original. It is, quite simply, the fastest thing on earth –

"Exactly," she said. "The fastest thing. Which means, however fast they chase us, they can't catch up."

"Agreed," I said. "It'd be ideal for our purposes, if we could use it. But we can't."

"My father used to talk about it," she said. "He was told all about it by one of our people who bred horses for the mail. Once you're on a mail coach, nothing can catch up with you and nobody can get to where you're going ahead of you. So if you're on a mail coach and you get somewhere and tell them something, they've got no way of knowing you aren't telling the truth."

Hatful of fallacies there, but I could see what she was getting at. "But we can't use the mail," I said. "It's incredibly tightly restricted."

"So there's no risk of stopping at a way station and finding the soldiers waiting for us with a warrant, because there's no way they could get there before we do. I say we use the mail. It's our only hope, being realistic."

"We *can't*. You need to be God or the emperor, *and* you'd have to have the right papers."

"Now then," she said, "it stands to reason, the mail station for the Imperial palace would be a big building quite near it, next to the road, with a very large stable out the back. That shouldn't be hard to find."

Even in the dark, no, it wasn't; mostly because, just as we poked our heads out of the shadows of the alley, a mail coach came thundering past us, nearly running us over. No mistaking it for anything else. Perfect lines, jet-black lacquered coachwork, drawn by eight of the most amazing horses you'll ever see, with two cavalry outriders front and back; and if that wasn't enough, the characters for Imperial Mail in gold leaf on the door. It had two running lamps on the back. I watched them hurtle away like twin shooting stars, then stop.

"That'll be it, then," she said. "Come on."

"Yes, but—"

"Come *on*."

Watch and learn. You're the duty officer in the post house. The evening mail from the northern stations has just come in; they've handed over the sealed bag for the palace, and that's all that's due in for tonight. The rest of your shift is peace, quiet, maybe a few drinks and a game of knucklebones with the watch commander. There are worse postings than this, you tell yourself.

All that is about to change. A weird-looking female in an amazingly expensive silk dress comes barging in through the door, ignoring the you-can't-go-in-theres of the sentries with that special selective deafness that only comes with the bluest of blood. Trailing behind her is a black man, ridiculously tall and skinny, scared out of his wits.

The female demands to speak to the duty officer. Unfortunately, that's you. Now, you've been in the service long enough to know that nobody throws their weight around in a government office unless they have plenty of weight to throw. Also, this female; you couldn't make her up. She's wearing the price of a porcelain factory, including goodwill and stock at valuation, but she's some sort of savage, with hideous birds tattooed on her face. She's got to be real. Nobody would dare try and fake something like that.

She talks very fast in a language you can't understand, but which sounds like a dog barking. The skinny black man translates for her. He has difficulty keeping up.

She is, she tells you through him, the queen of the Hus. She's had word that her father, the emperor of the Hus, is dangerously ill at Some-Place-You've-Never-Heard-Of. She has to reach him before he dies to receive his blessing, otherwise there'll be a disputed succession and a civil war and Echmen troops sent to shore up the loyalists and the sort of messy, expensive war that lasts twenty years, and all that will be *your fault* if you don't get her on a coach going south *right now*.

You tell her, sorry, I need a docket, duly countersigned. She points out that it's the middle of the night (slight exaggeration) and all the lazy, good-for-nothing, sons-of-bitches clerks have stoppered their inkwells and gone home, so there can be no paperwork. All she can offer by way of credentials is this; will this do?

You could have knocked me over with a feather; I had no idea she'd got it. Later she told me it had been sent to her father, as a token of good faith, and he'd given it to her when she was sent away. It's unmistakeable; a jade pheasant in an oval cartouche, about the size of your thumb. The Imperial safe passage. If I'd known she had that – why don't people tell me things? It'd save so much trouble in the long run.

"I didn't know," she told me, as we raced into the night, cushioned from the slightest turbulence by the most perfectly engineered coach springs ever made. "I knew it was pretty hot stuff, but I didn't know what it was *for.*"

"It guarantees your safety anywhere in the empire," I said.

"What, you mean I didn't have to leave after all?"

"Anywhere except the palace. And it can be taken from you. But, yes, it's big medicine. I really wish you'd mentioned it earlier."

"And have you steal it?"

"Oh, that's nice, after all I've done."

"Probably get a lot of money for it, if it's that valuable."

"Shut up," I told her. "I'm sick to death of listening to you."

"You can have the stupid thing if you want."

An Imperial pheasant. Dear God. "If only I'd known," I said. "I never for one moment dreamed you'd have something like that."

Scowl. "Really. You don't think much of us, do you?"

"What?"

"Us. The Hus. You think we're just a bunch of savages."

Yes. "No, of course not."

"Well, we aren't. And my father was a very important man. That's why they gave him one of these."

Doesn't work like that, I didn't tell her. It's not a prize or a medal, it's a bribe. What was it a bribe *for?* Highly unlikely that she would know; and whatever it was, it hadn't done her father any good. Maybe if he hadn't given it to her, he'd still be alive, and this horrible mess wouldn't have come bubbling up all around me. Probably not. The pheasant is only valid while you're holding it. While it's in contact with your skin, you're sacrosanct. If they snatch it from your hand, they can cut your head off. You can see why the Echmen make such good lawyers.

I looked at her. "What?" I said.

"It's just struck me," she said. "I suppose I must be very important, too, now that he's—" She froze, like a jammed mechanism, just for a moment. "I hadn't thought about that. Too much else on my mind."

"You're the queen of the Hus," I said. "And you're on your way to set your people free."

She glared at me. "Don't start that again."

Maybe I should tell you about my idea. The part of it, at least, that I'd told her about.

Getting her out of the palace didn't make her safe, not one little bit. If the Echmen wanted her dead, distance wouldn't save her, or armour, or disguise, or hiding in a deep, dark hole, or in a cave on the Moon. The Echmen would find her, disarm her and kill her, easy as winking. The only thing that could save her was politics. Fortunately, there's a lot of it about, at all times.

The Echmen enslave the Hus. The Hus are part of the Dejauzi family of nations. Like all families, the Dejauzi has some members who are hated like poison by all the others. But there's a difference between you hating your sister and somebody else hating her. Inside the family, it's fine and perfectly natural. When it's an outsider, it's different.

I had an uncle like that. We all loathed him, with good reason. He was horrible to his wife and children, he drank too much, he shouted at servants and when he came to stay with us he stole things. But when he was arrested for stabbing a stranger in a public place, the whole family mobilised, called in favours, spent a large percentage of its limited social and political capital to get him released and the charges dropped – not that he was the slightest bit grateful, and when he dropped dead of a stroke nine months later, we all felt like it was our birthday. Even so. It's cold scientific fact that the universe is composed of two basic elements, Us and Them, always opposed in fundamental, irreconcilable conflict. The fact that we may like individual Them loads more than we like any of Us is neither here nor there. When it turns into an Us-against-Them issue, we can no more side with Them than water can flow uphill.

So; the Echmen, who are Them, enslave the Hus, who to the other Dejauzi nations are Us in spite of everything. Now, if the Hus were to send a delegation to the other Dejauzi, reminding them of which side is which and pointing out that, on the timeless principle of divide and rule, one of them is bound to be next – something, I felt justified in believing, might just possibly get done.

Unlike the Sashan, the Robur, the Rosinholet and nearly every other variant form of tool-using biped, the Echmen don't like war. It's messy and the outcome is never certain, and it costs a ridiculous amount of money better spent on other things. Hence the desire for a big, thick wall, to keep the bastards out so they wouldn't need to fight them. Turn the Dejauzi into a big enough problem, with war a distinct possibility, and the Echmen will be open to a diplomatic solution. Once there's a treaty, trust the Echmen to abide by it to the letter (not the spirit, maybe, but punctiliously to the letter). Do that simple thing, and she'd be safe from the Echmen for the rest of her life. Easy as pie.

Not actually as easy as all that. I knew we'd need one more thing, one additional factor, to push the Dejauzi over the edge.

Otherwise, family or no family, they wouldn't risk picking a fight with the Echmen. One more thing. I hadn't told her about it yet. I'll come to it in a minute.

"So if I've got this," she said, turning the jade pheasant over in her fingers, "I'm safe, and we don't need your stupid plan."

I snatched it out of her hand and pretended to throw it out of the coach window. She screamed. I opened my hand, showed it to her and gave it back. "We need the plan," I said.

She sulked, affording me time to think. Outside the coach window, huge stretches of the world wound past us, like someone unrolling the longest scroll ever. I don't know if you've ever been in a coach or a chaise, but it's the weirdest sensation. You stay still and the world moves. I suspect mountains must see things that way, and very big old trees. It gives you a dangerous sensation of being the centre of things; of being the subject of the sentence rather than the object or, as is usually the case with me, a lowly preposition. I can understand how people who travel a lot in coaches – kings, generals, great officials, merchant princes – think and act the way they do. They sit still, in control, and all around them the world changes, for their benefit. Also, the world is a much faster place, if you travel by coach. One moment you're in Poor Town, surrounded by starving, desperate people to whom the boulevard five blocks away might as well be the summit of Mount Gebo. The next you're in the country, wheatfields and vineyards quilted with neatly laid hedges, all productivity and wealth with not a superfluous human in sight. A few hours after that you're looking out over a high mountain pass, whence you can see all the kingdoms of the earth. Wasted on me, of course, doomed to drag myself along with me wherever I go, like two men escaped from a chain gang; but someone with the right background, unsullied by insight and experience, a long ride in a well-sprung coach might lead him to make some truly awful decisions involving the destiny of his fellow creatures.

Like I said, doesn't apply to me. I'd made my decisions already. In a *library*.

She was about to say something. One of the books I'd read was Salmanazar's *Art of War*. I deployed my light cavalry for a pre-emptive strike.

"I can't believe you didn't tell me about the safe pass," I said.

"You didn't ask."

"It never occurred to me you'd have such a thing. Or you'd have one and *not tell me*."

She shrugged. "My father said, keep it secret. Uncle didn't know about it. Father said, keep it secret or someone'll take it off you. Like you just did."

"I gave it back."

"Shows you're not a complete idiot. Try anything like that again and I'll stab you."

So much for my pre-emptive strike. "For crying out loud, let's not bicker any more. It's pointless."

"I don't bicker."

"Tell me," I said, "about those tattoos of yours."

"No. It's private."

"I read in my book," I said, "that those particular markings are unique; the peacock standing facing right, left foot raised holding an orb flammiger. Nobody else among the Hus is allowed to have tattoos like that. Is that true?"

"Yes."

"So anybody taking a close look at you will know exactly who you are."

"I suppose so. If they know about all that stuff. Not every-body does. Lots of people think it's all just rubbish."

"But important people—"

"Oh, yes. But they don't need tattoos to know who I am. They've known me since I was a kid."

That, and now slavery. Life can be very hard. "So we won't have any trouble at all establishing that you're really you."

"I already said so, didn't I?"

"That's fine, then. Now, we need to figure out who we need to show you to. Who's likely to be in charge, now that your father's—"

I couldn't find the right verb. Choosing the exact word is important to a translator.

"The Echmen," she said. "You won't have any trouble recognising them. They'll be the ones with all the weapons."

"Who among your people? The leaders."

"We haven't got any. Oh, apart from me, of course."

"You know what I mean."

"There aren't any," she said. "Really. Not dukes and earls and commissioners and all that shit, like you people have." She'd said that in Echmen, because she needed the vocabulary. Point taken. "We have a king and a royal family, and then it's the heads of all the households. Didn't it tell you that in your book?"

"It was about the Dejauzi in general," I said. "I didn't realise the Hus were different."

"Well, we are. We're nothing like them, really."

Oh, don't say that, I thought. "Heads of households, then. These people who've known you since you were little. I'm guessing some of them are more equal than others."

"I guess," she conceded. "Some of them are smarter or talk better, so people listen to them."

"Right," I said gratefully. "Tell me their names."

I'd shocked her. "Did you actually read that book," she said. "Or did you just look at the pictures?"

I sighed. "I know," I said. "That was a really bad thing to ask and I'm sorry. But I need to know, and screw your deeply held cultural directives." I realised I'd broken into Echmen, too. But you try saying *cultural directives* in the language of goatherds.

"I can't just tell you their *names*. That's—"

"Force yourself."

She looked disgusted. "The man you want," she said, "is Heaven Thunders The Truth." She stopped to catch her breath. "He was my father's best friend, very smart man, father listened to him a lot. If the Echmen've got any sense, they'll have killed him already."

"Let's hope they haven't," I said. "He wasn't one of those specimens they brought to the palace, then?"

"Them?" She thought about it, then decided against spitting in a confined space. "Oh, they were heads of households all right, but nobody's going to do anything *they* say."

"But—" I scrabbled for words. "Your father's friend," I said. "They'd listen to him."

"Maybe. They'd listen to him if he was speaking for me."

I couldn't help admiring the Echmen. They'd managed to find a society perfectly suited to decapitation – kill the king and there's nobody to take his place. Ideal for enslavement. I wish I'd read the book they got that out of. Not on the open shelves, presumably.

"He'll do," I said firmly. "What's he like?"

"Like?"

"Describe him."

Her this-is-pointless look. Muscle memory, they call it; do

something often enough and you don't have to think about it, the relevant parts of your body just get on and do it. It's the basis for all archery and swordsmanship. "Well," she said, "he's about so high, and he's got white hair and a beard."

"And?"

She shrugged. "He's smart. But I already told you that."

Dejauzi. They like to think they're an egalitarian society; apart from the king and the royal family and the nobles and the generals and their families and the priests and their families and so on, all men are equal. Unlike every other nation professing such ideals, however, the Dejauzi actually believe it, some of the time. Equal means *the same*. Therefore all Dejauzi, apart from the categories scheduled above, are the same, or if they aren't they should be. I should've known better than to ask.

"What's he like as a person? Is he nice? Serious, or a sense of humour? Does he like children and animals? What's his favourite food?"

"I don't know, do I?"

"You said you've known him all your life."

"I have. What's that got to do with it?"

"It's all right," I said, "it doesn't matter."

We took on food and drink at the first way station and they changed the horses; we didn't stop. The food came in a wicker basket. Amazing stuff, even to someone used to the scraps from the palace kitchen. She picked at hers as though waiting for it to bite back.

"If you don't want that," I said, "I'll have it."

"Help yourself. What are those slimy black things?"

"Candied sea slugs. Not quite worth their weight in gold," I added, as she pulled the mother of all faces, "but pretty close. Actually, they're not bad."

"Slugs. Are you mad?"

"Sea slugs," I pointed out. "Really they're just a sort of shellfish. Without the shells. Sure you don't want some?"

"Do you want me to be sick all down your front?" She turned her head so she didn't have to see the delicious food. "What sort of people eat *slugs*?"

"Rich ones. And distinguished guests of the Imperial government. Could do with a little salt."

"Piss off."

Two more days like that. The Imperial mail is the fastest thing on earth, but it didn't feel like it. Still, we got there in the end.

Where we got to was the last way station before the labour camp. While they were changing the horses, we sneaked out and ran for it. We watched them looking for us; then they gave up, because they had Imperial mail on board and a schedule to keep. The coach thundered away. We started to walk.

I wouldn't let us use the road, just in case, but it's easy enough to walk parallel with it in those parts, which are mostly sand and rocks with only a few thorn bushes. We had just over seven miles to cover. She was wearing unsuitable shoes and no Hus likes to walk. Sand is miserable stuff to wade through at the best of times. I didn't say anything. She said plenty.

The labour camp wasn't hard to find; just follow your nose, because the smell made its presence felt long before we crested a dune and saw the tents. It was the smell of dead things, unmistakable and not very pleasant. It didn't bode well. As it turned out, the dead things were mostly oxen, which the Echmen had sent by the thousand to drag stone blocks for wall-building. Presumably nobody knew that oxen can't survive in those parts – there's a special sort of fly that bites them, and they get a fever and die. I didn't know that, and I'd read the relevant books. So the stupid creatures lay down in their pens and died, and the perfumed breezes guided us straight to where we needed to go. Providence; practically a miracle.

"Yes, they'll know who I am," she was saying, as we started down a long slope towards the dirty white sea of canvas. "But, no, that won't mean they're going to rise off and cast off their chains, just because I've turned up. It's a really stupid idea."

"You wait and see," I said.

"You're an idiot."

"I have faith."

The next smell was smoke. They lit the fire while we were still descending the slope. All I could see was what looked like a long ridge. As we got closer it didn't look right. It was dead level, and the ends were square. It turned out to be a brick clamp a mile long, and we'd turned up just as they were lighting the fire to bake the bricks. Soon the sky was black with smoke, enough to blot out the sun. It was like twilight in the middle of the day. No flame to be seen, apart from the very occasional spurt where there was a hole in the earth mantle, quickly stopped up by men with long shovels.

The Echmen like their walls built out of brick, with stone blocks for the foundations. A mile of clamp would be enough bricks for half a mile of wall. Oio had reckoned this job would take a thousand years, start to finish. I'd assumed he was exaggerating for effect. I should've known better. The camp was all tents – rags on poles for the workers, proper government-issue waxed oxhide homes-from-home for the soldiers, but there weren't many of those, I was pleased to see. Very little in the way of heavy plant and equipment, but roof-high stacks of long, straight softwood poles for scaffolding.

"This is all wrong," she said. "My people don't know anything about building walls."

"They're about to learn," I said.

She couldn't be bothered to swear at me. Bad sign.

We waited until it was dark ("You won't stick out so badly," she pointed out), then walked quietly down to the tents. My first taste of the Hus en masse. What joy.

We'd found a discarded tarpaulin and cut it down the middle, half for her, half for me, mainly to cover up her dazzling silk dress until we needed it, for effect. It turned out that scrap tarpaulin was very much in fashion in the labour camp; everyone who was anyone was wearing it that season. I'd read about how very cold it gets at night in the desert, but I hadn't really believed it. There were a few fires dotted about – broken spars and smashed crates, the Echmen weren't issuing firewood – each one with a dense crowd squatted round it. Time to say hello.

I left that part of it to her, not knowing how you ask where someone is if you're not allowed to say his name. Amazingly, she had no problem; gestures, body language. She kept a flap of tarpaulin across her face, to cover the peacocks. Someone went away, then came back with a small child. The child led the way.

Poor people huddled round fires all look the same to me, but the kid knew who he was looking for. He tugged my sleeve and pointed; him, over there. I nodded.

She brushed past me, sat down beside the man who'd been pointed out to us, and drew the cloth from her face. "It's me," she said.

He turned his head and looked at her. I held my breath.

"Fucking God almighty," said the man on whom all our hopes were pinned. "Do you want to get us all killed?"

6

Everyone likes to believe in something, though belief is a lot like sleep; when you want it, it won't come, no matter how hard you try; the harder you try, the less it comes. All my life, priests and monks and holy men have been urging me to turn aside from my licentious ways and *believe*. Invariably they neglect to tell me how I'm supposed to do it. I imagine that lecture was at the start of term, and I missed it.

It's amazing what people can believe, if they're blessed with the gift of faith. For example –

The Robur believe, sorry, *believed* that Omnipater created the world because his son and daughter, the Invincible Sun and the Eternal Moon, were always bickering and he couldn't get any sleep. So he made them a chessboard – that's the Earth – and two sets of pieces, one light and one dark; that's you and me.

The Blemyans, by contrast, believe that there is nothing, only emptiness and void, in which God sleeps. We and the world we inhabit are simply his dream, and when he wakes up we shall immediately fade and be forgotten.

The Vesani believe that the world was created as a place where Sechimundus and Sichelgaita, the primordial lovers, could be together; they were forbidden to meet in heaven, since they were brother and sister. The sun is their first kiss, and the sea was formed from Sichelgaita's tears when Sechimundus was struck dead for his sin.

The Dejauzi believe that the Great-Great created the world from the bones of an aurochs (sort of like a wild cow, only much bigger). The grass is the hair on the aurochs' hide, and the sun is the light of the Great-Great's countenance glimpsed through a hole in the sky.

The Sashan believe that the world was originally an orchard laid out by Agen for his pleasure; but maggots hatched in the apples and grew into men. To punish them, Agen sent down an angel with a golden box, which he forbade them to open. Needless to say, as soon as the angel had gone, they opened it, and out flew Death, Sickness, War, Poverty and all the other evils that plague mankind. All except one; Hope was too feeble to climb out of the box, and the stupid humans, not realising that Hope is the greatest torment and deceiver of them all, lifted her out and took her for their own.

The Hus believe the same as the Dejauzi, except that they call the Great-Great Skyfather, and are prepared to defend to the death their conviction that the Great-Great and Skyfather are not one and the same person, even though they're on record as having done exactly the same things in exactly the same way. To the Hus, Skyfather is the one true god and the Great-Great is an abomination whose very name is so despicable it can't be said out loud. Further or in the alternative, they maintain, the very first thing Skyfather did on emerging from the primordial egg was strangle the Great-Great and bury his bones in a shit heap. Where the shit heap came from they don't specify. Presumably it was in the egg, too.

The other thing the Hus passionately believe in is the Queen of Heaven. I'll come to her in a minute.

"It's very bad," said the old man, Heaven Thunders The Truth. "They took all our cattle. There's people with nothing to eat. People are dying."

We were sitting round a fire – call it a fire; a handful of twigs smouldering – at the edge of the camp, next to the rows of Echmen government-issue carts. Her, me, him, four old men who looked just like him and to whom I hadn't been introduced. Nobody so far had acknowledged my existence. Fine by me.

"What happened?" she asked.

"Damned if I know. We woke up one morning and there were Echmen lancers riding through the village. We were scared shitless. They told us the king's dead, you're all coming with us. Food for ten days, that's all we could bring, and round up all the sheep and the goats. Had to leave the oxen and the poultry. No tools, no bows, nothing, just what we stood up in."

"You just let them order you around?"

"Fucking lancers," he said, "in full kit. We thought they must be on their way to a war somewhere and they were moving us on out the way. They didn't tell us anything. When we'd been marching four days we figured it must be something else. Some of us tried asking, got a smack in the face. So we kept on marching, and the ones who made it ended up here. And now we're building a wall. We don't know shit about building walls. It's really bad, I'm telling you. And with your father gone—"

"How many died?"

He shrugged. "Don't know," he said. "There's people saying there's another camp, two camps, further down the river, but where they got that from I don't know. Could be they didn't catch all of us, could be we're all that's left. They don't talk to us, and if they did it wouldn't help. They don't know the language, bloody savages. Your father, he could talk Echmen."

"So can I," she said.

"Then you bloody talk to them," he said, "tell them we aren't standing for it any more. Tell them we want to go home."

"I don't think they'd listen."

"No, don't suppose they would. What's this wall about, anyhow? What do they want a stupid great wall for in the middle of nowhere?"

She grinned. "To keep us out. Us and the Dejauzi. And everyone else who isn't them."

He rolled his eyes. "So how long are they going to keep us here?"

"Till the wall's built. For ever."

"That's not right." He reminded me of a dog I saw once; a great big dog, tied up with a heavy iron chain, and there was this ginger cat who'd sit there for hours at a time, smirking, just out of reach, while the dog nearly pulled its own head off trying to get at it. All the anger in the world, and absolutely nothing you can do. "What right have they got, marching us out here and making us do their slave work? They can't do something like that."

"Your friend," I said, "has a real knack for saying things that aren't true."

Everyone turned and looked at me, in such a way as to make

me feel that maybe the strategy I'd decided to adopt wasn't so smart after all. "Who the hell is he?" the old man asked.

She didn't answer. Thank you so very much. "I'm a Robur," I said. "I was a translator at the Echmen palace. I saved your queen's life."

They looked at her. She nodded, as if admitting that, yes, it was her who left the gate open.

"I brought her here," I went on. "And she and I, and you lot, are going to save your people and get them out of here. I know what has to be done."

"He's got an idea," she said. "Actually, you might want to listen to him. It's not as crazy as it sounds."

With friends like her. I hadn't wanted to make a Big Speech, but apparently I had to. Oh well.

"I know the Echmen," I said. "I've been living among them for six years, right there in the Imperial court. I know how their minds work. They brought you here because you're expendable and you've got no friends. They want their wall built, and they want to be able to cross you off their list of possible future nuisances. They reckon, if you're dead you can't make trouble. You can grin and bear it if you like. I wouldn't."

I paused. They were all just looking at me, sad eyes, expressionless faces.

"What you need to do," I went on, "is find someone who'll help you."

"Oh, right," the old man interrupted. "Who?"

"The Dejauzi."

"Piss off."

I sighed. If I'd had a mirror, or even a puddle, I'd have practised it beforehand. "Yes, fine," I said. "You hate them and they hate you. You've got that in common, like everything else.

But if you and the Dejauzi got together – all the Dejauzi: the Cure Hardy, the Luzir Soleth, the Auzinholet, the Emportat, the Cosseilhatz – you could stand up to any power on earth, even the Echmen. You've got the skills and the resources and the manpower. You could do it. Also, right now I don't see you've got a choice."

"That's all very well," said one of the other old men. "I grant you, we're so deep in shit we ought to try anything, even making nice with those bastards. But what makes you think they'd want to help us?"

"Because they're next," I said. "I told you, I know the Echmen. I know how they do things. They don't want to fight all the Dejauzi at once, they might lose. But if they can pick you off one at a time, first the Hus, then the Emportat, while the others stay back and say, well, thank God they didn't come for *us* – until in the end what's left of you isn't strong enough to stand up to them any more, and then they come down on you and slaughter you like sheep. Make them understand that and maybe we'll get something done."

I got scowled at for that. "What business of yours is it, anyway?" another of the old men said. "You're Robur, right? Last I heard, the Robur weren't exactly putting themselves out there for justice and the rights of man."

I nodded. "The Robur would do exactly what the Echmen are doing," I said. "If they still existed. Or don't you people follow the news?"

"What's he talking about?" one of the old men said.

"The Robur have all been wiped out," she told them. "About three years ago. As far as anyone knows, this man is the only one left."

It went down big. They all went thoughtful-quiet, and I

could see why. A timely reminder about the fragility of existence; if it could happen to the Robur, so strong and rich and cruel, it could happen to anybody. "What happened?" her father's friend said.

"I don't know," I said. "All I know is, a huge army came along out of nowhere, conquered our empire and sacked our city. I gather it was because they didn't like us. And, yes, I can see their point. Good riddance and no great loss, before any of you says it, but that doesn't make it right. Any more than what's happening to you is right."

"The Robur, for God's sake," someone said. "I thought there were *millions* of them."

"There were," I said. "Doesn't matter. Let me tell you about something I saw once, in the desert, when I first came to Echmen from the west. We were riding through the desert, and our guide pointed to a hill and said, guess what that is. It's a hill, we said. No, he told us, that used to be a city. We know, because about a hundred years ago some of our lads found a gold cup on the side of that hill. So we came back with spades and picks and dug about a bit, and we didn't find any more gold, but we did find walls, twenty feet thick, and houses and a temple and a huge barn full of broken twenty-gallon jars, a whole city. But we've lived in these parts for a thousand years and we've never heard of anyone else living here, certainly not a big city. So I went and looked it up in books, where everything's written down so it won't get forgotten. But not a word about any big city in that part of the desert, or a great nation who used to live there. All gone, like they'd never existed. That sort of thing happens all the time. You haven't even got gold cups and city walls for anyone to remember you by."

"Like I give a stuff who remembers me when I'm dead," her father's friend said. "I just want to go home."

"That's not going to happen," I said. "Not unless you get help. Now, who else apart from the Dejauzi can we think of who might help you?"

Long silence. "You really think those bastards would help us?"

"Yes," I said. "If we ask them the right way."

"Bullshit," said one of the old men. "You honestly believe they're going to come out here and pick a fight with the Echmen army just to rescue us?"

"No," I said. "But if we get up and walk out of here into their territory, and the Echmen demand that they hand us over and they say no – that's a bit different, isn't it? It's saying to them, there may be a war if you help us and there may not, because the Echmen might find a way to save face and back down. But if you don't help us, sooner or later there *will* be a war, and you won't win it. Put like that—"

Her father's friend shook his head. "We can't just get up and walk out of here."

"Can't you?" I looked straight at him. "I think you can. How many soldiers are there in the garrison?"

He looked blank. One of the other men said, "Two hundred and fifteen. My boy counted them."

"And I'll bet you they sleep at night. Well, then. What does it take to bash a sleeping man's head in with a brick?"

"Oh, sure. And when they find out, they send the lancers."

"And by the time the lancers get here, you're across the border. A wise woman once taught me the merit of keeping one step ahead. The Echmen don't like crossing borders. Too much risk. Somebody's fault if it all goes horribly wrong."

I looked at them. Nearly enough but not quite; just as I'd thought it would be. One by one they turned and looked at her. "Well?" one of them said. "What do you think?"

"It sounds really stupid," she said, "but when you start thinking about it, maybe it's not so dumb after all."

"The *Dejauzi*, for crying out loud."

"Yes, that's what I said," she replied. "But if you're attacked by a tiger and all you can find to throw at him is a turd, you throw the turd. You might just get lucky and hit him in the eye."

"You're the queen," one of them said. "We do as you say. But I don't like this idea, myself."

"I don't either," she said. "I do a lot of things I don't like. Some of them are necessary."

"Isn't there anyone else we could go to?"

"Not close enough," I said. "That's the other thing. You can be in Dejauzi territory in fifteen days. Otherwise you're talking weeks, maybe months. Plenty of time for the lancers to come and cut you to ribbons."

Something I've noticed about the Hus. They make angry growling noises when you say something they realise is true. "We do what the queen says," her father's friend said. "That goes without saying. But do any of us really think the *Dejauzi* are going to help us? Even if it means saving their own necks? If it was the other way around, I know I wouldn't."

So there we were, at the place I knew we'd reach, sooner or later. Now came the bit that I thought was a cracking good idea and she thought was idiotic and refused to have anything to do with. Here we go, then.

"What if it's not up to them?" I asked.

"You what?"

"What if it's not their choice to make? What if someone tells them to do it and they've got to obey?"

They gave me a glare that would've stopped a heavy infantry charge. "Like who?"

"Like," I said, "the Queen of Heaven."

"You've done it now, son," the old man said, in that low voice that tells you much more than mere shouting. "You don't talk about the Queen of Heaven. You're not even one of us, you're a fucking blueskin."

"I've seen her," I said.

I think that if she hadn't been there, those old men would've killed me on the spot. Instead, they looked at her. She shook her head. "Listen to him," she said.

"I've seen her," I repeated. "Listen. You asked me why I was here, what business this is of mine. I'll tell you. I was happy. Things were going all right, for a change. I had a good job in the Echmen court. You people meant nothing to me. But I saw the Queen of Heaven."

"If you're lying," one of them said, "you're a dead man."

I did the big sigh. "I'm not sure you wouldn't be doing me a favour," I said. "Because the Queen of Heaven came to me and told me what I have to do. And when she tells you to do something, it's not like you have a choice. Being here has cost me everything, and if you all die, I guess I die with you. I can't go back to my nice fat job, that's for sure. Not now."

A sort of tortured look on her father's friend's face, stuck on a sandbank between outrage and the possibility I was telling the truth. "She spoke to you."

I nodded. "She told me I'd been saved out of all my race," I said. "All the Robur are dead, except me, because she needed me to do a job. I don't suppose need is the right word. She picked me out, like you pick a drowning fly out of a pail of water. That's why I'm here. I can't say I'm exactly happy about it. I don't know. Maybe if I can't make you believe me, I'll be let off and I can go on with my life. But I don't think it works like that."

The possibility that I was for real was physically painful to them, but they were listening. "Why you?"

"That's a question I keep asking myself. Why a Robur, for pity's sake? Why not one of her own? But there it is. I'm here to lead you out of slavery into the land given to your ancestors, whether I like it or not. Oh," I added, "and she said you wouldn't believe me. She said you'd be too pig-headed to listen and you'd demand to see proof, a sign. So she's going to give you one."

I kept my eye on her as I said this; I hadn't got around to mentioning it to her. She took it well; no change in expression whatsoever. "Are you serious?" her father's friend said.

"Perfectly," I said. "On the day you stand face to face with the chiefs of the Dejauzi, the Queen of Heaven will be there. That's what she told me, anyway."

"She'll actually *be* there."

"Yes."

She stood up suddenly. That meant everybody else had to stand up, too. "That's enough for now," she snapped. "You all heard what he said. I believe him. Whether or not you do is up to you."

I bet you were thinking, earlier on in the story: did he really spend three years reading in a library? The answer is, yes. It's a very fine library, quite possibly the best in the world, but even there it's not always possible to find what you're looking for straight away; particularly if you don't know what it is you're looking for until you've found it. In my case it took me eighteen months. The other eighteen months I spent reading what I'd found, making notes, copying things out, plus a certain amount of sitting staring into space, thinking about things. In fact, I could've done with another year, but events forced my hand.

One of the books I read – it was a real devil to find, and then it was only the Echmen translation of the Sashan translation of a book of Vesani travellers' tales quoting a Carchedonian source taken from a Mezentine encyclopaedia – had quite a bit to say about the Dejauzi Queen of Heaven. The Dejauzi only believe in one god, who is all-powerful, all-seeing and rather too busy with more important things to bother much with the affairs of mortal men. But he has a wife, and she's rather more approachable. Pray to the Skyfather and he may hear you and he may just possibly grant your prayers; he could just as easily fry you with a thunderbolt for disturbing him when he's busy. The Queen of Heaven is more soft-hearted, and she has the ear of her husband. Whatever your prayer may be, it sounds better coming from her.

Furthermore, no man living or dead has ever seen the Skyfather; probably just as well, because the sight of him would shrivel you like a leaf. But the Queen of Heaven has been seen, seven times. On each occasion it's been at a turning point in the destiny of the Dejauzi people. She appears, talks in a language nobody can understand, gives a sign. On five occasions the Dejauzi have interpreted the sign correctly and prospered. Twice they misconstrued the sign and suffered disastrous consequences.

The Queen of Heaven manifests herself as a tall woman, over six feet. Her skin is as white as chalk, which is why the Dejauzi paint themselves like they do. Her voice is like music, but nobody except a prophet can understand what she says. There's also another manifestation, but nobody quite knows what it is; the wording in the texts is ambiguous. It's something like *clothed in fire*, whatever that's supposed to mean, or it could be *armed with the thunderbolt*, depending on whether the final A is long or short.

Another book I read was the fifth volume of Zautzes' *Political Commentaries*. Tell you about that in a minute.

"You know what you are? You're a lunatic. You're out of your tiny mind."

I was shaking like a leaf, the reaction to all that talking big to strangers. "I know, you said."

"The Queen of *Heaven*. They're going to cut us both open and wind our guts out on a stick."

"No," I said. "I've got that covered. Trust me."

"*Trust* you. Trust *you*."

"Yes."

Had I got it covered? I hoped so. Everything depended on whether Oio liked me enough to send a letter, at vast personal inconvenience to himself, to someone I was fairly sure existed in the place where I hoped she would be, and that this person was sufficiently down on her luck and desperate to undertake a job so difficult I wasn't sure if even she could do it, in return for a reward I wasn't entirely confident I'd be in a position to provide. If that all happened, there was a slightly worse than even chance that the crazy scheme I had in mind would work;

in which case, I was letting myself and hundreds of thousands of perfect strangers in for a very rough time indeed. If it didn't work, any of it, I was dogmeat. The business with winding your guts on a stick wasn't just her being imaginative, by the way. It's a skill common to all the Dejauzi family of nations, very well documented, I read all about it in a book. They've been doing it for over a thousand years, and practice makes perfect.

I watched the proud Hus nation making bricks. There are worse jobs, at least four of them. Carts arrive from the river-bank, where they've been piled high with gleaming wet clay, dug from the seam the Echmen found there years ago. Men with wooden shovels stand on the carts and load the clay onto wheelbarrows. Four brickmakers to a barrow; each brickmaker has a sort of wooden paddle. He (or she; Echmen gangmasters aren't prejudiced) scoops clay into a wooden box with no top or bottom, resting on a wooden board. He presses it down firmly so it fills out the box exactly, then skims the surplus off the top so it's perfectly flat. Then he lifts the box up and gives it a little bang on the wooden board; the brick pops out, and he puts it on a stack with all the others he's made. Then he does it again, and again, and again. The stack's on a sort of plank stretcher, and every so often two men come and take the stretcher to the clamp. When the clamp's full, they set it alight, filling the air with smoke. The Echmen have figured out how many bricks a man should be able to make in a day, under ideal conditions, which these apparently are. This came as a bit of a surprise to me, in my professional capacity. I had no idea *ideal* meant that.

It set me thinking; define Man. Hitherto I'd always assumed that Man is a creature equipped and therefore designed to explore a wide range of possibilities and find those to which he's best suited. Watching the Hus, I wasn't so sure. Hundreds, maybe thousands of years ago, the ancestors of the Hus came to a place that nobody else seemed to want, where they were fairly sure they'd be left in peace. It was mostly hills and mountains, with shallow valleys and forested uplands. There were small pockets of flat land in the valley bottoms, where rivers had piled up silt; you could grow wheat and barley there, so they did. The upper slopes of the hills were scrubland, with just enough grass and herbage to feed a resilient breed of sheep, so they bred resilient sheep. The lower slopes had just enough topsoil to be useful if you went to all the trouble and effort of terracing them, so they built terraces and planted vines, fig and apple trees, olives in specially favoured locations. On the edges of their valleys were broad, dry slopes of sand and scrub, where the only animals that could survive were small wild horses. They caught the horses and learned to ride them. There were possibilities there; they explored them. They made the best of what they'd got. Then the Echmen came. They narrowed the possibilities down to one; you slowly work your way along a riverbank, sleeping in raggedy tents, eating one loaf of coarse barley bread a day, and you make bricks. That's all. Because, the way the Echmen saw it, the Hus were no use to the empire sowing wheat and herding sheep and pruning vines. They contributed nothing to the greater good, they were just parasites, fleas on the back of the Great Society. There's an Echmen saying: ask not what your emperor can do for you, but what you can do for your emperor. What the Hus could do for their emperor was make bricks. Well, then.

The Echmen explain it very well. Society is all one body. The Echmen are the head, the lesser races are the hands and feet and other extremities. The head conceives of the purpose and formulates the plan for achieving it. The rest of the body does as it's told. The hand alone can achieve nothing; it needs the head. The hand alone has no *purpose*. Cut off a finger and the body's diminished but it goes on functioning; the purpose is still attainable. Cut off the head and the body dies, simple as that.

It's a point of view, certainly.

7

The old man, her father's friend, came in from brickmaking and found me in his tent, sheltering from the sun. He'd been looking for me, he said.

He made a lunge and grabbed a handful of my hair. "I'm onto you," he said. "I know what your game is."

I reminded myself that this was unlikely. "Let go," I said.

"You're hurting me."

Always a silly thing to say. He tightened his grip. "I've been trying to figure you out," he said. "Why would a man like you, a blueskin, want to rescue our queen, bring her here and try and talk us into breaking away from the Echmen. Makes no sense."

"I told you why."

"Then," he went on, "I figured it out. It's her you're after. You *fancy* her. Or you want to marry her and make yourself king. Well, it won't work."

"I know," I said. "It's impossible."

Not what he expected to hear. "You what?"

"And I can prove it," I said. "If you'll just let go of me."

Ah, the power of the simple conditional clause. If X, then Y; it's a bait nobody can resist. "Go on, then," he said, and let go of my hair.

I put a yard or so between him and me. He might look old, but he was fast and very strong. "You think," I said, "that I'm doing this because I'm in love with the queen, or I want to marry her and be the king. That's not true."

"You said you can prove it."

I nodded. Then I put my hand on the hem of my tunic and lifted it. He stared and pulled a face. "Oh," he said.

This bit isn't really something I wanted to talk about, but apparently the narrative requires it. I go where the narrative takes me, like driftwood on a river in spate. Oh well.

I was seventeen. My first posting was the Seventh Lancers, a very prestigious regiment, based at Scoira Limen. Our family is old and distinguished but no longer affluent, so I knew that if I wanted to fit in and shine, I'd have to be good at something and make myself popular. Fortunately, there's one thing I'm good at. I'm a crack shot, and the army loves its archers.

That's why I spent my legacy on the bow, and it turned out to be a good investment. I wasn't the very best, but I was in the top ten. In my first year I won two silver medals and a bronze, and I made sure I was a good loser; people like that. When the news of my father's death broke, that did me no harm either. He'd died defending a pointless outpost on the wrong side of a river we should never have crossed in the first place, after the main expeditionary force had been routed by a superior enemy; my father's garrison bought the idiots enough time to get back into Robur territory, but it was deemed necessary to break down the bridge, to stop the enemy streaming across it, and my father and his men were stuck on the far side. Official despatches said he died a noble and honourable death. I happen to think there's no such thing. But it made me sort of a hero's son – by no means a rarity, because there was a lot of noble and honourable death about at that time, a minor epidemic – and so people liked me, as if I'd somehow persuaded him telepathically to stay at his post and die with his boots on.

Strange things start happening inside your head when people like you. At first you feel smug and a tiny bit guilty. Then, without realising it, you begin to believe. If they like me, you find yourself thinking, there must be something there to like. In vain you try reminding yourself where all this comes from; they like me because I happen to be able to group all six inside the inner gold at thirty yards, or because my father got killed because of the incompetence of the joint chiefs of staff. You start to spin cobwebs of rationalisation; ah yes, but what they really like is how modest and unassuming I am as I walk forward to pull my arrows out of the target, how bravely I took the news about his death. It somehow slips your mind that you practised that modest and unassuming stuff beforehand until you were pitch perfect, and that one of the first things that crossed your mind when the adjutant told you the news was, *act brave, they'll love you for it*. Instead, you see someone different in mirrors, a likeable man, a good man, someone who's worth something.

I started getting invitations to dinner. I didn't mind that at all, since a free meal is one you don't have to pay for, and money was tight. My father, it turned out, had been living beyond his means; he was the hare and his means were a pack of old, tired hounds struggling to catch up. The house and the land covered his debts and there would have been a bit to spare, only he'd left that to the Golden Spire monastery, to endow a chantry for his soul. My mother's brother reluctantly gave me an allowance, enough so I wouldn't look bad and let the family down, but it wasn't all that much and, besides, it didn't feel right. I decided I'd have to get an early promotion. When you make full lieutenant, the army starts paying you, rather than the other way round. Since we weren't on active service, the only path to promotion was popularity. Just as well, I decided, that I was such a jolly good fellow.

Advancement at Scoira Limen centred around the adjutant general, a sensitive, cultured man who collected old porcelain and early Mezentine folksongs. His more mundane responsibilities were mostly carried out by his elder son, Colonel Theudahad, a born administrator, prematurely bald. His younger son, Lieutenant Carloman, was a keen archer, almost but not quite as good as me. Colonel Theudahad's only weakness was a fondness for gambling. He was a slave to it but, as befitted a born administrator, he preferred to bet on sure things. Carloman and I made the semi-final of the regimental summer knockout competition.

I was sitting on my bunk polishing my helmet when Carloman came in and sat down beside me. He wasn't his normal cheerful self.

"My brother," he said.

"What about him?"

"He's ordered me to throw the match."

That made no sense. I said as much.

"He's got a lot of money on you," Carloman said. "The thing of it is, because I'm his brother everybody thinks the fix is in and you'll throw the match so I'll win. So you're three to two and I'm sixteen to one."

"That's not fair," I said.

Carloman shrugged. "Lot of it about," he said. "Look, I'm only telling you because for crying out loud, whatever you do, don't have a headache or an off day, all right? There's only so much I can do to make it look convincing, so it'd be a great favour to me personally if you shot really, really well."

"I'll do my best," I promised him.

I was as good as my word. I slaughtered him. It was one of those days when everything is perfect. There was a very slight left-side wind at fifty yards, just enough to be a problem unless you knew precisely where to hold, which I did. Halfway through the fifty yard, I'd only dropped two points. I was narrowing the whole world down into a coloured ring, a rainbow reflected in a lake on a still day; all I had to do was concentrate every fibre of my being on the target and my eyes and hands and arms and back would do all the rest. My final score was 142 out of 144, with twenty inner golds. I don't think anyone on earth could've beaten me that day.

Talk about the conquering hero. I was invited to dinner at the adjutant general's lodgings in the Prefecture. Carloman was thrilled because he hadn't had to screw up deliberately and hadn't lost face. Theudahad was delighted because he'd just made a very substantial sum of money. The old man was beside himself with joy because he'd just paid a small fortune for a tiny plain white jug, which he assured us was genuine Three Clouds period. And the old man's daughter, Lady Melaxuntha – did I mention her? No, I don't suppose I did.

They didn't have anything like her where I came from. It wasn't just that she was beautiful; in fact, looking back, I'm not sure she was beautiful at all. But – there's this theory, about dogs. They can't really see things when they're still, only when they're moving. Lady Melaxuntha's face was never still, never the same two seconds together. It changed with every word, every expression, every emotion. I imagine that if she held perfectly still, she'd be handsome going on plain. I expect the wind would be very different if you caught it when it wasn't blowing. But if it wasn't blowing, it wouldn't be the wind.

Like her father, she was a collector. She collected junior officers. You know what collectors are like; they want you to look at the exhibits, but you mustn't touch them. By the same token, she wanted to be looked at, gazed at in speechless adoration, but finger marks were definitely not allowed, in case they spoiled the patina. All very harmless and innocent, and a source of gentle amusement to her and her family.

My father knew a man whose wife kept a leopard. Her husband had been given it by a Sashan diplomat. It's a very special, prestigious gift in Sashan society. The idea is, you turn it loose in your deer park, chase it with hounds and kill it, preferably on foot with a sword. Barbaric, said his wife, we're not doing *that*, and I guess her husband, who'd have had to take care of the on-foot-with-a-sword side of things, didn't give her much of an argument. Instead, she tamed the horrible thing. It was just like a big pussycat. It curled up in a basket and slept a lot. It held still while she tied bows round its neck. If you were very patient and gentle, it would eat bits of cake from your hand; its tongue, she said, was slightly abrasive, like fine sharkskin. And then one day it killed her, and by the time they were able to get into the room and kill it, it had already eaten her head and both legs. Moral: don't play with savage things that are stronger than you are.

Such as love. I have no idea what Lady Melaxuntha saw in me, as against the sixteen or so other subalterns in her collection. Maybe it was my ability to read crosswinds, or my fairly pleasant speaking voice, though I doubt it. Something about me snagged in her long, luxurious fur, and then into her flesh. To begin with she was subtle and discreet, so much so that it went over my head like a flock of geese; but her brothers, who knew her well, must have noticed something, because their manner towards me changed. When she invited me to dinner at the house they were perfectly pleasant, but they looked at me, just making sure I was where they could see me. Gradually the stress and tempo of the flirtation changed. Junior officers don't actually receive formal training in flirting. It's something they're expected to know already or pick up as they go along. But there's definitely an orthodox way of going about it, like good form in fencing. I always reckoned I was a bit of a duffer at it; good enough to get by but not one of my strong suits. I really don't like doing things I'm not good at. I'm pretty sure I wasn't in love with her, certainly not like she was with me. But when she was in full flight she was irresistible.

There was a sort of summer house out at the back of the adjutant general's lodgings. It was based on a pavilion, which is a sort of tent you pitch when you want to watch the tournament or the archery contest in comfort. Nobody used it in autumn, once the evenings started drawing in and there was a nip in the air, so it was ideally suited to the purpose. We met there four times, no bother at all. The fifth time was different.

I remember looking up and seeing Carloman, and five other junior officers who I thought of as my friends. The look on Carloman's face was indescribable. She caught sight of him, put two and two together and started to scream – thank God you're here, look what he's doing to me, I told him to stop but he wouldn't. He told her to shut up and get out. I don't think he believed her, but that wasn't the point.

I tried to stand up, but one of the men I thought of as a friend hit me so hard I could scarcely breathe, and I flopped down again. Carloman had brought a knife. He showed it to me. "If thine eye offend thee, pluck it out," he said.

"Carlo," I started to say, and got a mouthful of toecap.

"But it's not your eye that's the problem, is it? Not to worry, I'm going to cut it off, and then nothing like this will ever happen again."

It was a knife ideally suited to the purpose, one of those hooked jobs they use for pruning roses and cutting leather. The men I thought of as my friends hoisted me up and held my arms. I couldn't help noticing a certain squeamishness, a reluctance on Carlo's part actually to touch it – perfectly normal male reticence, I suppose. But grab hold of it he did, and I watched him align the curve of the blade to the radius of the shaft for a quick, clean slice.

It wasn't deliberate on my part; purely instinctive, combined with some pretty sloppy work on the part of the men holding me down. I don't actually remember what happened, not well enough to give a coherent account, the sort that would satisfy a historian. I squirmed or bucked or did something. The knife didn't go where it was supposed to. The pain was horrible and there was blood everywhere.

"Shit, Carlo," someone said behind me, "you've killed him."

Not really what you want to hear, and the fact that they let go of me made it worse. Carlo had this terrified look on his face; he dropped the knife and backed away. "We should get the doctor," someone said. "Don't be bloody stupid," someone else said. "We've got to go, now." Carlo was thinking about it, making a quick decision, like he'd been trained to do, while his heart and soul went all to pieces. I could see what was going through his mind. If we leave him, he'll bleed to death in no time flat. No witnesses. She won't say anything. We can get away with this if we just keep our heads.

He looked at me; furious hatred and a deeply sincere apology, all rolled into one, like a haggis. Then he turned and ran, and the men I thought of as my friends followed him.

So there I was, on my own. I looked at the damage. Between us, them with the knife and me flinching, we'd contrived to sever the top knob, and then the hook of the knife strayed or was deflected into my stomach, about a thumb's length shy of my navel; a long slit, pumping out blood like crazy, running diagonally up onto the ribcage, petering out before it reached the nipple. I could see why they'd reasoned as they had. The hell with it, I remember thinking. That's that.

For some reason that now escapes me, it was important at the time that I shouldn't be found dead in the summer house. I suspect I was trying to be considerate. After all, this mess was essentially of my making, or at least I'd contributed significantly to it, and in spite of everything these people were still my friends, so if I could help them before I died, I would. I stumbled out onto the lawn, then through the back gate into the stable yard, from there into the back alleys. Last thing I recall was finding an open door, lurching through it and hitting the ground.

I remember I had a lot of dreams, which seemed very real. One of them I can actually remember. I was doing something or other, and I looked up and there was this very tall, beautiful woman standing over me. I had a feeling she might be an actress or something like that. Her skin glowed bright, like a candle. "Who shall I send?" she said, "And who will go for us?"

"Here I am," I remember saying. "Send me."

Which seemed to settle the matter, because then I woke up. There were people crowding round me, staring at me. One of them said, "Fuck me, he's alive." I remember, I was disappointed.

They called a doctor, who told me I really shouldn't have survived. Sorry, I told him. I meant it. Then they took me to the hospital, where army surgeons sewed me up like a patchwork quilt.

I remember I felt weak as a kitten. The adjutant general came to see me. This is all very bad, he said. I agreed; it was. He'd written to my uncle, he went on. Obviously, I couldn't remain in the service, and it was probably best if I went abroad for a while. A posting in the diplomatic corps seemed to fit the bill quite nicely; what did I say to that?

I felt sorry for him. I was making a lot of trouble, which he'd done nothing to deserve. I wanted to ask him to tell Carlo, no hard feelings, but I didn't have the strength to speak.

They sent me to a monastery to convalesce. While I was there, one of the brothers came to see me and asked if I felt like learning Echmen; he understood I was being posted out there, and knowing the language would be useful.

Echmen, then Sashan, then all the languages they had grammars for; I soaked up languages like water, which surprised me. Some people have the gift, I know, but it never occurred to me that I might be one of them. Which is how I came to be a translator, something I'd never even have considered if my best friend hadn't sliced me open. It only goes to show; silver linings.

"What the hell happened to you?" the old man said.

"I can pee through it," I told him, "though it hurts like stink. Other than that, it's neither use nor ornament. So you see, nothing to worry about on that score."

"Put it away, for fuck's sake," he said, and I did. "What happened?" he repeated.

I grinned at him. "It's the price you pay for seeing the Queen of Heaven," I replied.

He went very quiet.

"You're serious, aren't you?" he said.

"Yes."

"And that—"

"Nothing worth having comes for free," I told him. "She said to me, I'm going to spare you, out of all your race, but there's a price. I'm not complaining."

He was having a bad time, I could tell. "I owe you an apology," he said. "I thought—"

"Of course you did. I don't blame you. You're just watching out for her. That's good."

"I never thought—"

"Well, you wouldn't, would you? And as for me wanting to make myself king, I know that among all the Dejauzi tribes the king has to be physically unblemished, so it's no good if you're blind in one eye or you're missing a foot, or—" I smiled at him. "Whatever. Not to mention the utmost importance of the line of succession. There's no way the queen could marry someone like me. I suggest you tell everyone. It'll set their minds at rest."

He lifted his eyes and looked at me. "You really saw her."

"Yes."

"What was it like?"

"You'll find out for yourself soon enough," I said. "If you do as I told you."

That was like a slap round the face, but maybe he'd asked for it.

8

One jump ahead. I hadn't realised the importance of it before, until she showed me. I owe her for that.

We had no weapons as such, but we had spades, picks and shovels. The guards weren't expecting trouble. Most of them were in their bunks when we did it. We killed the sleepers first, quietly. That left about thirty. We told them that if they put down their weapons and didn't make a fuss, we'd let them go. So they did that, and then we killed them.

It's a breathless sort of feeling, when you've done something irrevocable and there's no going back. But we were one jump ahead, so provided we kept our nerve we'd be fine, or so I told them. People like to hear that sort of thing. Another conditional clause, you'll have noticed; if X, then Y. One of these days I'll find myself operating in a language that doesn't have conditionals, and then I'll be screwed.

Bless the Echmen for their organisational skills. We had food for three weeks, courtesy of the Imperial commissariat, and water jars, and carts to carry them in, and Imperial horses to pull the carts. The Hus would have to walk and they hate walking, but never mind about that. I don't much like walking either, which may have had something to do with my decision to ride ahead and open talks with the Dejauzi.

"You can't just barge in and expect them to listen to you," she said. "They'll take one look at you and start throwing stones."

That thought had crossed my mind. "So send someone with me," I said. "Not you," I added quickly, "your people need you with them."

That got me a huge scowl. For some reason I don't think she relished the thought of leading a large convoy of people, many of them very much like her, out into the desert on foot. "Who else are they going to listen to? Use your brain."

Ah well.

There were eighteen riding horses, formerly the property of Echmen officers. She chose three, one each and a spare to carry the water.

I rode a lot when I was young, but Echmen saddles are – well, different. I can see the rationale behind them, they're very cleverly designed, but not at all what I'm used to. We muffled our heads up against the sun, which made conversation difficult. Small mercies.

There's a room in the Echmen Imperial library which is full of nothing but maps. To the Echmen they're works of art rather than objects to be used. They like to gaze at them, enjoying the sinuous curves of coastline, the delicate and distinctive shape of rivers, like the veins in a dried leaf. Many very fine Echmen poems have been inspired by looking at maps. I'd gone there with a wax tablet and a stylus, and committed my notes to memory. I could close my eyes and see all the country between the Echmen border and the Dejauzi heartlands, spread out in front of me like a neatly laid table at a formal banquet.

The trouble with maps drawn by people who appreciate them for their aesthetic qualities is that very occasionally they're tempted to improve on nature. My plan was to follow the river south until we came to the dried-up bed of another river, which only runs wet in the rainy season; that ought to lead us straight to a convenient pass over the mountains, on the other side of which we'd find the stronghold and principal trading post of the Luzir Soleth. I now suspect that the dried-up riverbed was added in the interests of symmetry, because it wasn't actually there.

When I shared my suspicions with her, she wasn't impressed. I let her talk herself out, then asked if she had anything to suggest.

"I knew you'd balls it up," she replied, "so I brought this."

From around her neck she drew a sort of pendant, which proved to be a bone tube with a copper loop glued to it, on a bit of sinew string. There was a stopper in one end, which she picked out. Then she opened her palm and shook out a small, thin needle.

"We need a bowl of water," she said.

I poured water into a bowl. "Now what?"

"It's called a lodestone," she said, dropping the needle into the water. It sank, then bobbed up again and turned, as if twisted by unseen fingers. "The blunt end points north."

"You're kidding."

"Belonged to my mother," she said. "It was her dowry. They offered my father a choice, three hundred sheep or this. By all accounts, he didn't hesitate. Don't ask me where it came from, I don't know. It works."

I got up and lined myself up the best I could behind the needle. "It's pointing towards that mountain," I said. "So we need to go—" I calculated. "That way."

She retrieved the needle, put it away, and drank the water. "Problem solved," she said.

"You seem to have lots of incredibly useful things which you don't tell me about," I said.

"Yes."

We went that way, and, sure enough, it wasn't long before the mountains appeared, and the pass through them. "You'd better leave the talking to me," she said. "Actually, I don't know why you had to come at all."

I was beginning to think that. Now that I'd seen the territory at first hand I was heartily glad I hadn't had to cross it on foot. That said, I wasn't looking forward to meeting the Luzir Soleth.

The Echmen haven't got a lot to say about them, so you have to go to the Sashan accounts, which are somewhat biased on account of the fact that four hundred years ago the Luzir invaded the Sashan homeland, sacked three major cities and killed every living thing they could find. A certain degree of negativity, therefore. Of course the Sashan retaliated, which is why the remnants of the Luzir ended up here, two thousand miles south of where they'd started and greatly diminished in both number and self-confidence. Since their great adventure they hadn't been any real bother to anyone except their fellow Dejauzi, but they were reputed to have long and vivid memories. I was hoping therefore that the message that the Echmen were about to come for them would go down big. On the other hand it might not. Seventy years ago they made a bit of a stir at the Echmen court when a political dissident sought refuge with them and the Echmen demanded his extradition. What they got was the dissident's head, perfectly preserved in a jar of wild honey. I happen to like honey, but not as much as that. There's no word for *diplomat* in Dejauzi. You have to use a loan word from another language or a paraphrase. "If we'd gone a couple of days further south," she was hissing in my ear as we walked up to the main gate of the castle, "we'd have been in Cure Hardy territory. At least you can talk to them without getting your throat cut. These people are *savages.*"

"Fine," I said. "If you're so smart, you think of something."

I like people who thrive on adversity, like the trees that grow in the cracks between the stones in a wall. They can be hard going the rest of the time, but when the steel bashes into them, they strike sparks. "Looks like I'll have to," she said. "Watch."

She strides, no other word for it, right up to the nearest man. He's standing with his back to her, checking the girth on a pack horse laden with two bales of wool. She prods him in the back. He turns round. She smacks him across the face so hard it makes my teeth hurt.

There's a small trickle of blood at the corner of his mouth. "You crazy bitch," he says. "What did you do that for?"

"What are you going to do about it?"

He looks her up and down, notices the peacocks. "You're Hus," he says.

"So I am."

I can practically hear him think. A strange Hus woman socks him for no reason, then stands there bold as brass. She doesn't make a grab for the horse's reins or try to run away. Therefore she's either mad or somehow important. Either way, she's too complicated a problem for him to solve. Without breaking eye contact he calls behind him; quick, run and fetch the magistrate. A boy, presumably his son, darts off at high speed. And, not long after that, we establish communication with the proper authorities. It's not the way I'd choose to do things, but apparently it works.

It went rather better than I'd expected; mostly, I fancy, because I did as I was told and left the talking to her. It was a real stroke of luck that one of the Luzir king's uncles happened to be in town. It meant that royalty was talking to royalty, so no mucking about.

She explained the situation and offered him a choice. Either the Luzir could fall in with our plans, or else we'd bring all our people into their territory regardless. In which case, if we all starved to death or they handed us over to the Echmen, it would be an eternal shame on the Luzir Soleth and a wonderful pretext for the other Dejauzi to gang up on them and give them a kicking. He argued, of course, but I could see his heart wasn't in it. Later I found out that he'd been on at his nephew for years about the Echmen threat and how someone ought to do something about it. More luck.

He didn't have the authority to make treaties, he said, but he wasn't about to let seventy thousand people starve to death in the desert or get carved up by lancers. Besides, if we chose to gate-crash his territory, being realistic there wasn't a lot he could do about it, so why the hell not?

"But you need to talk to my nephew," he said. "The boy's an idiot, but he listens to me and my brothers. Then I suppose we'll have to talk to the Aram Chantat. That's not going to be fun."

It wasn't. Their emissaries arrived very quickly indeed, not a good sign. You must be out of your minds, they told us. What the hell do you think you're playing at, annoying the Echmen? When she answered them, I realised (among other things) why, hundreds of years ago, the Robur adopted the medium-length, double-edged, broadly fullered Type 14 sword, originally invented by the Mezentines. When a weapon's been used against you to devastating effect, you know how good it is. You want it on your side.

First, she said, the Echmen were coming anyway. They'd already started, as witness the enslavement of her people. Second, if fighting for their lives annoyed the Echmen, tough. Third, if the Dejauzi stood up to the bastards *now*, maybe there wouldn't be any fighting. Fourth, she was the queen of the Hus and this man here is the king of the Luzir Soleth, and neither of them were in the mood to talk to *subordinates*, so why didn't they make themselves useful and go and fetch their king?

So they did that, and with him came the crown prince of the Rosinholet, because his father was too old and frail to travel. Extraordinary; much more than I'd hoped for. Dejauzi kings don't pay calls on their neighbours unless they absolutely have to. But here they were. Maybe, just possibly, someone had tried listening instead of shouting.

It's odd for me, sitting in on a high-level conference and not translating. It's like those dreams where you talk but nobody can hear you. I felt like a ghost, or a minor diplomat without portfolio wandering round a great palace, or a scavenger. She'd told me to get lost, go and sit somewhere else until it was over, but I didn't feel I could do that. Nobody had actually asked who I was or what I was there for, ever since we arrived on Luzir turf; some sort of ornament, lucky piece or pet, I imagine they assumed. That part of it didn't bother me. I don't like being involved if I can help it. If you're not involved, you can't screw up. During negotiations I often saw her shooting glances my way, reassuring herself that I was docile and under control, not about to say something provocative or stupid. Fine. The simple fact was, she knew what she was doing. In the blood, I guess.

Four Dejauzi rulers sitting in a circle under an apple tree; nothing like that in living memory. It should have been the Hus and the Luzir against the Aram and the Rosinholet, because that's Dejauzi geometry; assemble an even number of Dejauzi and they'll naturally fall into symmetrical opposition. But she wouldn't let it happen. She wouldn't take no for an answer. An hour into the talks and we were way past the point where someone should have stormed out in a huff, closely followed by someone else, leaving the other two to celebrate how unreasonable the offendees were being. But she kept them all there, hammering at the weak points in their arguments like a woodpecker, keeping to the point like a drill, and when they insulted her she ignored them; their taunts weren't worth the bother of a reply because that's obviously all they were, taunts, parries to deflect the argument. Smart. Finally, when tempers had rubbed down through skin and flesh to the bone, she smiled at the Aram and the Rosinholet and said, "We're not getting anywhere, are we?"

"Only because you won't listen."

"Well," she said, "if you don't believe me, maybe we should ask someone you will believe. How about it?"

They looked at her. "Who might that be?"

In passing; she was sitting with her back to the apple tree, having made a point of getting there first. There's a rigid Dejauzi protocol about where people sit, based on where the original homelands of their nations used to be. A thousand years ago, the Hus lived north of the Aram, with the Luzir to the south-west and the Rosinholet to the south-east, though of course there were loads of other tribes in between, and since then everybody's moved about all over the place. Never mind. All Dejauzi meetings sit in a circle, oriented by ancient tradition. Rather sweet, don't you think?

"The Queen of Heaven," she said.

Intakes of breath so sharp you could've used them for surgery. She's done it this time, I thought.

"Wash your mouth out with ashes and water," said the Rosinholet. "That's not funny."

"Wasn't meant to be." From round her neck she produced the little bone tube. "Know what this is?"

"Bit of shin, at a guess."

"In here," she said, "is the greatest treasure of the Hus people. It's the Queen of Heaven's needle. It was given to my mother's family, a thousand years ago."

Long silence. Then someone said, "What about it?"

"Get me a bowl of water."

Humour the stupid bitch, said the Luzir king's expression as he nodded to a bystander. A bowl duly appeared. "It works like this," she said. "I put the needle in the water and it'll turn and point at whichever of us is right."

"It'll sink," said the Aram.

"If it sinks, I'll go away and never come back. If it does what I say it does, we all abide by the decision. Agreed?"

If she'd dropped the needle at that moment, we'd all have heard it clatter on the ground. "Well?" she said.

"If this is a trick," said the Rosinholet, "there won't be any Hus left to hand over to the Echmen. We'll see to that."

"No trick. My word of honour."

Big medicine. "All right," the Aram said. "But if it's a needle, it'll sink."

It didn't. It bobbed up, then slowly swivelled round and pointed at her; due north, with her back to the tree. Now that really was smart.

Later she told me, "It really is the Queen's needle. That's why it's a lodestone. It points to her, and she lives in the north, everybody knows that."

I nodded. "And it's been in your family a thousand years."

"More or less."

"Your lot have managed to keep something like that a secret for a thousand years."

"Yes. Otherwise somebody might've stolen it."

Well, quite.

So they sent for the kings of the Cure Hardy, the Maudit and the Emportat, who agreed to come. Extraordinary. Wild times among the Dejauzi, but I was bored. I had nothing to do. I hadn't even brought a book with me.

But I had brought the bow; so, when I saw a bunch of men setting up a straw target, I wandered over and asked if I could watch. They scowled at me but didn't tell me to go away. I watched.

All the Dejauzi are archers, or so they'll tell you. The bull on their target is about half as big again as the one I'm used to, and they shoot from twenty yards, not thirty. The men I was watching were getting three or four out of five in, and seemed to think they were doing well. I noticed that they drew to the corner of the mouth rather than the ear, possibly explaining their tendency to drift to the right.

After a while I couldn't stand it any more. I slipped across to the stable where I slept, retrieved the bow, strung it and wandered back. I didn't say anything, just stood there with the bow hanging from my hand at my side.

After a while, one of the men said, "What's that supposed to be?"

I raised it so he could see.

"What's that? A kid's bow?"

I smiled. I hadn't had much experience with the sort of bow they used – all-wood (what we call a self bow), as tall as the archer or slightly taller. The Sashan guardsmen I'd shot with for a while used something similar, only better; theirs were slightly recurved, and the limbs were thin and flat. The Dejauzi bows were straight, thicker and narrower with a D cross-section, about the least efficient geometry there is. "May I?" I said.

"Oh, go on, let him have a shot," one of them said. "Then maybe he'll go away."

I had the arrows her uncle gave me. I put six in the dead centre of the bull, touching. They looked at me. "Do that again," one of them said.

My arrows had gone in so deep that only the nocks were showing. "I'm afraid I'll ruin your target," I said. "I think maybe my bow's a bit too strong for it."

"What, that little thing?"

Fine. I shot another six, same result. Straw was coming out of the back of the target in handfuls, and one arrow had passed clean through and buried its head socket deep in a stable door. "What weight do you draw?" I asked.

They gave me a blank look. Question not understood. "Could I possibly have a shot with one of yours?"

As I thought, their bows were much lighter; fifty-five, sixty pounds. I was able to make the necessary allowances, so I didn't disgrace myself. It was like using a toy compared to mine. A kid's bow.

They'd gone all quiet. "Here," one of them said. "Let me have a go with that thing of yours."

Under normal circumstances the answer would be no. Never lend a good bow, even for a single shot. Something told me, however, that it would be all right. "Sure," I said, and handed it over.

Needless to say, he couldn't draw it. None of them could. My bow draws a hundred and fifteen pounds; on the light side by Robur standards, nearly double what they were used to. They stared at me.

"That's why it's tearing up your target," I explained. "Sorry about that. It didn't occur to me."

"You can actually shoot with that thing? And hit stuff?"

I gave them another demonstration. It cost me, because my fifth arrow hit the nock of my second and smashed it to hell. Never mind. Six in the middle, touching. I had an idea that I was beginning to get through to them. And I'd just understood something about the Dejauzi, and the course of history.

"Actually," I said, "it isn't really about strength. It's a knack."

They gave me dubious looks. "Is that right."

"Yes. You draw with your arms and shoulders and a bit of help from the back. We draw with everything – arms, body, legs. Watch me and you'll see."

Later, I explained the difference to them. They made bows out of wood, from the trees that grew everywhere you looked.

Where the Robur originally came from there were very few trees; the odd stunted, wispy thorn, and that was about it. So we learned to make bows from other materials. On the side that stretches we use sinew – think of a deer bending its head down to drink, how strong in tension its backstrap must be. On the inside, which compresses, we use horn, the most resilient material in the world. In those far-off days we were a nation of horse archers, so we made our bows short, to be shot from the saddle. Not having good material led to a better product; our poverty made us stronger. It takes three months to build a Robur bow; a Dejauzi can whittle one out of a seasoned log in an afternoon.

"The most you can get out of one of your bows is sixty-odd pounds at full draw," I told them. "Otherwise it'd have to be so tall you'd need a ladder to reach the handle. Also the shape's all wrong."

"It works for us," someone growled.

"Sure it does," I said, "because you want it to stop a roebuck in the woods at thirty yards. Whoever designed this thing couldn't get closer than a hundred, because game can see you coming out in the open. So he needed a lot more power."

More to it than that, of course. I read about it in a book. For most of their history, the Dejauzi only fought other Dejauzi, and only ever about practical things – grazing rights, access to water, the sort of issue where it was in everybody's interest to reach a decision quickly and with the minimum of disruption to everyday life. Since the Dejauzi have never liked talking to each other, war seemed a reasonable alternative – provided it was conducted in an efficient and sensible manner. Which it was.

When two Dejauzi nations couldn't agree, they turned out en masse and faced each other at extreme range, precisely calculated through long experience. The key to success was the weather; whoever managed to get the wind at his back had an overwhelming advantage. So the two armies would trace and traverse about, wise and skilful generals would stand on hilltops throwing handfuls of dust in the air, and, when the time was right, the two sides would launch volleys of arrows into the air at forty-five degrees to the vertical, the elevation that makes for maximum carry. The upwind side's arrows naturally went that bit further; they could reach their target while the other side's shots were falling short. After a dozen or so hits had been scored, the downwind side reconciled themselves to the fact that today simply wasn't their day and ran for it, leaving their enemies to declare victory, pile up a cairn of stones to confirm the fact and go home. On a bad day, a few men would be killed, which was a pity; that sort of thing causes bad feeling and a wasted life is no use to anybody. Generally speaking, however, the cost in life, time and resources was slight compared to the advantages of vexed issues settled and decisions reached. So the Dejauzi nations were at war almost constantly, giving ambitious men a chance to shine as wind-savvy generals and boisterous youths their opportunity to show how far they could shoot. It was a good system, quite possibly the best way I've ever come across of settling disputes with foreigners.

But then the Echmen came, and the Sashan, and other monsters. They came with huge armies of armoured men mounted on big, fast horses. The arrows from the Dejauzi bows lodged in their shields or bounced off their armour, and then came the bloodbath. The Dejauzi tried shooting at the horses, but their effective range was no more than seventy yards; a warhorse can cover seventy yards very quickly. One volley, and then the lancers were on top of you, furiously angry because you'd shot up a dozen very expensive horses.

So the Dejauzi turned to other weapons. They went up the mountains and cut long, straight poles, and when the lancers came back they found themselves facing squares of pikemen. The Dejauzi couldn't hurt the armoured lancers, but the lancers couldn't get in close enough to break the squares. Then for a couple of hundred years or so the lancers were too busy fighting each other, Sashan against Echmen, and the Dejauzi were left with the vague impression that they'd won, along with a vivid memory of how much that victory had cost. Bows, they decided, were no use on the battlefield; pikes were the answer. This had an unfortunate effect on the traditional Dejauzi way of settling squabbles. Wars between the Dejauzi nations suddenly cost far too many lives, and they took to hating and resenting each other but not actually fighting. Not fighting is, of course, always best, but the way they reached that point left a certain amount to be desired.

So; they were still a nation of archers, but they were beginning to forget why. Every night in every Dejauzi village, some old fool would start singing one of the old ballads, preserving the memory of battles long ago; clouds of arrows that blot out the sun, the exceptional cunning of this or that adept at reading the fall of wind-blown dust. But that was the olden days. In real life, war is about very long poles, people getting hurt and enemies who may well decide to come back any day now, and nobody feels inclined to sing songs about it.

It was very different for the Robur, who came as horse archers into a country where good land was too scarce to waste on pasturing horses. Once they'd shot all the natives, they settled down, ate the horses and learned to grow wheat; and when the Sashan came on their mighty chargers, they greeted them on foot with locked shields, javelins and the Type 14 sword. What prevailed in the end wasn't the technical advantages of this or that weapon. The Robur were simply more violent, more prepared to trade their lives for those of the enemy. The Sashan like to win but the Robur loved to fight; in consequence the better man lost – that's if you define better as possessing more admirable qualities, and not loving bloodshed for its own sake has always seemed pretty admirable to me.

In time the Robur professionalised their armies and spent a horrifying proportion of their national wealth on the very best armour that money could buy for their darling heavy infantry. That would appear to have been a mistake, bearing in mind what happened to them; they grew to be so good at war and conquest that the rest of mankind decided they had to go. But in straight military terms they went with what had always worked: heavily armoured foot soldiers standing in straight lines with locked shields. Archery had its uses, but there was always a lurking suspicion that it was somehow cheating; besides, where was the point in killing a man if you don't get to feel his dying breath on your face? I was a Robur soldier for a while. I didn't think that way, but I pretended I did. So did everyone else, and what everybody pretends has a habit of growing into the truth.

And there's my bow, a masterpiece of design and construction. I watched it being built. Its natural enemy is tightly rolled straw. I wouldn't willingly have it any other way. But how would it be if—?

*

The Hus arrived.

They were in pretty good shape for people who'd just walked across a desert. For a start, they were alive, and most of them were still on their feet. The rest were slumped in the carts that had started the journey full of food and water. If they'd been sheep or chickens you'd have been merciful and put them out of their misery, but mercy means something else when applied to human beings.

The Luzir reacted to the arrival of their suffering brethren by demanding to know what these people were going to eat, where they were going to sleep and at whose expense. Good questions. I was acutely aware that I'd gambled their lives on my plan and her debating skills, and it remained to be seen if I'd won my bet. Without the lodestone, I think the sight of all those hungry mouths would've tipped the balance and condemned the Hus to death by starvation and exposure. But a twitch from the Queen of Heaven was something else. The Luzir king gave orders for every family to contribute a jar of flour and a blanket. It wasn't quite enough, but it was better than nothing.

All those sad people sitting round with nothing to do. Since my archery exhibition I'd become an object of interest; the Hus queen's performing dog, rather than just her dog. I went to see the king of the Luzir, who looked at me and said, "What?"

"I was wondering," I said. "What happens to all the bones and sinews and other odds and ends when your people butcher a goat?"

"I don't know, do I? Do I look like a butcher?"

"Would it be all right if I found out?"

He shrugged. "Do what you like."

I'd been hoping he'd phrase it like that. When you're a

translator, precision matters. The right words in the right order. The Mezentines used to believe, before they got rid of all their gods, that in the beginning the Almighty spoke the exact specifications for earth, air, fire, water, the various plants and animals, minerals and their properties, the height and footprint of every mountain, the speed and vector of every wind; and behold, as he said it, so it came into being. That's the Mezentines for you. Even their god is an engineer. But at least they grasp the fundamental importance of absolute precision in your choice of words.

I went away and did what I liked. There is, of course, no waste when they butcher a carcass, but some body parts are more useful than others. The sinews, for example, can be dried and thrashed and woven into very strong twine, but there are easier ways of making string. Horn is useful for knife handles and the like, but bone does just as well. By making a thorough nuisance of myself, I quickly got hold of as much horn and sinew as I wanted. Then I went to see the Hus.

Just as well I'd hung around when my bow was being made, watching every stage of the process like a hawk. This, I explained, is how you crush the dried sinew, very much like crushing flax; then you comb it out into strands. You can do that for me? Sure, they said, but why would we want to? Likewise, with sawing horns into strips and boiling them till they're soft. It's not exactly chariot science, just time-consuming.

"They need something to do," I told her. "Otherwise they're just sitting round feeling unhappy and resentful."

She knew her people. "Fine," she said. "I'll tell them to do it. What are you up to?"

"Destiny," I said.

"Oh, that."

You also need glue, which you get from boiling down hooves. By the weirdest coincidence possible, four hooves produce enough glue to stick two horns and a backstrap tendon; one good-sized eating goat equals one bow. The wood for the cores grows on trees. Apart from that all you need is time, a good hot sun for drying and skill.

Some nations are all thumbs. Others are naturally handy. Lacking a developed economy and not even having a word for industry, the Hus were used to making everything they needed themselves. They could therefore saw a straight line and shape a piece of wood by eye with a knife or even a sharp bit of stone. I implied that the skills needed for advanced bowyery were beyond them. They resolved to show me how wrong I was. Perfect.

Some things needed real skill, such as making the forms and jigs. The Luzir king, who by now was starting to take an interest, lent me a dozen tentmakers, who turned out to be able to turn their hands to anything. I explained what I needed and left them to it. I can't even knock a nail in straight.

It takes three months in a temperate climate to make a high-class competition bow, but there are corners you can cut, or so we learned as we went along. Searingly hot sunlight definitely helps. By the time the remaining three kings arrived, we had our first two dozen prototypes. One of them snapped like a carrot as soon as I tried to string it. The other twenty-three were just fine.

Now that I was a person of some importance, the assembled kings of the Dejauzi were prepared to listen to me. "It'll make all the difference in the world," I told them. "An arrow from one of these bows will bring down a warhorse at a hundred and fifty yards. In practice, that means you get at least four shots before the lancers reach you. Now suppose two of your shots miss. That's still two lancers out of action for every archer."

They did the sums in their heads. I had their attention.

"Actually," I went on, "it's much better than that. Echmen lancers are the best in the world, but they aren't going to press home an attack against a hedge of pikes when half of them won't even get there. They'll break and run. And if the lancers run, so will the rest of the army. We can beat the Echmen, simple as that. Now stop a moment and think what that means."

So they did that; and it was like when you reach the top after a long, weary climb and look down into the valley. What you see there may be good, bad or both, but the perspective takes your breath away. "That's all very well to begin with," someone said. "But they're not idiots. They'll adapt."

"Only if they have time," I said.

There's a difference, of course, between being able to do something and wanting to do it. That was a difference I wanted to blur over, the way you smooth plaster into a crack. But they were sensible men, not easy to fool. "That's a hell of a thing you're suggesting," said the Maudit.

"It can be done," I said. "It happened to the Robur. Think about it."

"You're talking about a huge war," said the Rosinholet. "Why would anyone want to start something like that?"

"A war to end all wars," I told him. "Come on, think. There's been a shadow hanging over the whole Dejauzi nation for as long as any of you can remember. One day, the Echmen are going to come for you. It's at the back of your minds every day of your lives. Isn't it? Right, then. It's like you've built your house under a mountain, and every day you look up at a great big outcrop of rocks and you know that sooner or later it'll come tumbling down and squash you flat. Fine. You can live like that, for a while. Or you can go out with picks and crowbars and your friends and neighbours and you can dig out those rocks so you'll know they'll never bother you again. Like the milkfaces did with the Robur. People shouldn't have to live like that, waiting for the enemy to round them up like sheep and herd them away. It happened to the Hus, it'll happen to you. Unless you put a stop to it, once and for all."

They looked at me as if I was the angel of death, perched on the end of the bed. "Just how far do you suggest we go?"

"As far as it takes."

"A war to end all wars," the Aram Chantat said. "That's like saying death makes you immortal."

I rather liked that, but I had to ignore it. "You saw what they did to the Hus," I said. "And you know what the milkfaces did to the Robur. Think about it, that's all I'm asking. How many of you do they need to pick off singly before the rest of you combined can no longer stand up to them? Say they take the Luzir next. That's all right, the rest of you say, we never liked them much anyway. Then they take the Cure Hardy, march them a thousand miles away to the other end of their empire. Who's next after that? And when do you reach the point where all of you put together will hardly slow them up, let alone stop them? All right, you say, but let's not start anything, let's wait for them to come to us. Sure. You let them come at you in their own time on their own terms, fully prepared. Now that's really smart."

"War is one thing," someone said. "I think you're proposing something more than that."

"That's right, I am. I'm proposing peace. The peace that comes when your enemy can't hurt you any more, because your foot is on his neck. It's the only kind worth having, believe me."

The Rosinholet turned to her; reluctantly, I thought, like a husband admitting to his wife that he's wrong. "You brought this character here. What do you think?"

She shrugged. "I think the only thing the Echmen are good for is bonemeal," she said. "But they murdered my family, made slaves of my people and came this close to killing me through sheer carelessness, so I may not be the right person to ask. And, yes, I happen to believe that the best time to attack someone who's bigger than you is when he's asleep."

For a moment I thought they might actually be convinced, thereby saving me an infinity of danger, risk and work. Too much to ask.

9

The fifth volume of Zautzes' *Political Commentaries*; you may remember I mentioned it earlier. A masterpiece of historical analysis, though a bit dry. I had to keep pinching myself to stay awake while I was reading it, but it was worth the effort.

Nestling in the middle third of the book is an anecdote, designed to illustrate the stupidity and credulity of the common man (a leitmotiv in all Zautzes' works, bless him), even supposedly sophisticated people like the Perimadeians. When Auxen the Great was exiled for the second time, the story goes, he went away into the mountains, where he happened to come across a very tall, striking looking shepherd drawing water at a well. He offered the man more money than he'd ever imagined could possibly exist, and enlisted his help in a cunning subterfuge.

The Perimadeians have a legend. At the hour of the city's greatest need, so the legend runs, when disaster stares them in the face and all seems lost, the greatest hero of all time,

Breuxis the Dragonslayer, will return, in the flesh, to save them and lead them to victory. Auxen therefore dressed up the tall shepherd (he was, apparently, just shy of seven feet) as the hero Breuxis, in meticulously researched period clothing and armour, put him in an ivory chariot drawn by four milk-white horses and paraded him through the streets of Perimadeia to the shrine where the hero's body is buried. He had the lid prised off; the tomb was empty (reasonably enough, since Auxen's friends had broken into it a few days earlier). Wild with joy, the people clamoured for Breuxis to set them free of the cruel oppression of the Senate, whose heads shortly afterwards made a pretty display on pikes in front of the main gate of the Prefecture. Breuxis then bade them farewell, entrusting them to the care of his good friend Auxen, who shortly afterwards declared himself dictator for life and lived happily ever after.

In Perimadeia, mark you, not some rustic backwater. I heard the story years ago and assumed it wasn't true. Zautzes must've thought the same, because he researched it thoroughly. He found out the shepherd's name and what became of him; he'd used his earnings to buy a massive ranch in the Mesoge, his children married into the local landed gentry and their descendants were still there when Zautzes came hassling them; they showed him letters and title deeds and family trees (anything, presumably, to make him go away) and even the grave of their illustrious ancestor, inscribed, in typical Mesoge fashion; *here lies Tamanidas, who made a great deal of money pretending to be Breuxis.* He came away convinced, and Zautzes was the sort of person who wouldn't take your word for it if you told him his name.

From what I'd seen of the Hus, I got the impression that

they'd be far less likely to fall for a stunt like that than the Perimadeians, or any other urban society. Living in cities tends to breed the smarts out of people somewhat, and the Hus prided themselves on their earthy common sense, their resistance to clever speeches and charisma, their robust scepticism, their knack for the awkward question, their downright rudeness. If they'd had a heraldic crest or a Great Seal, the motto on it would've been *No Flies On Us*. Still, the harder they are, the more and smaller the pieces into which they shatter, and one can but try.

I mention this because a stranger turned up, tottering out of the desert in a hell of a state, which is perfectly normal in those parts. He told them, once he'd swallowed a few mouthfuls of water and could speak, that he was a holy man. Is that right, they said. No, he replied, he wasn't here to convert anyone or sell anything. He was a pilgrim looking for an even holier man, a prophet, rumoured to be in those parts. We don't get many of them, they said. I'm not surprised, he said, but this one's easy to spot. He's a Robur.

"You didn't say you're a holy man," they pointed out, when they came to fetch me.

"No," I said.

"Well, are you?"

"Yes."

They were impressed. A holy man who keeps his vocation a secret rather than making a pest of himself on street corners was a new one on them, and they rather liked the idea. Why hadn't I mention it, they asked. I only preach to the chosen people, I told them. That's not us, then. I don't know yet, I replied. I'll let you know when I find out.

The less you try and sell something, as every conman knows, the more they want to buy. I was already a figure of considerable interest, the crack shot who'd taught them to make the new improved bows, the right-hand man of the Hus queen who wanted to start a war with the Echmen. It wouldn't be long before this latest piece of the puzzle was common knowledge. A holy man; that puts a different complexion on it. A holy man. A prophet, for crying out loud. What's he up to?

I went and saw the pilgrim. He was in a bad way. "Hello, Oio," I said.

He called me various names until I had to urge him not to overtire himself. "You got here all right," I said.

"No. I got here. Definitely not all right."

"Did you bring her?"

He sighed. "Yes," he said. "She's cosy and snug in a tent at the oasis, painting her toenails."

I nodded. "You shouldn't have set out to cross the desert on foot," I said.

"I didn't. The horse died."

"Ah."

"I've changed my mind," she said. "We're not going to do this."

I sighed. If patience is a virtue, why do so many bad people have it? Me, for instance. "Yes, we are," I said. "It's all set up, and the whole thing's going to fall to pieces if we don't do it."

"Good. It's a crazy idea anyway."

"Fine," I said. "If you want to withdraw the Hus from the Anti-Tyranny League, that's your prerogative. The rest of us will just have to carry on without you."

I might as well have punched her in the solar plexus. "Don't be stupid. It's me they listen to, not you."

"Not so sure about that any more. I think they'll listen to me, even if you chicken out."

"I'll tell them all about you."

"You could do that. You could tell them how you conspired with a Robur to mislead the entire Dejauzi nation. I suspect it'd be the last thing you ever did, but you could do it, yes."

She hated me, very intensely, for about fifteen seconds. "If it wasn't for me," I said, "you'd be dead. Twice over."

"It's a really stupid idea. Something will go wrong. It won't work."

"There is that possibility. And if it doesn't work, we'll be torn to pieces and they'll feed the scraps to the dogs. Big deal. My life has been so universally shitty that either I lose it or improve it, I'm not really bothered which, just so long as it doesn't carry on the way it's been so far. Your life, which I saved twice, belongs to me. Now shut up and stop making difficulties."

The last word. Precious, like diamonds, on account of its rarity.

When I told the Hus elders that I'd seen the Queen of Heaven, I was telling the truth. I was fourteen at the time, and my uncle took me to the theatre to see a show. It was a typical Notker farce, I don't recall which one; it was some pot-boiler, garbage. But there was this actress.

For one thing she was very tall; six feet one, I later discovered. And she had this knack of staying perfectly still in such a way that you ignored everybody else on stage and just sat there gazing. She didn't have many lines, and what she did have to say was tripe, but that voice: you could hear every syllable right at the back of the hall, even when she was whispering.

She didn't do all that swooping and thrilling you get nowadays; when she spoke it was ordinary human speech, no chanting, cooing or declaiming. But no matter what she said, the finest blank verse in Saloninus or pass the mustard, it sounded marvellous; it was a beautiful voice, and every word that came out of her mouth was beautiful. So was she, even though she was a plain woman, ordinary looking, you'd be hard put to it to describe her to the police. Her features were plain enough that they didn't get in the way of her beauty, which came from deep inside, like a demon.

When I first saw her, she was just starting out. She went on to be the second most famous actress in the City. My brother officers and I used to ride down from Scoira Limen whenever we had the chance and see whatever show she happened to be in. We all adored her, it goes without saying. Maybe not quite as much as we adored the first most famous actress in the City, the divine Andronica, but anyone who tells you it's impossible to be madly in love with two people at the same time clearly doesn't go to the theatre.

I was thinking about her as I sat in the Imperial library – Hodda, her name was – and it occurred to me that I was probably the only human being still alive who'd seen her, or Andronica, or any of them; that the extraordinary branch of commercial magic they'd specialised in existed only inside my head, and that when I died it'd be gone for ever; like the names of great-grandparents or the history of a nation or a language. It wasn't like someone would come along a thousand years in the future, dig it up with a spade and soak off the verdigris in vinegar. Nobody on earth apart from me knew what it was like to hear Hodda say the opening soliloquy from *Leucas and Galatea*, and nobody would ever know again. Now that's more than sad. That's unbearable, like watching God die in your arms.

Then I sat down at my usual seat in the library one day, and someone had left a piece of paper there, a playbill. I ought to mention that the Echmen have theatres, very fine ones. But they don't have plays. They have opera. At least I suppose you could call it that, because all the dialogue is sung, not spoken; there aren't any tunes, though, nothing you can hum. And the Echmen are mad on it, from the highbrow stuff they put on at the Imperial court down to the rather more coarsely accessible variety that working people pay good money to see; all sung rather than spoken, and I gather they don't move about a lot, just stand rooted to the spot warbling at each other until the curtain falls. It's what you're used to, I suppose. Besides, I've never actually seen an Echmen opera in an actual theatre, so what would I know?

You know what's on at which theatre by means of playbills, which are bits of paper stuck up on walls; one of the benefits of a society with the highest level of literacy in the world. This one was interesting.

Echmen theatregoers like value for their money. You turn up at the theatre in the late afternoon and you come out again in the early hours of the morning, having seen two curtain raisers, the main event, a melodrama and a farce. The big deal about this show, according to the playbill, was the main event. Entirely new and original foreign drama without music, it said, the implication being: be there or be square.

Only two societies on earth have traditions of theatrical drama, the Echmen and the Robur. This show-without-music clearly wasn't Echmen. Therefore –

I asked around. Oh yes, people told me, it's the latest thing.

There's this mad woman, about seven feet tall and black as your hat – sorry, no offence – and she stands there and talks, with no music. Everyone's going to see her, but it'll never catch on. I mean to say, no *music* –

Everyone (except me) went to see her, but it didn't catch on. Apparently the mad woman had blown into town with a ridiculous amount of money, all of which she'd invested in the show to end all shows. It ran for a long time, but not nearly long enough to cover its costs. Then she put on another show, but nobody went. They'd already seen what a tall black woman looks like talking with no music, they didn't need to see it again.

"This mad woman," I asked. "Does she have a name?"

"Hudda," they told me. Close enough for government work.

How she'd got there and what she thought she was doing I had no idea, but she *existed*. A bit like God, you might say. Or the Queen of Heaven.

It was Oio who arranged for the playbill to land on my desk, it goes without saying, and he knew I was going to ask him a favour before I put my head round his door. He had her traced. Yes, her name was Hodda and she was Robur and she'd spent all her money and nobody would lend her any, so she was living in a fleapit in the Old City trying to figure out what she was going to do next.

Could he, I asked, possibly get a letter to her? And I might need some money.

Oio didn't have any money and neither did I, but the Imperial Treasury had any amount of the stuff, so that was all right. The letter was a bit harder, but Oio managed it somehow. I waited anxiously for Hodda's reply. It came. No way, she said.

I wrote another letter. How would it be, I suggested, if you got money *and* a free pardon? But I'm not in any trouble, I haven't done anything, she replied. Leave that to us, I said, and, sure enough, a few days later Oio had secured a warrant for her arrest, all perfectly genuine and legal and sealed with the double entwined dragons of the Department of Justice.

Once she was in jail, of course, she needed a translator. She was a trifle steamed to begin with, but I was in a hurry. "What are you doing here?" I asked her.

"Trying to interest a load of barbarians in classical Robur drama," she said. "How stupid can you get?"

I explained about the singing. "I can sing," she said bitterly. "I can sing a damn sight better than they can. Why didn't anybody tell me?"

"Possibly you forgot to ask. How the hell did you get out of the City? What happened?"

So she told me. I found it hard to believe, but she was there, so she ought to know. Apparently, the huge army of savages lured the City garrison out into a forest and annihilated them, leaving the City defenceless. But a gladiator by the name of Lysimachus organised the people and kept the savages at bay until eventually the navy turned up and saved the day. Lysimachus got himself made emperor and kept things running for several years, but it was obvious the City was going to fall sooner or later, so he evacuated the entire population in barges, leaving the empty bricks and mortar to the savages. Then it all went wrong. The place he led them to – he didn't make it, unfortunately – turned out to be less than ideally suitable for a quarter of a million City folk without the faintest idea how to grow food. It ended badly – starvation, disease, that sort of thing; all that ingenuity and effort for nothing.

Hodda wasn't with them by this point. She'd lucked into a certain amount of money (she was reticent about the details) and resolved to try her luck in what was now the only place in the world that still had theatres.

"All of them?" I asked.

"I don't know, I wasn't there. But I can't imagine any of them survived. I heard there are diseases there which the locals were all immune to. And besides, you know City people. Food comes from shops. No shops, no food. I heard a rumour that some of them left the colony before the end to try and find Olbia, but even if that's true, what possible chance would they have had? Nobody even knows where Olbia is."

I'd accepted the extermination of my people once already. Having to accept it a second time was much harder. The tiny annoying part of you that harbours hope had been insisting all the while that the City hadn't fallen, that a great leader had sprung up out of nowhere, fought off the savages and led the people to safety. That had turned out – incredible miracle – to be true. But they'd all died anyway. No, wait, said the tiny annoying part, the intolerable plague that was too smart to climb out of the box with the other plagues, some of them are still alive and they found Olbia. Fool me twice, shame on me.

I happen to know where Olbia is. It's on a creek that flows down from snow-capped mountains into the armpit of the Friendly Sea, and many years ago the Robur set up a colony there, which reported back for a while and then was never heard of again. But I know where it is because it's marked on Sashan military maps, copied by Echmen spies at the risk of their lives and smuggled back to the Imperial library sewn into the backings of carpets. A few desperate Robur survivors wouldn't have known that. Nor would they have seen the

Sashan geographical survey report, which describes the faint traces of ruins that are all that's left of the Robur colony. That was an old survey, hope whispers, you know what the Sashan are like, they copy out stuff that's two centuries old and serve it up as new data. Or it's a different Olbia, or they had the map upside down and the ruins they found weren't the Robur city at all.

"What do you think?" I asked her.

"I neither know nor care," she replied. "If there's any of them still alive they're no good to me, not until they start building theatres again. All I know is, my life's turned to shit and landed me in prison when I haven't even done anything. I don't have any sympathy to spare for anyone else."

"If you cared," I rephrased, "what would you think?"

"Well." She thought about it for a moment, possibly for the first time. "The rumour I heard said that the expedition to find Olbia was being organised by someone called Sisinna. I'm guessing that would be Admiral Sisinna, who was head of the navy and about a million times smarter than anyone else in authority. And Olbia's supposed to be on the sea, and navy people have loads of maps. So if the navy were running the show and Sisinna was in charge, then, yes, it's possible that they found Olbia. It's even possible they're still alive. Who the hell cares?"

"I do."

"Really." She was looking at me. "What did you say your name was?"

"Felix."

"Aemilius Felix Boioannes the younger."

Five words I was sure I'd never hear again. "Yes, as it happens."

"Thought so. I remember hearing about you. Carloman Ahenna was a friend of a friend of mine." She grinned. "Got in a spot of trouble, I seem to recall."

"There was a degree of unpleasantness."

The grin widened. "So much for you and me being the parents of a new Robur race. Not," she added, "that I'd have been interested under any circumstances whatsoever. So why all this interest in the last of our people? You'd never be able to show your face among Robur again."

"Maybe not," I said. "Or just possibly, nobody would care any more."

"Don't you believe it," she said. "If there's still anyone alive, it'll be because the military are running things. And so long as there's one Robur officer left, you wouldn't be welcome. Come on, you know those people. Forgive and forget isn't their way."

"You're probably right," I said.

"And the last thing I'd ever want to do," she went on, "is that whole pioneer thing, hoeing turnips and carrying firewood and sleeping in a tent. Screw it. Life without a certain level of comfort and refinement isn't worth living. Talking of which," she added, "will you please get me out of here? The food's actually not bad and the architecture is amazing, but there's other things I should be doing."

"I'll be happy to," I said. "And I'll give you money. Provided you do one little thing for me."

She gave me a look that really ought to have turned me to stone. "How little?"

"Acting job," I said. "Right up your alley, believe me."

"Singing?"

"No singing," I said. "And not in a theatre, but definitely acting. The part you were born to play. In fact, there's nobody

else in the whole world who could do it, apart from you. That's
assuming Andronica didn't make it, of course."

"Who?"

"Exactly. A few hours of your time, and you can go on your
way rejoicing. Or you can stay here. Indefinitely."

"Bastard. What harm did I ever do you?"

"None whatsoever."

Perhaps it's time I came back to some of things I said I'd come
back to later.

Olbia, for crying out loud. It's a place, a sad case history of
Robur administrative incompetence, an article of faith. When
I left the City there were people who'd vaguely heard of Olbia,
had studied the pathology of what went wrong at Olbia, who
earnestly believed in Olbia; the latter two categories being
scholars and lunatics respectively. What went wrong at Olbia
is actually quite simple. Something like this.

Head up the coast from the City, past the straits, and you
come out into the large patch of water we call the Friendly
Sea. If it wasn't for all the salt you'd call it a lake, since it's
surrounded by land on all sides, apart from the tiny little
bottleneck at the straits; which is why the City was built there,
of course, and how it came to rule a vast and unhappy empire.
Everything on the shores of the Friendly Sea was our turf.
Originally we came from the steppes right up at the top, and
worked our way down, taking the land as of right and killing
anyone who objected. Later we conquered other places and
deported the people who lived there to work the empty land
we'd depopulated. They were only milkfaces, so the argument
ran, and it was nice to think that someone had finally found a
use for them.

Centuries later, when the City had outgrown its original footprint and overcrowding had led to catastrophic fires, plague, riots and all manner of aggravation, someone in authority decided to export the surplus urban population to some place a long way away; a colony. The idea was that our tired, our poor, our huddled masses yearning to breathe free would be much better off living as simple, self-sufficient yeomen farmers. They'd be surrounded by fresh air and open countryside, every man sitting under his own vine and his own fig tree instead of kettled up in narrow, unsanitary alleys choking on the smog from foundries and tanners' yards. It was a nice thought, a genuine desire to do good. The road to Olbia was paved with the very best of intentions.

The City proletariat weren't farmers. Even the government knew that. Naturally they could learn farming (if country people can do it, the logic ran, it can't be difficult) but it would take a while, several years maybe. During that time, the colonists wouldn't be able to feed themselves, so their loving mother the state would have to feed them. Mighty grain freighters were commissioned to carry huge cargoes of flour, beans and dried fish, everything anybody could possibly want. The government asked for quotes to supply ploughs, harrows, picks, shovels, hoes, saws, axes, buckets, carts, yokes, big hammers, little hammers, crowbars, scythe blades, rakes, pruning hooks, every damn thing you could think of, and a thousand contractors responded with yelps of delight. For five years practically everybody in the City was busy and money flowed like a river in spate.

The geographers, meanwhile, had had a look at a map and found what looked like the ideal spot, a point on the northern coast of the Friendly Sea where a river rolled down from the mountains across a flat plain into an estuary. It didn't have a name, or not one anyone could pronounce, so they called it Olbia – the City of the Blessed.

In due course, the First Fleet sailed, led by a retired general with years of experience in commissariat, construction and supply. It was pity that he died before the fleet made landfall, but his second in command, by some strange coincidence his nephew, made a pretty good fist of things, all things considered, and soon the saws, axes and hammers were busy as bees turning limitless forests into neat rows of identical huts. Oxen were unloaded from gigantic livestock barges and yoked to the plough. The great experiment was underway.

It takes three weeks to sail up the coast from the City to Olbia. But, for technical reasons I don't understand, tides or prevailing winds or something, it takes four months to come back. Six months later, the first news reached the City. It wasn't wonderful.

Olbia would be a great place to live, the reports said, if it wasn't for the insects. There was a certain sort of fly that bit the cattle and a certain sort of mosquito that bit the people. Nearly all the oxen were dead, and a third of the settlers. Not to worry, though; relocating half a dozen miles or so down the coast would make everything right as ninepence, and what was one extra year in the grand scheme of things? Meanwhile, please send more food, more oxen and, of course, more people.

So they did that. Six months went by, during which harvests failed, rebellions in the provinces severely hampered trade and the collection of revenues, war with the Sashan ate up ridiculous amounts of money and conscription drew men away from the plough and the workbench, leading to economic depression and famine. Then news came from Olbia. The new site was much better than the old site, but there were problems. For a start, there were bands of local savages, under the impression that they owned the place. They'd been slaughtered like sheep, naturally, but not before they'd killed about a fifth of the settlers, annoyingly mostly women. Furthermore, the bean and pulse seeds sent out from the City wouldn't germinate there – too cold or too hot or something – and there was a certain sort of mite or bug that had killed off all the poultry. The wheat and barley had ripened in record time and would've produced a grand harvest if the disgruntled savages hadn't set fire to it, just before running off most of the oxen, just before being wiped out. Now that the natives were dead, clearly those problems would not recur and it ought to be plain sailing from now on. In the meantime, please send more food, more oxen and, of course, more people.

At any other time the emperor would have been only too happy to oblige. But with food riots in the City and all available shipping tied up with supplying the army on the Sashan frontier, his hands were tied. As soon as the situation eased, the reply went, everything the colonists needed would be despatched, maximum priority. Until then, do the best you can.

The Sashan war didn't go too well. That was the occasion on which twelve successive assaults with heavy equipment failed to breach the City wall – something to be very proud of indeed, but we wouldn't have had anything to be proud of if the Sashan hadn't been camped under the City walls for eight months, until plague and supply problems forced them to give up and go home. By the time all that was sorted out, the economy was in such a terrible mess that it was touch and go whether the empire would survive at all. It did, and eventually the situation was sufficiently eased that someone remembered about Olbia, and sent a fleet of freighters. When they got there, they found the place deserted. The rows of huts were still there, but when you pushed open the doors you couldn't go inside because they'd filled up with brambles and cow parsley. There weren't any bones lying about, animal or human, and no signs of destruction by fire. Instead, the relief party found a big stone in the middle of what would have been the town square, on which someone had chiselled a brief note. Site uninhabitable, the note said, survivors have moved upstream to where the red apple trees grow; please find us and take us home.

The relief party followed the river right up into the mountains, but found no apple trees and no settlers. Nor did they find skeletons, abandoned equipment or anything else. It was getting late in the sailing season; if they stayed much longer they'd be stuck there all winter until the really nasty winds stopped blowing. They gave up and came home.

So much for Olbia. It had achieved its main purpose, getting rid of troublesome surplus citizens, and its undeclared secondary purpose, generating enough blame to justify a thorough cleanout of the middle and upper-middle levels of the Imperial bureaucracy (there were just as many bureaucrats in office a year later, but they were different bureaucrats; Robur definition of progress) The eye-watering cost in money and lives was a drop in the ocean compared to the losses suffered during the Sashan war, so that was all right. An unintended third objective, providing employment to scholars and historians, was in full swing by the time I left the City. And the fourth objective, giving dreamers and lunatics something to believe in —

Dreamers and lunatics like me. And, just possibly, Admiral Sisinna, generally reckoned to be the shrewdest man in the empire; had he really led the survivors of the City exodus to Olbia, sincerely believing it was really there somewhere? Was it possible that somewhere, among the mountains and the non-existent red apple orchards, there were Robur ready and willing to take in their destitute countrymen, feed and clothe and protect them until the situation at home had eased?

Anything's possible.

"You lied to us," her father's friend said.

Glue is wonderful stuff. You slap it on and go away, and a few hours or days later, two separate objects have turned into one object. But it can be a bit like a big, friendly dog; all over you, wet and annoying. I was setting a newly assembled bow into a jig, which would give the limbs the shape I wanted. "I don't think so," I said.

"You told us—" He stopped and lowered his voice. "You told us, if we came here, she'd be here to meet us."

"You mean the Queen of—"

"Don't say the name."

"Sorry. But that's who you mean?"

"Who else?"

I nodded. "My fault," I said. "I must've phrased it badly. You think you know a language, but that doesn't stop you making the occasional mistake. What I meant to say was, once you get here, she'll come."

"When?"

"Soon."

"How soon?"

"Soon. When she's ready. I don't know, do I? I'm just passing on the message."

He glared at me furiously. "We did what you said. Exactly what you told us to do. People *died*. And now you've got us all sitting around making stupid bows for some war we never agreed to." He stopped himself with an effort. "They're saying you're a holy man. A prophet."

"I can't help what people say."

"How can you be a prophet? We've never had prophets before. What do you do, tell fortunes?"

"I never said I was anything of the sort."

"You didn't deny it, either."

"There's lots of things I haven't denied. Doesn't mean I did them."

"You are a prophet, aren't you? Admit it."

"This is pointless," I said. "If I told you I'm a prophet, you wouldn't believe me. You don't even know what a prophet is."

He breathed out loudly through his nose. "You'd better be right, that's all. Otherwise—"

I waited for the rest of the sentence. He scowled at me and left.

Things that interest me don't interest other people, and vice versa, so I'll spare you the technical details of the bow-building project. There were problems. We sorted them out. Getting hold of materials was difficult. We managed. Persuading the Hus to stick at it and persevere was harder still. I managed that as well. The breakthrough came when the assembled kings of the Dejauzi watched me giving a demonstration of the new-style bow in action. I'd managed to track down an Echmen lancer's cuirass – it had been given to her grandfather by someone or other and sat at the bottom of a trunk ever since – which I tied round a sack tightly stuffed with hay and shot at from thirty yards. Six arrows in one minute. An Echmen cuirass is made out of about a thousand D-shaped steel scales, tinned to stop them from rusting and sewn onto a jerkin so that they overlap. Generations of Dejauzi had been taught that Echmen armour is proof against anything, up to and including dragons. All six of my arrows went straight through. One of them went through and out the other side. Dead silence; not even birdsong. Then the king of the Maudit asked me in a rather shaky voice if I was interested in selling those things.

Needless to say, if the Maudit had them, all the other Dejauzi had to have them, too. I explained that it wasn't up to me, all I'd done was teach the Hus how to make the things, mostly to give them something to do. If anyone wanted bows made, they'd have to talk to the queen of the Hus, who no doubt would be happy to oblige, in return for good-quality raw materials and a generous supply of food and clothing for her starving, homeless people.

It made no difference, however. Even with bows that could shoot through Echmen scale –

"At thirty yards," someone pointed out. "We went back to seventy-five and the arrows just bounced off."

"Absolutely," I said. "That's why you don't shoot at the men, you shoot at the horses. Not until they get up really close. Sorry, *unless* they get up really close. But they won't get that far. And if they do, you'll slaughter them."

"Sorry," they said. "Not interested."

Well, now. I'd found useful paying work for the Hus menfolk, but not the women. Fortuitously, I'd read a book;

Aechmalotus' *Elements of Botany*. In the section about flax – you have no idea how much there is to say about flax – Aechmalotus describes how the Blemyans used to make armour out of linen cloth, about a thousand years ago. Sixteen layers ought to do it, he says, laminated together with flax-seed glue, doesn't even have to be new cloth, you can use old clothes, sheets, worn-out sails, anything you like. Of course, he adds, he'd never tried it himself, but the Blemyans swore by it, a thousand years ago.

I'd come across a bunch of men starting a bonfire. What's that you're burning. I asked. Old tents, they told me. Old canvas tents? Yes, what about it? I smiled. Tell you what, I said. Give me those useless stinking old canvas tents you were about to set fire to, and I'll give each of you a beautiful new horn and sinew bow. How about it?

Glue we had, bucketfuls. Sixteen layers did just fine, and in that heat it set like a rock. This time, I had no trouble getting the kings of the Dejauzi to spare me five minutes. I handed the king of the Rosinholet a spear. "If you can stick it right through so it comes out the other side and pierces the sack," I told him, "you can have all the bows you want for free."

He looked at me. "Seriously?"

"Go ahead," I said. "It's just a few bits of old tent."

I'm sorry to say he hurt his arm trying, and all to no avail. Needless to say, if the Rosinholet had linen armour, all the other Dejauzi had to have it, too. Back to the glue kettles. Over the course of the next few days, the Hus became the stickiest nation the world had ever seen.

Why can't human beings be more like chemicals? In an alchemical experiment you add X scruples of A to Y drams of B and stir slowly over a gentle heat, next thing you know you've got what you want, predictably and reliably. Into the crucible I'd placed the weapons, the armour and the manpower, and even the most exacting critic couldn't fault me on my gentle, persistent stirring. Even so. Sorry, they still said, not interested.

When all else fails, they tell you, pray. Time to do just that.

Just when I was starting to wonder where the hell Oio had got to, he came back.

Maybe I should tell you about me and Oio. What did I ever do, you've probably been asking yourself, to deserve such a loyal, devoted friend? To answer that, let me take you back a few years, to shortly after I first arrived at the Echmen court. Oio is, as I think I mentioned, a Lystragonian, and he and I were the only Robur-speakers, below senior administrative level, in the palace. I don't think he liked me much. I was, therefore, mildly surprise when he pounced on me as I was walking through the cloisters one morning and dragged me behind a pillar.

"If anyone asks," he said, "I was with you all last night."

I thought about that. "Doing what?"

"I don't know. Playing backgammon."

"Chess," I said. "Where?"

"Your quarters."

"Have you got a chessboard?"

"Yes. Why?"

"Because I haven't. But that's all right, because you brought yours and we used that. What's it made out of?"

He had to stop and think. "The board's sycamore and ebony and the pieces are bone. One set is dyed black."

"What does the rook look like?"

"The what?"

Lystragonian, I forgot. "The castle."

"A man with a pointed helmet carrying a sword. Pointing up."

I nodded. "One of the chessmen wouldn't happen to have a chip or a scratch or something like that."

"One of the fleurets of the white queen's crown is missing."

"Of course it is," I said, "I remember now."

He looked at me. "From after third watch till the call to prayer."

"That's right. I won quite a lot of money, I seem to remember, which you didn't have with you. But that's all right. You can pay me when you see me next."

He was about to say something, but a captain of the guard and two sergeants in full armour came along and arrested him. Later that day they came to see me. "You're sure about that," they said.

"Yes. Why? Is he in any trouble?"

The captain was looking round my room. "You were playing chess."

"That's right."

"Doesn't seem to be a chess set here."

"He brought his."

"Describe it."

So I did that. "It must've cost a lot of money," I said. "Actually, I feel guilty about that."

"Really?"

I nodded. "I dropped the white queen and broke one of the little points off her crown. I had a look for it after he'd gone but I couldn't find it."

Housekeeping had swept my room that morning. Would the captain know that? "When did he leave?"

"Not sure," I said. "Call to prayer, or not long before that. To be honest with you, I was half asleep by that point."

"You look quite bright and breezy for a man who was up all night."

"I'm a junior diplomat. I sleep a lot during the day."

It was a while before I saw Oio again. "How much money did you win off me at chess?" he asked.

"Thousands," I replied. "I don't suppose you've got much money."

"No."

"Oh, well, in that case forget about it." I smiled at him. "Look," I said, "I know we spent that night together playing chess, but if we hadn't been what might you have been doing?"

"I don't know what you mean."

I heard later that one of the other clerks in his department had been found head down in a rainwater barrel, though what killed him was probably the blow to the head. The hell with it; I didn't kill him, so he wasn't my fault. Oio has been very kind and helpful on many occasions, and what did truth and justice ever do for me? I did ask Oio once, though; why me?

"I couldn't think of anyone else," he said. Good reason.

Anyway, he came back. "Is she all right?" I asked him. "Did you bring her?"

"There's a fallen-down old lime kiln about half a mile up the road," he replied. "I left her there. She's not happy."

"I'm sorry to hear that," I said. "When it's dark, you and she make your way to the top of that hill over there. When you see a bonfire, it's time."

"She wants to know about the money."

"Lie to her," I said.

"She's incredibly suspicious."

"Lie convincingly."

He was looking very worried. I'd made him certain promises concerning his future. "It is all right about the money, isn't it? It's all there and everything."

"Trust me," I said. An exhortation, rather than a statement of fact.

I realised as I walked back to the courtyard where the kings were holding their next meeting that I'd forgotten to ask Oio about the stuff. I try so hard not to make assumptions, but from time to time I slip up. You assume that people, especially professionals, know their job and don't have to be reminded about every single little thing. For instance, if I know I'm going to be translating in a dispute over fishing rights, it wouldn't occur to me to turn up for work without having read something about what sort of fish people catch and how they go about it, so that at least I'd be familiar with the technical terms. Then I'd have either looked those terms up in a lexicon or asked someone who knew the language, so I'd be able to translate them as and when they came up in the talks. It's my job to know the Permian for gurnard and the southern dialect words in demotic Vesani for the three different kinds of deep-water long series tangle nets, not to mentions the reasons why someone would want to use one of them and why someone else would want him not to. Sitting down with a bunch of busy, important people without knowing all that kind of thing would be simple incompetence, like a soldier forgetting his shield. But I've known translators who get caught out and blame it all on someone else. I should've been properly briefed, they say, someone should've seen to it that I was given all the materials beforehand. I can't be expected to think of *everything*. And do they get fired for being useless? No, some clerk gets the blame. So; if assumptions can vary so widely within one profession, how much more likely that they're different as between one profession and another – translating, for example, and the drama.

Nothing I could do about it now, of course, as men and women pushed past me with faggots and bundles of dried herbs, to scent the bonfire. It was the night of the Old and New festival, celebrating the return of the flocks from the mountain pastures to the valley. It's a festival common to all the Dejauzi. There's a truce, and a special sort of cake only baked for the occasion, music and rather dreary traditional poetry, followed by a sort of general assembly where forthcoming marriages are announced and important issues likely to arise during the next six months are discussed in very general terms and put to a pretend vote – the king votes first, then everybody agrees with him. It's rather a tame affair compared with most Dejauzi festivals: no bloodletting, animal or human, no violent sports, not even bull-jumping or two blindfolded men trying to brain each other with sticks. The evening concludes with a hymn to the Queen of Heaven and the lighting of the bonfire. But all the Dejauzi, and the Hus especially, take it very seriously. A promise made at the Old and New can't be broken, or that's the theory, at least.

Properly speaking, the bonfire should be made of the desiccated bones of your vanquished enemy, or at least generously garnished therewith. In which case, the Luzir Soleth had just pulled off a spectacular victory against the king of the thorn bushes – fair enough, I suppose, nobody likes the things, especially the very tips of the thorns, which work their way into your fingers and hurt like hell for weeks. Exterminate all the brutes, say I. No mercy. Or it could be because thorns burn nicely when dry, or the king's people had just cleared a large patch of scrub on the hill slope ready for planting olives. It'd be diplomatic to say it was probably a combination of all three. The festival side of things was all right, I suppose. It kicked off with a choir of Luzir under-twelves singing a long hymn very slowly. Then we had a choir of Hus under-twelves singing the same hymn very slowly, followed by another hymn from a slightly older Luzir choir, followed by the same hymn from their Hus contemporaries, followed by what passes for dancing in those parts – demonstrating yet again the difficulties of my trade, given that the Robur word for dance doesn't mean to stand on the same spot for ten minutes undulating slightly at the hips. Never mind. They seemed to enjoy it, which is what matters.

Then we had the poetry. Lots of that. The poem, which I had the opportunity to study in some detail, since I heard it once from the Luzir and once from the Hus, word-for-word identical, tells of how the great-great-great-great-grandfathers of the Dejauzi were promised a land flowing with milk and honey by the gods, on condition that they behaved themselves, which they signally failed to do. Accordingly they ended up in the land next door to the promised one, adequate but milk-and-honey-deficient, where they were periodically smitten by heaven every time they got above themselves, roughly once a generation. I didn't think much of it to start with, but once you got into it, it's actually rather good, particularly the inventive ways heaven found for punishing the chosen people. I'd read a rather garbled and inaccurate precis of it in an Echmen text, but not the thing itself, which has never been written down.

Then we had the cakes. They tasted odd rather than nice, and they made my head spin. Later I found out that they season the batter with funny herbs, the same sort they use to perfume the bonfire. The cakes made me thirsty. There was plenty to drink; milk or beer. I opted for the milk.

Next we had forthcoming marriages, which seemed to go on for ever. The names were called out by the respective heads of families, and each announcement was greeted with solemn foot-stomping and slow hand-clapping, neither of which mean the same to the Dejauzi as they do in the Hippodrome or the theatre. My head stopped spinning and started hurting. I was feeling jumpy, and the noise of the foot-stomping made my teeth ache.

After the marriages came the important issues. The Luzir king got to his feet. Apparently he did it exceptionally well, because he got a big round of applause for it. The Luzir and the Hus, he said, haven't always seen eye to eye. But they're here now and they haven't really made nuisances of themselves, so things could be worse. The Luzir have been incredibly generous with food and shelter and everything anyone could possibly need, and likewise the Maudit, the Aram, the Rosinholet and the Cure Hardy, all giving selflessly to poor destitute unfortunates who had no right to expect such generosity, considering the awful things they've done in the past, but that's the Dejauzi people for you – generous and forgiving to a fault. For their part, he went on once the cheering from half the crowd had died down, the Hus have kept themselves occupied and out from under people's feet, and we should all be grateful to them for that. An unexpected side effect of all this industry has been lots and lots of fairly useful-looking armaments, which may well come in handy at some point in the future. But (here he paused again and peered round as if looking for someone; I have an idea it might have been me) any silly rumours anyone might've heard about a war, especially a war against the Echmen, are completely unfounded. He spoke for all the kings on this point. There wasn't going to be a war. Absolutely not.

Loud applause from everyone. Oh well.

Accordingly, he went on, it was his honour and privilege to propose the usual vote: that everything should carry on pretty much the same as it is at the moment. He raised his hand in favour, then sat down.

Carried unanimously, which was the signal to light the bonfire. I felt my stomach churn and my knees go loose; just as well I was sitting down and nobody was looking at me. I wondered what it would feel like to be kicked to death. Most likely it wouldn't last very long, but you don't know, do you? Perhaps it wouldn't be so bad. I think half of the trauma of pain and injury is the fear; am I going to die, am I going to be left paralysed, how much permanent damage will there be? If you know it's that time and the damage won't matter, all that leaves is the pain. Regarding which, you can either fight it or scream. I've always found that screaming helps you cope.

Picture the scene. The towering heap of thorn branches catches and crackles. There's a wave of heat, as physical as a shove, and a bright red light. Then a breeze makes the fire roar. It's a sound of many voices rather than just one. A cloud of sparks, like burning rain falling up rather than down.

Shouts and swearing as glowing embers light on necks and the backs of hands.

After its first flush, the fire pipes down a little and settled into the bales of that funny herb, which smoulders rather than burns, gushing out dense, sweet smoke. It wouldn't be to everyone's taste but the Dejauzi must really like it. They're smiling, laughing, suddenly cheerful for no obvious reason. The glare dies down as the sides of the fire burn through and fall into the core.

Someone notices something. Others turn and look. Someone screams. At first you can't see because there's too many people in the way, but the crowd draws apart, falling away like water off perfectly clean metal, leaving an empty space.

Into which steps something or someone. You've never seen anything like it before but it's perfectly, overwhelmingly familiar. It is or it looks like a very tall woman, taller than a man. She's stark naked and her chalk-white skin *glows*; sort of green, sort of blue, you can't make your mind up which. Her hair shines, too, piled up on top of her head like a tower, or those pointed hats the Sashan wear. In one hand she has a knife, and in the other something that looks like a short log of wood.

Dead silence except for the crackle of the fire. She stops in the exact centre of the crowd, smoke hanging round her shoulders like a cape, her glow shining through the smoke like sunrise. She turns her head, looking for someone. She finds him: the skinny Robur belonging to the Hus queen, the one who's supposed to be some sort of prophet. She beckons. He comes forward, unsteadily, like a drunk, and drops to his knees in front of her. She points the knife in her right hand at his heart, then takes one step forward and drives the knife into his neck, right up to the hilt.

He falls sideways. She says something in a weird language you can't understand. The dead Robur stands up; not like a wounded man with blood pumping out of a breached artery, but perfectly normally, as though what you just saw never happened. She hands him the log of wood. They talk to each other in the language you don't know.

"When do I get the money?" she said in Robur.

"There isn't any money," I replied. "Keep perfectly calm," I added, "they're watching you."

I took the scroll from her hand. Funny to see it again, after all that time, in such a very different context.

"Don't piss me around," she said, in that wonderful, amazing voice, like honey mixed with starlight. Her delivery was even better than I remembered, or else she'd improved with age. Part of me was enraptured, away with the angels, just from hearing her speak. "Seventy thousand nomismata, cash. We agreed."

"Sorry," I said. "No money. Look, you've done me a great favour, and in return I'm not going to tell all these people that you're a fraud plastered in whiteface and luminous paint. If I did they'd tear you apart. But we don't want that, do we?"

"Thank you so fucking much, you treacherous little shit."

I bowed my head, dazzled by her radiance. "It's the least I can do," I said. "So, when you're finished here, I suggest you go back to Echmen and forget any of this ever happened. Once you're back there, you can say what you like. These people will just assume it's the enemy telling lies."

"I've met some real arseholes in my time," she said, her voice soft and low but filling all the available space like floodwater, "but you're something else, you know that? You're so full of shit I don't know how you live with yourself."

"You could learn to juggle," I said. "The Echmen love jugglers and acrobats. You could earn good money."

"Piss off and die."

The shining woman – who are we trying to kid? Call her by her name. The Queen of Heaven flings her arms wide. There's a thump, like a heavy rock falling on the ground, and behind her the fire surges and blossoms, filling the air with sparks and hot cinders, then collapses. Suddenly it's dark. She's gone.

They look round for the Robur, who's collapsed in a heap. He looks like he's having some kind of a fit. They fetch some water. He swallows a mouthful, retches violently. He's got the log the Queen gave him gripped tight in his hand, only it's not a log. It's parchment, like you'd cover a drum with, rolled up tight.

The Luzir king has been pushed to the front of the crowd. "What did she say to you?" he asks.

I opened my eyes. My head was swimming. I wasn't acting the shortness of breath. "It was her," I said.

"What did she *say*?"

I took a few deep breaths. The lining of my throat and mouth were raw, from bile. "Help me up," I said. "My legs are all weak."

They got me a stool to sit on. I had their attention.

There was going to be a war, I told them. The Echmen had sworn to wipe them off the face of the earth – not just the Hus, all the Dejauzi. But the Dejauzi were her chosen people. She would give them victory and lead them to the promised land.

The king was staring at me as if I was a hole in the sky he might fall through. "Did she say that?"

"I think that's what it meant, yes."

He looked up, over my head, to his fellow kings standing behind me. They'd heard. I guess the implications of being chosen were starting to sink in. "You're sure."

"As sure as I can be. It wasn't a language I know. I was sort of hearing it inside my head, if that makes any sense."

"What's that she gave you?" I heard the Maudit king's voice. I looked at the scroll in my hand as though I'd never seen it before. "I don't know," I said. "Writing."

"Can you read it?"

"Let me see." I unrolled the top few inches. "I think so."

The uncertainty was genuine. I have difficulty reading my own handwriting, even in broad daylight.

"Well?"

I looked round at him. "Do you want me to read it to you?"

"Yes, of course."

I took a deep breath. "In the beginning," I read out, "Skyfather created the heavens and the earth."

If that sounds familiar, please don't give me a hard time. I'm not exactly a master of prose style, as I'm sure you've discovered by now, and I needed something powerful and profound, of proven efficacy. The chances of any Dejauzi having encountered the Permian Book of the Dead in any shape or form were, I'd decided, slight. Besides, if imitation is the sincerest form of flattery, plagiarism is practically a declaration of love.

I said a few words a moment ago about the value of preparation, and I hope you'll agree that the goings-on at the Old and New festival bear me out. It helped, of course, that I'd had the Imperial library at my disposal. It was there I cobbled together and wrote out the text of the scroll, which I entrusted to Oio once I knew we had Hodda on board. It was in the library that I solved the mystery of luminous paint and thunder-flashes, which have been the most jealously guarded trade secrets of the Robur theatrical profession for two hundred years, and which had always been one of Hodda's trademarks. Apparently, luminous paint is made from some very peculiar rocks that can only be found on a mountainside in Scona. You grind them up, cook them in a crucible with loads of charcoal, then spread out the resulting mess in the sun to soak up the light. Thunderflashes come from a recipe in one of Saloninus' notebooks, written in code. The notebook in question is now lost or at least unavailable for inspection; rumour has it that Attalus, the greatest actor of his day, bought it at an auction and decoded it, and the secret has stayed in the profession ever since, each generation prising the formula from the cold, dead hand of its predecessor. I knew that whatever else Hodda might have lost or sold during her vicissitudes among the Echmen, she'd keep with her to the bitter end her pot of luminous paint and half a dozen thunderflashes. It was a bit of bunce that she also had one of those trick daggers where the blade slides up into the handle, but I should have remembered seeing her in the suicide scene in *Marpessus and Otia*, one of her best ever performances.

It's true that when I offered her a huge sum of money I had no intention of ever paying her. Oio had embezzled me a modest down payment, but that was as much as he dared abstract all in one go, and we were on a schedule. I felt and still feel guilty about that, though I imagine the jade go-anywhere-and-get-out-of-trouble pheasant which I gave Oio to pass on to her will have fetched a tidy sum once she'd finished with it herself. I make trouble for people, I know. But, then, people (admittedly different ones) make trouble for me, so in the grand scheme of things we're quits.

I rolled up the scroll. I was hoarse from all that reading aloud. Nobody had moved or said a word all through the performance. Not even a cough. I'd have said it was physically impossible and a violation of the laws of nature for anyone to read out anything in front of an audience without somebody coughing. Shows how much I know.

I'd had my eye on the page and my horrible spidery handwriting, barely legible by the glow of the dying fire, so I had no idea of how it had gone down with the Dejauzi people. I was afraid to look up. If they hadn't bought it, these would be my last few moments on earth. If they had, the world was about to change, nations would be torn apart, empires would fall. All I ever wanted out of life was modest comfort and peaceful obscurity. The hell with it.

So I looked up. Every eye was fixed on me; the archer's stare, where you concentrate every fibre of your being on the target, just before you loose. Moving my eyes only, I located her; the queen of the Hus, She Stamps Them Flat, looking daggers at me from behind the shoulder of the King of the Aram Chantat. Hers was, as far as I could tell, the only negative reaction. Everybody else just looked gobsmacked.

Being a prophet isn't something I'd recommend to the self-conscious. You get stared at an awful lot. The thing to remember is that, having gazed into the eyes of God, you hardly notice anything else. A bit like looking straight at the sun: for a long time afterwards, everything is shiny blurs and splodges. I decided that the best way to act would be to pretend I'd just been knocked down by a runaway horse.

For the next few days, therefore, I took it very gently, only speaking when spoken to and usually having to be spoken to twice before I registered anything. Gradually I came back to life. Yes, I admitted when pressed, I'd talked to the Queen of Heaven. Yes, she killed me, I remember that now. I died, and she called me back to life. It was the weirdest feeling, I told them, and refused to go into details. The scroll? Oh, that. She gave it to me and told me it was all the Law and the prophets, whatever that means. Presumably it's what she wants us all to do. I can't remember any of it, I told them, what did it say?

They brought it to me. They'd found a Sashan carved ivory box, somebody's prized heirloom, to keep it in, so they wouldn't have to look at it. Can you still read it, they asked, or was reading it all part of the . . . you know? I frowned like crazy while they held their breath. Yes, I said, it's coming back to me. I can read it.

The trick when fabricating doctrine is to keep it simple. You don't want complex theological issues such as transubstantiation or the dual procession of the holy spirit. That can come later, when you've got ten thousand full-time monks looking for something to do. I'd looted the Permian stuff first because they wouldn't know about it, second because Permian religion is so vague and open-ended, practically anybody can bend it to fit their existing beliefs, even atheists. A simple creation myth, then straight into the dos and don'ts. Love God with all your heart and soul and your neighbour as yourself; be nice to strangers and foreigners (guess why I put that in) because you yourself were once a slave in Echmen; no murder, rape, stealing or antisocial behaviour; I thought about forbidding them to eat insects and fermented food, mostly because I loathe sauerkraut, but then I thought, no, let's keep it simple.

Honour the black men, because they're holy; make them your priests. That's about it, really.

What about the promised land, they asked me. I don't know, I replied. Where is it, they asked, how do we get there, what's it like? I'm sorry, I told them, I have no idea.

10

"You've gone too far," she said. "If I'd known you were thinking of something like this, I'd have stayed in Echmen."

"And got your throat cut," I said.

"You keep saying that. And I don't suppose it'll matter much in the long run. You're going to get us all killed anyway, so what the hell?"

"I wish you didn't have to be so negative all the damn time."

She gave me that you're-a-real-piece-of-work look I'd come to know so well. "I thought you were on my side," she said. "I honestly thought you did it all to save me. Save my life."

"Did you?" I said. "Why would I do that?"

"Because you—"

Someone said, Saloninus probably, that you can't really hate someone else unless you first hate yourself. As a general rule, I think that's garbage, but in her case; maybe. "I'm sorry," I said.

"Is it true? What they told me about you."

"Yes."

"Just once," she said, "I'd like to meet someone who doesn't make things worse for me. Just once."

"You don't need anyone else for that," I said. It just slipped out. She took it well, considering.

Even so, I was anticipating further negativity from her when the kings of the Dejauzi held their next summit conference under the walnut tree. I was pleasantly surprised.

"The Echmen killed my father," she told them, "and my whole family. They put my people in chains. Now they're coming to finish the job. I don't want a war, nobody in their right mind would. But there's going to be one, so let's do everything we can to win it. Otherwise—" She had this clever gesture, a very slight droop of the hands that said it all. She sat down. The king of the Luzir looked at me. "Well?" he said.

"So now you're all agreed," I said.

"We were wrong," said the Maudit. "What do you want, an apology?"

"Don't look at me," I said, "I'm just a representative."

That got me a hatful of dirty looks, but anything else would've been out of character. "You're all agreed," I repeated. "That's good. Now, what are you going to do?"

"You tell us," said the Rosinholet.

"Oh no you don't," I said. "I'm not in charge. I'm not even Dejauzi. And if you're under the impression that She's hovering about somewhere invisibly whispering the answers in my ear, forget it. I don't even know why you want me sitting in on these meetings."

She breathed out through her nose. "You were in the Robur army."

"Yes, for a while. I was a junior lieutenant. Cockroach level."

"You went to the Robur war school," one of them said.

"True."

"So you know about war."

"Never been in one," I replied. "And all we did at military academy was read books. If you're looking for a general, leave me out of it."

They weren't expecting that. "But you're the prophet."

"So everyone keeps telling me."

Eventually, after heated argument and angry words, I finally let them browbeat me into leading the army, which was what I'd intended all along. Dejauzi politics, I'd come to realise, is pretty straightforward if you've ever tried to get a horse on board a ship. It's the only useful thing I learned in the army, but it made the whole experience – almost the whole experience – worthwhile. The horse doesn't want to go aboard the ship, reasonably enough. If you tug at his bridle, he starts backing away, and he's stronger than you. So you turn him round and tug at his bridle the other way; whereupon he backs away right up the gangplank, and there you are. Same with the Dejauzi. Refuse to do something and they'll bully and badger you until you agree to do it. The extraordinary thing is that the Dejauzi have never figured that out for themselves. The benefit of a fresh perspective, I guess.

"On one condition," I said. "I won't be your commander-in-chief, but I will be joint commander. With her." I pointed. "Otherwise, you can forget it. I mean it."

"Fine," said the Luzir. "Anyone got a problem with that?"

"Because," I explained to her, "the Hus are outsiders among the Dejauzi, as you well know. If I'd chosen one of the kings, all the others would've been nervous as cats, in case someone got an advantage over someone else. But nobody's friends with the Hus, not even now. It's good to be the outsider sometimes."

That wasn't the reason, of course, but she accepted it at face value. "You've got everything you wanted," she said. "What I don't understand is what you want it for."

That was a bit too close for comfort. "You said it yourself," I told her. "The Echmen slaughtered your family. They were about to kill you. They marched off your people in chains. That's not right."

"What business is that of yours?"

"Just because I – can't love you doesn't mean I don't care." Had I judged the little catch in the throat just right? I really wish I'd studied acting rather than Sozen III's innovative use of light artillery. "I couldn't just do nothing. Trouble is, doing something meant doing this. Nothing less would be any use." I made a show of pulling myself together, after all the mushy stuff. "You know all that. I told you. We talked about it. You agreed."

"A *prophet*."

"They weren't going to buy it without a dirty great shove," I said. "Now we've got them eating out of our hand. And you're leading the army."

Her cold look. "I was going to ask you about that. What the hell are you playing at?"

The cold look back at her. "Your people don't like the other Dejauzi. Well?"

"No."

"Well, in two shakes of a lamb's tail, you'll be the queen of the entire Dejauzi nation. Don't say I never do anything for you."

Her eyes opened wide. "You're kidding. Tell me that's your idea of funny."

"Isn't that what the Hus have always wanted? Your boots on their necks? It's the only way you can be safe from them. Just as it's the only way you'll be safe from the Echmen."

For a count of five, dead silence. "Why are you doing this?" she asked.

I knew it was coming, sooner or later; like the Echmen, only harder to deal with. "Because it's what you want," I told her. "What you really want, deep down. What you deserve."

"Fine," she said. "Don't tell me, see if I care. I'll just have to guess. You're doing this because you want to be the king of whole world."

I smiled at her. See above under muscle memory. "Really."

"I know," she said, "it sounds crazy. It's such a totally crazy thing to want. But I think you want it." She was shredding a scrap of linen offcut in her broad, stubby fingers. "Otherwise I can't think of a reason why you've done all this. I'm guessing it's all to do with your people being wiped out, the almighty Robur empire, so much better than everybody else that God even made them a different colour, so there'd be no excuse for not knowing. I think that really got to you."

"I'm not denying that," I said.

"So," she went on, "you figured it something like this. The world belongs to the Robur. I'm the only Robur left. Therefore the world belongs to me."

"That's a syllogism," I said. "I didn't know you'd learned logic."

"I read a book about it," she said. "It was all bullshit."

"You mean you couldn't understand it."

"I understood it just fine. But it was bullshit. Like all the stuff you've been trying to kid me into believing. I think you believe that because you're the last of your incredibly superior kind, you've got the right to be king. Maybe even God, some of the stuff you pulled. You're going to make yourself a god-king and punish the world for what it did to your darling blueskins."

I nodded. "It'd be a plausible scenario," I said, "except for one thing. I hate the Robur."

Sometimes, however hard you try, sincerity seeps through. She had an amazing ear for sincerity. On her day she could detect one part of it in a million parts of bullshit. "Do you?"

"Oh yes," I said. "Because of what they did to me. They made sure that I'd be cut off, pun fucking well intended, from my family, my people, the entire human race, for the rest of my life. And do I blame the Robur for that, or just specific individuals? No, I blame the lot of them, because the ones who did this to me were about as representative as you can get. They stood for everything my people believe in; know your place, respect your betters, do your duty, my only regret is that I have but one life to lose for my motherfucking country. They took my father, they made my mother despise me, and they made me into—" Deep breath. "What I am. That's what they do. Did. So they're responsible. I'm their fault. Just look at me, will you? No, really, look. No wonder I hate them."

If I didn't know better I'd have said she was shocked. "You swore."

"What?"

"You used foul language. I've never heard you do that before."

"I'm sorry."

"You must've had a reason. You always choose your words carefully."

"Do I."

"Yes, you do. And Dejauzi isn't even your language."

"It is now," I said. "And the Hus are now my people. I don't think you can have a nation of one, it's a grammatical impossibility."

"That would matter to you. The grammar."

"Yes," I said. "Nation is a collective noun." I was using the Echmen words, of course, but she understood them. "So if I belong to a nation, it's got to be plural, not singular. Therefore I may have been born Robur, but now I'm Hus."

"I don't think so. People aren't words, you can't just translate them." She considered me. It wasn't a comfortable experience. "Actually, hate them? Really and truly?"

"Really and truly," I said.

"And you'd rather be Hus than Robur?"

"Hus wouldn't have been my first choice," I said. "But, yes. Every time."

"Because we're dumb savages and you can kid us into doing what you want us to."

I sighed. "You want the truth?"

"Yes."

I let my shoulders slump, as though I'd just put down a heavy sack. "All right, then," I said. "I was the lowest form of life in the Robur diplomatic mission. I got sent to Echmen because I was an abomination to my own people and they couldn't stand the sight of me. Fine, I told myself, I screwed up, I deserve it. Then one day, no more Robur, gone, ceased to exist. I wasn't sorry, but I was terrified. So scared I couldn't hardly breathe. Imagine you're a little kid, your parents take you to the big city and you get separated from them. They've gone off and left you behind. You're surrounded by huge strangers, and all you know about strangers is that you're not to talk to them, because they're dangerous. That's how it felt.

I was this close to standing on a chair with a rope round my neck and jumping, only I was too frightened. What if I did it wrong and instead of dying I broke my neck and ended up paralysed? The Echmen might've kept me alive, out of pity, they do stuff like that. It's my worst nightmare, lying there not able to move."

She was weighing the evidence. "Go on," she said.

"Then you rescued me," I said. "And suddenly I wasn't a lost kid any more. You were rude and thoughtless and you made it clear you didn't like me—"

She scowled. "You singular?"

"You plural," I said, "which includes the singular. But that was fine. Like I said, not necessarily the nation I'd have chosen, but beggars can't be choosers. At least I *existed*." I paused, then went on; "And then the Echmen wanted some throwaway people to build a wall, and they chose mine. Oh, sure, I could have stayed on as a jobbing translator, made myself useful, earned enough money to keep myself fed and have a tiny little room all to myself. But I could never be Echmen, not with my unfortunate skin condition."

"True," she said.

"I know it's true. It's worse than leprosy to the Echmen, because before you got leprosy you were a human being. But *this*—" I drew a fingertip down my cheek. "I might as well have scales, or feathers. I could never be human to them. And," I went on, "it wasn't like I was spoiled for choice. I could stay with the Echmen and be an animal all my life, or I could throw in with you people. Did I tell you my name means lucky?"

"You did mention it, yes."

"I chose your lot," I said. "Unfortunately, the choice came with a problem. Your lot were being marched off as slaves.

My only link to the Hus was you, and you were on the point of being discreetly murdered. Which meant if I wanted to be a Hus rather than a non-human biped I had to save you. And to do that I had to save the Hus, and to do that I had to take control of all the Dejauzi. And to do *that*, I had to start a war. Not just any war, but the Dejauzi against the Echmen empire, the worms of the earth against the lions. It's like I'm locked inside a building and the only way to get out is to smash down all the walls and scramble out over the rubble. I ask you, though. What the hell else could I have done?"

She gazed at me. "That's a very strange way of looking at things," she said.

I shrugged. "You wanted the truth," I said. "You got it."

"Fine. Now what?"

"That's up to you," I said. "It wouldn't be too hard for you to get rid of me. There's poison, or someone who wants to do you a favour. If you can get rid of the body quietly, you can say you saw me carried up to heaven in a fiery chariot." I smiled at her. "Nothing I can do to stop you, if that's the way you want to go."

"Or?"

"We do it my way," I said, "and see where we end up. Could be an absolute bloody disaster, for all I know. Or we could end up ruling all the kingdoms of the earth. Would you like that?"

She thought about it. "I can't see the point," she said.

"Nor me. But you never know. Maybe it's like what my mother used to tell me when I got invited to kids' parties and I didn't want to go. You'll enjoy it when you get there, she used to say. Maybe we'll get there and find it's fun."

She looked at me. "How would it be," she said, "if I asked around and got enough bits of gold and silver junk to fill the saddlebags of a mule, and you just went away and never came back?"

I shook my head. "If I wanted that, it'd already have happened."

"Two mules."

"There isn't enough gold in the Dejauzi nation to fill four saddlebags. And if there was, the answer would be the same. I happen to have brought with me," I added, "Sirupat's *Concerning Poisons*. It's the standard reference, and it's in Echmen, so you wouldn't need a translation. Lend it to you if you like."

"Maybe later," she said. "All the kingdoms of the earth."

"What you control," I said, "can't hurt you. You'd need bodyguards and a food taster, but apart from that you'd be free and clear. Or you can spend the rest of your life glancing up at the skyline, it's up to you. But if you have me killed, I won't be there to save you the third time."

"Do you really think you can beat the Echmen?"

"I think *we* can," I said.

"But you're only a little soldier. All you've done is read books. And we don't even like fighting."

"Exactly," I said. "And that, I do believe, is why we can beat the Echmen."

One of the reasons people get irritated with me is my incurable flippancy. Everything's a joke to you, they sooner or later say, you can't be serious about anything. Which, I think, betrays a fundamental misunderstanding of the nature of humour.

There's a sort of cuttlefish, so they tell me. When it's chased by a shark or whatever, it squirts ink in its eyes and dashes for cover. For ink, read joke. The whole world scares me. A lot of the time, even thinking about who's coming for me next makes me ill with fear. So, because I assume everything and everybody is hostile, I spend my life behind a screen of floating ink. Of course, the danger I'm most afraid of is the one I carry around inside my head. And sometimes the screen is so thick I can't see a damn thing through it.

Trust me on this: behind the screen I'm deadly serious. You can't look at a sharp knife that close to you and see the look in the eyes of the man holding it and not be. The knife is there with me every day. It's like you've got a terminal illness and every morning you wake up and it's the first thing you remember.

No matter. Always the good-natured jibe and the merry quip. See? I'm harmless.

It started with a shepherd. They brought him in shortly after dawn. His jaw was smashed and half his face had been cut away, which made him hard to understand.

He'd been with his sheep, about ten miles out into the hill country. There'd been nothing to see or do all day, and he'd gone to the brook to fill his cooking pot with water. From over the brow, where he'd left his flock, he heard bleating, so he went to look. What he saw was a dozen horsemen. They wore long, shiny metal coats and rode the biggest horses he'd ever seen in his life, and they were driving off his sheep.

He dropped down and tried to edge back over the skyline, but one of the horsemen saw him and whistled to the others. Three of them broke off and came after him. He jumped up and ran like a hare. Obviously they closed in on him before he could get away, but he saw a big old disused anteater's hole and hurled himself into it feet first. It would've been a good idea, if only he'd been a handspan shorter. As it was, the top of his head stuck out, just the scalp and the hair. He couldn't see what happened next, but he heard hooves thumping towards him and felt the ground shake, and then the most terrible pain and his eyes were full of blood. He passed out, which probably saved him, the lancers assuming that he was dead.

When he came round, he realised that he was wedged in the hole, his arms pinned to his sides. He'd have died there, sure as eggs are eggs, if his cousins hadn't come looking for the sheep and followed the trail of hoofprints. They managed to get him out and onto the back of their donkey, and here they all were to tell the tale.

I had a look at the wound before they plastered it up with turmeric and plantain, and my guess is that the lancer jabbed at him as he rode past and thought he'd connected fair and square when in fact all he'd done was slice the skin off his face with the cutting edge of his spearhead. The last twist to free the blade must've been what broke the shepherd's jaw, levering against it in a confined space. He was lucky, and it should have been far worse. He'd be fully entitled to change his name to Felix.

I explained what it meant. A small party of lancers, a routine patrol or a scouting party, carries its rations with it. You only get foraging parties when a large body of men is out on an extended operation. Since there'd been no other reported encounters (at least, not yet) we could assume this party had come a long way from its parent column, which made sense if they were following the course of the old caravan road, which hadn't been used for a long time but which was still marked on the Echmen ordnance maps. In which case, I could make a fair guess where they were now, and which direction they'd be coming from once it had dawned on them that maps sometimes lie.

"They must think the Hus went that way," I explained, "following the old road. It'll lead them to the river, at which point they'll know you didn't come that way after all. So they'll follow the river upstream, right here. They know about this place because traders come here from all over to buy stuff to sell in Echmen. They should be able to cover thirty miles a day, easily. So, two days, give or take. Then they'll be here."

The Aram said: "My people may be here by then."

"That's good," I said, "but I'm not counting on it."

She stirred ominously. "It sounds like you've got something in mind," she said.

"I had a few thoughts," I said. "You know, just in case."

The Maudit said; "Let's hear it."

"If you like," I replied. "Basically, we can't go on the defensive, this town simply isn't big enough to hold all the country people, even if we could round them up in time. The technical term is chevauchée, which is Sashan for cruising around at your leisure burning houses and barns, driving off livestock and trashing standing crops. Oh, and killing people, of course. It's how the Echmen prefer to fight less developed nations, and they're very good at it. The idea is to force them into a pitched battle, which the Echmen inevitably win because of their superior equipment and training. All of you are wide open for it, and they know that. And, obviously, you can't possibly win."

I was sitting in the middle, with the kings in a circle round me. I couldn't join the circle since I wasn't their equal, but they wanted me where they could all see and hear me. Hence the seating arrangements; they the planets, me the sun. I didn't plan it that way. Just occasionally, things fall right without being pushed.

"So?"

"So," I said, "we do what they aren't expecting. We take the field against them."

She glared at me. "You just said, if we fight a pitched battle, we lose."

She was in the half of the circle that was outside the shade of the walnut tree, hot and dazzled by the sun. "That's not quite what I said. I choose my words carefully. If we're forced into a pitched battle, then yes, we'll probably lose. But if the battle happens when we want and where we want, that would be different."

The Rosinholet laughed. "I thought you said you weren't a general."

"I'm not," I said. "All I ever did was read books. Very good books, some of them."

So we talked about what we'd got, and what we could get in time, and what we were going to have to do without. So far, the Hus had made about twelve thousand of the new-model horn and sinew bows, but they'd made them to sell to the other Dejauzi. We had just under five thousand finished but not yet delivered. Similarly with the linen armour; the Hus had made thirty thousand linen breast and backplate harnesses, but twenty thousand had already been shipped. The Luzir had twelve thousand pikes in store, nearly all of them serviceable, and any amount of arrows, mostly unsuitable for the new bow, but what the hell. I'd taught the Luzir drill instructors to shoot flight rather than precision; what that means is, rather than trying to hit an individual target, which takes a long time to learn and is very difficult, you shoot at a linen sheet pegged down a hundred and fifty yards away. When you can hit that, you move the sheet back fifty yards. The idea is to learn the elevations you need to put an arrow there or thereabouts at a given distance, and most people can get the hang of it in an afternoon, assuming they already know the basics of archery. The real problem should have been getting them to draw the bow at all, given that it was twice or three times the weight they were used to. But they got on top of that remarkably quickly, presumably through wounded pride and spite. If I could do it, they sure as hell could; so they did. Anyhow, you can shoot flight with a hundred and twenty-pound bow and arrows spined for sixty pounds; they won't go straight and they won't hit as hard as properly spined ones, but never mind. A damn sight better than nothing.

We spent that evening and most of the night sorting out provisions and things to carry them in, sorting people into units, some very quick and dirty drilling in the three or four simple manoeuvres that I'd chosen to rely on. Keep it simple, it says in the good books, be realistic, never overestimate the courage and resolve of the ordinary fighting man; within those limitations, you can actually achieve a great deal, if you're smart. The next morning, we marched out, sorry, we shuffled out to war.

The scouts were gone a long time. They found the Echmen more or less where I'd hoped they'd be, working their way up the river, slowed down by the lack of things to forage. Any Dejauzi could have told them that at that time of year the flocks would be on the lower slopes of the hills, not down in the river meadows, but it hadn't occurred to them to ask. Yes, they were driving a substantial herd of sheep and goats, but not really enough to keep such a large army – twelve thousand lancers, God help us – going for any length of time. Pretty soon they'd need some more. Splendid.

Always, says the book, give the enemy what he wants, within reason. What he wanted just then was large, poorly defended resources of livestock. I arranged for that. We drove everything we could round up in the time available out onto the lower slopes, where their outriders could see them. The column changed direction with a whoop of joy, and rode off towards the herd. By the time they got there the shepherds were long gone, so no fighting required. They drove the herd back down the hill towards the river, only to find that while they'd been gone, ten thousand Dejauzi pikemen had slipped in between them and the river, the only drinking water within two days' ride.

It's bad enough at midday in that part of the country if you're wearing nothing but a light tunic and a hat. An Echmen lancer sports a collar-to-ankle oxhide coat, to which are laced more than four thousand small steel plates, shaped like fish scales and overlapping. On his head is a wraparound helmet weighing six pounds, with a faceplate down to his chin. Think how hot anything made of metal gets when you leave it out in the sun. The lancers like to stay close to water whenever they possibly can.

I had the pikemen fan out along the riverbank with their backs to the river. The Echmen must've smiled when they saw that, because I'd made a really stupid mistake: no escape route. Absolutely. Carrying those pikes were roughly ninety per cent of the adult male Hus, about whom I had few illusions. If they could run, they would. The Hus are fine athletes, very proficient runners, not so good at swimming. Luckily they didn't appreciate the truly awful situation I'd put them in until the Echmen lowered their lances and charged and it was far too late to do anything about it, or they'd never have followed my orders.

I got them lined them up in three rectangular blocks about a hundred yards from the riverbank. When the Echmen began their charge, with the impetus of riding down the slope in their favour, I'd told the middle block to pull back. We'd rehearsed it a dozen times. All I want you to do, I said, is turn around, walk fifty yards, stop, turn round again. That's all. Even so, I don't know if I could've done it if I'd been there with them, which needless to say I wasn't. Turning your back on twelve thousand charging lancers and walking, not running, in the opposite direction. I really admire them for doing that.

Fifty yards, stop, turn. To the Echmen, of course, it looked exactly as though the centre of my line had given way and started to retreat, exactly what they were expecting. So they bunched up to concentrate their impact on the centre block, expecting to plough into the backs of terrified retreating men. What they got, when the centre block turned and stood, was a hedge of sixteen-foot pikes, and no horse ever bred will throw itself onto something like that and get spiked. I saw the moment when the steel wave dissolved into foaming breakers of rearing, terrified horses, the front ranks stopping dead, the ranks behind crashing into them at top speed. Lancers have far more sense than to try and charge a hedge of pikes, but they hadn't been doing that, they'd been running down fugitives, until it suddenly all went wrong. That was the point at which the other two blocks of pikemen wheeled in on them through ninety degrees and started to close up the space.

Faced with pike hedges on three sides, the lancers knew

when to quit. They dragged their horses round and made for the one open side. At which point, the archers I'd concealed in dead ground two hundred yards back stood up and started to loose.

A short while later, a knot of about seventy lancers who still had horses managed to squeeze through the gap between the middle and the left-hand pike blocks. I was happy to let them go. I wanted witnesses. The rest of the lancers weren't so lucky. Their fault, not mine.

I watched the performance from a hilltop on the other side of the river. A long time ago, someone had built a cairn and set up five prayer flags, the rags of which still rattled in the stiff breeze. I'd chosen it because I could see the whole of the action from up there, and also because it put a broad, fast-flowing river between me and the fighting. It was far enough away for the people to dwindle down into dots, flashing bright Echmen stars in a sandy sky, thickets of spears, ragged geometrical shapes, nothing recognisably human. I could hear the noise, but it blended together into a confused symphony. Better that way.

When I was sure it was safe I came down, the conquering hero picking his squeamish way through thousands of dead and dying horses scattered everywhere. Their riders had nearly all died in one place. Dismounted, they'd huddled together in a square, but their lances were seven feet shorter than our pikes. The Dejauzi were fine about it. They weren't close enough to see individual bodies and faces through the hedge in front of them; all they had to do was walk forward until they felt resistance on the ends of their pikes, then grip hard and shove. When there were too few Echmen left to be a threat, I pulled the pikemen out and brought up the archers. We had about six thousand newly made arrows, bodkin heads – a flying nail rather than the usual flying knife. I wanted to prove to the Dejauzi that the new bow would shoot through Echmen scale armour at close range. It did, just fine. It took less than a minute, and I was too far away to see anything that might disturb me.

The dead horses were lying everywhere, spaced like trees in an orchard. A long-range hit with a broadhead, slanting down at an angle of around sixty degrees, wasn't nearly enough to knock them down. Instead, it opened a wide cut about two inches deep. They went wild with pain and fear, rearing and kicking and thrashing around till they bled out, which took somewhere between one and five minutes. I spent a summer in the City when I was young, just downwind of a slaughterhouse, so the smell of all that blood made me feel homesick.

"Can you tan horsehide?" I asked one of the Luzir who was acting as my bodyguard.

"You bet. Makes great shoes, among other things."

"There's enough material here for a whole industry."

Well, you've got to be practical. Quality leather goods weren't the only harvest of victory, of course. We now had best part of ten thousand sets of Echmen heavy armour; also boots, shirts, trousers, saddlery, tents, blankets and the round felt pillbox hats they wear under their helmets as padding. All made to Imperial specifications, the very best money can buy. Even the kings of the Dejauzi could never afford to dress that well. I decided that armour and weapons belonged to the state, everything else to the individual private-enterprise looter. Nobody seemed to mind that. A gilded parade helmet with velvet lining and an ostrich feather plume makes an attractive keepsake, but trousers are trousers.

There were about a hundred survivors. I went and had a look at them. They looked stunned mostly, as though they couldn't believe what had happened. About a third of them were badly carved up. The rest were walking wounded. "What unit are you?" I asked in Echmen.

"Third Lancers," someone replied.

"Go home," I told them. "Tell your superiors what you saw here today. Don't take the road you came by, there's a much quicker route with an oasis about halfway. Here, I'll draw you a map."

I sketched some squiggles in the dust with the toe of my boot. Close enough.

"What about the wounded?" one of them asked. "They won't make it on foot across the desert."

"Take them with you or leave them here and we'll patch them up."

"We'll take them with us," said someone I took to be an officer. "I'm not leaving my men in the hands of savages."

"I knew a drill sergeant like you once," I said. "He's dead now."

I like the Echmen; some of them, some of the time. They limped away into the desert, carrying their dying brethren. I found out later, quite by chance, that six of them made it. Six more than I expected, to be honest.

Twenty-seven Hus had been killed, forty more cut up or trampled by horses. Nobody could remember the last time twenty-seven people had all died on the same day. Fortunately for me the Hus tradition favours quiet, secluded mourning. You shave your head, stay indoors and don't eat for a week, and family and friends stay the hell away from you, like you've caught something nasty. Meanwhile, cousins in the second degree take the body away and dig a hole somewhere and don't tell you where, and the dead person's name isn't spoken for five years. There's no Dejauzi word for grave, tombstone or funeral. I guess there's no sensible way to behave around death, though some ways are more repugnant than others, to me anyhow. The Echmen burn their dead on enormous bonfires and throw expensive parties. The Sashan take the body out into the wilderness and leave it for the vultures, and they hire people, widows and orphans for choice, to sit on their doorsteps and scream for three days. In Permia they act as though nothing's changed; a place is laid at table, the dead man's clothes are washed, pressed and put out ready for him to wear, when he condescends to come back from wherever he's popped out to, for a whole year. In Blemya the corpse is gutted, sun-dried, embalmed and transferred to an underground house with everything as nice as the family can afford to make it, and you go once a month and visit your elderly relatives in their beautiful home; just like we do, I guess, only they don't talk so much.

11

"Of course we won," I told them. "It's not like anything else could have happened."

The Aram Chantat had arrived, a day late, just in time to lend a hand with piling up the dead lancers for compost and skinning the horses. They'd come in a hurry, empty-handed, so the Luzir had to find food for them and places to sleep. All the other Dejauzi nations were on their way. There's precious little surplus food in a Dejauzi community at the best of times. Luckily, nobody seemed to regard the problem as my fault so I wasn't called upon to deal with it; just as well.

The mood under the walnut tree was a sort of muted, bewildered joy. It's like you just inherited a million gold stamena from a distant cousin you'd never heard of. It's so unexpected you can't really believe or understand it, and you know there's got to be a catch somewhere. "What happens now?" one of them asked.

She answered for me. "This is the worst defeat the Echmen have suffered in eighty years," she said. "It'll have to be avenged. Letting us get away with it is unthinkable." She shot me a savage glance, then went on, "If you think we were in trouble before, you just wait."

"Which is precisely what we're not going to do," I interrupted. "She's right. They'll be coming for us, as soon as they've called in their forces from the provinces. To give you an idea of what we're up against, last time anyone counted, there were a little under a quarter of a million Echmen lancers, divided up into five regional armies. We've slaughtered a twentieth of them. It's a start, but we've still got work to do."

Stunned silence, which I took advantage of. Four hundred years ago, I told them, the Echmen invented head-to-toe armour, heavy horses and the lance charge. They annihilated anyone stupid enough to stand up to them, because all their enemies fought on foot, with light armour, self bows and javelins. By the time their territorial expansion brought them into collision with the Sashan, the Sashan had developed heavy cavalry of their own. For three and a half centuries, therefore, the definition of war in both Sashan and Echmen was waves of lancers crashing into each other with a thump you could hear a mile away. It's a difficult way to fight, needing a lot of training and skill, and both sides were now very good at it. Any other form of armed conflict, however, was by now far beyond their contemplation. Fighting on foot, for example, or using bows or long pikes, simply wasn't war. It was something else; probably a kind of criminal activity akin to banditry, and therefore the civil authority's pigeon, nothing to do with the military.

"Right now," I said, "the Echmen generals who haven't been hanged for incompetence will be explaining to the emperor that the reason they lost was that they didn't send enough lancers.

We won't be making that mistake again, they'll be saying. Which means," I went on, "three things. One, they'll be back, in force. Two, it'll be a while before they're back. Three, when they come back, we can wipe the floor with them."

A rather shaky voice said: "Are you sure about that?"

"Absolutely," I said, and I think I may even have smiled. "It's something called diminishing returns, or you could think of it as the right tool for the right job. Suppose you want to knock in a nail. You fetch a hammer. Now, if you're an Echmen general, you say to yourself, if a little hammer works for driving in nails, a fifteen-pound sledgehammer must be even better. And the next thing you know, you've smashed the thing you were making and crushed your thumbnail to pulp. There's a tipping point where more men and bigger armies make things worse, not better. They're a liability. They make it pretty well certain that you'll lose. All we have to do is set things up so that we reach that tipping point. Which is what we did yesterday, in case you hadn't noticed."

After the meeting I was shaking like a leaf. "You need to get a grip," she told me.

"Yes," I said. "I'm sorry."

"You look awful."

Did I? No idea. "I'm fine," I said.

"Liar." She put both hands on my shoulders and pushed me down onto my knees, then sat down beside me. We were in the shade of a chestnut tree. I had a lot of things I should've been doing. "I've seen healthier looking corpses. Admit it, you're exhausted."

It hadn't occurred to me. "No, I'm not. I've just got the shakes a bit after doing my big speech. I get nervous. I always think someone's going to hit me."

"You're trying to do too much," she chided. "Most of the day you're drilling the troops or doing bow training, and when it's not that it's something else. You're running yourself ragged, you know that?"

"I'm not, really." I stifled a yawn. "I don't have a farm to run or cattle to look after, I don't earn my own living, I don't even have to translate for anyone. I'm unemployed. Gentleman of leisure."

"And when you're not doing that you're reciting that stupid scripture for people."

"Reading aloud isn't work."

"You need to rest," she said firmly. "Come on."

It occurred to me, as I closed my eyes lying on a heap of pillows in the Hus royal pavilion, that I hadn't slept for three days. Proving that I didn't need sleep.

They woke me up an hour or so later. The Maudit had arrived.

Just when you think everything's about to collapse in on top of you, someone quite unexpectedly shows a glimmer of common sense, and it sort of lights up the world, like a sunrise. The Maudit had brought food with them, jars of flour, barrels of apples and sides of bacon, in carts; also tents, blankets, you name it, everything they needed and we couldn't provide for them. I was so grateful I nearly burst into tears.

They also brought arrows, bundled up with string in faggots, and their own home-made copies of the horn and sinew bow. It was, if anything, better than the ones I'd taught the Hus to make, which put noses out of joint but what the hell. There were eighteen thousand Maudit, three divisions of six thousand, of whom five thousand were archers. I have no idea what their king had said to his people, but it must've been something pretty good.

After the Maudit came the Rosinholet, closely followed by the Cure Hardy. The Rosinholet had somehow contrived to get hold of thousands of bales (I can't think of a better word offhand) of dried fish – weird, since they live a very long way from the sea, but I didn't ask. They'd traded it for furs, apparently, thinking it might come in handy, and did anybody know what you're supposed to do with it?

Just so happens I'd read about it in a book. Your dried fish is baked in the sun until it's indistinguishable from a slab of tree bark. Try and bend it over your knee; it's stiff, then it snaps. All you do is soak it in water till it turns soft, then boil it or grill it or do what the hell you like. It's light to carry, it keeps practically forever so long as the damp doesn't get at it, mice won't touch it, and in an emergency you can shove it up your shirt as a really quite functional form of armour.

The Rosinholet are like that. They love buying and selling things, and it's rather a shame they're not better at it. But it means that traders from all over the place battle their way across deserts and over sky-high mountain passes, knowing that when they finally get there they've got a chance of off-loading all that stuff their brother-in-law bought when they were out of town and which they never thought they'd ever see the back of. In return the Rosinholet supply furs: brown bear, white fox, black hare, ermine, rabbit, beaver, caracole, muskrat and sable, all derived from the prolific hordes of vermin that make agriculture next thing to impossible in their neck of the woods. At age six a Rosinholet can hit a running rat at twenty yards, but the multitude of furry horrors still devour every spring lamb, ear of corn and blade of grass in the river valleys as soon as it appears. It was a glorious day for the whole nation when it turned out that there were people who actually wanted the waste products of dead pests. The supply is inexhaustible, so they never could be bothered to haggle. They heaped up ramparts of pelts and were pleased and grateful for whatever they got given in exchange. In consequence they're a nation of fatalists, resigned and accepting, firm believers in wild swings of fortune, stoical endurers, fine shots and absolutely the people you'd be glad to have at your side if ever you wanted anything skinned.

The Cure Hardy aren't as straightforward as the Rosinholet. Ask the other Dejauzi about them, and they'll all immediately tell you the same thing; the Cure Hardy eat people. Which is true, up to a point. If someone dies under the age of thirty, not from an infectious disease, it's the duty of the next of kin to roast the body and eat certain parts of it – the heart, the brain, the liver and the bone marrow, which is where they reckon the soul lives. The idea is to reabsorb the essential part of the deceased into the family so that he or she can live out their full term, unnaturally cut short, through their closest relatives. It's all very respectful and loving and I could foresee the most dreadful problems once the Cure Hardy started fighting the Echmen. How the hell were we going to get dead bodies from the front back to the home villages before they went off? The idea of not eating their honoured dead was so appalling to them when I suggested it that I was almost tempted to send the lot of them home. But they're gritty fighters, cheerful and resourceful when the going gets tough, and they'd brought food and a ridiculously large quantity of arrowheads, so I didn't want to lose them; a compromise was therefore necessary. We discussed various options – salting, pickling in brine or vinegar, preserving in honey, air-drying into biltong (my preferred option, because it didn't call for additional materials or large storage vessels, but no good because of the marrow) – before settling on a form of representative adoption. All Cure Hardy, so their traditions say, are descended from one original patriarch; therefore, all Cure Hardy are related to each other, and by extension to the king. Adoption inside the family is common practice – you can hop from one branch of the family tree to another on a whim, if you're so inclined – so it was perfectly legal and proper for the king to adopt all Cure Hardy on active service as his sons; illegitimate, naturally, so as not to confer succession rights, but in every other respect flesh of his flesh and bone of his bone. It would then be his responsibility to take at least one token nibble of all the warriors who fell in battle, and that was that problem sorted. Cannibalism aside, the Cure Hardy are an amiable bunch, musical, kind to strangers and with a great sense of humour, though they tend to be sore losers at organised sports.

So everyone who was coming was here. Between them the six nations mustered a whisker over sixty-five thousand men; eighteen thousand archers with horn and sinew bows, the rest pikemen. We cut the skirts off the Echmen scale coats, and those combined with our home-made linen breastplates provided armour for nearly half the pikemen. We'd scraped together nine thousand carts but only eight thousand teams of oxen to pull them and not nearly enough flour, beans or cured meat –

"You're the prophet, right?"

Four Cure Hardy sitting round a campfire, roasting some kind of meat on skewers. I was getting used to being told who

I was, but it still felt strange, like jarring your back when you slip and fall.

"That's me," I said.

"We thought it must be. Tall skinny black man, see?"

"Ah."

They grinned at me. "You stuck it right up those Echmen bastards."

"We stuck it right up," I amended. "The queen of the Hus is commander-in-chief. I'm an adviser."

"Sit down and join us," one of them said. "There's plenty."

Four Cure Hardy offer you a bit of meat on a stick.

"Thanks," I said. "I already ate."

That made them laugh. "Try some," they said. The 'or else' was silent, like the P in psalm.

I sat down. They passed me a skewer. A bit chewy and slightly too sweet for my taste, but edible. "Not bad," I said. "It's been a while since I tasted beef."

More laughter. "That's not beef."

I told you they had a sense of humour. "Tastes like beef," I said.

"Horse."

"Ah."

I chewed up another bite, then said, "You people like horse, then."

"When we can get it," one of them said. "Bit of a delicacy back home. I mean, you don't go killing good horses just to eat. But when we got here we saw a couple of guys skinning a dead horse, and we asked, do you want that, and they said, go ahead, help yourselves. So why not?"

I chewed a bit more. "It definitely grows on you," I said. Then I nodded at the cart they were sitting next to. It was laden with barrels. My guess was, they were the carters. "What's the load?"

"Salt," said one of them. "We figured, someone might want to buy it."

Another thing about the Cure Hardy. In the back end of their territory, there's a mountain of pure salt. It's a bitch to get to unless you actually live there, so it costs outsiders more than it's worth to mine and ship it. The locals just turn up with picks and shovels and help themselves. "Did many of you boys bring salt with you?"

One of them nodded. "To pay for those fancy new bows. We figured someone might want it. It's all we've got."

Salt, and – assuming we won – an inexhaustible supply of dead horses. And if we lost, we wouldn't be needing food anyway. Another problem bites the dust.

"I've been thinking," she said. She stopped and looked at me. "What are you doing?"

I had a shovel in my hands and I was standing over a narrow, steep-sided, flat-bottomed trench about three feet deep. Beside the trench was a mound of earth, liberally studded with fist-sized flints. Stout denial would be pointless. "Digging a hole," I said.

"Why?"

On the other side of the trench was a wooden crate I'd knocked up out of bits of plank I'd scrounged from the Hus wainwrights. Sawn timber is nothing at all in the City, barely one step up from junk, but if the Hus want a plank, they have to start with a tree and keep going with a saw. I've known important men who've put less work into building their entire careers than a Hus devotes to a simple piece of lumber. Inside the crate was an oilskin bag. Inside the bag was my bow.

"I'm storing something."

"You're not very good at digging."

"I came to it relatively late in life."

She looked at the box, considering its dimensions. "How do you reckon on finding it again?"

"I thought a pile of rocks."

She shook her head. "Someone'll come along and take them for hardstanding," she said. "Or dig up whatever it is you're burying. A tree would be better."

"It's rocks or nothing," I said.

"When we want to hide something," she said, "we dam up a river, dig a hole in the riverbed, line it with three sheets of lead, then break the dam. You can hide something real good that way."

"What have any of your people ever had that would be worth all that effort to hide?"

She sat down on the bank of spoil, preventing me from finishing the job. "That's more or less what I've been thinking about," she said.

I sat down opposite. "In what way?"

"Something you said," she replied. "About us and the Echmen. The worms of the earth against the lions."

"It's a quotation."

"Thought it must be. All the clever things you say turn out to have been said by someone else. What does it mean?"

"Once upon a time," I told her, "the lions declared war on the earthworms. Everyone was sure the lions would win, but the worms were clever. They dug deep holes in the ground so the lions couldn't get at them. Then, at night when the lions were asleep, they came back up, crawled in through the lions' ears and ate their brains. It's an old Robur fable."

She nodded. "And that's your idea, is it?"

"Basically, yes. The worms won because they figured out a new way of fighting. Which is what we've done."

She thought for a moment. "In the story, the lions started it."

"The lions always start it," I said. "By being lions."

That shut her up for several seconds. "You believe that."

"Yes."

"Is that why you're doing this?"

I chose my words. "I don't like predators," I said.

"This is about those friends of yours who cut you up."

It was a question that deserved a thoughtful answer, maybe even a true one. Or maybe not. "Partly," I said. "Yes and no."

"This *is* about those friends of yours who cut you up."

"Partly. And it's about what the milkfaces did to the Robur. And what the Echmen did to you. You singular and plural. To us."

"And?"

"A war to end all wars," I suggested. "Reorganising the world so wars don't happen any more. Wars and genocides and whole nations marched off into slavery—"

"Like the Robur used to do."

"We called it spreading civilisation and core Robur liberal values, but yes."

She nodded again. "Why you?"

I acknowledged the merit of the question with a nod of my head. "Because I suddenly realised I was in the right place at the right time with the right materials all within easy reach. Meaning you. The Hus. And the Echmen. And if not me, who else? The opportunity might not occur again, ever. It sort of came to me, in a flash."

"In a dream, maybe?"

"I had a dream once. I think I saw the Queen of Heaven. Of course, back then I didn't know it was her. But I was off my head through blood loss at the time. That wasn't the flash, though. I was wide awake, in the library."

"You want to rule the world."

It was like a slap in the face. "I suppose so," I said. "Like they say. If you want something done properly, do it yourself. And from what I've seen, nobody else is fit to be trusted with it."

"And you are."

"Me, no. You, maybe. But even I couldn't make a bigger hash of it than everyone who's tried so far."

"I see. What gives you the right?"

"Self-defence."

She sighed. "So you picked on me to be your crowbar."

"Do you want to know what I really think?" The words came out like blood from a wound, a sight I'm familiar with. "I think you and I are very much alike. The lions came looking for us, we didn't start it. They murdered your father and all your family, and me—" I grinned. "They cut me up. But that's a thing about worms. You cut one in half, all you achieve is two worms."

She frowned. "We're not really all that alike," she said. "For a start, I'm a queen and you're—" Her turn to choose her words with care. "Nobody."

"True. But being a queen wasn't doing you a lot of good when you were sitting in that cell. And the queen of the worms is still a worm."

I could see her thinking it over, weighing one consideration with another. "If you'd told me this was what you had in mind at the start, I'd never have gone along with it, I'd rather have died. But you've been so smart and fixed things up so well for yourself that the only way I can see to stop it is to kill you. And that would be—"

"Yes?"

"Ungrateful," she said. "And, yes, the lions are bad. It's time something was done about them. I expect that if we win, in a hundred years we'll be lions ourselves, but I won't be here to see that, so fuck it." She looked at me. "Is it possible the Queen of Heaven really did choose you, only she forgot to tell you? Or maybe she figured that if you knew, you'd screw everything up."

"Of the two," I said, "that's the more likely. Why? Do you think I really—?"

"It's a weird thought," she said. "And, no, I don't think that. But if she was going to choose someone to be her prophet, maybe someone like you would be the sort of person she'd go for. An outsider, cut off from everybody else, nothing to live for, left with nothing to want, no desires." She paused, as though doing mental arithmetic. "There's wealth, of course, money. But money's only good for buying things. If you had all the money in the world, what would you buy with it?"

"I don't know. Armour, possibly. A castle. Or I'd build a pillar."

"A what?"

"Couple of hundred years ago," I said, "there were these holy men, out somewhere on the Robur–Sashan border. They persuaded devout believers to build enormously tall pillars, with a platform on the top. The holy men took a pillar each.

They climbed up a ladder to the top, then pushed the ladder away. When they needed food or a particular holy book, they lowered a basket on a bit of string. When eventually they died, they toppled off and the devout took them away and buried them. Possibly the single most selfish thing I've ever heard of, but there are times when I can see the attraction."

She nodded. "The danger would be someone coming along with a ladder while you're asleep. But you're not a holy man, are you?"

"Not to my knowledge. Though who says the Queen of Heaven has to choose a believer? Like you said. A believer would probably make a mess of it."

She stood up. "I wouldn't bury it if I were you," she said. "The damp'll get into the glue and it'll all come apart. You'd be better off lodging it up a tree."

"I'm scared of heights."

"Then take the stupid thing with you."

I shook my head. "If I did that," I said, "someone might expect me to shoot someone with it. Or it'd get lost or left behind or stolen. It's all I've got."

"Then it's one thing too many, if you're serious about being a prophet. And you're never going to shoot anyone. You'd be too scared to get close enough."

She said it like it was a bad thing, but I think fear is wonderful, in its place. It keeps you out of all sorts of trouble. On the other hand, it gets you into all sorts of other trouble, so maybe it's as broad as it's long.

Real generals working for proper countries have spies, who keep them up to date on what the enemy's doing wherever he's doing it. We had scouts, who flatly refused to go further than twelve hours' ride from home. Accordingly, if we wanted to figure out the enemy's plans, we had to use our imaginations.

If I was the Echmen chief of staff, what would I be doing? Well, now. I have a paper strength of a quarter of a million lancers, according to the annual military review, as presented to the emperor on his birthday each year, illuminated vellum exquisitely bound in gilded calfskin. In practice, things are a little different.

What I actually have is a quarter of a million legal obligations. Every Echmen subject who owns property worth more than a certain amount is legally required to do thirty days of military service, for which he provides his own horse, armour, grooms and batmen, at his own expense. There are a number of recognised exemptions; benefit of clergy is the main one, and you can also opt out if you're the last male in your family, so that if anything happens to you, your family name dies out; there are a few others as well, but they're complicated. If you're exempt, or too old and fat, or you simply don't fancy killing and getting killed, you can hire a substitute, provided he's of acceptable social standing. This would usually be one of your neighbour's or cousin's younger sons – no use to anyone, no great loss if he doesn't come back, and unlikely ever to amount to anything except by virtue of a successful career in the military.

The sad fact is, though, that not everybody fulfils their legal obligations. A quarter of a million paper lancers probably represents two hundred thousand real ones. Furthermore, twelve thousand of your lancers – real, not paper – are dead, thanks to some tiresome savages who now have to be dealt with.

That still leaves a hundred and eighty-eight thousand, and with an army that size you could comfortably storm heaven and slaughter all the gods. It's not quite as simple as that. It's a legal requirement that twenty-five thousand men should be stationed at the capital at all times, to protect the person of the emperor, and even suggesting that all or some of them should be seconded to other duties is treason, punished by death. Each provincial governor – there are five of them – has an army of forty thousand paper, thirty thousand actual soldiers, to guard his terrifyingly long and vulnerable borders and remind the subject nations of the benefits of civilisation; the twelve thousand we killed came from the eastern provincial army, now standing at eighteen thousand strong. Even if the governors of the northern, north-eastern, western and south-western provinces could be persuaded to part with their forces, it would take time to get them to where we were. The soldiers themselves were lancers and could cover forty miles a day if they absolutely had to, but food for them and their horses moved on oxcarts, which can do ten miles a day on good roads.

In practice, therefore, the Echmen commander-in-chief has at his disposal the army of the governor whose province he's operating in, plus his reserve, the field, as opposed to provincial, army. On paper, the field army is twenty-five thousand men, the second best in the service after the Imperial guards garrisoning the capital. But there's a catch.

In theory, the Echmen emperors are descended in an unbroken line from God. Actually, there have been twenty-six dynasties, completely unrelated to each other. Twenty-one of those dynasties were founded by generals, following military coups or civil wars. There is, accordingly, a certain reluctance on the part of the emperor to leave large numbers of fighting men under the direct, unsupervised control of a general, particularly if he's any good at his job or if his soldiers like him. The field army (a large number of fighting men under the direct, unsupervised control of the commander-in-chief) is never allowed to reach its nominal strength, and is normally kept at around five thousand, including clerks, storekeepers and administrators.

I did the maths. General Alyattes, supreme commander of the Imperial forces, would have at his disposal the eighteen thousand men left in the eastern provincial army, plus between two and three thousand of his personal reserve; something over twenty thousand lancers actually available to slaughter us like sheep and grind our bones into dust. I, on the other hand, had sixty thousand Dejauzi.

It goes without saying that odds of three to one are meaningless in such a context, since one Echmen lancer is worth a hundred savages, and no mob of half-naked barbarians would ever dare to challenge the might of the greatest nation on earth. Even so.

"That's a map," said the king of the Rosinholet. "How does it work?"

The Rosinholet know their own territory like the backs of their hands and they never go anywhere else, so the need for maps has never arisen. "Imagine you're a bird," I said, "very high up in the air."

He shrugged. "Where are we?"

"Here," I said. "And here's where the enemy are most likely to be, where my thumb is."

"That's very close."

About a hundred and twenty miles, but I wasn't going to undeceive him. "It's only a rough sketch," I said. "It's the best

I could do. But, yes, that's us and that's them. And this here is the mountains, and that's the river."

"That sort of squiggle."

"Yes. We can be here—" I pointed, keeping it vague "—in five days. The supplies he needs to feed his army will be coming down this road here. If we cut him off from his supplies, he's screwed. He'll have to fight us or starve."

"I thought the Echmen foraged for supplies," said the Maudit.

"Yes," I said, "they do. But there's nothing to forage out here, where they're coming from. The nearest sheep and villages are here, look, so they'll be coming down this road. And here's where we'll be, right between the Echmen and what they need."

"It's what you did before," she said. "Only last time it was water and this time it's food. Won't they be expecting that?"

"Probably not, if they're underestimating us, which they will be. Also, they can expect till they're blue in the face, there's nothing they can do about it. Not unless they go all the way round through here, where there's plenty of stuff to forage. But by the time they've done that, we could be across the border and burning major cities."

"So what?" she said. "Better that than fight a battle you might well lose."

"Not if you're an Echmen general. If you lose a battle, that's not necessarily fatal. You might be able to put the blame on someone else. But if an important city gets burned down, one the emperor's heard of, and you made no effort to save it, your head will be stuck up on a pike somewhere faster than butter melts."

Silence. Then: "That's stupid," said the Cure Hardy.

"It's how they do things," I said. "It's why they're civilised and you're not. If we shade our line of march a bit south, along here, we'll look like we're making directly for one of these cities here, in which case he'll have to stop us before we reach the border. Here," I pointed. "Which is where I want us to be. With your approval, of course."

Nobody spoke. I waited. I knew what they wanted to say – can't we forget about it and go home? Five divinely anointed kings of five fiercely independent nations. "That's settled, then," I said. "Let's get weaving."

Some people have no luck at all, and General Alyattes was one of them. He'd been supreme commander of the Echmen army for about eighteen months, after a lifetime in the military. Received opinion around the Imperial court was that he'd got the job because of his proven skill and expertise in keeping costs down and improving response times and connectivity in the upper-middle echelons of the army clerical corps; under his iron governance, memos were getting from desk to desk in half the time it had taken under his predecessor, the endemic culture of fiddling that had plagued commissariat and supply for as long as anyone could remember had suffered a mortal blow, and major contractors were now charging the government the going rate for supplies and services, rather than double less a colossal sweetener for the relevant officials. At the time of his appointment he'd been exactly what the service needed, and ever since then he'd been doing a marvellous job. Of course, nobody back then had imagined that the Echmen would shortly find themselves fighting a serious war, let alone one against a completely unknown quantity who played by different rules.

But Alyattes was nobody's fool, and he took his duties seriously. He'd never been in combat himself, but he knew plenty of people who had, and he wasn't too proud to take advice. He got together the best, most experienced commanders in the army and asked them, how do we beat these people? Simple, they said. You avoid pitched battles. Instead, you evacuate all the major cities between the border and the capital. You confiscate or destroy all food stores, livestock and standing crops. You let them go where they like, shadowing them every step they take with a large mobile army but never getting close enough for them to engage you. The rest of your troops you send to their homelands, where you kill, smash and burn everything. Give it nine months and they'll give up and go home. Then arrange for their leaders to be assassinated and make sure to get the right people to replace them. Easy as that.

It was the right advice and Alyattes knew it. Unfortunately, he couldn't take it. His rivals would have his job and his head if he even suggested doing something like that. He was an honourable man, prepared to die for his country, at least in the vague abstract – but not like that. And even if he did, he rationalised, it wouldn't do any good. Whichever of his colleagues got his job would immediately launch a full-scale attack seeking a decisive pitched battle. The battle was therefore going to happen, it was inevitable, there was absolutely nothing anyone could do about it. So; either he led the army into this hopelessly ill-advised battle, or someone else would, somebody incompetent, arrogant, downright stupid, absolutely certain to fail. But if he led the army himself, there was always the chance that he might think of something clever on the day, or the savages might make a mistake.

Things like that did happen. They'd happened in the past, surprisingly often. Old Echmen proverb: when falling off a high tower, try to fly. You never know your luck and what've you got to lose?

Early in his three-year course at the Echmen Imperial Military Academy, Alyattes would have read and learned by heart the thirty-six axioms of warfare, attributed to the Diamond Emperor but more likely composed during the interminable wars of the Fourth and Fifth Dynasties. The seventh axiom states that out of every ten battles, two are won by the victors whereas eight are lost by the losers. Sometimes – more often than you'd think – the first half of the battle is lost by side A, whereupon side B makes an even worse mistake, making it possible for A to snatch victory out of the jaws of thoroughly deserved defeat. Generals and their subordinate officers make mistakes all the time. Trouble is, you can't predict or rely on the other man's errors. Not unless you lead him into temptation.

In his second year at the academy, Alyattes would've studied the battle of Merope in the Second Mercantile War between the Sashan and the Ordoac. He will have been told to mark, consider and inwardly digest how the recklessly arrogant Sashan king committed his entire army to a frontal attack, only to find that he'd walked straight into a trap. So completely was he fooled that his entire baggage train – carrying among other things the royal pavilion, wardrobe, dinner service and privy purse, about twenty heavily laden wagons – was snapped up by the enemy before he could do a thing to save it. Luckily for him. Confronted with wealth on a scale they'd never imagined was possible, the Ordoac heavy infantry forgot about the battle and settled down to some serious looting. Meanwhile, the commander of the Sashan light cavalry somehow managed to rally his decimated troops and lead a counter-attack, catching the Ordoac infantry just as they'd started fighting among themselves over the spoils. That's why you've never heard of the Ordoac. A few months later, they ceased to exist.

Alyattes didn't go in for solid gold dinner services, but he did have six million gold tremisses, the tax revenue for the entire eastern province, on the point of being sent up to the capital in a fleet of heavy wagons. The problem was making sure we knew about it, which he solved by prompting a dozen or so of his Aram no Vei auxiliaries to desert. The no Vei made sure we knew all about the gold, then headed home.

It was a good plan. It's the sort of thing I'd have done myself in his shoes, if I'd been smart enough to think of it.

What the no Vei said to us was: You want to watch those bastards. They're up to something.

"Really?" I said. "Such as what?"

The oldest no Vei, spokesman by virtue of seniority, grinned at me. "They've got a load of big carts, and in them they've got all the gold money they screwed out of the towns and villages on their side of the line. You want to tell me why they're taking that with them into the desert, into harm's way, instead of sending it to the emperor?"

I nodded. "Bait," I said.

"Our colonel was dead keen you heard about it," said the spokesman. "So much so, we got sent home early with double pay, just so we could tell you. Six million tremisses, he said, if that means anything to you."

"It means a lot of money."

"We gathered that," the old man said with a grin. "Six million of anything's got to be worth something."

"A tremissis is a chunky gold coin the size of your thumbnail."

"No shit." The old man was impressed. "Six million of them. What would anyone want with all that?"

I smiled at him. "It'll all go on administration," I said. "That means hiring a lot of people to do things that don't need doing instead of growing wheat and raising sheep. It won't do any good to anyone, it'll just sort of melt away. The Echmen are like that."

"Screw them," said the no Vei. "Thanks for the soup."

About the Aram no Vei. You'd assume from their name that they're something to do with the Aram Chantat, but they aren't. They're not Dejauzi. They live north-east of the Luzir Soleth, half in and half out of Imperial territory. They don't like the empire much, because of its habit of taking their sheep and their people and not paying for them, but they've adapted. Whenever the Imperials come tax gathering, they simply up sticks and move in with their cousins on the other side of the fence until the nasty men go away. They're short and slightly built, the only milkfaces east of the Friendly Sea, with hair the colour of rust or flax and slate-blue eyes. They're easy-going, hard-working, generous people, down to earth and very reluctant to get involved with violence. The Echmen military use them as porters, carters, latrine diggers, grooms (they're good with horses), stockmen and general fetchers and carriers. The Echmen pay them good money, but it's worth bearing in mind that the no Vei language uses the same word for *employee* and *slave*.

"If you felt like it," I said, "you could do me a favour."

The old man looked at me. "Such as what?"

"It wouldn't take you five minutes, and it'd be a poke in the eye for the Echmen."

"Such as what?"

The south-eastern border of no Vei territory consists of a high ridge topped by a plateau, the home of the Suessonians. It's a godawful place to live. It's bleak, windswept, practically nothing grows there and you have to carry your drinking water a long way uphill along tracks too steep for donkeys even. But it's a magnificent natural defensive position, which is why the Suessonians went there.

Everybody hates the Suessonians, and with good reason. Originally they were followers of one Suesso, a lecturer at the Imperial College of Theology, who founded an extreme religious movement. He predicted that the end of the world was nigh, at which time the righteous would be transfigured in glory while the unrighteous fried; since the unrighteous were as good as dead already and dead men can't take it with them, why bother observing their property rights? Their neighbours hate them because when they arrived as refugees from Echmen justice and took possession of their impregnable plateau, where they felt they needed to live to be safe from the vindictiveness of the unrighteous, they quickly found they couldn't feed themselves by agriculture, so went back to robbery with violence instead. Mostly they steal food, but they're not averse to pretty shiny things of all sorts, and since they sincerely believe that the world is about to end and we'll all be dead this time next year anyhow, they're not afraid of anybody or anything, even Imperial lancers.

Because of how their nation came to be, the Suessonians

don't have a king. Instead they have a professor, the Chair of Applied Theology. When the current Chair heard from a party of no Vei returning home that a huge sum of money was practically passing his door – two days' ride for his lightning swift light cavalry – he decided that it would be wicked ingratitude to Providence to let it trundle past unmolested, even though it was being escorted by an Imperial army. Normal business practice for the Suessonians is to sneak up under cover of darkness, cut out what they want and run for it, and they've got it down to a fine art. Carthorses are far too slow to keep up with the Suessonians' hill ponies, so they take their own specially trained draught teams with them and couple them up to other people's carts, using a highly ingenious form of linkage that'll fit on practically anything with wheels. They reckon to be able to get the wagons hooked up and moving before the enemy's even awake; then they stampede his horses, shoot up his camp to sow a little confusion and head for home as fast as they can go. By the time the enemy's ready to follow they've usually got a handy head start, and they station ambushes and diversions along the escape route to slow them up further. You've got to admire people who do their job well, and, when it comes to stealing things, the Suessonians are the business.

Highway robbery was quite some way down on Alyattes' list of things to worry about. He was more concerned with the sequence of events in the carefully planned trap he'd designed for us. He'd arranged his order of march so that, when we broke through, we'd carry on right through the centre of his formation to get to the gold wagons, where we'd then be outflanked, enveloped and cut to ribbons. To achieve this, he'd positioned the wagons at the rear of his column, practically sticking out at the end, therefore highly vulnerable to a late-night smash and grab raid. If the security implications occurred to him, he dismissed them. Thanks to his highly efficient corps of scouts he knew exactly where we were: heading north-west to cut off his supply line. We had no cavalry to speak of, and were therefore in no position to conduct lightning raids.

Imagine his fury, therefore, when he was dragged out of bed to learn that unidentified hooligans had crept up in the night, murdered the sentries, stolen the tax money, driven off the horses and butchered a hundred or so lancers in their bunks before galloping away into the darkness. He'd signed for that money. If he lost it – not to the enemy, to *criminals* – he'd be recalled and executed long before he even came in sight of a Dejauzi. One damn thing after another, I imagine he thought, and why did he ever want to be a soldier in the first place?

He had to wait for dawn before he could pick up the trail, and of course the thieves had done everything they could to make life interesting for him: false trails, roads blocked with boulders and fallen trees, infuriating hit-and-run ambushes that wasted time and utterly demoralised the men. There was also the humiliation of chasing after a bunch of lowlifes when he ought to be saving the empire. At least he knew where we were, which was something. We'd have to wait until he'd caught and stamped on the thieves, and then he could take out his feelings on us, which would be a positive pleasure.

It was unfortunate for him that I'd learned from a wise and perceptive woman the merit of getting where you need to be ahead of the messenger. The further Alyattes galloped in pursuit of the thieves, the further his scouts had to go to report on our movements. Consequently, they never got a chance to tell him that we'd moved out and gone. They were still chasing after him when he found us for himself.

Or, rather, we found him. Under normal circumstances he'd never have allowed himself to get caught in that hoariest of poison chestnuts, the narrow canyon with steep, unscalable sides. When he scrambled to a dead stop because the road ahead was blocked with a landslide, he was still thinking about bandits and six million gold coins. It was only when our pikemen fell in at the other end of the canyon, and our archers appeared on the two facing skylines and started shooting his horses, that it dawned on him that he'd been had.

There was nothing he could do and, to his credit, he did it very well. Heaped ramparts of dead horses provided a modest level of cover from our archers, and he had the comfort of knowing that our pikemen, standing undisturbed in full armour for hour after hour, must be getting very hot, whereas it was shady and cool for his men cowering under the canyon walls. But our men had plenty of water and he didn't. As the noonday sun peeped down squarely onto his soldiers' helmeted heads, he decided that it was probably a good time to talk to the enemy, if any of the savages could speak Echmen.

"The battle of Merope," I said to him. "Good idea. It should have worked."

He looked at me. He was dripping with sweat, and his beautiful Imperial court hairdo was plastered to the top of his head in a melange of melted lacquer. I'd brought a leather bottle of water with me, and he kept looking at it out of the corner of his eye. "We surrender," he said.

"Not so fast," I replied. "We don't take prisoners."

I could practically hear the voice inside his head; *oh well*, it was saying, *this is it, then*. Followed by, *at least I won't have to go home and face all that*. I felt sorry for him. But I had a job to do.

"Not because we're bloodthirsty butchers and cannibals," I added, "but because we simply aren't set up for that sort of thing. Feeding and guarding all this lot. We don't have the resources. I've got enough on my plate looking after my own people without playing nursemaid to the enemy as well."

A little fly of hope started buzzing in his mind, too fast and erratic to swat. "Fine," he said. "Let us go."

"I'd like to, really," I said. "But if I let you keep your horses you'll come after us and fight us, and if I don't you'll run out of water and die. Unless, of course—"

(Those conditional clauses. A syntactical form that can change the world.)

"Unless, of course, you want to talk about politics. I've got the time, if you have." I held out the water bottle. He hesitated, grabbed it and guzzled. Water went all down his face and neck, but he didn't seem to mind.

"Politics," he said. "Fire away."

"I think," I said, "that if you go home, they'll kill you. Am I right?"

He nodded. "I've made a pretty thorough mess of things, so yes."

"That would be a pity," I said. "You haven't done anything wrong. A Merope-type trap was a great idea, it's just bad luck we happen to have read the same books."

He looked at me. "Who are you, anyway?"

"Me? I'm just the translator. But the queen doesn't speak Echmen, so you've got me instead. Don't change the subject. You were unlucky. I don't regard that as a capital crime, do you?"

"I should've known better," he said. "Anyway, what's that got to do with it?"

"Oh, nothing," I said. "It just seems to me, a system where a man like you should be forced into a position where he's fighting with one hand tied behind his back all the time can't really be much good, can it? The system sets you up so you fail, and then it blames you and off goes your head. That's just stupid, surely."

"I can't say I like it much," he replied. "But it's not up to me."

"Here's one scenario," I said. "We all sit here until your men shrivel up and die. Then I take my seventy thousand soldiers and start picking off big cities, until some other poor fool is sent to stop me and ends up where you are now. Sooner or later the empire will fall, and tens of thousands of good Echmen soldiers will be dead. Probably hundreds of thousands of civilians, if that matters to you. I have no real problem with that, but it strikes me as wasteful."

"Or?"

"Join us. No, don't be like that, I'm serious. We don't want to sweep through the empire killing and burning, we're not monsters. All we want is to put things right."

"Really."

"Yes, as it happens. You know what your emperor did to us? He rounded us up like sheep, marched us away from our homes and made us into slaves, building his fucking wall. Is that what you signed up to protect? Civilisation?"

He shrugged. "I don't make decisions like that," he said.

"No, you don't. If you did, maybe that sort of thing wouldn't happen. Maybe a lot of things would be different. Maybe you could even go home one day and see your children."

There's a convention, of course, that all fathers long to see their offspring and will go to any length to be near them. I don't think that would've cut much ice with my father. But you never know. It's a good argument when you're arguing with yourself, even if you don't actually mean it.

"What's all this leading to?" he said.

"It's very simple," I said. "We've come to make sure the empire never does anything like that to us ever again. We can do it by stamping on your heads till you're dead. That's fine, we can do that. It's well within our capability. Or we can adjust the empire so it works properly. No more forced labour, no more extortionate taxes, no more government by corrupt bureaucratic elites. Maybe even an empire that helps people once in a while."

"You must be out of your mind." He peered at me. "I read about you in the briefing," he said. "You're some kind of mad religious zealot."

I nodded. "People will insist on telling me who I am," I said. "It's very sweet of them to care, but I wish they'd get their facts straight. But don't let's talk about me. Let's talk about the empire. Do you believe that, under the current management, everything is for the best in the best of all possible worlds?"

He sighed. "This isn't getting us anywhere," he said.

"All right. In that case, let's talk about history. The history of the Echmen empire, from the earliest times to the present day. How long has the present dynasty been in power?"

"What?"

"You heard."

He shrugged. "A hundred and sixty years."

"That's right. Five emperors. Now, what did the first of those emperors do for a living before he got crowned?"

He looked at me for a while. "General Lydas," he said. "He commanded the Fifth army on the north-eastern frontier."

"He was a soldier," I said. "Just like you. Now there's a coincidence."

I had his attention. "What are you suggesting?"

"History tells us," I went on, "that when General Lydas made a real mess of a border skirmish with the Sashan and was informed that he'd been condemned to death *in absentia* for incompetence by the Imperial court, he rallied his troops and marched on the capital. Along the way he was joined by three of his fellow divisional commanders, who were sick to death of the cruel and arbitrary regime of the Twenty-Fifth Dynasty. It was a practically bloodless takeover, and apart from the emperor everybody lived happily ever after. Lydas got to go home. He got a better job. Not bad for a man living on borrowed time."

"You talk a lot, for an interpreter."

"You listen a lot, for a general. That's good. It means you might learn something."

It was very hot, and I'd taken back the water bottle. I offered it to him. He swallowed three gulps and handed it to me. "Let's see if I've got this right," he said. "You came all this way and went to all this trouble and killed thousands of Imperial lancers just to make me the emperor."

"Not my primary objective. An incidental benefit."

"You're full of shit."

"So people tell me. That doesn't mean I'm not serious. I can be trusted implicitly so long as our interests absolutely coincide. What about you?"

He looked at me again. "I need to think about it."

"Take all the time you need." I emptied the water bottle and put it down next to him. "We're not going anywhere." I stood up. "By this time," I said, "the Suessonians – that's the bandits who robbed you – will be miles away and the money will be in a safe place where you'll never be able to get it back. So, even if you come home in triumph with my head dangling from your saddlebow, you're for the chop. My way, though, you may yet live to smell the spring flowers. Think about it."

We took their weapons away, of course, and a third of their surviving horses, which we needed for eating. Their function was to march by our side, comrades in the glorious cause, rather than do any actual fighting; at least until they were so thoroughly compromised in the eyes of the empire that they'd have no choice but to join with us for real. As a wise man once said, when you have them by the balls, their hearts and minds will follow.

"You did what?" the kings said, but she was onto them before I had a chance to open my mouth. Why were we doing this? To make sure the Echmen never bothered us again. How? We had a choice: kill the lot of them, and she didn't know about them, but she wasn't going to be party to that, even if it was possible, which it wasn't. Or control them; and what better way of doing that than put our own puppet emperor on the throne, someone who'd do exactly as he was told. Or did we want to leave our lives behind, move to the Echmen city and live there till we died, spend all our time signing things and organising things and negotiating and arbitrating and sorting out all their endless stupid quarrels about money and making nice to diplomats and merchants and guilds and commercial attachés – and even if we did, we'd make a total fuck of it, since we have no idea about that shit, so we'd have to rely on Echmen advisers anyway, so why the hell not have a pretend emperor do it for us? Really it was no different from hiring a steward. And the alternative was to fight all five of the Echmen armies, one at a time or all together, and the hell with that, she personally had better things to do and who knows, we might lose. Whereas this way, if there had to be any more fighting, we could get the Echmen to do most of it for us, which would be perfect. Well?

"You said that like you meant it," I said.

"I did mean it."

Something in the way she said it bothered me. You have to listen carefully for nuances when you're a translator. People often say one thing and mean another. I don't know if you've noticed it, but it's true.

12

I was dreaming, I remember, about a certain incident in my past. I reached a familiar bit, then woke up and found it wasn't a dream.

That would explain, I thought, why the men in the dream were Dejauzi, not Robur. "On your feet," they said, and someone produced a knife and showed it to me, just close enough to my nose to be out of focus. "You're coming with us."

They were Maudit by the sound of it, though Dejauzi accents are notoriously hard to pin down, and I'd never dare try and do one. The Rosinholet flattened A, for example, is almost but not quite the same in Aram Chantat; you need a really good ear to distinguish between them. "What's wrong?" I asked. "What did I do?"

"Shut up."

Not likely. With my mouth shut, I'm nobody, I don't exist. "Is this the king's orders?"

"We haven't got a king any more."

Ah, I thought. "Let me put some clothes on, for crying out loud."

"No. Move."

They shoved me out of the tent into the bright sunshine. Served me right, I guess, for oversleeping. I could feel the knife pricking the small of my back. Here we go again, I thought. But it was fun while it lasted.

There was a crowd of Maudit standing around, closely packed so I couldn't see past them. They looked scared and angry, in that order. When they caught sight of me, some of them started yelling things, mostly self-evidently accurate references to my anatomy. People telling me things about myself. I ought to get YES, I KNOW tattooed on my forehead.

A man I vaguely recognised seemed to be in charge. He was sitting on a three-legged stool, formerly the property of the king. He scowled at me with a melodramatic thunder face, but I could see he was as frightened as I was. "So you're a prophet, are you?" he said.

"People keeping saying I am."

"Prove it. Prophesy something."

I took a deep breath. "I can do that," I said. "Question is, do you want to hang around here till it comes true? Only it's about your grandson."

At the back, someone laughed. I like the Maudit. They're easily amused.

"You're no prophet," the scared angry man said. "You're just some bloody chancer."

"Your king didn't think so."

"He's dead, isn't he? For listening to you. And her."

"You murdered your king."

"For selling us out to the Echmen, too bloody right we did."

"Are you going to kill me, too?"

He didn't answer. It was the question he didn't want to be

asked. "I'll take that as a yes," I said. "That's fine. I've been killed once, it doesn't hurt." I jerked my arms free and folded them in front of me. Something warm and wet was trickling down my leg. "Get on with it, then. I won't bite you." I paused, mostly because my throat was full of reflux. Then I added: "It's not me you need to be worried about."

Apparently I'd played right into his hands. "You mean," he said, "the Queen of Heaven."

There was a sort of sigh when he said it, as though he'd picked up a turd and bitten into it. I made a show of wincing. "You tell me," I said.

"I'll tell you something, you lying bastard," he said. "That wasn't the queen we saw that night. It was some blueskin whore called Hodda."

The truth, I've found, is like an annoying little dog that takes a fancy to you in the street and follows you home, barking. I can count on the fingers of one hand the number of times I've been glad to be confronted with the truth. "What makes you say that?"

He grinned so much I thought the corners of his mouth would split. "There's one of the Echmen soldiers who can talk Pirzoi," he said. "And so can one of our lads. The Echmen told him that your fucking Queen of Heaven is some blueskin tart who came to the city doing singing and dancing. Name of Hodda, he said. Well? What do you say to that?"

It's going to hurt, I told myself, but it'll be quick, with so many of them joining in. "And you believed him. An Echmen."

"He saw her, he said. In a singing and dancing place in the Echmen city."

"You killed your king on the word of an Echmen prisoner of war."

"Too right. And now we're going to do you as well."

"No, you're not," I said. "Let's do this properly." I turned to the man closest to me, who I'd never seen before. "In my tent," I said, "there's a stool next to the bunk. On the stool there's a wooden box. Fetch it."

He looked at the angry, scared man, who said, "What's that got to do with anything?"

"In that box," I said, "is the writing She gave me. I need it if we're going to do this properly."

Left to himself he'd have ignored me, but he wasn't by himself, not by a long chalk. "Fine," he said. "Get the liar his box. We're not fooled. He thinks we're stupid but we're not."

Someone brought the box. I touched it to my forehead and opened it, not looking inside. "Here's how we go about it," I said. "This scroll is my witness, before Her. I'm now going to stab myself. If I die, I was lying and you were right. If I don't, the Echmen soldier was lying, trying to make trouble. Does that sound fair to you?"

I'd made it sound so calm and reasonable that he couldn't refuse. "Go ahead," he said. "You'll save us the trouble."

I reached into the box, not drawing attention to my hands by not looking down, and felt for the trick theatre knife, which Hodda had palmed on me to get rid of it on the night of the big show. Bless her, I thought, I owe her so much. I found the knife, took it out, placed the point in the hollow of my throat, where the collarbones meet, and pushed it as far as it would go. It was an awkward moment for me – I don't know if I mentioned it, but I have this thing about knives getting close to me – but I kept my eyes fixed on the sad, angry man, even when I toppled over. I lay still, counted to ten, then got up again.

Perfectly still and quiet. My skin tingled where the tip of

the blade, slightly rounded, had almost broken through. The scared, angry man had jumped up off his stool. He was staring. He'd seen the knife go in, up to the hilt.

"It's a trick," he said. "There's something funny about that knife."

"I don't think so," I said. "Let's test it, shall we?"

Years ago, there was this accident at the theatre. I remember hearing about it. An actor was stabbed and nearly died. With those trick knives, if you jam your thumb against the base of the blade, you can stop it sliding up into the handle. Not enough to stab someone properly, but you can use the edge to cut something. I'd put a good edge on the blade, in my spare time. One of the books I'd read in the Imperial library was an anatomy textbook. There was a useful drawing showing all the main arteries.

At the last moment I remember thinking; I can't do this, me of all people. But it takes much less pressure than you think to cut human skin. The blood squirted out right into my face. I was blinded and staggered back. I wiped my eyes clear with the back of my wrist. Then I cleaned the blade quickly, got the knife back in the box out of sight and closed the lid. Everybody was looking at me.

"You murdered your king," I said loudly, "on the word of an enemy soldier. You said the Queen of Heaven is a blueskin whore. Anything that goes wrong from now on will be your fault. I thought you ought to know that." I looked down at the body. "We don't have to wait to see if the prophesy about his grandson comes true. The prophesy was, he won't have one. Now, if you wouldn't mind getting out of the way. You make me sick, the lot of you."

I went back to my tent, pulled the flap closed, fell onto the bunk and lay there shivering. That man's blood on my skin was like spiders walking up and down, but I couldn't make myself wash it off, even though there was water in a jug and a cloth right next to me. I felt like I was the one who'd been cut up, again. I really don't understand why people go on about how wonderful the truth is. In my experience, all it does is make trouble.

After some indeterminate period of time, I heard rustling at the tent flap, and someone bustling in. When someone's standing in the doorway it blocks out the light, so you can't see who it is. "Are you all right?" she said.

"Fine," I replied. "Where the hell were you?"

"The Maudit wouldn't let us through, and nobody wanted to pull a weapon on a Maudit. I had to get some of the Echmen."

"Bad move," I said. "You shouldn't have done that."

"Fuck you," she yelled. "They could've killed you."

"Give me a minute and I'll come out and deal with it. Is their king really dead?"

She nodded. "He refused to believe what they were saying about you, so they kicked him to death."

I closed my eyes. "That's a shame," I said.

"He really believed in you." She hesitated. "What happened?"

"Excuse me?"

"They're saying you did a miracle. What happened?"

I looked up at her. "I'm not entirely sure," I said.

"What do you mean, you're not sure? What fucking happened?"

She knew about Hodda, but I hadn't bothered to tell her the details, such as the trick knife. "I stabbed myself," I said. "Then I cut that man's throat."

"You stabbed yourself."

"That's where all this blood came from, presumably. I haven't looked to see."

"Stand up."

"Do I have to? I'm tired, I want to rest."

"Fucking stand up."

So I did that. "There's not a mark on you."

"Really?" I looked down at my neck. "You're right. Now there's a thing."

She was so angry I thought she'd burst. "Did you stab yourself or didn't you?"

"Oh, I stabbed myself all right. Ask anyone. But you're right, there doesn't seem to be a mark." I frowned. "That's crazy."

"Where's the knife?"

"What? Oh, that. I don't know, I must have dropped it out there. Why's there no mark? I don't understand."

"Show me the place."

I pointed. She looked closely.

"I don't understand," I repeated. "I thought, if I stab myself, at least it'll be quick, better than being kicked to death or watching my guts rolled out on a stick. Then I wasn't dead, so I thought I'd take the opportunity to get rid of that bloody nuisance, while I had the chance. Then I came in here. I didn't realise—" I sat down, with my best gormless look on my face. *Don't pull faces*, my mother used to say, *you'll stick like it*; then, *Too late, you've stuck*. And I'd rush to find a mirror, in case she was telling the truth. She never was, though. Did that make her a bad person?

"Did you really stab yourself?"

"Oh, for crying out loud."

"Did you?"

"*Yes.*"

She was staring at me, scared and angry. Strange. All I want is a quiet life, albeit on my terms. "It's true, then. You're a prophet."

"Oh, come on."

"What happened that night? I saw it. She stabbed you, but you didn't die."

I frowned. "I assumed it was sleight of hand."

"I saw the knife go in."

"Don't ask me," I said, "I wasn't looking. I assumed—" I stopped. "I honestly don't know," I said. "That woman was an actress. I *thought* she was an actress."

I stopped there and let her do the rest. She duly did it, I could see it happening in her face. "You told me," she said, "you told me you saw her once."

"Yes, on the stage, when I was a young subaltern."

"Not her, the queen. You said, in a dream."

"I saw someone," I replied. "In a dream. I see all sort of weird shit in dreams. So do you, I imagine. Doesn't mean you're a prophet, too."

"I saw it go in. I thought it was a trick."

"Pull yourself together," I said, "for pity's sake. I don't know if you've noticed, but we've got a crisis on our hands. Who's the new king of the Maudit?"

"What?"

"The Maudit," I said. "Who'll be the new king?"

She frowned, forcing herself to concentrate. "His son, I guess. But he's a kid. Five years old."

"That's no bloody good," I said. "We need somebody now. Close relatives?"

"He had a brother."

"Had?"

"You just killed him."

That was the king's brother. Oh boy. "So there's a five-year-old kid out there who's just lost his father and his uncle, both because of me, and we're supposed to do business with him. Wonderful." I scowled at her. "These lunatics are your people, you tell me. What are we going to do?"

"I don't know, do I?"

"Think."

So she did that. "We need a regent," she said.

"Great. Who?"

She shook her head. "The Maudit have to decide that for themselves," she said. "All the heads of families get together and they choose."

"See to it," I snapped. "In case you've forgotten, we're in the middle of a war. This is not a good time to be holding elections."

"It doesn't work like that. I'll see what I can do."

After she'd gone I felt bad, of course. I felt bad about deceiving her, manipulating her, killing the Maudit king's brother, getting the Maudit king killed because he believed in me; various other things, too, but not nearly everything I should've been feeling bad about, because there's only so many things you can hold in your mind at any one time. I felt bad, really I did. Bad enough to do anything about them? Maybe not. But I washed the dead man's blood off me, before the stink of it drove me crazy. That blood smell; very familiar. Made it seem just like old times.

As to whether it would be safe for me to leave the tent, or safe to stay in the tent, I really had no idea. I'd pulled what I'd have said was a blatant and pretty unconvincing stunt, but of course I know all about theatres and trick daggers. Therefore I believed that what I'd done was all a lie; and the Maudit had seen the same thing, and believed it was the truth. It occurred to me that maybe they knew something I didn't know, or at least could perceive something I wasn't capable of perceiving. Just because I think something I tell you is a lie doesn't mean it isn't actually true. What do I know, after all? I'm nobody.

I don't know how long I stayed in the tent. I was thinking about various things, so I guess I lost track of time. I was still thinking when the tent flap was pulled back and the light was blotted out again. It's a design fault with tents. Someone ought to do something about it.

It was General Alyattes. He'd brought his own stool to sit on. You can see why he was such a firebrand as a supply officer.

"What are you doing here?" I asked him.

"Some of your people have got one of my men," he said, in a sad, I-shouldn't-have-to-deal-with-this voice. "They've got a rope round his neck and they say they're going to hang him. There's some more of your people trying to stop them. You seem to be very popular right now. I was wondering if you'd come and sort it out."

"Let me rephrase that," I said. "What are *you* doing here?"

He smiled bleakly. "Apparently they think you're so holy they don't dare disturb you. So I elbowed my way past them and came in. They didn't stop me, and here I am."

I nodded. "You've got a translator."

"No," he said. "The man with the rope round his neck can talk some strange foreign language which one of your lot can understand, so everything's having to go through them. Hardly ideal. Unfortunately, nearly all our chaps who can talk Dejauzi were assigned to the labour camp, and when you broke out, you killed them. It makes communication rather difficult."

"Just as well I'm here." I stood up. "What do you want to learn Dejauzi for, they told me, you'll never find a use for it."

Something in his expression made me feel we'd never really be friends, but I'm used to that. "If you don't mind," he said.

"Sure. Lead on."

The Echmen soldier was terrified, reasonably enough. "What've you been telling people?" I asked him.

It wasn't his fault, he told me. He'd been sitting in a bar, just before he came on this expedition. He got talking to someone, who told him that someone had told him that the Dejauzi goddess who'd sparked everything off was really a Robur actress. They'd had a good laugh about it. How do you know? he'd asked. Because the actress is going round telling everybody. Apparently she didn't get paid and she's mad as hell about it. That was what he'd heard. Then, when he found there was a Dejauzi who could talk Pirzoi, he thought it'd be a laugh to tell him about it, just to see the look on his face when he realised he'd been made a fool of.

"I see," I said. "And now the Dejauzi want to hang you."

"They told me there's been a miracle or something. Look, I didn't mean any harm. I just wanted to put that guy in his place."

"Of course you did," I said. "All right, I'll see what I can do. Just for the record, though, it's not true. I don't know any Robur actresses."

He looked at me. "Straight up?"

"Cross my heart and hope to die in a cellar full of rats."

He grinned through his terror. Why would he lie to me, he was thinking, I'm not anybody. I turned away from him and held up my hands. "This man hasn't done anything wrong," I said loudly. "Let him go."

Someone called out something about blasphemy. I shook my head. "He repeated a lie somebody told him," I said. "He wasn't to know. Let him go. We all make mistakes. And if you lynch him, it'll only piss off the Echmen."

Nobody said anything. I lifted the noose from off the poor fool's shoulders, then gave him a shove. The crowd let him through. They did the same for me, which was a blessing.

"If I'd known being a prophet was going to be like this," I told her in Echmen, "I'd have been something else. A military genius, something like that. Much more of this and all my hair'll fall out."

"I wish you wouldn't say things like that. You think it's funny and smart, but it isn't."

You can't help but admire someone who can turn even a declaration of faith into a telling-off.

"We had a meeting," she told me later. "The kings and the Maudit heads of families."

"Good," I said, pulling my boots off. "Who did you choose?"

"You."

So help me, I really didn't see that one coming. "You did what?"

"As regent," she said, "till the prince comes of age, in nine years. It had to be someone everybody trusted and respected."

For crying out loud.

We caught a couple of Echmen scouts. I got hold of some pig bones and had them put in a big brass cooking pot. "See those?" I said.

They told me they could see them just fine.

"That," I said, "is you, unless you're absolutely straight with me. The Dejauzi aren't nice people. Do you understand?"

They understood. Among the interesting facts they were only too pleased to share with me was the news that General Alyattes and his army had formally been declared traitors and sentenced to death for treason and cowardice. I frowned. "That's no way to talk about your emperor," I said.

"Excuse me?"

By rights, I explained, Alyattes was the emperor. It was a little-known fact, covered up by the corrupt and treacherous regime, that Alyattes was the true son of the previous emperor's sister; furthermore, she and her brother were both poisoned by the present incumbent to clear his path to the throne. Alyattes was therefore the rightful emperor, and all we were doing was helping him take back what was his. They've probably been telling you, I went on, that this is a barbarian invasion. Nothing of the sort. This is justice in action. Please pass it on when you get back. I also gave them a letter to give to their commander, saying the same thing but peppered with a few uncheckable allegations masquerading as evidence. Time to get the ball rolling, I thought.

We followed the course of the Spring and Winter River, bypassing the large towns, which were undefended, and helping ourselves to the supply stores in the Imperial roadhouses, maintained for the benefit of the provincial army. Well, that was all right because the provincial army, what was left of it, was now part of us, so we were entitled.

At station 27 we were met by a small group of horsemen, unarmed and in civilian clothes. They'd been sent by General

Carcamela, who'd been ordered to seek us out and destroy us. Carcamela, they told us, didn't know the secretary of state who'd assigned him the mission, because there had been a major upheaval at the palace and all the old familiar faces had disappeared. But he did know Alyattes, who'd been his adjutant fifteen years ago, and he knew which of them he preferred to trust. Alyattes read them a prepared statement, all that stuff about being the old emperor's nephew, and added a personal message to Carcamela; rather nicely phrased, though I do say so myself. There was a lot about change we can believe in and draining the swamp and yes we can, and the messengers trotted away looking cheerful, having met someone they felt they could do business with.

Carcamela joined us four days later with twenty thousand lancers and a supply train. I let Alyattes' men have their weapons back. Half of them now believed that I was a prophet, and the other half were looking forward to looting the Imperial palace. Emperor-elect Alyattes appointed Carcamela commander-in-chief of the Imperial army in exile, and his first job after the fake emperor had been deposed was to be dealing with the Suessonians, with the proviso that his loyal troops would get to keep anything of value they found in the hilltop stronghold; six million in gold, for example, things like that.

By this point we were deep into Echmen territory. Supply wasn't a problem, thanks to Alyattes' splendid reorganisation of the Imperial commissariat. We also had full use of the Imperial intelligence network, since news of Carcamela's defection, though common knowledge on the ground, hadn't yet filtered through official channels; which is to say, the joint chiefs in the capital knew about it just fine, but the orders rescinding his commission were still percolating through to divisional level.

Until that happened, district intelligence officers still reported to him, and they did, volubly. From them we learned that the northern governor and the Imperial guard were still loyal to the old emperor, and the other three governors were sitting on the fence, waiting to see what would happen.

"Saloninus," I told her, "says that there are basically two kinds of invasion. There's conquests, where you get hordes of savages streaming across a frozen river, cities burned to the ground, every living thing slaughtered right down to chickens, the end of civilisation as we know it, followed by a dark age, followed by something very much like what you had before. The other kind is called a takeover. That's where you clear out the people at the top and take their place and everything else goes on as normal. Takeovers are better because you inherit all the nice things your predecessors had, which is why you wanted to rob them in the first place. Otherwise it's like breaking into a rich man's house, smashing everything up and torching it, then walking away empty-handed. I think this ought to be a takeover, don't you?"

She gazed at me. "You're really into all this, aren't you?" she said. "Right now you're telling yourself, this is what I was born for."

"Maybe I was."

"There you go," she said. "Actually, I have a horrible feeling you were. It'd explain a lot. Like, why everything's been set up perfectly for you, waiting for you like a pile of neatly folded clothes."

I thought about that. It worried me. "I don't follow," I said.

"Yes you do." She poured herself a drink. The Hus drink wine, beer, mead and something really disgusting made from fermented quinces, which they distil through copper pipes in the bright sunlight. She'd been doing a lot it lately. "It's like all of history has been leading up to you, making sure everything's ready for when you turn up." She nibbled her drink and pulled a face; definitely the quince liqueur. "You're going to argue, so let me lay it out for you. Once upon a time there were three empires."

"Four," I said. "You're forgetting Blemya."

"Fuck fucking Blemya. Three empires; and they bash into each other over and over again, until they're like three rocks hanging on a clifftop, and one little shove will set them toppling. Even a little kid could set them rolling. Even you."

"I had nothing to do with what happened to the Robur."

"Never said you did. That was the rock that pushed *you*. But the point is, everything's perfect. Everything's just right. It's like the Echmen went out of their way to engineer their stupid empire so it could be collapsed by pulling one simple lever. Now you can quote Saloninus and tell me how it got that way because of the course of history and loads of problems they never got around to fixing until they'd gone too far to fix, but that's not the point. And I'll bet you anything you like that when you've finished with the Echmen and you start beating up on the Sashan, it'll all fall beautifully into place like – what's that stuff they had in the palace with little spiky wheels that made things go round?"

"Clockwork."

"Clockwork." She nodded. "There you go."

"I don't think so," I said. "I think things got that way because that's what things do. I think I saw what nobody else had seen, because nobody else was looking."

"Bullshit." She swallowed her drink, had a coughing fit and poured another. "I don't think that's how it is at all."

"Tell me," I said, "how you think it is."

"I will." She paused for a moment and took a sip of disgusting quince liqueur. This time she didn't pull a face. "That wheels-going-round thing."

"A clock." I nodded. "Invented a hundred and seventy years ago in Scona by Prosper of Schanz. The example in the Imperial palace is one of only seven complete units completed by Prosper before his death. What about it?"

"Suppose," she said, "a Dejauzi's walking along the riverbank, and he finds a what you said, a clock. He looks at it and realises that the steel finger goes round in a circle precisely twenty-four times every day. What's he supposed to think? Maybe he thinks that what he's found is a stone that's been in the river for hundreds and hundreds of years, and the water's bashed the stone against other stones and chipped bits off and eaten away the soft parts, and by sheer coincidence the result just happens to behave in that funny way. Or maybe he thinks, somebody made this so he could tell the time."

"I think," I said, "that you've got a wonderful imagination."

"You did see her, didn't you? That time when you thought you were bleeding to death and you were going to die."

"No," I said. "I made that up."

She shook her head. "You think," she said, "that just because you don't believe in her, she doesn't exist. Well, fuck you. I don't know if this needle believes in me or not, but if I want to sew something, I use it. I couldn't give a shit whether the needle has faith."

She was really starting to get to me. "Pull yourself together," I said. "You know perfectly well that what you saw was a Robur actress called Hodda with no clothes on."

"Do I?" She grinned at me, like I'd just made a stupid chess move. "Explain to me, I'm just an ignorant savage. What's an actress?"

"You know perfectly well—"

"Explain to me."

"Fine. An actress is a woman who plays a part in a theatre."

"I don't know what that means. Explain some more."

"All right. A man writes a play. He writes out what all the actors are going to say. They learn it by heart. Then they stand up in front of an audience and pretend to be the people in the play."

"That's what I thought," she said. "So, when your Hodda goes out in front of the people watching, she's not Hodda any more. She's someone else."

My head was starting to hurt. "She's pretending."

"Really." She glared at me. "You go to one of these plays and you see a woman stand up and say and do things. Has she got a name?"

"Yes."

"And the other people in the play. They can see her?"

"Well, yes."

"And hear her?"

"Yes, unless she's mumbling."

"And you can see and hear her?"

"Yes."

"So there's a woman standing there, and you can see and hear her and she's got a name and she talks and does things. So she's real. Not pretend."

It was like trying to argue with a small child. "Hodda is not the Queen of Heaven."

"Maybe not. But maybe the Queen of Heaven was Hodda. For a little while."

"That's stupid," I said. "So where was the real Hodda all this time, while the queen was using her arms and legs?"

"Where's the real Hodda when she's being someone in a play?"

"You've got that back to front," I said, then realised she hadn't. "Look, it's not like that. It was all a trick."

"But when you got stabbed, that wasn't a trick. I saw the knife go in. Right up to the hilt."

I came this close to telling her, but then I thought; no, better not. "I can't explain that," I said.

"Of course you can't. But I was there. I saw it. And I think I saw the Queen of Heaven. Not some blueskin tart in shiny paint."

I drew a long breath so I could point out to her all the fallacies in her argument, but then I thought; why? Out of an overwhelming duty to the truth? Fuck, as I may have observed before, the truth. If it was here, would it go out of its way to defend me? Unlikely. The truth is utterly selfish and doesn't give a damn about anyone else. Serving the truth is like serving the empire. Nobody thanks you for it and you die poor.

Besides, what is the truth, anyway? In a court of law, it's the testimony of credible witnesses corroborating each other. She'd been a witness and she knew what she saw. So was I, but even my mother wouldn't say I was credible. And there'd been hundreds of people there, all rock-solid upright pillars of Dejauzi society. And when I stabbed myself, there were loads of people watching, and they saw what happened with their own eyes. And, come to that, Alyattes was now the nephew of the old emperor and the rightful heir to the throne. He hadn't been until quite recently, but pretty soon anyone who could testify against his claim would be dead or singing a very different tune, and what was once a lie would become the truth, official, carved on the lintels of triumphal arches; and if you can't believe what you read on a government arch, what can you believe? All the books would tell it that way, and in a thousand years' time it *will* be the truth, just as what was once the bottom of the sea is now a mountaintop. Ask the wise men at the university what truth is and they'll tell you it's the consensus of informed and qualified scholars, based on the best evidence available. Availability is governed by what gets burned in the meanwhile, but I see no real problem with that. All living things change or else they die, and why should the truth be any different?

13

We swung south until we reached the Great East Road, then headed west towards the capital. I put the Echmen at the front of the column, then us, then the food carts; not that I doubted Alyattes' commitment to the cause, but you can't be too careful.

We were marching across the wide, flat plains between the Red and Summer rivers. They call it the garden of the empire. The soil is deep and rich, and there's the most amazing system of irrigation channels, built up over the course of a thousand years of intelligent planned investment. Two-thirds of the grain grown in the empire comes from there, not to mention all the luxury stuff to supply the capital. There's thousands of acres of orchards if you happen to like fruit; over a thousand acres just growing asparagus, for crying out loud. We rode through a gently sloping combe and everything on either side of the road as far as the eye could see was an ocean of beans in flower. The king of the Rosinholet was riding next to me. "That's amazing," he said. "Just look at that."

"A bit different from home, then," I said.

"No kidding."

I waited for a moment or so, then I said, "You could live here."

He looked at me. "You what?"

"You could bring your people and live here," I said. "It'd be much nicer than where you live now."

He didn't say anything and I let well alone. Once you've planted an idea, you don't want to kill it by overwatering.

That night, he and the king of the Cure Hardy came looking for me. "What you said earlier," he said.

My mouth was full of coarse barley bread. "Mphm."

"We've been thinking about that."

I swallowed. "It's worth thinking about," I said. "It's generally accepted, this is the best farmland in the world. I think you deserve it. What do you think?"

"Depends," said the Cure Hardy, "on who we've got to fight to get it."

"Nobody," I said. They made rude noises. "No," I said, "straight up. All this beautiful land. Who do you think it belongs to?"

The kings looked at each other. "The people who live here?"

"You really think that? How sweet. No, it belongs to the Imperial nobility, all of it, from here to the mountains. Once upon a time it belonged to some people called the Cleroe, but then the Echmen came along and that was the end of them. The idea was that the Cleroe's land would be divided up among the poor and needy Echmen who didn't have any land of their own, but somehow or other it all ended up being owned by twelve very rich families, and that was two thousand years ago, and nothing much has changed since. It used to be parcelled out to tenants, but the Echmen nobles realised they could make bigger profits if they got rid of the tenants and brought in slave labour. So if I hadn't come along and made all this trouble, I expect you and your people would've ended up living here after all. But I don't think you'd have liked it very much."

The Cure Hardy stared at me. "All that belongs to twelve men?"

"Basically, yes," I said. "The twelve most powerful men in the empire. And if Alyattes has the sense he was born with, the moment he gets his bum on the throne he'll have them rounded up and chopped, because if he doesn't they'll chop him. So," I added, after a very brief pause, "you might want a word with Alyattes, at some point. Remind him who his true friends are. I expect he'd far rather have friends than enemies living on his doorstep controlling the food supply to the capital; you know, people he could count on in a crisis. I know I would, in his shoes."

Which set me thinking. Of course I knew all about the vast slave plantations of the Two Rivers plain. I'd known about them long before I sat down in the library to think, and using them to pay off the Dejauzi had been a fundamental part of the plan from the very beginning. It was a part I was proud of. The resettled Dejauzi would be simultaneously a sword in my puppet emperor's hand and a knife at his throat, making him secure and keeping him scrupulously honest. And, of course, I'd free the slaves and give them jobs working for the Dejauzi settlers, and that'd be another hundred thousand people who love me and my pet emperor, which couldn't be bad, could it? Smart, or what?

Indeed. Well, there's a scene in one of Saloninus' plays where the great hero, who's just killed the dragon and won its golden hoard, bumps into the god who designed his destiny. How did you kill the dragon, asks the god. With my amazingly wonderful sword, says the hero, who has no idea who he's talking to. Where did you get such a very fine sword? I made it myself, boasts the hero, out of useless splinters of a broken sword I found under a bench. The god smiles. And who made those useless splinters? he asks. The hero doesn't see the point of the question, not knowing that the god had put them there for him to find. Like it matters, he says. All I know is, they were no good for anything till I came along.

Absolutely right. But I had to ask myself, now that she'd set the idea buzzing around in my head. Who made the useless splinters? And who put them where even a clown like me couldn't help but find them?

The loyalists, led by the depressingly competent General Samodattes, had decided to make their stand at the 37th milestone. There's a bridge there, the only place you can cross the Red River without going fifty miles out of your way and leaving yourself vulnerable in flank and rear. It was designed to stop anyone doing what we were trying to do. Time to think of something clever.

"Well," Alyattes said to me, "let's hear it."

"Excuse me?"

"You must have some brilliant stratagem gleaned from the pages of history for doing this," he said, as we stared from the closest high ground at the monstrous brown bulk of the river. The Red swells and floods two weeks after the start of the monsoon season in the mountains, nine hundred miles away. For six weeks after that, nothing can cross. Swimmers would be swept away, boats smashed into kindling. It's too wide to shoot an arrow across, so you can't get ropes over to build a cable bridge. The only way to get from one side to the other is the military bridge, a brutal, colossal thing made out of concrete. Six men can march abreast across it, or two carts, or three horses. Its span is over four hundred yards, and every fifty yards there's a pair of guard towers, with arrow slits, a portcullis and a tilting section of roadway that functions like a drawbridge. Fighting your way over it isn't really an option, as various fools have found out over the centuries.

"Sorry," I said. "No idea."

"We assumed you must have."

"Me? I'm just the interpreter."

So I found her in her tent. There was a jar of the horrible quince liqueur in front of her, the resin seal unbroken. "What do you want?" she said.

"You told me," I said, "about how the Hus hide things."

"Did I? Oh, right, yes. What about it?"

"You split a river in half, you said."

She reached for the jar but didn't quite get there. "So what?"

"How would a person go about doing that exactly?"

The Red River is called that because it runs past a large deposit of iron ore. Past, please note, rather than through; the veins of ore run through the base and middle of a mountain, through which the river cut a gorge long, long ago. Most of the year the river flows well below the level of the veins, but when the monsoons start in the Table Mountains and the river is in spate, its level rises dramatically as it's forced through the gorge, and it washes red ore out of the cliff, turning the water a sort of reddish brown. When it's that colour it's poisonous. Anything that drinks from it dies, and the vegetation along its banks shrivels away. There are no trees beside the Red River, apart from a few spindly willows that just about manage to shake off the toxic effect of last year's floods before being poisoned all over again.

The Echmen, however, are smart. They draw a huge amount of water from the river to irrigate their slave plantations, so they've built a series of wonderfully ingenious filters at the mouths of their irrigation channels, which not only clean the water but trap the iron, which can be dug out and smelted. From this iron they made the legendary Echmen watered steel, out of which incredibly skilful smiths make marvellous unbreakable swords for the nobility, who are too fat to use them.

We chose a spot about twelve miles upstream of the 37th milestone. I hadn't had an opportunity to study detailed maps of this area, but we got lucky. One of General Carcamela's adjutants was distantly related to the nobleman who owned the estate, and his father had been the steward there. I told him what I was looking for, and he grinned and said, no problem.

What I needed was a large pit, or at least a dip; somewhere that was lower than the level of the river, not too far away from it. Carcamela's adjutant took us to a disused gravel working. For a hundred years, thousands of slaves had dug out a crater, about half a mile in diameter, until the gravel gave out and they moved on somewhere else. You need gravel to make concrete, apparently, and the Echmen dearly love concrete.

At the closest point of its circumference the pit was about six hundred yards from the river. Well. It could've been worse, I guess.

Next thing on my list was free all the slaves. When I told him what I was going to do, General Alyattes let off a yowl they must have heard in the palace, but I explained and he shut up, though he wasn't happy. I sent messengers out with a proclamation. Every slave on the plantations would henceforth be free, men, women and children. There was a little job we wanted them to do for us first, but they wouldn't mind that.

The job was to dig a sap, under the supervision and direction of a battalion of the Echmen Imperial engineers, which Carcamela happened to have by him in case he needed to lay siege to any cities. It was a long, wide sap and it had to be done very quickly, but one thing we had was manpower. With sixty thousand pairs of hands, you can shift a lot of dirt in no time flat, especially if the workers have an incentive. Tools and carts, liberated from the plantations, weren't a problem, and the engineers really knew their stuff, as engineers tend to do.

The idea was simple enough: to dig a sap, about fifty feet down, connecting the gravel pit to the middle of the riverbed. We felled a hundred acres of mature pear and plum orchards for pit props, and it cheered my heart to see the slaves who'd spent their lives nurturing and tending those trees getting their own back on them with axes. The branches and brash we dragged down the sap to fill the chamber we dug directly under the riverbed. Then all we needed was oil (about two hundred gallons, premium-grade extra virgin, no problem) to drench the firewood with. Light a fire, then run very fast back down the tunnel. The fire burns through the props holding up the roof of the chamber. The roof collapses, and the river goes crashing down a hole in the floor, along the sap and out into the gravel pit. Simple as that.

We had to be quick. It wouldn't take long for the floodwater to wash away the pit props in the sap, at which point the whole thing would cave in and fill up with dirt, and the river would resume its usual course. I figured we had an hour. Actually, the engineers had done better work than I'd given them credit for. The props held for an hour and a half, which was just as well. If we'd only had the hour I'd bargained on, half the Dejauzi would've been swept away and drowned. But they weren't, so that was all right.

What we did, by the way, bears no relation to the way the Dejauzi split rivers to hide things. Their method involves wading halfway and driving in piles, and I stopped listening at that point because it wasn't going to be any use. No, I got the idea from a book I read about building ornamental fountains, using hydraulic pressure to move water uphill. We didn't have to do too much of that, in the event, thanks to the fortuitous gravel pit. Otherwise we could have ended up with a waterspout two hundred feet high, which would've been a sight to see and I'm sorry I missed it. But the gravel pit was better, so the hell with it.

Anyway, that was the river crossed. I reflected as we rode away that the lake we'd accidentally built would probably be there for ever, long after Alyattes' puppet dynasty had been swept away like the pit props, and I'd found an excuse for freeing a hundred thousand slaves, whose lives would never be the same again, simply in order to move a body of men four hundred yards from A to B. Unintended and partly intended consequences, which often end up being far more important than the silly little thing you were actually trying to do. As for what I did, I don't know what will become of it. I imagine that in the story, if it survives and grows, what happened was that I called on the Queen of Heaven and stretched forth my hand over the waters, which parted miraculously to let us cross, then resumed their course just in time to drown the entire enemy army as it rushed after us in hot pursuit. For all I know, by the time you read this, that version may well have evolved into the truth; in which case, don't believe a word of what you've just read. It's all lies. I made it up, just to be annoying.

When he woke up to find us behind him and Carcamela (who I'd left behind) in front of him, General Samodattes, commanding the loyalists, gave up. It wasn't just that he was surrounded and outnumbered three to one. He was an Imperial general, and fighting your way out of fixes like that is all in a day's work for men of that calibre. It was the fact that I'd somehow miraculously spirited two-thirds of my army across an uncrossable river that broke him. When I told him later how I'd done it he just looked at me, and I think he thought I was lying. Anyway, faced with a choice between starving to death on a bridge and joining us, he made the sensible decision. It helped that I promised him the governorship of the northern province, but I think he'd have signed on anyhow. He had the stunned look of someone who's just had a silk scarf pulled out of his ear by a skilful conjuror, and I think he'd made up his mind that I was going to win.

Next on my list: march on the capital. So we did that.

Alyattes wanted me to send him on ahead with a thousand fast horsemen, but I told him to calm down and tie a knot in it. He was afraid the emperor might escape. I reminded him that I'd spent much more time in the palace than he had over the past six years, so I had a better idea of how things worked there. More to the point, I wanted Alyattes where I could see him, though I didn't tell him that, in so many words.

In the event, my way of doing it worked out quite well. When the news reached the palace that Samodattes had surrendered and joined the rebels, the department heads of the Imperial civil service went to the emperor's private apartment and locked him in. If there was anything he wanted, they told him, just let them know. The emperor thought about it for a while, then asked for a gallon jar of the '76 spring wine and an ounce of a certain sort of rather special powder, reserved since time immemorial for the emperor's exclusive use. It kills you stone dead, but first you get to enjoy the most amazingly wonderful hallucinations, and when they find you, there's a grin on your face like a summer sunrise.

While the emperor was away with the fairies, the heads of department got down to the job of sorting through the Imperial archives. A lot of documents got burned – you could see the plume of smoke rising from the North tower right across the city, apparently – and a whole lot of other documents that should have been written but were somehow never got round to miraculously appeared, so that by the time we got there, Alyattes' claim to the throne was meticulously and unimpeachably documented and laid out ready for inspection, alongside the late emperor's full confession, sealed with the Twin Dragon seal and therefore definitively authentic.

I'm glad we didn't rush things, because it gave the people of the city a chance to get ready. It takes more time than you think to source a million flowers and weave them into garlands, organise street parties on every block, hang up a thousand miles of bunting, form choirs of smiling children and teach them the words of the Hail-the-Liberators song you've just written. There was a slightly anxious edge to all this jubilation, almost as if the city people were worried we might cut loose at any moment and start spit-roasting children in the street; but in the event everyone behaved themselves and it all went very well. It probably helped that Alyattes had promised a thank-you present of five years' pay to every soldier in the army in lieu of looting rights, and that the Dejauzi were too stunned by the sight of all those tall buildings crammed in next to each other to think about anything much. I think they were probably more scared than the city people, though I don't suppose there was much in it.

Once we'd got there, though, I was keen to press on with the coronation and get it out of the way, since I had the feeling that things were about to start happening, and I didn't want to get bogged down. I insisted that the queen of the Hus should be the one to place the Imperial crown on Alyattes' head, and that he should be handed the rest of the Imperial regalia by the other Dejauzi kings (except me; I can't stand fuss). Otherwise I was happy to leave everything to the priests and the men from the Ministry of Ceremonies, provided they kept it reasonably short.

One thing I wasn't expecting was to find the streets of the capital thronged with crowds of fanatical disciples of a new religion, which turned out to be the one I'd made up. But there they were, dressed in brown wool habits with rope belts (where they got that from I have no idea), reciting great chunks of my mix-and-match scripture in loud voices, apparently from memory. It was, people assured me, going to be the next big thing. There was already a temple, with six more under construction, and a clergy with a fledgling hierarchy and millions of tremisses promised as donations by the faithful, and if I'd care to drop by and say a few words, that would be the most wonderful thing that ever happened in the history of the world.

I had to find out about that, so I hired a couple of Alyattes' sergeants to make discreet enquiries. It turned out that Hodda had been going round telling anyone who'd listen about what I'd done to her and how I'd ripped her off, and as usual, the public had fought tooth and nail for the wrong end of the stick. The truth, it turned out, was that Hodda had witnessed a miracle out there in the desert, and had been spreading malicious lies about it because she was a bad person. Once she figured out that there was a chance of making money from this, she changed her tune. Yes, she confessed, she'd lied about her part in what had happened, because of a long-standing grievance going back many years. The miracle had been a real miracle, and she'd said what she'd said because bad men had paid her to do so, threatening to harm her if she refused. But it so happened that she'd memorised the holy scripture I'd read out on that occasion, recognising it to be the word of God, and had had the presence of mind to write it all down while it was still fresh in her mind, and copies could be had at a reasonable price. What she'd got hold of was my rough draft, which I suppose Oio must've found when I did my flit. There were a few clerical errors here and there, probably due to my lousy handwriting, but on the whole it was pretty accurate.

I caught up with her at one of the nearly finished temples, where she'd just been appointed archbishop of Echmen. "I'm not talking to you," she said.

"Oh, come on," I said. "You're making more money than you've ever dreamed of."

"You underestimate my dreaming capacity," she said. "And no thanks to you if I am. You abandoned me in the desert to *die*."

"Be that as it may," I said. "You can't stay here, it's too risky."

"Balls to that," she said. "This is a good thing, and it's all my own work. Fuck off and conquer something and leave me alone."

"Sorry," I said. "But there's no need to get upset about it. What you want to do is build a monastery in the desert."

"Fuck you," she said with spirit. "I hate the desert. It's hot. There's scorpions."

"I said build it, you don't have to live there. I suggest you have a nice villa somewhere. Just not in the city where anyone can see you."

"Arsehole," she said. "Just think of the favour I've done you. You're practically God because of me."

"Nobody asked you to," I said, but she did have a point. "Tell you what," I said. "I appoint you my apostle to the gentiles. Go out and spread the good news. Somewhere else."

She thought about it. "Apostle to the gentiles in places where they have clean bedlinen and decent plumbing."

"Of course. They need saving, too. And it's only right that the mother church should fund your mission. Say sixty per cent of the net."

"The gross."

I shrugged. "Not my money. If you can swing it, why the hell not? Give it six months, you'll be able to afford to build your own city."

She frowned. "Actually," she said, "that's not a bad idea. The City of God. Preferably somewhere cool, not too far from the beach." She smiled. She has a nice smile. "You're still an arsehole."

"I never said I wasn't. Go in peace."

I turned to leave, then thought of something. "You wouldn't

happen to know where I can find Oio?" I asked. "I've had people looking for him, but he's hard to find."

"He's dead," she said. "Didn't you know?"

Oio was dead. He'd tried to keep his head down when he got back, but somebody recognised him and he was arrested, charged with assisting a fugitive and strung up on a gibbet. The best friend I ever had, and he died because of me; no greater love, as I think I said somewhere in my hastily cobbled together book. Still, it doesn't do to dwell on things like that.

So far, so good. But, as I told them all, the one thing we couldn't afford to do was stand still.

The emperor was dead and the civil service had accepted Alyattes without a murmur, and the three fence-sitting governors had sworn to back us to the death the moment they heard we'd won, but the old Imperial nobility was still out there and they hated us like poison. Taking away their slave plantations had weakened them, but they still controlled most of the factories and large workshops and owned most of the ships, and dispossessing them entirely would be a step too far for a fundamentally conservative nation like the Echmen. Two-thirds of the officer class in the army were poor relations who owed their commissions to some mighty distant cousin. Their first loyalty was to their careers, but you can't expect an Echmen to forget who he's related to; it'd be like casting a man adrift in an open boat on a vast and empty ocean. There's only so much that can be done with poison and unfortunate accidents, so we had to find a way to get the nobility on board, or better still bypass them. The way to do this, I told Alyattes and his new council of ministers, was war. Same as it always has been.

The new council was unlike any gathering of ministers the empire had ever seen. There were the kings and queen of the Dejauzi, General Carcamela, the department heads of the civil service and the official interpreter, namely me. "War against who, for crying out loud?" she asked in Echmen, before Alyattes could open his mouth. "We won, didn't we?"

"That's like saying you don't need dinner because you had breakfast," I said. "Also, war with the Sashan is unavoidable. There's always a war with the Sashan every time there's a change of dynasty. Ask him," I said, pointing at Alyattes, rather rudely. "He'll tell you if you don't believe me."

"It's true," Alyattes said. "They'll assume we're weak, and that we lost far more men than we're letting on. They'll think that if we could be conquered by a bunch of savages, no offence intended," (smirk), "our army must be in a hell of a state and we're ripe for the picking."

"They must have spies," said one of the bureaucrats, and I started translating for the Dejauzi. "Surely they know what state our army's in as well as we do."

Carcamela laughed. "Yes, but their reports won't reach the top brass, because the top brass won't want to see them. The last thing you want going the rounds when you're planning a big offensive is anything negative. It puts people off."

"You're saying they're coming whether we like it or not, so let's give 'em hell," she said in Dejauzi. "Where have I heard that before?"

"Does it have to be a big war?" asked the king of the Aram Chantat. "Can't you just make a show of strength along the border till they go away?"

"We could stay on the defensive," Carcamela said, once I'd given him the gist. "We'd probably lose a few forts and a bit of territory, mostly the places we took off them in the last war. They'd probably be satisfied with that. But what sort of message is that going to send about the new regime? We're telling everybody we're strong. We've even got God on our side," he added, glancing at me, "apparently. No, we need to give them a smacking they won't forget in a hurry. Otherwise, our rich and powerful friends will have all the ammunition they need to make our lives miserable."

"Get rid of them," said the Luzir Soleth.

"Can't," Carcamela replied. "They're still too strong. There'd be a civil war, a real one this time. My officers would line up according to family allegiance, which means most of them would be against us. And before you suggest it, I can't just slaughter the entire officer corps. Even if I got away with it, the army simply wouldn't work without them."

I translated; then I said: "He's right. We need a big war, which'll give us a chance to tax the bastards into the ground, to pay for it all. When they can't or won't pay their taxes, we take over their assets. That way we get hold of manufacturing, transport, shipping and trade. The nobility's big thing is how patriotic they've always been, generations of selfless service to the state. Fine. If they pay their taxes, we bleed them white and they're no longer a problem. If they don't pay, they're selfish hypocrites stabbing our brave fighting men in the back, and then we take over all their operations. Either way they're gone and we can call our lives our own." Then I took a deep breath and said it all again in Echmen. I'd have thoroughly earned my translator's fee, if I'd been getting paid.

"Hell of a reason to have a war," said the Rosinholet, "to defeat your own people."

"Maybe not the main reason," I said, "but a useful extra benefit. The main reason is not getting overrun by the Sashan."

Alyattes could see the look on the Rosinholet's face. "What's he saying?"

"Just a minute and I'll tell you. She's right," I went on in Dejauzi, pointing at her. "The war's coming whether we like it or not. That's the main thing. It's a bitch, but there it is. Anything else is just making the best of a bad situation. But if we can do that, why the hell not?"

Afterwards the Rosinholet and the Luzir Soleth hung around rather than rushing off as they usually did. "We need to talk to you," the Rosinholet said.

I looked at her. "Let me guess," I said. "Something's bothering you."

"Too bloody right," the Luzir said.

"They don't want to be in this war," she said. "They don't see why they should have to."

I sat down on the edge of the table. It was beautiful thing. It was made from a special sort of wood, a sort of honey colour with a complicated black figure. Someone told me the trees only grew on one island in the middle of the sea, miles off the south coast of Echmen. When the prince of the island sent him the table as a gift, the emperor liked it so much he had all the other trees on the island cut down and burned, so that this table would be unique. Looking at it, it occurred to me that if I played my cards right, at this particular juncture of my life, I'd be able to do things like that. A very strange thought indeed.

"They're quite right," I said. "Why should they?"

Not the answer the kings had been expecting. She looked at me sort of sideways, like she had a bet on with herself about what I'd say next.

"So far," I went on, "things have worked out pretty well. Better than they should have, to be honest with you. We've really only fought one battle, and we got out of it quite lightly. And because of the time of year and being able to help ourselves to Imperial supplies, we've not had as many people dying of hardship and disease along the march as we should've done, though even one is too many, if you ask me. So now you're saying, let's not push our luck. Well, fair enough. I agree."

She made that tooth-sucking noise, but the kings took no notice. "Seriously?" said the Luzir.

"Absolutely," I said. "I think the Dejauzi people have done their bit and now it's time they enjoyed their reward. If I were you, I'd start getting your people moved out here to the plains, those of them who want to go. It's your promised land," I added. "Get on and take possession, before some bastard tries to stop you."

The Rosinholet gazed at me. "What about this big war?"

"Let the Echmen fight it," I said. "There's more than enough of them, and we're all on the same side now, all good friends. They're the ones who need this war so they can sort themselves out. It's nothing to do with us. If they want to go around killing and getting killed, let them. We've got better things to do, like farming."

"Just a minute," the Luzir said. "You talked them into this war. I was there. I saw you do it."

"Sure," I said. "Because they need it. Something weird just happened to them. They got taken over by a bunch of savages, but then it all turned out all right. They need to reassure themselves they're still God's own people, and the way they do that is by kicking the shit out of somebody else. It'll do them good," I added, as the Luzir frowned desperately at me, "and it means we can get rid of the old nobility once and for all, so we won't have them making a nuisance of themselves trying to get their land back."

"But don't you need us? I mean, don't they need us? To beat these Sashan?"

I looked at him. "It'd be much easier for them to win the war if they had you with them," I said. "I think the pikes and archers combination would really mess up the Sashan lancers. But that's beside the point. You can make it easy for them to win the war, yes. So what? Just because you can do something doesn't mean you should. Not if it involves putting our people in harm's way with no benefit to us. No, screw them."

The Rosinholet was looking worried. "You're going to teach the Echmen to fight on foot with pikes and bows," he said.

"Not likely. That'd be giving away our advantage. The whole point of war," I told him, "is to get what you want. It's not about killing the maximum number of people. That's a bad way of going about it. That just shows you're incompetent, or lazy. We could've slaughtered the Echmen like we did in the first battle, sure we could, but that would have made taking over their empire much, much harder. So naturally I'm not going to give the Echmen the secret of our success just so they can kill a shitload of Sashan lancers. If we turned them into infantry they'd be better soldiers, but think of the mess it would make of their whole society. The Echmen have their way of doing things and seeing the world, and it's nothing at all like ours. You'd be taking power away from the horse-owner class and giving it to the common man. I can't think of anything that would do more damage, except maybe plague."

The kings looked at each other, then at her, then at me.

When there wasn't anybody left to look at, the Rosinholet said, "That's fine, then. We're happy with that."

"Except," she put in, "if any of your men want to go to the war, you ought to let them."

I think she shocked them. "You reckon there'll be people who want to go?"

"Yes," she said. "Because of him."

Meaning me. Everything is my fault. "Why?"

"Because they want to fight for the prophet," she said, "and the holy cause, and shit like that. So, if they think like that, let them go. Maybe they'll get killed, and we'll be shot of them before they make nuisances of themselves."

I think the kings expected me to flatten her with a thunderbolt. Instead I nodded. "She's right," I said. "When people get themselves worked up into a state like that, it's best to let them get it out of their system. And a thousand or so Dejauzi archers would make a big difference."

More like five thousand, and three thousand pikemen. They insisted on dressing up in white smocks with the sign of the Scroll (at least, I think it was a scroll, though it looked more like a sausage to me) painted on their chests. They called themselves the Spear of the Prophet and they made me very nervous, but by this point they were trained and experienced soldiers, so on balance I was glad to have them along.

Not like the crusaders. That could have been a serious problem.

Bloody Hodda. Her twenty-*dael*-a-copy scriptures had indeed turned out to be the next big thing. I think I told you a bit about Echmen religion. It's all very well and it keeps everyone docile, tranquil and pleasantly bored, but there's nothing you can really get your teeth into if you're that way inclined, which of course many people are. Hodda's stupid religion, which as it grew and evolved turned out to be as much or more about the holy prophet, poor bastard, as it was about God, was something you could get really steamed about, while at the same time being largely compatible with what the Echmen already believed. Two consequences: one, Hodda had become exceedingly rich and had retired to the Serimandil coast to build her holy city; two, there were tens if not hundreds of thousands of new true believers milling about trying to get a glimpse of the prophet, which was a pest, and yearning for a holy war against the unbelievers, which was a disaster waiting to happen. Another very good reason for a proper war, conducted along traditional lines by the Echmen professional military, and the sooner the better. A hundred thousand inadequately armed and chaotic civilians roaming about in the desert and either dying of thirst or being slaughtered by the Sashan could ruin everything.

The Echmen have these little cakes, which I simply can't get enough of. I call them cakes, but maybe they're more like dumplings, I don't know. They're fluffy, white and slightly savoury on the outside, stuffed with meat in a slightly sweet sauce, and you never put anything more delicious in your mouth, trust me. Some observant person in the catering department noticed that I was partial to them and saw to it that they turned up at every meal. I have no self-control when it comes to yummy food. I guess it comes from six years of eating what was basically pigswill. Anyhow, I had a tendency to let myself go whenever they showed up on the table, and as a result, I'm convinced, I started having this dream.

I'd had most of it before. The first part of it was actually just the usual same old same old, with a sharp knife and pain and blood everywhere, and the second part I think I may have mentioned already, with the Queen of Heaven asking who will go for us. The third part, though, was new. In it, I saw a new heaven and a new earth, for the first heaven and the first earth were passed away, and there was no more sea. Then I saw the beautiful city of the Robur, coming down from heaven, dressed as a bride adorned for her husband, and a voice from heaven saying there will be no more death, nor sorrow, nor pain, for the former things have passed away. I got the impression that somehow I was supposed to be something to do with it happening, but you know how it is in dreams. And then I woke up, sweating, thinking; no more late-night savoury dumplings for me.

14

I got a letter.

It was from the king of the Sashan, delivered by a royal messenger wearing more red velvet than should ever be concentrated in any one place at any one time, and addressed to me personally. Hold your horses a moment and consider that. Imperial protocol requires that emperors write to emperors. You don't send a letter to a fellow emperor's subject, just as you don't put your hand down the blouse of a fellow emperor's wife. It's not respectful.

The letter started off telling me a lot of things about myself that I already knew; I was a false prophet, a deceiver, I'd stirred up the people with a lot of lies about God and induced them to murder their rightful sovereign, I was a blasphemer and an idolater – I'm not entirely sure what an idolater is, but it's probably safe to assume that I'm one, I'm everything else, after all – and there was an unspeakable punishment lined up for me some time real soon. That punishment, he went on, it would be both his duty and his pleasure to carry out; to which end, please note that a state of war now existed between the Sashan and the Echmen. Followed by the royal seal, love and kisses conspicuous by their absence.

Alyattes wrote back telling him to go to hell, and that was that. Game on.

Sashan names are a pain in the bum. Properly speaking, my recent correspondent was called Shekelesh son of Ahhiyawash son of Meshwesh, Brother of the Sun, Husband of the Moon, so on and so forth; you try saying all those sh's and anyone within a yard's radius will end up covered in spit. So inconvenient and awkward is the true authentic Sashan language that they don't actually use it any more. They speak Apiru, which they stole from some people they conquered seven hundred years ago, and they write in Shasu, the language of the glorious and sophisticated people who flourished for thousands of years in the territories that now make up the heartland of the Empire of the Sun before the Sashan came along and exterminated them. But when the Great King writes to a brother monarch, he writes in Sashan; which means he composes his letter in Apiru in his head, dictates it in Shasu, then sends for a scholar who translates it into Sashan so it can be translated into Echmen or Vesani or Robur so that its recipient can understand it. From which it follows that skilled interpreters are esteemed and valued in Sashan society, and if my uncle had fixed it for me to be posted there instead of Echmen, the history of the world would be very different.

Nobody who doesn't live there has any idea what ordinary Sashan are really like. It's not a question anybody's supposed to ask. Instead, so the orthodox view goes, the Sashan nation is a mighty oak tree alone on a mountaintop. The trunk of the tree is the king, immovable and unimaginably strong, and from him branch off the scholars and the nobility; supported by his strength, they're able to turn their leaves to the sun and bring forth fruit, or at any rate acorns. The people, meanwhile, are the roots, extending for miles under the ground, drawing vitality and power from the good earth, and permanently out of sight.

Everything Sashan is about the beauty of strength. All Sashan men are strong, with arms like other people's legs and necks like bulls. That's why Sashan men go about muffled from head to foot in flowing robes, so that if by some miracle there should chance to be a weedy one somewhere, nobody would have to look at him and be appalled. All Sashan women, by the same token, are beautiful, and wear veils. The Sashan are probably the most accomplished artists in the world, and they have more painters and sculptors per capita than anyone, all earning good money. This is because every building in a Sashan city is profusely decorated with exquisite murals and sculpted reliefs, all showing the Great King smiting ten kinds of shit out of the enemy. Even private houses are practically built out of art – walls, doors, ceilings, window frames, you name it, every conceivable surface marvellously wrought to convey one transcendent message: don't mess with the Man. Interestingly, there's no word in Apiru or Shasu for strong. It's just implied in everything, and having a word for it would be tautology.

Now, when you know something's true, you don't feel the need to go around all the time proving it. The Great King knows he's the strongest creature on earth and in heaven, and nothing can ever possibly change that. But he's not stupid. Harsh economic truths can't just be waved away, and one such truth is that keeping a large standing army costs a lot of money. The Great King is no fool. Why keep a dog, he reasons, and bark yourself? Since everybody knows that the king is so strong that his sneezes flatten mountains, why spend an absolute fortune on soldiers and equipment that probably won't ever be needed? Should the need arise, of course, the mighty Sashan nation will surge up like a river in spate and annihilate the enemy as though he'd never existed. Until then, better to keep the money in the Treasury, or spend it on a nice bit of art for the palace courtyard.

There is therefore something of a discrepancy between the Sashan army on paper and the Sashan army in the field. A bit like the Echmen, only more so, because the Sashan actually *believe*. If the king has an inscription carved on a wall saying THIS PROVINCE IS DEFENDED BY A HUNDRED THOUSAND MEN, it inevitably follows that it's true. Furthermore, it always was true and it always will be, because the king says so. That notional hundred thousand is represented on the ground by twenty thousand. Note the word *represent*. The hundred thousand are the truth; the twenty thousand stand for them, just as the idol in the temple stands for the god, but the god is infinitely more real in any meaningful sense.

Now the twenty thousand representative Sashan lancers are pretty hot stuff, never doubt that. They're Sashan, they're strong, they have the honour to have been chosen out of a hundred thousand ultra-real soldiers to represent the king's right arm out on the frontier. What we were up against, in the slightly inferior level of reality in which people actually live, was the best equipped, best trained and best motivated army in the world; significantly smaller than the Echmen army, but blessed with an edge of sheer ferocity that the Echmen tend to lack. They know that the Sashan have never lost a battle; not *really* lost, anyway. Anything other than total victory would be unthinkable.

The thing about people who believe defeat is unthinkable is that they tend not to think. My kind of enemy.

Which brings me, inevitably, to Mecho son of Terupat. A man with a vision. A man who changed history.

When Terupat died, Mecho and his brother divided the old man's estate between them, which is how they do things in Blemya. The brother took the land, the sheep, the house and its contents. Mecho took the camels. Both brothers reckoned Mecho had got the better part of the division, because the old man had been the foremost camel breeder in north-east Blemya, but that was all right. The brother was happy to stay home and tend the farm. Mecho wanted to conquer the world.

In commercial terms, at least. Mecho was educated. He knew that there were other countries and other races of men out there, on the other side of the desert, beyond the mountains. He'd read books and talked to travellers, and he knew about the people who lived far away to the east: the Denyen, the Tieker, the Lubu, and, beyond them, the sophisticated and fabulously wealthy Echmen. About the latter he knew one particularly important, shocking, wonderful thing. The Echmen had no camels.

Which was odd, because they had deserts all round them, to the west, north and east, and they were a trading and manufacturing nation, needing to transport goods long distances through the desert. But no camels. Instead they used mules and a network of wells and oases, which worked fine but which meant you had to cross the desert in a sort of meandering stagger, hopping from water to water and taking three times as long as you would if you could go in a straight line. Which you could do, if you had camels. Which they didn't. Very odd.

So Mecho set out with the seven hundred pedigree camels he'd inherited from his father. It can't have been an easy journey. First he had to cross the endless white sand of the Blemyan Ocha. Then he faced the rampart of the Ganz Mountains, the ascent of which took him from the blistering heat of the plains to the murderous cold of the high passes. The other side of the Ganz was Denyen territory; he was wounded three times in skirmishes with raiders, and seventy-two of his herders were killed, but he battled through, only to find himself confronted with the River Cobryas, in full spate. These days there are bridges over the Cobryas, built by Robur engineers. Back then, you had two choices. You could sit on the west bank until the flow subsided and get picked off and harried to death by the Denyen, or you could try and cross. Mecho tried, and succeeded; it cost him another seventeen men and fifty camels, but he made it, and the altar he built to give thanks to heaven is still there to this day.

Crossing the Cobryas brought him into the rocky, hostile lands of the Tieker, where for centuries rival clans in mountaintop strongholds had conducted their incredibly bitter feuds with their neighbours. The Tieker pay lip service to the sacred laws of hospitality, but in practice there's never enough food to feed the Tieker, let alone strangers. The Tieker despise money. Their only legal tender is arrowheads. Forty of them bought a sheep or a quarter of oats. Mecho knew this and had brought three hogsheads of arrowheads with him, but one hogshead had been washed away crossing the Cobryas and the other two turned out to be the wrong sort; he'd brought broadheads for hunting, but the Tieker wanted bodkins for punching through armour. It was lucky for him that he'd lost so many men and therefore had fewer mouths to feed, or he'd have been in serious trouble.

The Tieker, of course, were a walk in the park compared to the Lubu. They live on the wide, bleak treeless plains of the plateau the Echmen call the Roof of the World. It rains for two days every week, but it might as well not bother. The howling winds scrubbed away the topsoil a long time ago. There are books in the Echmen library that talk about the vast forests of Lubu, which goes to show how old they are. There were vast forests there once, but the Lubu cut them down and floated the lumber down the Gold River to fuel the charcoal pits of Echmen. It'll be fine, the Echmen promised them; once you've cleared the land you'll have pasture for a million million goats, you'll live like kings. And so they did, for a while, until the goats ate all the roots of the heather and gorse that held the soil together, and the wind and the rain carried it away to form the fertile silt pans of the Valley of Joy in the north-west province of the empire. These days the most valuable resource the Lubu have is a species of large white hawk, greatly prized by discerning falconers. They snare them, train them and sell them, travelling thousands of miles on foot with the hawks sitting on their hands, because the Lubu have nothing to make baskets out of.

If you're not interested in buying hawks the Lubu don't want to know you. They won't actively harm you, but they won't sell you food, since they have none to spare, and their past experience with foreigners has left them surly and suspicious, so your chances of a roof for the night to keep out the wind and the rain are fairly poor. Lubu territory is immense. It takes three months to cross it under ideal conditions, and conditions there are never ideal. Also, screaming gales and driving rain aren't good for camels. Twenty of Mecho's precious stock in trade died of a pernicious variety of footrot before he eventually reached the eastern edge of the plateau and began the long, slow descent into the empire.

On the frontier there's a castle, built long ago to collect tolls and keep out bandits. It spans the road, which is blocked by the castle's enormously wide bronze gates. When Mecho got there, he was greeted by a hundred archers drawn up across the width of the road, with bows strung and arrows nocked. News of his arrival had preceded him.

The officer commanding the castle garrison walked out to meet him. "Go back," he said.

"I don't understand," Mecho said.

"Piss off," said the officer, "and take those fucking animals with you."

There was a reason, it turned out, why they don't have camels in Echmen. It's because horses can't stand the way they smell. One whiff of camel is enough to drive even the best trained and seasoned warhorse mad. They buck, rear, throw their riders, barge into each other and stampede, injuring themselves and anything stupid enough to stand in their way as they race to get away from the intolerable stench. When the first ever camels appeared in Echmen, three hundred years earlier, they caused such havoc with a detachment of Imperial lancers sent to escort them through the Lubu country that the emperor issued a decree. Bringing a camel into the empire was a capital offence, and any camel seen within the borders was to be shot on sight.

It was no use Mecho pointing out that horses quickly get used to the smell – a week or ten days at the most and then they're good as gold. The archers raised their bows and the garrison commander started counting to ten. It was obviously no use trying to sneak across the border at some unguarded spot. All Mecho could do was turn round and head back the way he'd come.

Going home turned out to be even harder than getting there. By this point Mecho had no food, money or trade goods, most of his drivers were dead and so were most of his camels. It was either pure serendipity or the mercy of heaven that led Mecho to run into a convoy of salt miners at a crossroads in the Tieker Mountains. Every year the miners made the long and arduous journey from their base of operations just north of the Tieker country across the desert to Beloisa, where they sold to Robur merchants. They'd never seen camels before. What, they asked, are those extraordinary creatures?

Mecho explained, and sold his remaining hundred and six camels for just enough money to get home with. Legend has it that when he arrived at the gate of his old home, his brother came running out to meet him, burst into tears of joy and gave him half the farm, and they lived happily ever after. Anything's possible.

The salt miners, meanwhile, found camels were ideal for their transport needs. The breed derived from Mecho's original hundred and six are shorter and sturdier than the true Blemyan camel, apparently. They don't carry quite as much freight and they have a reputation for foul temper, but since they're the only camels anywhere east of the Cobryas, nobody worries about it very much.

*

She came looking for me.

She found me mending my boots with strips of parchment snipped from Olybrius' *Commentaries* and a rather clever sort of glue the Maudit make from the sap of a certain sort of lime tree. "You arsehole," she said.

I looked at her. "Now what have I done?"

She sat down on a log and glared at me. "You've inspired eight thousand Dejauzi to volunteer to fight the Sashan. That's obscene."

I could see her point. Dejauzi don't fight unless they have to, it's one of the things I like most about them. They swear and threaten and bluster, if they think it's an efficient method of getting their own way, and tempers occasionally flare to the point of blows and even weapons, though not very often. But they don't see any merit in fighting. To them, it's a bit like peeing. You do it when you have to, but you don't make a song and dance about it, or pretend you enjoy it, or that your peeing skills make you a superior human being. Rather, they feel it's somehow distasteful and dirty, to be ashamed of.

"They volunteered," I pointed out. "Nobody twisted their arms. They want to go."

"Exactly. That's what's so gross. Dejauzi wanting to fight, in a war that's got nothing to do with them. You realise, you've turned my people into a race of murderers."

I don't know what I'd do without her, really I don't. The exact same point had been bothering me somewhat; did I really like the idea of being the man who made war-in-a-good-cause an acceptable idea for an otherwise enlightened nation? No, not really. But with her blustering in my face and calling me an arsehole, I was able to muster all sorts of good arguments for why it was a good thing really, simply in order to refute her, simply in order to win the next round of our perpetual battle. The good arguments then allowed me to kid myself that I was right, when I knew in my heart I wasn't. And I really couldn't have performed that miracle of ethical acrobatics without her help. Bless her. Like a sort of counter-productive conscience, giving me an excuse to do the really bad thing. "It's purely temporary," I said. "Once this war's over, they'll go back to being how they've always been. It's their nature."

"Says you."

"We need them," I said. "In case the fighting turns bad. The combination of pikes and horn and sinew bows is unbeatable."

"Fine," she said. "Why do we have to do it? You could teach it to some of your pet Echmen, and then we could stay home in peace."

"Oh, sure. You want me to tell the Echmen how to be invincible. This, ten minutes after we used those same tactics to beat the shit out of them. How sensible."

"They're our friends now. You keep telling me that."

"They're our friends because we've got an extra-special unbeatable knife at their throats. You don't want to give them that knife, trust me. So," I went on, before she could argue, "we keep the secret to ourselves. We don't give it to our worst-enemy-turned-best-friend. But we need those archers and pikemen for the war. Therefore, some Dejauzi have got to go. And it's only eight thousand."

"You should listen to yourself."

"No, thank you. All right, since I'm saying bad things, let's add in a few more. The sort of man who volunteers for a job like this probably isn't the sort of man who makes a model citizen in the Great Society. So it's probably better to have him out on the frontier doing a useful job than back home making trouble."

"And then the enemy kill him, and he's not a problem any more."

"Since you put it like that, yes."

She rolled her eyes. "You don't give a damn, do you? You read books and make plans and shake the world like an earthquake—" She stopped and looked at me. "Of course you do. How stupid of me, I'm sorry. It's just, I always assumed the messiah would be one of the good guys."

I did a big fake yawn. "That joke's getting a bit old, if you ask me."

"You make me sick sometimes."

"In which case," I said, "obviously I'm not the messiah. The chosen one inspires love and loyalty, not nausea. Therefore—"

"How can you be so *blind?*" she said, and stomped off in a huff.

As it happened, I'd figured out a way of beating the bows and pikes combination, purely out of academic interest, just in case it might come in handy one day; lighter mobile versions of the stone-throwing artillery used for bashing down city walls, to smash the pikemen from a safe distance, protected from the archers by a screen of heavy infantry with pavises. But the Sashan don't think like that, and even if they did, it'd take them at least six months to design and build the artillery.

I got an even bigger surprise when I asked her to lead the army and she said yes. "That's great," I said. "Thank you."

"I'm not doing it as a favour to you," she said. "I know why you asked me and I think it's a good idea."

Somehow I doubted that. "You might want to expand on that."

"You figure that if this turns into a bloodbath, it looks better if I'm in command. You're expected to perform miracles every time you go out of the house. So, if it all screws up, it's better for it to be my fault than yours. And if it all goes to plan, everyone will think it was really your doing anyway." She grinned. "That's what they want to think. So, why not? It's a good idea."

"Thank you."

"Besides," she went on, "if I stay here without someone to keep me from doing something violent, by the time you get back there'll be four new kings of the Dejauzi. I'm sick to death of their incessant bloody whining."

I frowned. "What are they whining about?"

It occurred to me that I had no idea what she looked like under all that chalk makeup and egg-white-stiffened hairdo. Not that it had the slightest relevance to anything. "They're tired of hanging about," she said. "They want to get settled into their new land. I keep telling them it'll still be there tomorrow, land is like that, it stays there. But they just snarl and look pathetic."

"Who's stopping them?" I said.

Her turn to frown. "What, just let them go? What's the soldiery word, demobilise."

"Why not?" I said. "The sooner they're settled in, the better. If they get a move on, they can probably get a wheat crop in the ground for next season. Probably a bit late for barley, but I'm no expert. No wonder they're itching to get on. I wouldn't want to be sitting on my arse doing nothing if it meant losing a whole growing season."

"But we need them."

"I don't think so," I said.

She nodded slowly. "So you've finished with us, have you?" she said. "That's interesting."

"I'm not sure what you're getting at."

"Don't be stupid. You've finished with us. The hoe goes back in the tool shed because now you're going to use the rake. That's fair enough." She stood up. "I'll tell them, they'll be pleased."

"It's not up to me," I said. "What your people choose to do," I added. "It was never up to me. I made suggestions, which they chose to follow."

She had her back to me. "Yes, I suppose you could see it that way. Everybody's always got a choice, after all. I can choose to disobey my master's orders and get beaten to death with a stick, or I can do what he tells me to do. Entirely up to me. Therefore, not his fault. That's what you always say, isn't it? Not my fault?"

"For crying out loud," I said. "What have I done now?"

She turned and looked at me. "You know perfectly well," she said, and walked out.

About three-quarters of the Dejauzi had chosen to move into the new territories. The remainder said, thanks but no thanks; we've always lived here, so we're staying. There didn't seem to be a problem about it. For the ones who'd decided to stay, it meant plenty of land for everyone but a great deal more work. Nearly all the Maudit decided to move, but over a third of the Rosinholet chose to stay. I suggested – just a suggestion, that was all – that if there was going to be a labour shortage, they might care to take on some of the recently freed slaves as hired hands or, better still, tenants. They didn't belong anywhere in particular, and they were keen to work and better themselves, so why not? The suggestion met with approval on both sides, I'm pleased to say. I suggested to Alyattes that it might be a nice gesture if the Imperial Treasury helped out with the costs of the relocation and general settling down and settling in. I thought he was going to have a stroke when I first mentioned it, but he chose to agree, in the end.

I had one other suggestion to make, and at first it didn't go down at all well. I suggested that, now that most of the Dejauzi nation was making a new start in a new and better place, it might be a good idea to forget about Maudit and Rosinholet and Luzir and Hus and concentrate on Dejauzi. It's what we have in common that makes us strong, I suggested. Our differences make us weak, like splits and shakes in a plank of wood. Naturally, I added quickly, we wouldn't be forgetting the great old traditions that made us what we are. But what we are, fundamentally, is Dejauzi. So why not put that front and centre, where it belongs?

What the hell are you on about, the kings asked, knowing full well. A united Dejauzi nation, I said. Of course there would still be the six nations, with their six kings, but united under one overall leader, a queen for all Dejauzi everywhere. And, since I'd been given the undeserved honour of leading the Maudit, I'd be happy to lead the way and pledge my loyalty to the new queen on behalf of the Maudit nation, both here and in the old country. It was entirely up to them whether they joined me or not, but I suggested it would be the right thing for them to do.

Stony silence. Then one of them, I forget which, asked if it was true that the queen was leading the army against the Sashan. Perfectly true, I said. So she's going away and won't be back for some time. Quite possibly. And you're going to be taking on the entire Sashan army, just you and the Echmen horse-botherers. That's right, yes. And you're going, too? I am, yes. He looked round at his fellow kings, who nodded. We accept, he said.

I'd given up eating the yummy dumplings but I was still getting the dreams, so I consulted a doctor. Echmen medicine is so much better than anywhere else. They have cures that frequently work and doctors who sometimes make you better. Rather startling for someone brought up on Robur medical practice, which tends towards the view that the doctor's job is to help finish what nature started. The Echmen also know a bit about what goes on inside people's heads. I've been getting these weird dreams, I told the doctor.

He looked at me carefully. "You're the prophet, aren't you?" he said.

"People say I am. Look, can we not talk about that?"

He asked me about the dreams. I told him.

"My first instinct," he said, "would be that you were quite right and it's all to do with eating rich food late at night. It overheats the digestion and produces too much blood, and that's what gives you nightmares. But you say you've stopped all that and you're still getting the dreams?"

"Yes."

He frowned. "In that case," he said, "I would think it's probably because you're worried about something."

"Ah."

He steepled his fingers. "Worry does funny things to the human brain," he said. "There's all that stress and tension building up inside your head and nowhere for it to go, you see. So your mind has to find a way of dealing with it, and it turns it into imagery. What sort of imagery depends on a lot of things; who you are, your past history, what your major concerns are, all that kind of nonsense. Your head's stuffed full of prophets and God and the destiny of great empires, so naturally you choose to interpret your stress in those terms in your dreams. Probably if you were a sausage-maker by trade you'd be dreaming about sausages. Same principle."

I nodded. I liked the way he'd chosen the word *interpret*. I could relate to that. "So ought I to be worried? I mean, about going mad, anything like that?"

"Oh, I don't think so," he said with a smile. "Just try and get some rest and fresh air now and again and drink plenty of liquids."

As opposed to drinking solids; yes, right. "Thank you," I said. "That's a great weight off my mind."

"That's what I'm here for," he said. I stood up to go. "Just one thing."

"Yes?"

He smiled awkwardly. "Forgive me," he said, "but I've got to ask. You're not really the prophet, are you?"

No, I told him. I don't think he believed me, though.

15

Imagine you're General Turshen, commander-in-chief of the Sashan army. You've been chosen, in preference to the other six senior generals, to lead the invasion of Echmen. It's the greatest honour imaginable and clearly marks you out as the most distinguished soldier of your generation. Furthermore, everybody tells you, it's going to be a piece of cake, a walk in the park. The Echmen military machine, once so formidable, has clearly decayed to the point where a mob of barbarians can punch a hole clean through it and grab hold of the Imperial throne; which is why now is the time to settle old scores, avenge past disgraces and grab Echmen for the Great King.

To make matters worse, they haven't just given you what you asked for – three divisions of seasoned veterans with experience of operating in the Echmen theatre. No, they've entrusted you with nine divisions, leaving just one to defend the fatherland. With that kind of force at your disposal, they tell you, you'll be able to sweep aside anything those effete and decadent silk-fetishists throw against you, they won't stand a chance. We only wish we were going with you, they say with a barely suppressed smirk, but you know how it is. Someone's got to stay home and mind the store. An army that size brings with it a whole new world of difficulties. Food, water, fodder for the horses; the three divisions you'd asked for could've lived off the land, happily thieving and burning their way through the Echmen border country and forcing the enemy to give battle much earlier than he'd have chosen to because of the damage you're doing and the political pressure that creates. Nine divisions are a different matter entirely. You need a supply train that's almost as big as your fighting force and which moves at the speed of oxen. You have to stick to well-maintained roads and pray it doesn't rain, because if it does, all those ox-hoofs and solid iron-tyred cartwheels will turn the road into a swamp, and nothing will be able to move at all. Instead of being fast as the wind and elusive as a dream at daybreak, you're a huge, lumbering monster whose dust cloud can be seen for ten miles in any direction. Geography is now your mortal enemy. Roads that would have been broad enough to dash along at top speed have suddenly become narrow passes and defiles where you're in deadly peril of ambush and massacre; and as for crossing rivers, you really don't want to think about it. You could, of course, send one or two divisions ahead, to fight the war the way you'd have fought it if the people back home hadn't been so bloody generous, but that would create its own horrible opportunities for disaster. Do you go with the expeditionary force and leave the bulk of the army in the hands of some idiot who'll let them all starve to death while your back's turned? Or do you put the idiot in charge of the two divisions, knowing you'll be the one who gets the blame when the enemy picks him off and cuts him to ribbons? Meanwhile, when you're preoccupied with all of that and have more than enough on your plate as it is, some clown in the civil service back home discovers that military activity on the grand scale has led to a catastrophic cash-flow problem, so calmly announces that your men are going to have to wait for their pay for another six months.

You're careful not to call it a mutiny, or even let the M-word cross your mind, because mutiny is so desperately serious that you'd have to take extreme measures to deal with it so it'll never happen again. The punishment for mutiny is laid down in the military statutes and can't be altered. You drive a lot of tall posts in beside the road, precisely twenty-five yards apart, and you sharpen them. Then you choose every tenth man from the mutinous units and impale them. Because of this, the army hasn't had a mutiny for four hundred years. That's not to say there haven't been lapses in discipline here and there, some of them involving a reluctance to obey orders, but none of them have been officially declared as mutinies. Which goes to show how well the system works.

You didn't get to be commander-in-chief by being stupid or lacking in imagination, so you get the money to pay the men by auctioning off looting futures to a syndicate of forward-looking businessmen; anything lying on the battle-field after victory is formally declared as theirs to carry away and sell, buyer arranges his own transport. It bothers you a little that the winning syndicate will now go to the enemy and buy the same rights from him, but you know it's just business and they don't mean to imply any lack of confidence in your abilities.

Then it turns out that the mustn't-call-it-mutiny wasn't

about pay, or at least there was more to it than that. The men are scared. They've heard that the enemy is some sort of mad religious prophet, and he can do miracles. Your junior officers are doing the best they can to calm them down, but the more they talk about it, the more they get to hear. They start thinking: just how did a bunch of barbarians overthrow the Echmen empire with hardly a drop of blood spilt? Wild stories about walking dry-shod across a mighty river, about city walls collapsing at the sound of a trumpet; it's all bullshit, the junior officers tell the men, but then the officers themselves start thinking. Something weird must have happened, so is it bullshit or is it really miracles? Not a matter of abstruse metaphysical speculation, since any day now we're going to be up against these people, and if they really can divert the course of rivers and bring walls tumbling down –

Don't be such a girl, you tell them. But you can't help but wonder.

Then things improve. The enemy have been sighted. They're headed this way, and by the looks of it they want a pitched battle as soon as possible, which suits you fine. Their general can't be too bright, because if you were him you wouldn't be looking to fight here, in the open, with no tactical edge from the geography. True, he outnumbers you three to two; no matter. It means he's brought along practically his entire army, so if you can beat him here and now, the war's effectively over. The man must be an idiot, you say to yourself, and then you find out he's not even a man, he's a *woman*. For the first time in months, you can feel your shoulders start to unhunch. Looks like we're going to win this after all.

As you make your troop dispositions on the day of the battle you keep asking yourself: what have I missed, what is he, sorry, *she* up to? You stare at the broad shapes slowly creeping into place in front of you, but damned if you can see it. She's trying to do something, sure enough. She wants the battle to be spread out; no, scratch that. She wants you to be spread out, while she bunches her forces up to match you, as though she's deliberately trying to negate her own numerical advantage. She must know that the Sashan win their battles with an unstoppable charge of heavy lancers, smashing through the enemy centre, then hooking up to attack in flank and fold the two halves in on themselves. Clearly she knows that, because she's doing everything she can to make it happen. Why would she do that?

You call in all your best people and ask them that question. They think about it. No idea, they say. Yes, now you mention it, it does look like the stupid bitch wants to lose. Don't knock it, they say. If she's got some far-fetched scheme rattling about in her empty little head, so what? It won't work, whatever it is. It can't do. Just come out here and look for yourself. With the armies set out like they are now, there's no power on earth that can make us lose.

Put it like that and you can't argue. So, since Sashan generals traditionally lead from the front, you strap yourself into all that horrible armour and scramble up into the saddle, and off you go. The men cheer you as you pass, but it's not quite as deafening as you've come to expect. They're worried. Fine. In an hour it'll all be over, and then we can go home.

The enemy, you observe as you start off at a gentle trot, are just standing there. That's all right, you know all about Echmen tactics. When you're two hundred yards away from them they'll do their celebrated charge from a standstill. It was something that worked with devastating effect a long time ago, because it was unexpected, and they've been doing it ever since, predictable as the phases of the moon. Never mind about that. The decisive factor will be the balance of weight and speed, something the Sashan know more about than anyone.

You give the signal to increase the pace, and behind you the lancers shift from line to wedge formation. The distance closes. You reach a certain point. Now the enemy don't have time to change position; if they try they'll be caught in disorder. You relax. The outcome is now inevitable, and only one thing can possibly happen.

Your horse stops dead. You're shot forward, and its neck hits you in the face as it rears up. Something slams into you from behind, skewing both of you sideways. Now the stupid horse is trying to turn round. You shorten the rein, but it's pulling too hard, ignoring the pain in its mouth. Another horse cannons into you, riderless, mad with fear. Your horse rears again, and while it's upright and off-balance something else bashes into you from the other side, and you both go down. You hear and feel your bones break at the same moment. You try and pull yourself free, because there are stampeding horses all round you, you can see them surging up towards you, filling your field of vision. One of them is very close indeed. You can see the ends of the nails, driven through the shoe into the hoof and clipped off short by the farrier –

And now I must ask you to stop imagining, because you're dead.

The moment the Sashan wedge collapsed in on itself, I sent forward our right and left wings for an enveloping sweep. The Sashan reserve didn't need to be told what would happen if they let themselves get hooked and wrapped up. There didn't seem to be anything they could do for the centre anyhow. Then the horses in their own front rank started freaking out, just as the wedge had done. Enough is enough, they said to themselves, and ran for it.

I'd been hoping they'd do that, because the road they'd come in on an hour or so earlier, which passes through a narrow gorge between two steep ridges, was now blocked with pikemen. The tops of the ridges were lined with archers.

I was as sure as I dared be (but you never can tell, can you?) that I'd read them right. Stuck in a classic trap, the sort you know can only end one way, and with some sort of weird and horrible sorcery closing in on them fast from the rear; they were Sashan, there was always risk they'd make a stand and fight for it, but I was sure, I *hoped*, they'd do no such thing. There's Sashan and there's just plain dumb. The difference is slight but real.

They sort of slumped, and I knew we'd done it. I gave the signal to move the camels right back to the rear. I didn't want all those Sashan warhorses panicking in the confined space of the classic trap, where somebody might get hurt.

What camels? Oh, those camels. I'd hired them from the Denyen salt miners, at ruinous expense but worth every *dael*. It was sheer luck or divine providence that the wind chose to blow right in the Sashans' faces, and that the camels should be at their absolute peak of scented ripeness. I'd had them fed double rations of fermented apple pulp just to help matters along, but that probably wasn't necessary. Sometimes I have a tendency to overegg the pudding.

General Turshen and most of his senior officers were dead, and it took a while for the survivors of his staff to figure out which of them was now in command. By that point it didn't matter. The soldiers had thrown away their weapons, stripped off their armour and flattened themselves on the ground in the excessively melodramatic conventional pose of surrender familiar to anyone who knows Sashan monumental art. Eventually I accepted a rather beautiful watered steel sword from a petrified young man who announced himself as Colonel Weshesh. You could tell by looking at him that he was somebody's son-in-law, but no matter. All he had to do was say, *We surrender.* He managed it, just about. I gave him a reassuring smile and asked him to step over and join the other prisoners.

Kudos to whoever thought up the Sashan order of battle. Because of the leading-from-the-front thing, a large proportion of the casualties were senior officers and their adjutants. They got ridden over by the rank and file behind, who mostly managed to keep their seats and let their bolting horses carry them out of harm's way. Somehow I don't feel so bad about the slaughter of the Sashan top brass, who'd wanted the war and looked forward to it and taken bets with each other the night before as to who could skewer the most Echmen. All human life has value, even the lives of shitheads and arseholes, but then again, you can't make omelettes, so on and so forth. On balance I'd rather see six dozen senior officers trampled into squashed bags of broken bone than the same number of other ranks. No real logic to that, of course, but there you go.

I'd wanted the war, too, of course. But at least I had the sense to keep as far away from the action as I could possibly get without emigrating.

Fortunately, the Sashan had brought plenty of food with them, enough for us and them as well. We were about to sit down to a well-earned meal when I was told there was someone to see me. Not now, I said. They insist, I was told. What the hell, I said, bring them through.

Shortly after that I was confronted by six politely furious men in expensive clothes. They explained that they were the contractors who'd bought the plunder rights. They'd paid a great deal of money, they said, in all good faith, and they had the paperwork (waved under my nose) to prove it. Here was the seal of the late General Turshen, look, and that was the seal of some Echmen officer I'd never heard of who was allegedly responsible for health, safety and public hygiene, which I guess includes clearing up dead bodies. Fine, I said, that all seems to be in order, what's the problem? The problem, they said, keeping their tempers with an effort, was that they'd paid for a battlefield full of dead bodies, and there wasn't one. Congratulations, they went on, on your amazing victory, it was either a stroke of strategic genius or a miracle or both, probably both; be that as it may, they wanted their money back. From us in the first instance, and also from us, as conquerors of, and therefore successors in legal title to, the Sashan.

I pointed out that they were entitled to the dead. There were fifty-odd of them, so hopelessly trampled and mangled that I didn't suppose they were worth anything, but if they wanted them, they could help themselves. That made the businessmen very sad. Tell you what, I said, if you take the loss on this battle I'll give you thirty per cent discount on the next one. They thought about that. There's going to be a next one? they asked. Bound to be, I said, sooner or later. Take it or leave it, I said. They looked very sad indeed, but they took it.

*

I couldn't spare the men to escort the Sashan prisoners back to Echmen, so we took them with us. I didn't anticipate any trouble, or at least not the sort that guards could do anything about. The problem, such as it was, lay in another quarter. Almost to a man, the Sashan prisoners had got religion. Guess which one.

Maybe it would've been different if they'd known about the camels. But I'd made sure that was kept completely hush-hush, just in case I had to use them again, so as far as the Sashan knew, their immaculately bred and trained horses had gone mad with fear because of a miracle, and divine clemency had saved them all from getting killed. Blessed, I always say, are those who have seen and yet have not believed, but it's a big ask under circumstances like that. Shortly before we left for the campaign, Hodda had come up with a simple but impressive baptism ceremony. Much against my better judgement I performed it for them, omitting the fee, and it made them very happy.

"It was a stupid risk to take, though," she said. "If the horses hadn't been spooked by the camels, they'd have torn into us and cut us to ribbons. You gambled all our lives on some shit you read in a book."

"Which turned out to be true."

"You believe everything you read in books."

I sighed. "No, not always. But in this case I consulted all the available accounts of the incident, considered whether they were trustworthy, considered if there were any extraneous factors which might have contributed to the outcome, and based on all of that, I made the decision—"

"To gamble all our lives on some shit you'd read in a book." She gave me her hard stare. "Nobody in their right mind would do that, unless—"

"Unless what?"

"Unless he *knew*. Unless someone had *told* him."

I rolled my eyes. "Oh, come on," I said. "You might at least try and be consistent."

"I'm always consistent."

"No, you're not. If you're really a true believer, you ought to show some respect. Awe, even."

"Like hell."

"You believe I'm a holy prophet and you're always so damned *rude*."

She gave me the sort of scowl that's guaranteed to shift stubborn verdigris off copper. "I'm not saying I believe. I suspect. There's a difference."

"All right," I said, "I admit it. Since I'm not the prophet and nobody told me anything, it follows that I gambled all our lives, recklessly and stupidly, on some shit I read in a book. Luckily we got away with it this time. Next time—"

"Who says luck had anything to do with it? You *knew*."

And so on and so forth, for three long days, until we reached the Blue Gates. There, if anywhere, what was left of the Sashan army would make its stand, and if they did, we were in dead trouble. The Gates are the only pass in the mountains you can get a horse through, and, about a third of the way in, the road's just wide enough for two carts to pass, if they don't mind jeopardising their wheel hubs. Going the long way round would take months and take us through places we really wouldn't want to go. She called a halt and we pitched a carefully-fortified camp, with a proper ditch and palisade and everything. We even sent for a water diviner in case we needed to dig a well.

While the well was being dug, two horsemen rode up with

a white flag. Oldest dodge in the book; you send out your spies and they get given the run of the camp and a guided tour, just because of a bit of rag on a stick. But the camels were safely behind the lines, so I had nothing I didn't want spies to see. In fact, the more comprehensive their account, the more shitless the enemy would be scared. Bring them to my tent, I said, the long way round.

They weren't spies. They were priests. The Great King of the Sashan, they told me, wanted to talk to me. I managed not to bruise my jaw on my collarbone. Fine, I said, I'd like to talk to him, what arrangements do you propose? No arrangements, they said. He's here, just inside the gates. We'll go back and fetch him.

Which is how, a very long hour later, I came to meet Shekelesh the Strong, Brother of the Sun, Bridegroom of the Moon, Great King of the Sashan. He rode into camp on a white donkey, accompanied by the two priests and an old man, very tall and dignified with a white beard halfway down to his navel, who turned out to be the king's uncle.

"His majesty," said the old man in actual Sashan, "is here to surrender."

A priest stepped forward to translate. I waved him back. "You're kidding," I said.

The old man looked bitterly offended. "His majesty," he repeated, "is here to surrender."

I realised I hadn't spoken yet. "Surrender accepted. Would one of you please tell me what's going on?"

The figure on the donkey was swathed in purple, with a purple hood over his face. He peeled it off, slid off the donkey and stumbled badly. The old man helped him up and tried to take his arm, but he shook his head, tried to walk forward and sat down again. He took off the heavy purple gown and sat there in a plain tunic of unbleached linen, with the purple all round him like a puddle. Then, slowly and painfully, he got down on his knees, then pressed his forehead to the ground. Slowly and painfully because he had that thing – the Echmen have a medical name for it which slips my mind – where your spine is bent like a pear sliced longways. He was about sixteen years old, skinny as a rake, with a pleasant, intelligent face apart from a lower lip that stuck out. I don't know when I've ever been more shocked in all my life.

He lifted his head off the ground. "Would somebody help me up, please?" he said.

The priests carried him to my tent. The effort had been too much for him and I could see he was in considerable pain. He sat down on a low stool, which was all I had to offer apart from the chair, which he refused, because he couldn't be seated higher than me now that he'd surrendered. The priests and the old man looked scared to death; not of me or the entire Echmen army, but in case he overdid it, or tripped and fell. It wasn't just duty or respect. They loved him.

"Thanks," he said. "I'll be fine now."

Translated: go away. They didn't want to, but they left, and I was alone with the king. He raised his head, looked at me and grinned.

"It was camels, wasn't it?" he said.

"Yes."

He beamed at me. "I knew it had to be camels," he said. "I thought I was the only man living who's read the *Secret History*, but apparently not. You know, I never believed that story. Shows how wrong you can be."

He was terrified, and pumping out charm like a squid squirting ink. Also, something was hurting him very badly. I guessed it was arthritis, something like that. "Sorry," I said. "What secret history?"

"The – it's a book," he said. "About how Kushro the Great conquered the Marcoman. The Battle of the Chains. All that." He frowned. "You haven't read it."

"No."

"Good grief."

"Is it any good?"

He laughed, but it hurt. "I love it," he said. "It's full of great stories. But it's in Old Shasu, which only about seven people can read."

"Eight," I said. "I'm a translator by trade," I explained. "I'm good at languages. Maybe you could lend me a copy."

"Of course." He looked at me. "So you thought of camels all by yourself."

"Sort of. I found an Echmen military report and got the idea from that."

"Well," he said, "that certainly corroborates the *History*. A proper scholar would say that made it all worthwhile. Trouble is, I'm just a dilettante, so I mind terribly."

I smiled. "I'm sorry," I said.

"Not to worry." He'd started to shake. I wanted to call a doctor, but I knew he'd be offended. "Business," he said firmly. "I surrender."

"So I gather. Would you care to explain?"

He nodded. "It's more of a business proposition than a surrender," he said. "Not to put too fine a point on it, you're making my life very difficult."

That made me feel bad. "I'm sorry," I repeated.

"The Great King," he went on, in his high, rather pleasant voice, "is invincible. That's a fact. Noting can defeat him. He's stronger than anything in the world except God."

"There's different kinds of strength," I said.

"Sweet of you to say so. Not where I come from. It's a matter of historical fact that the Sashan have never lost a battle. It says so in the histories, so it's got to be true. And then along comes you and your dratted camels."

"I can see the problem," I said.

"Mercifully," he went on, "you're putting yourself about as a holy man, and thanks to your confounded camels you won the last one with practically nobody killed, which means it was a miracle. Well, then. Since only God can beat me, you must be God. Or his officially accredited representative. Therefore I'm allowed to surrender to you, which I've done. With me so far?"

"I think so."

He nodded. "Good man. All right," he said, "I'll tell you what I want. I want everything to carry on as near as possible to how it's always been. What do you want?"

"Your army," I said. "For a little while. I'll give it back when I've finished with it."

"And?"

"You'd need to swear fealty to the queen of the Hus."

He pulled a sad face. "Can't do that," he said. "Sorry."

An idea occurred to me. "Let me work on that," I said. "We'll sort of leave that paragraph blank and come back to it. In addition, I'm afraid I'm going to need a lot of money. And stuff in kind – food and boots and hay and all that sort of thing."

He shrugged. "The Sashan empire is effectively bankrupt," he said. "But it's been like that for three hundred years and we soldier on regardless. Try and keep it down if you possibly can. Is that it?"

"More or less," I said. "Other things may occur to me, but they won't be substantial."

"I asked you a question," he said. "Would you mind awfully answering it? What do you want?"

So I told him. When I'd finished, he thought about it for a while. "Really?" he said.

"Really."

"Whatever lights your candle, I suppose. Fair enough. In return for what you want from me, you accept my surrender."

I grinned at him. "We're talking about surrender in a strictly theological sense."

"Neatly put. Actually, what I had in mind was more sort of an endorsement. By you of me. Believe it or not, there are some people who reckon I'm not the most suitable king ever to sit on the Dragon Throne. A pat on the head from the holy prophet would do no harm at all."

"I think I could manage that," I said. "And when I've finished my bit of business, I solemnly undertake to stay out of your hair."

"Subject to the paragraph we left blank just now."

"Subject to that, yes. But I think I can see my way round that. I need to talk to somebody else first, though."

He closed his eyes for a moment, and I got a fleeting impression of a body in which life was clinging on out of sheer bloody-mindedness. But it was a strong life. His father had died when he was three, leaving no other offspring. Three mighty lords had served as regent, one after another, during the ten years of his minority. All of them had intended to get rid of him and take the throne for themselves. They were all dead now, but he was still here. A very strong life. "Excuse me if it's a rude question, but I've got to ask. Are you the prophet?"

"Yes and no."

That earned me a chuckle. "Let me see," he said. "Is it three major miracles or four? Our intelligence boys are pretty good, but they may have missed something."

"No miracles."

"According to orthodox doctrine, you need three major miracles to qualify as a recognised prophet. Two only makes you especially blessed of God. One miracle and you're just another smartarse. So, we've got this last battle, the crossing of the Red River, the manifestation of the Holy Mother, that's three. And didn't you bottle up the entire Echmen army in a ravine with not a drop of blood shed? That sounds pretty miraculous to me. That's four. Oh, and the assassination attempt, five. That, if you don't mind me saying so, is a lot of miracles."

I shook my head. "Camels," I said. "And other stuff like that."

He stopped to catch his breath, lifting a hand to ward off any offer of help. "You don't understand," he said. "I don't blame you, you're not Sashan. You need to be Sashan to understand this sort of thing. Take me, for instance."

"The Great King."

"Exactly. The strongest man on earth. When I'm not tearing down city gates with my bare hands, I'm strangling lions. And that's true. It's true because people believe it."

"I suppose it depends on your definition of—"

He shook his head. "No," he said. "The truth's the truth, that's it's defining quality. Either a thing's true or it isn't. But tell me this. If I don't believe in a thing and everybody else in whole wide world does, what then?" He smiled. "A thing is true because we believe it. If we stop believing, it stops being true."

"We stop believing because new evidence comes along."

"You think that? How sweet. No, really it's all about fashion, like hairdos and hemlines and tassels on cushions. We believe something because people we think are really cool tell us it's true. Then we shape the evidence to fit, like a blacksmith bending iron. Or we just believe, because the truth is so self-evident it needs no proof, and no proof can shake our belief." He stopped and caught his breath again. "Listen to me, nattering on. But you're not a subject of the empire, so you don't have to listen to me. Lucky you. The long and the short of it is, the fact that a miracle was really all camels doesn't stop it being a miracle. From time to time, God uses tools and instruments. He makes use of you, just as you make use of camels. It was a pleasure to meet you," he said. "I'd best be getting back now. They worry about me, and it's way past my bedtime."

"Just a moment," I said. "Are you saying you actually—?"

"Believe?" He smiled. "Yes, of course. Mostly because it's politically expedient and it gets me out of the fix you made for me. But also because it's true." He looked at me. "You don't believe, I take it."

"No."

"Weird. Ah well, you'll come to it in time, I expect. Ask yourself this, though. Who told you about the camels?"

"I read about it in a—"

"No, you're missing the point. Who *told* you to exploit the fact that horses can't stand the smell of camels?"

"Nobody."

He looked at me. "Like I said, you'll come to it in time.

Thanks ever so much for talking to me. I'll send someone over to sort out the details. Now, if you wouldn't mind."

They brought a covered litter to take him back. The white donkey, I learned afterwards, was liturgically correct for the Great King paying homage to the gods, but it must have been excruciating.

"What was all that about?" she asked me. "And why didn't you call me?"

"We won," I explained. "But there's something I need you to do for me. It'll only take you five minutes and it's no big deal."

"What?"

I told her. Then she hit me so hard it made my head spin.

Eventually, though, I managed to talk her round. It wouldn't be a real marriage, I explained, not in that sense. And she wouldn't have to live in Sashan, or even see him again after the ceremony if she didn't want to. And it really did tick all the boxes, political and military.

"It's grotesque," she said.

"It's politics," I told her. "And there's tautology for you. This sort of thing happens all the time."

"Yes, but supposing I really wanted to get married. To a real person."

"It's not like that. It's just pretend. Besides, you're the most powerful human being in the world. It's the Great King or nobody. Anybody else would be the most outrageous slumming."

She didn't hit me again, mostly because I took a long step backwards. "Fine," she said. "You're the holy fucking prophet. I'll marry you instead."

"Sorry," I said. "Not the marrying kind, you know that."

"It's just pretend," she snarled at me. "And what do you mean, the most powerful person in the world? Bullshit."

"You are, you know," I broke it to her gently. "And when you marry the Great King, there won't be any doubt."

"You make me sick," she said. I took that for a yes.

The Great King sent his uncle. We hadn't really hit it off before, and my idea that his nephew should marry a Hus didn't really improve matters. But he could see the merit in it, he told me, and besides, it wasn't up to him. His nephew thought it was a splendid idea, so that was that.

"He does?"

"It's what you want, he says. Apparently that's enough." He glared at me. "He believes in you," he said.

"So he told me."

"But he means it." He breathed out through his nose. "This religion of yours is sweeping through our cities like—" A plague, he didn't say. "The high priest has designated you a true prophet. He didn't really have any choice. There have been a number of incidents."

Luminous paint, a stage dagger and camels. I wanted to tell him, but I could see he wouldn't want to be told. "I'm no expert," I said, "but from what I know of Sashan orthodoxy, there's nothing actually incompatible—"

"That's the line we're following," he said.

"Can I ask you a question," I said, and when he nodded I went on; "Why aren't you the Great King? It would be—"

He gave me a look that made me wince. "The king is the king because he's the king. I have the honour to serve him. Can we talk about something else, please?"

*

It was a charming wedding, in the Sashan sense. That's to say, it's right and proper that the wedding of the Great King and the queen of the Hus should be a delightful occasion, uplifting and life-enhancing. So it was.

In actual fact, it took place in the chapel of the border outpost at Cedesh (she'd announced that she didn't hold with long engagements, meaning longer than a week, and unless she got it over and done with straight away, she fully intended to change her mind). The room was built as an armoury, with racks for lances and rows of pegs for helmets, and a three-inch-deep channel running the length of the floor for rinsing the sweat out of padded gambesons. Remarkably for a Sashan interior it was almost devoid of sculpture, the only exception being a wonderfully realistic basalt frieze of soldiers crossing a flooded river on inflatable rafts made from the flayed skins of their enemies. Someone had hastily daubed up a mural of me and the Queen of Heaven, which covered the whole of the north wall, where the altar stood. The paint was still wet, so my face gleamed like I was sweating; a nice touch, I thought. I was kneeling and she was handing me what looked like a savoury flatbread, but which the inscription revealed to be all the kingdoms of the earth. Being a Sashan artefact it was actually rather good, but I could've done without it.

I had to go to a lot of weddings as a kid; I was always being chosen as a pageboy, because I looked so cute. This one wasn't like the ones I was used to. The bride arrived first, escorted by me. She was wearing her old black sheepskin coat over the suit of lamellar armour she'd taken to prancing about in ever since the start of the Sashan campaign. It only came down to her hips, and to cut down the weight so she could stand up in it the plates were so thin a bird could peck through them, but useless armour is still armour, just as a good-for-nothing man is still a man. Under that she had her old white gown, the one she'd worn when I first knew her. She was many things in many different ways; a clothes horse wasn't one of them.

The groom, by contrast, was a sight to see in the roustabout travelling version of the royal regalia. He wore a chin-to-toe purple gown embroidered in gold thread and seed pearls with scenes of mayhem and slaughter with lace cuffs at the wrists, gold slippers and a magnificent sort-of-hairnet of interwoven gold serpents, with rubies for eyes. He managed to walk all the way down the ten yards of aisle, with a lot of help from his uncle and an enormous man in armour. Then they fetched him a chair with a high back. He was bone-white with pain by the time he sat down, and I made up my mind that my wedding present would be the best Echmen doctor money could buy. She took one look at him and pulled a face that needed no interpretation. He smiled pleasantly in return, having no doubt seen her real expression, in the Sashan sense.

They made me perform the ceremony. All the way through, I felt like the ground was about to swallow me up.

The Great King's wedding breakfast lasts ten days, round-the-clock feasting to which every man, woman and child in the kingdom is invited, though invariably quite a few of them have previous engagements and can't come. Even though this was a bit more hole-and-corner than your typical Sashan royal wedding there are some protocols you just don't mess with, and the interminable banquet is one of them. I didn't stay for it. I had other things I had to attend to.

I was very specific about what I wanted. Ten thousand

lancers, Sashan, volunteers. No more or less; less wouldn't be enough, more would be too many. Sashan, because they were even more fanatical converts than the Echmen. Volunteers; some of them reckoned I had the golden touch and wherever I chose to go must be the next big thing, some of them just liked to fight, but most of them were believers, enough said. Other people's motives aren't my fault. For every two lancers I specified a cavalry horse loaded with supplies like a pack mule. I wanted us to be fast and independent, no shopping, no stopping. The Great King sent home for some maps I wanted, with instructions for the couriers to take a short cut through the mountains and meet us on the way.

The first three weeks were on Sashan roads in Sashan territory. With me I'd taken General Shardana, a loyal and experienced commander who'd really volunteered, in the Sashan sense. He knew all the district and area hierarchy, they knew him, and everything ran like the proverbial well-oiled machine. It was fascinating to watch Sashan administration at work. Everything is governed by plump little blocks of baked clay. They look exactly like meat and onion pasties: same size, rectangular, convex surfaces, golden brown and slightly glazed. When the clay's wet, you write on it with a bit of reed or whittled stick; not letters or characters, but little wedges, with the occasional dot made by the pointed end of the reed, mostly punctuation. You can get a hell of a lot of text onto a mud pie that way, baking overnight makes them pretty much indestructible, they don't tear or smudge, they're waterproof and fireproof, and the material for making them is dirt, literally, cheap and available everywhere a man can sink a spade. Written Shasu is a bitch to learn but once you've got the hang of it, it's a wonderfully flexible and expressive language. You can say things, and therefore by implication think things in Shasu that can't be said, or thought of, in any other language. If the Sashan really are superior to every other form of life on Earth, as they confidently assert, it's because of their language. I've already touched on the Sashan concept of truth. That's just the start of it.

Give you an example. One evening two weeks into the expedition, a young captain came and loomed over me while I was eating lentil porridge. He was too shy to speak – a man nearly seven feet tall, and with all the lean meat on him he'd have easily fed a family of six for a week – so I gave him a reassuring smile and asked what I could do for him.

He opened his mouth and stammered for a bit. There was a real possibility he'd choke himself to death if I didn't do something. "What's that you've got there?" I asked.

That, it turned out, was the Gospel According To Me, translated into Shasu by the bashful giant. It was an awful lot to ask and he wouldn't dream of bothering me with it when I was so busy, but could I possibly see my way to just glancing it at, and maybe even pointing out some of his more catastrophic blunders?

It was that or watch him boil to death inside his own skin, so I said yes, I'd be delighted. He backed away and went off to die of joy, and I started to read. It was what I'd written, pinned and tacked and cobbled together on the scrounged backs of memos in the palace library; but in Shasu it – well, *made sense* is the nearest I can get to it (and me an interpreter, supposedly competent at finding the right words). I don't know; maybe generations of Great Kings had been telling the truth and God really is a Sashan. He certainly appears to think in Shasu. That, and the fact that you can get the whole thing onto a single slab of clay the size of a roof tile, with no scope for rubbing things out and altering them, made me realise I was holding the first ever copy of the Authorised Version. It'd be a sweat and a drag for the faithful having to learn Shasu but the faithful seem to like that sort of thing, perversely enough. And the translation was so much better than the original.

16

General Shardana had been a fighting soldier for thirty years. Then he had a nasty fall from a horse and broke his leg, so the Great King put him in charge of Intelligence. His leg was better now (really) so he could ride without too much agonising pain, and he was the man I needed to talk to. So he volunteered.

Yes, General Shardana told me on the third evening out, he'd tried to get as much information as he could about the catastrophe that had wiped out the Robur, but it hadn't been easy. Information had been hard to come by, and what little he'd managed to gather didn't make sense. He was pretty sure that there was a man called Ogus, some savage from some unimportant place a very long way away. Somehow or other, Ogus had put together a massive coalition of many diverse nations, apparently by sheer force of personality –

Here he looked at me without speaking for a moment, then went on:

– Sheer force of personality, because all they appeared to

have in common was a burning desire to wipe the Robur off the face of the earth. This they'd succeeded in doing, in unbelievably short order. It had helped that sixty per cent of the Robur armed forces were foreign auxiliaries recruited from (as Shardana put it) the slave races. Magnificently trained and superbly equipped, they'd changed sides and slaughtered their blueskin comrades in arms in their beds, and that was the end of the mighty Robur empire. You had it coming, he didn't say. He was a great one for not stating the obvious.

After that, he went on, it got stranger and harder to believe. The entire garrison of the City –

"What's it called, by the way?" he asked. "I'm ashamed to say I don't actually know."

"Excuse me?"

"Your capital city," he said. "What's its name?"

"We call it the City," I said.

"Ah."

The entire garrison of the City had been lured out by a trick and massacred, leaving the place open and defenceless. But – and here was where everything clouded up – it hadn't fallen. Some accounts said that a small but sufficient number of regular troops somehow appeared in the City and organised a defence. Other accounts mentioned some local sports hero called Lysimachus, who rallied the ordinary working people. Anyway, the City didn't fall, and Ogus laid siege to it for a number of years, with no success. Then – and here it got really weird – the population of the City seemed to have slipped out quietly in the night and gone away, led by this character Lysimachus, who then either died or disappeared without trace, depending on who you believe.

"So where did they go?"

He shrugged. "That I couldn't tell you," he said. "I think they didn't want to be found, understandably enough. The last reliable information I had was that most of them died of hunger or plague, and the few that survived sailed off up the top of the Friendly Sea somewhere. We don't have much in the way of intelligence assets in that region, so that's all I know. I've sent my best men to find out what they can, and they'll report back as soon as they've got anything."

"Thank you," I said. "What about Ogus and his army?"

He frowned. "Nobody's seen or heard anything about Ogus himself for a while now," he said. "His empire didn't last long. Large parts of it broke away, either shortly before or shortly after the Robur did their flit and the siege ended, we aren't sure which. Last we heard, the coalition still controls the heart of the old Robur empire, the coastal provinces on the east coast of the Middle and Friendly Seas. But they never seem to have had a fleet to talk of, so they'll have their work cut out keeping any sort of order with only land communications. It's a bit odd that they've been so quiet, but, frankly, we aren't particularly interested. By all accounts they're a rabble of savages, no possible threat to our interests and too far away to be worth conquering. We miss the trade, naturally, but it's no big deal in the grand scheme of things."

I wanted to be angry with him but I couldn't think of a reason why. Besides, he wasn't a believer, which was a good thing as far as I was concerned. "Find out everything you possibly can," I told him. "And where are those maps I sent for? They should have reached us by now."

We made record time, so they assured me, through Sashan territory, but once we were across the border, inevitably we slowed up considerably. It wasn't hostile country exactly, because nobody in their right mind would pick a fight with the Sashan unless they absolutely had to, and we tried not to make nuisances of ourselves, but it wasn't exactly friendly either.

First we came down off the Shordovan Heights, the foot of which marks the frontier, into the densely wooded uplands which the Sashan call the Vincul Forest; what the locals call it, nobody seems to know or care. General Shardana had profound and entirely valid reservations about taking ten thousand lancers through a forest, but we pressed on and came out the other side without any trouble, emerging into a broad valley cut by the Siaxar River. The Siaxar is the longest river in the world. It starts way up north in a mountain range where the snow never melts, and winds down in the creases between lots of other mountains until it comes out into the Friendly Sea. All we had to do was follow it. Piece of cake.

Piece of cake in the Sashan sense. In practice there was more to it than that. There are large stretches of the Siaxar where you can float along comfortably in boats, but there are also large stretches where you can't, and the hundred-odd miles from the Vincul to the Blue Falls is one of the latter. Nor can you ride along the riverbank, because there isn't one; it's all ravines and steep water-cut cliffs. We had to go the long way round, through yet more bloody forests and then out onto rolling uppy-downy expanses of rocky scrub. It was all forest once, but a nation called the Murru or something like that chopped them all down and burned them for charcoal to use in their great cities, not a brick of which has anyone seen for the last two thousand or so years. The Sashan have copies of various treaties they made with the Murru before they died out, thanks to the unlimited longevity of baked clay. Without them, nobody would know they'd ever existed. Their legacy, however, is a major pain in the arse. It was just as well we'd brought the packhorses loaded with supplies or we'd have starved.

Once you're past the Blue Falls the road gets easier and the country is flat and fertile. That makes it worse, because people can live there. They're called the Gorsin, and they don't give a damn. They liked jumping out at us from thickets and spinneys along the roadside, shooting arrows at us and running away; not, as far as I could tell, because they thought we were an invasion, but just for the hell of it. Status in Gorsin society is achieved by martial prowess, and the bravest man is the one with the biggest collection of heads, pickled in vinegar or brine or preserved in honey and proudly displayed in pottery jars on windowsills. Killing them doesn't seem to discourage them, since they believe that if you die in battle you go somewhere nice. Luckily they're not very bright, so if you send scouts ahead to burn off all the spinneys and copses you don't get bothered too much, but that sort of thing takes time. I didn't feel too bad about looting their villages and running off their herds for supplies. Given their mentality, they probably enjoyed it.

On the other side of Gorsin territory the ground rises, then flattens out. Then you're into the Great Salt Plain, a series of arid, broken uplands that stretch as far as the eye can see. The salt flats are actually further east, but it's a miserable place and nobody much lives there. The good thing was that we could make up time; if you enjoy riding fast, it's heaven. The Sashan lancers love that sort of thing. I clung on as best I could and endured.

On the southern edge of the plain we veered east and rejoined the river. Mesembrotia isn't exactly an earthly paradise, but it's a wonderful change after the salt plains. Things actually grow there, and the people aren't ferocious lunatics. We bought food with money, and when we asked them the way they told us. They were glad to see the back of us, but you can't blame them for that.

South of Mesembrotia is the empire of Drazimene. They call it that because a long time ago they were a great nation and ruled everything from the desert down to the sea. Things have changed since then. Their city still stands, but when you ride in through the massive basalt gates, flanked with thirty-foot-high statues of eagle-headed lions, you don't see streets and houses; it's all little fields divided up by neat hedges and the occasional fruit orchard. The Drazimenes had a knack of making themselves unpopular, so the city was more often under siege than not, and as their population dwindled away they knocked down the empty houses, ploughed up the streets and planted barley and oats (they're too high up for wheat). Drazimene City is now a little village about a mile and a half in from the walls, surrounded by barley and turnips. There's still an emperor, but he can't read or write and at harvest time he turns out and lends a hand along with everyone else.

We bought barley flour, pease porridge and oats for the horses from the Drazimene, the biggest injection of foreign exchange they'd had in two generations and probably giving rise to runaway inflation. Then we followed the river south into the territory of the Jasechite Alliance, where Shardana's messengers finally caught up with us, bringing the maps I was so keen to see.

The Jasechites are an odd lot. You can tell as soon as you look at them that they're Echmen stock, and how they got there nobody knows. They stoutly maintain that they've always been there, so I suppose it's possible that the Echmen are descended from Jasechites with itchy feet, but their language is totally different, and if we hadn't brought along a couple of Drazimene interpreters we'd have had no way of communicating. I dare say we wouldn't have missed much. Nobody I talked to had heard anything about a bunch of people who looked like me, or any place called Olbia, which they couldn't pronounce. They weren't happy about letting us march through their country but there was absolutely nothing they could do about it apart from raise all their prices by thirty per cent.

The maps were beautiful, precise and up to date, and none of them showed any such place as Olbia. Ah well.

Down through the Jasechite Alliance and into Cataboea, affectionately known to Robur mariners as the Armpit of the Friendly Sea.

The Cataboeans are all right. They believe some truly weird stuff. They believe that they're the only people on earth, and all the other anthropoid entities they meet are the spirits of the dead. When a Cataboean dies, they load his body onto a door and lay it down on the other side of the frontier, taking great care to keep one foot on their side at all times – the borders are clearly marked with stones, placed three yards apart and painted with limewash twice a year. Outside the white dotted circle is the land of the dead, and anyone coming from there must be a resident. There's no way of persuading them otherwise, though I don't suppose many people have bothered trying. They refuse to set foot (to be accurate, both feet) on alien soil, because anyone who did that would instantly die. A Robur merchant with a sense of humour captured one once and carried him across the line, counted to ten then took him back. The poor devil spent the next hour or so wandering about in a daze, ignored by everyone, then drowned himself in the sea.

Dead men don't need food, so trying to get provisions from the Cataboeans isn't easy. Don't bother talking to them even if you know their language, and nobody does, because why would anyone want to teach a language to the dead? After a number of frustrating attempts at silent barter, during which they just stared past us, we lost our rag with them and helped ourselves. They made no effort to stop us, even though provisions for ten thousand men for a month was a nasty dent in their national economy.

About midday, our second day in Cataboea, we rode over a small hill and found ourselves looking at the sea. The sight of it made me feel like the abducted Cataboean must have felt: a dead man surrounded by the living, painfully out of place. If Olbia was anywhere, it ought to be in Cataboea, close to the mouth of the Siaxar, whose course we'd been following closely. If the colony had retreated into the back country, inevitably they'd have followed the river, just as we'd been doing, because apart from the river there is no fresh water for miles on either side.

"Why have you brought us here, prophet?" a young subaltern asked me, head reverently bowed. "Is this a holy place?"

I wasn't in the mood. "Piss off," I said.

Just when I thought I was never going to drop off to sleep, I had a dream.

It was a new dream, same as the old dream – except that when it got to the Queen of Heaven she wasn't Hodda, she was She Stamps Them Flat, dressed in the full regalia of the Great King and holding a knife. It was the same knife my friend Carloman used to cut me open. Believe me, I'd know that thing anywhere. She looked at me but this time she didn't speak, and a voice came from heaven. It said: this is my beloved wife, with whom I am well pleased. Then she stuck the knife in me and I woke up.

I lay on my back staring at the tent fabric, which I could just make out because the dawn light was starting to glow through the weave, and the oddest thing came into my mind. A snippet of comparative theology, which I'd read in some Echmen commentary on scripture. The Dejauzi Queen of Heaven, it said, was originally a moon goddess, before her aspect as intercessor and intermediary came to dominate the belief systems of the faithful. Well, I remember thinking, with that cockeyed logic you go in for when you've only just woken up, that explains that, then.

What had in fact woken me up was raised voices. The Massani sect believe that human life is God dreaming, and when you wake up, it means that God has fallen asleep. I yawned and rubbed my eyes. For crying out loud, I thought, keep the noise down. I threw some clothes on and went outside.

The noise, I soon realised, was coming from at least two, possibly three Meshtuns. Which was odd, since the Meshtuns live a very long way away and never show up east of Beloisa. I closed in on the source and found about a dozen soldiers in a ring around three thin, battered-looking men in rags, who were demanding to talk to the manager.

Meshtun is easy; it's basically just colonial Vesani with a lisp. "What's the matter?" I asked.

They looked at me and shut up like clams. They were terrified.

"They jumped out at the sentries and started jabbering," explained a hassled-looking young lieutenant. "We can't understand a word of it."

"That's fine," I said, "I can," and the lieutenant nodded and stepped back, mightily relieved. The prophet, of course, has the gift of tongues. He can even understand the birds in the trees and the soft mutterings of worms deep inside the earth.

It wasn't at all fine with the Meshtuns. Something about me clearly bothered them a lot. I've seen happier birds sticking out of the mouths of cats. "Gentlemen," I said. "What seems to be the problem?"

I like the Meshtuns. They're one of those put-upon, kicked-around nations that turn up everywhere and nobody seems to notice, but once upon a time they were great navigators and traders, opening up the first island-hopping trade routes across the Middle Sea. Then the Robur came, and the survivors ended up scattered all over the place, doing odd jobs for rubbish money. They're smart, resourceful, articulate and generous, and they complain about everything all the time. These Meshtuns, however, clearly didn't like me.

"We're not going back," one of them said. "You'll have to kill us first."

A tiny sun rose in the back of my mind. "You don't have to go back," I said. "I promise you on my honour, and I'm in charge here. Back where, exactly?"

They told me all about it. Unfortunately, they insisted on beginning at the beginning. Meshtuns are born narrators and hate leaving anything out.

They were fishermen, they told me, with a sideline in pearls. One day they were pearl-diving off the coast of Lysembatene (which is out west, a very long way away) and they got nabbed by a boatload of Sherden pirates. The Sherden took them to a town on the east coast, about eighty miles south of the City, and sold them to a milkface, claiming they were skilled ship-wrights. It didn't take long for the milkface to find out that they were no such thing, and he sold them on to another milk-face as field hands. They didn't like being field hands much. Luckily they were only about five miles from the coast, so one night they broke out and legged it, found a boat and cast off. There followed a long and harrowing account of five men in an open boat, the long and the short of which was that three surviving men were wrecked by a squall and landed up on a beach. They were just about to thank the Heavenly Twins for their deliverance when it proved to be no such thing. A bunch of blueskins with weapons showed up and dragged them away by their hair –

"Blueskins," I said.

Yes. Sorry, Robur, no disrespect. Anyway, these blueskins set them to work chopping down trees and hauling logs, which they didn't enjoy at all, until eventually they'd had about as much of it as they could take and decided to –

"How many blueskins?" I asked.

Loads of them, they said. Decided to make a run for it, so one dark night –

"How many blueskins? Dozens? Hundreds?"

They didn't honestly know. Could have been hundreds, maybe more. A thousand, for all they knew. Anyway, they ran away and got here and saw soldiers who palpably weren't blueskins, so they decided to claim asylum, only to find –

"Where?"

The man I was talking to looked at me. "You said you wouldn't send us back."

"I won't. It so happens that I'm the ruler of the known world, and I give you my solemn oath that you're free men. But if you show me where to find these blueskins, I'll give each of you a thousand gold nomismata and a city to govern. How about it?"

I took fifty men with me, on foot, since we were going up into the mountains. Sashan lancers don't like walking. They regard it as something of an admission of failure, as if the age-old symbiosis of man and horse had turned out to be a lie. But they were believers, and if the prophet ordained that they should get blisters which turned septic and they all died, so be it.

We were going deeper and deeper into the Cataboean heartland, the main characteristic of which is, the higher up you go, the fewer people you meet. It occurred to me that a whole bunch of foreigners could show up and settle down here and the Cataboeans wouldn't notice them, on account of them being dead. I couldn't stand how slowly the Sashan lancers were walking. I wanted to run.

Not far now, the Meshtuns told me, for the fifth time in as many hours. The lancers, of course, were still in full armour. I'd have told them to take it off and throw it away, but that would be like telling them to cut off their own legs. I was vaguely aware that my feet were killing me, but it didn't really matter, like vague reports of a drought in a faraway country. At the top of a steep rise I saw a thin line of smoke rising straight up in the air. I felt like I'd just swallowed a very big stone.

"Over there," said the Meshtun, pointing at the smoke. "Look, would it be all right if we went back now?"

"Fine," I said.

"And you meant it, about the cities?"

"My word of honour as the messiah," I said. "Scoot."

They scooted. The Sashan had taken advantage of the pause to sit down and start taking their boots off. "Come on," I said. They looked very sad, but they were true believers.

It was no more than half a mile to where the smoke was coming from. As we came down the hill we saw hundreds and hundreds of freshly cut tree stumps, some of them still oozing sap. The first thing a Robur would do in a place like this was chop down trees to make charcoal to forge iron to make weapons. I don't think I ever saw a more beautiful sight in all my life.

We were about a quarter of a mile from the smoke when we came upon people: a dozen or so Cataboeans, chained together, slowly brashing a felled tree. Their backs were bleeding. The second thing a Robur would do in a place like this would be to use his newly forged weapons to enslave the locals. I smiled at them. They didn't see me.

Sure enough, the smoke was coming from a charcoal kiln; the blue smoke that means it's time to close up the vents. I could see men with shovels digging. I tried to call out to them, but my voice didn't work. I couldn't run because the ground was covered in the brash from the felled trees. It was like one of those dreams where what you want is so very close but you can never get there. I wanted to thank God, just as those Meshtuns had done when they got washed up on the beach, but I didn't believe in Him, so how could I?

There was a man, a blueskin, ten yards in front of me. He'd

been kneeling, so I hadn't seen him, and now he stood up. He hadn't seen me. Maybe I was dead, like the Cataboeans believe. I opened my mouth, but I had no idea what to say.

I must've trodden on a stick or something. He looked round and saw me. "Hello," he said, in Robur. "Who the hell are you?"

Take me to your leader, or words to that effect. Sure, he replied, and who are all those soldiers? Never mind about them, they're with me. He gave me a funny look. You'd better talk to the boss, he said.

There was a tent. Rather a fine one; those finely woven textiles came from the mills of the old country. I held my breath. I had no breath to hold. "Hey, boss," he shouted, "you'd better come out here."

The tent flap opened. A man came out. I recognised him. He recognised me.

"You," said my old friend Carloman, with all the hate in the world. Then he pulled a knife and stabbed me.

Two minutes later, there wasn't enough of him left to bury, more a sort of mulch. So ended Carloman, brother of the only woman I ever loved and one of my dearest friends; sort of a pattern there, don't you think?

One of the Sashan lancers saved my life with some pretty nifty pressure-applying and bandaging. I had just enough strength left to stop a general massacre. Then I went to sleep.

I woke up to find I'd started a war. The Sashan had cleared and fortified a defensible space. They'd shooed away the Robur, piled up logs to form a pretty effective redoubt and found a stash of bows and arrows, with which they were able to keep my Robur brothers at bay, barely. The Robur had left enough men to keep them pinned down and withdrawn to gather reinforcements for a frontal assault. Marvellous.

"Let me talk to them," I said, because, of course, none of the Sashan spoke Robur and none of the Robur spoke Apiru, but they said I was too weak and I should just lie there and do nothing while my Robur brothers and my Sashan disciples killed each other. They were right. I was too weak. Life is like that sometimes.

I was reflecting on the irony of it all when I heard shouting in the distance. I'd grown so used to thinking in Apiru that it took me a moment to realise that that was what the shouting was in. One of the lancers who'd been kneeling beside me deep in bloody prayer jumped up and went to see what was going on. He came back to say that the cavalry had arrived, literally.

Later I found out that the Meshtuns, distrustful of the Robur and anxious to make sure nothing came between them and their promised cities, had hurried back to the camp and somehow communicated by signs, gestures and non-verbal nagging that the holy prophet had reached the camp of people who weren't very nice, and they were worried about him. The army saddled up and rode out straight away. It shows what good horsemen the Sashan are; I wouldn't have thought you could've got horses along that trail, but they managed it, and here they were. A miracle, you might say.

Unfortunately, I chose to use this stage in the sequence of events as an opportunity for more sleeping, so I missed all the excitement. When I came round, the first face I saw was General Shardana's. He had a deep cut running from his left eye to the corner of his mouth, and he was grinning; because, it surprised me to discover, he was pleased to see me alive. "We thought you'd had it," he said. "We should have known better, of course. You can't be killed, can you?" I decided not to answer that. "What's happening?"

"We got the blueskins surrounded and they've surrendered," he said, with a certain satisfaction. "We had to kill about a dozen of them, and one of my men's got a bad concussion, but he should be fine. You shouldn't be alive with a hole in you like that, but the quack says you're going to make it."

I glanced down and saw a long line of very near stitches. We'd brought along an Echmen-trained doctor, just for luck. He'd done good work.

("The hardest part," he told me later, "was all those idiots wanting to dip bits of cloth in your blood, for holy relics. I can't operate under those conditions. How anyone could get a knife in that deep without hitting anything important, I really don't know. I couldn't do it, and I'm a surgeon.")

That wasn't the end of the war, not by a long chalk. What we'd captured was only the lumber camp, under the command of the First Citizen, the late Prince Carloman. The rest of the Robur nation, about five thousand of them, were safe inside the palisades of their log city, provisionally named Lysimachea.

As soon as I could move – rather earlier than that according to the quack, who was worried about his beautiful needlework – I had myself carried to the main gate of the stockade. The Robur shot a few arrows at us, but I told the men carrying me that they were safe so long as they were with me, and the idiots believed me. Luckily the Robur were bad shots or not really trying.

The gate opened and a man came out. I recognised him as

one of Carloman's friends. On the day in question he'd had his arm across my windpipe. "You," he said.

"Yes, me."

"Your towelheads killed Carloman."

Towelheads. There are times, believe it or not, when I wonder why I bother. "He tried to kill me," I explained.

"Don't blame him. We should've finished the job back at Scoira Limen."

Suddenly I felt weary. I really didn't want to talk to this idiot. Unfortunately, I was the only man on our side who could speak Robur. I suppose I could've sent for General Shardana to conduct the negotiations and translated for him, but that would've been silly.

"Shut up," I said, "and listen. These Sashan aren't your enemy. They're your friends. They're the advance guard of a great army that has come to drive out Ogus and his savages and restore you to your homeland, so that you can take back everything that was stolen from you. Why anybody would want to do that for a bunch of poisonous shits like you I really couldn't say, but there it is. If you don't want the City back, that's fine, we'll all leave you here and go home. Entirely up to you. Personally, if I never see another black face as long as I live, I'll be overjoyed about it."

He stared at me. "Seriously?"

"No, I'm making the whole thing up. Seriously."

"A great army?"

"Yes. Forty thousand Sashan, eighty thousand Echmen and around sixty thousand Dejauzi if we need them. That's not counting auxiliaries and people to do the laundry."

"Why?"

I felt sleep coming on. "Don't ask," I said, and passed out.

*

By some miracle there was a Robur who could speak Meriot. Meriot is a bit like Tarsi, and there was a Sashan lancer who knew just enough Tarsi to make himself understood. By the time I woke up, General Shardana and two interpreters had reassured the new First Citizen that I was telling the truth. The war was over.

I was too sick to move, they told me. I liked the way they said sick, like I'd caught malaria. What they should have said was, I'd been carved up by my own people too badly to move. But that's me; I like to choose precisely the right words. A hazard of the profession, I guess.

The Robur were in two minds about me. On the one hand, they were thrilled to be going home again, with the entrancing hope that some day soon things would be back as they were before the late unpleasantness, which was exactly how things should be in a properly ordered universe. On the other hand, I was a man of proven bad character and their First Citizen was dead because of my henchmen. Also, I gave every appearance of having thrown in my lot with the Sashan, the Echmen and some savages they'd never even heard of. There was a word for that. Not a nice word, begins with T. As for this religion I'd concocted, they wanted no part of it, even though large chunks of its scripture were either looted word for word or closely paraphrased from orthodox Robur liturgy. No matter. It was blasphemy or idolatry or heresy or all three rolled up into a ball, and it was only the fact that I was taking them home that stopped them from nailing me to the nearest tree.

One of them condescended to talk to me, though, and from him I learned the weird tale of how one Lysimachus, an arena gladiator, had organised the defence of the City, usurped the throne and evacuated the entire population in the nick of time, just as the walls had finally been breached, using large barges fortuitously available for the purpose. Lysimachus had died of dysentery before they reached Olbia, which was probably why things had gone so badly. Admiral Sisinna? Oh, him. He brought them to Olbia in the fleet but shortly afterwards scratched the back of his hand on a thorn, got blood poisoning and died. One damn thing after another, really.

No, they had no idea what had happened back home after they left. Given that the prime objective of Ogus and his savages was to exterminate the Robur race, they'd thought it wise to avoid contact with anyone who might tell Ogus where they were. They'd given no news and received none. Presumably the bastards were still there, in which case they were in for a nasty shock, weren't they?

He also told me that last time anyone counted, the invincible Robur nation now consisted of nine thousand four hundred individuals, slightly more women than men. All the rest were dead. He didn't say it, but I think he blamed me for not getting there earlier.

The question then arose as to how we were going to get home. Practically the entire fleet had brought them to Olbia, together with two hundred enormous barges. But the first winter had been bitter cold and there wasn't much in the way of firewood at the original site, so they'd broken up a lot of the ships for fuel, and shortly afterwards most of the rest of them were blown adrift in a violent storm and smashed to bits on the rocks. No matter, I said; the Sashan had plenty of ships and so had the Echmen. Alternatively, if they didn't fancy waiting for them to arrive, we could go overland, reconquering former Robur provinces along the way. My man went away and took instructions from Theudomer, the new First Citizen, who said he'd wait for the ships. His people, he said, had had enough to contend with recently without dragging all that way across country. The provinces could wait to be liberated until the Robur were back home and settled in. Rough on them, of course, but they'd just have to be patient.

I'd prefer not to dwell on the next few weeks, if it's all right with you. The Robur ignored me, the Sashan fawned on me, even General Shardana, to whom faith had come in a blinding moment of revelation when he saw me weltering in my own blood, like (as he so vividly put it) a duck in raspberry sauce. The more the Sashan fawned on me, the more the Robur shunned me. They were getting decidedly tense about having to feed an extra five hundred hungry mouths. Providing food for nine thousand Robur with nothing except exceptionally deep, rich soil and abundant wild game to work with was a constant headache for First Citizen Theudomer and his ruling council of old army buddies, and we most certainly weren't helping. Meanwhile, I was plagued in my convalescence by an unending stream of earnest young Sashan who just wanted to stand there and gaze, knowing that the sight of me would be enough to wash away their sins and make paradise a dead certainty. I don't know if any special spiritual merit accrued from getting sworn at by the prophet; if so, quite a few Sashan lancers were profoundly blessed. A prophet, says Saloninus, is not without honour, save in his own country. What he said, in spades.

Then the ships came. Before we left, I'd gently hinted to the Great King that it might be nice if he could arrange for the Fifth Fleet to come and loaf about in the safe anchorage at the northern end of the Friendly Sea, and he'd been good enough to oblige. The Fifth Fleet is mostly galleys, monstrous vehicles with five banks of oars one on top of another, plus three enormous square sails. The oarsmen double as marines, and a single galley can accommodate four hundred passengers and a surprising amount of cargo. We got everyone on board with room to spare and didn't have to wait for a favourable wind. We were off.

Admiral Peleshet was a bit concerned about the enemy having a fleet, even though there was no evidence to suggest that such a thing existed. Better safe than sorry, however, so we followed the coast down the eastern shore of the Friendly Sea rather than making a straight dash for the City. What we saw as we cruised along was unexpected, to say the least. Last time any of us had been there, Sashan or Robur, the eastern seaboard was one thriving coastal city after another. Instead, we saw no ships, big or small, no livestock grazing on the hillsides, no crops growing in the fields. When we stopped at harbours big enough to accommodate us we found dense thickets of brambles. Your bramble loves to grow in ash and climb over tumbledown masonry. At some point, somebody or something had made a lot of brambles very happy.

"Thirty-six cities can't just disappear," the admiral said. "They're marked on the map. They should be here."

Eventually one of the Robur condescended to explain. He'd heard that during the latter stages of the siege, Emperor Lysimachus had sent the fleet to sack and burn the enemy's coastal cities, with a view to weakening his resolve and disaffecting his allies. The scale of the initiative hadn't been widely known since it was an active operation and there were security issues. Presumably what we were looking at was the result, in which case the emperor had done a better job than anyone had ever given him credit for.

"But they were Robur cities," Peleshet said. "You burned down your own cities."

"No," the Robur said, offended. "They'd fallen into the hands of the enemy. They were enemy assets. So we destroyed them."

Well, they were the brambles' cities now. We didn't get to take on supplies, but we'd brought plenty from home, so it didn't matter. I couldn't help thinking, though, that in spite of desperate cutthroat competition for the title from practically every nation on earth, the Robur were still, as they'd always been, their own worst enemies.

It's always widely been accepted that the best way to see the City for the first time is from the sea. The classic description is in Teuderic's *Elegiacs*. At first, he says, there's only a blur, a smudge on the flat, blue horizon. Then, as you draw closer, you begin to make out landmarks: the columns of the saints, the blazing gold domes of the temples, the forest of masts in the Great Harbour. If you come in from the landward side, the City doesn't want to know you. The Walls of Florian rear up in front of you like a hand, palm outward – go back, thus far and no further. But if you approach by sea, the harbour is the City's arms thrown wide to receive you and draw you in, so that you're instantly at home.

I hadn't come in by sea before, so I was looking forward to it. There was a risk, Peleshet said, that the enemy might have raised the great bronze chain to block the harbour mouth, but he'd prepared for that. He'd had a specialist crew of engineers working on the problem, and they'd figured out a method using a giant crosscut hacksaw running between two long-boats, while six galleys broadside on provided covering fire from ship-mounted artillery.

There wasn't a chain. Nor were there warships or barges loaded down with enemy soldiers snapping at our throats. There wasn't anything. We rowed into the harbour on a clear, still morning and there was nobody to meet us except seagulls.

And a notice, flaking paint on a weather-beaten board. Nobody could read it, so they lifted me into a boat packed with cushions and rowed me ashore. I could read it just fine. It was in Sherden, the lingua franca of pirates everywhere, and it said: QUARANTINE WARNING. PLAGUE. DO NOT LAND UNTIL FURTHER NOTICE.

We had Echmen doctors with the fleet. Three of them went ashore, swathed in silk gauze from head to foot, and poked around until they found some bodies. Then they wrote us a letter, which was read out to us, because the boat crew couldn't come back on board, not ever.

It was, they said, plague all right; the nastiest possible form of plague, which meant they were staying ashore and we should get the hell out of there as soon as possible. The bodies they'd examined had been dead for over a year, but that didn't matter. This form of plague stayed fresh and virulent for at least eighty years, in some cases up to two hundred. We could forget about the city, us and our children and our children's children. It was one big killing bottle, and the best thing we could do was forget about it entirely.

*

We put a lot of food in a boat, set its sail and pointed it towards the shore. Then we sailed away, back the way we'd come. Nothing else we could do. A pity about that, but there it is.

The Robur insisted on renaming the colony Carloman City, in memory of their martyred founder. For obvious reasons, I wasn't welcome there. Fuck them, I thought, and asked Admiral Peleshet to take me home.

Home: I used the word when I spoke to him, but what did it mean? I'd spoken instinctively, so I guess that deep inside I knew what I meant by it. Take me back to Sashan, or Echmen, or the Dejauzi territories; anywhere but here. Home defined as everywhere on earth except for one place, the place I originally came from.

We sailed in a long loop, taking it easy. At that time of year you can go all the way from the Friendly Sea through the Straits into the Sashan Ocean. I spent the time talking with General Shardana, who believed, and Admiral Peleshet, who originally didn't but was gradually coming around. I didn't try and talk them out of it. They were both extremely intelligent men, educated and well-read, much more so than I was. I kept trying to steer the conversation round to other matters, but with no great success.

The fleet put in at Kurosh, a huge trading city on an estuary. Official estimates put the size of the crowd gathered to greet me at four hundred thousand. They wanted to carry me ashore in a litter but I felt that walking on my own two feet was the least I could do. I managed two hundred yards and then something tore or split. They carried me into the newly consecrated temple and put me down at the feet of my own statue, a vast thing with an outstretched right arm and a beard. I do have a right arm, so it wasn't all that inaccurate.

She sent a trio of excellent Echmen doctors to patch me up. Then she came to see me. "You idiot," she said.

"Hello."

"You couldn't resist showing off."

"Was that what I was doing?"

"Anu wanted to come and see you," she said, "but I told him, don't be so stupid. So he sends his regards."

"That's really sweet of him. Who the hell is Anu?"

Anu, apparently, was the private, or real, name of Shekelesh the Great King. It turned out that she and the king were getting on like a house on fire; probably an apt simile, if you think about it. He's not like anyone I've ever known before, she said. He's calm and quiet, very intelligent, nice sense of humour, he listens when I talk, there's none of that stupid macho bluster, he's not really like a man at all. And his whole attitude to life has changed since he found the true faith. He says he understands now.

I nodded. The Dejauzi Queen of Heaven is essentially a moon goddess, and the Great King is the brother of the Sun and the bridegroom of the Moon. I'd have figured it out a lot earlier if I wasn't so damned stupid.

"Which leaves us with the question of what to do about you," she said.

I looked at her. They'd tied me to the bed to stop me moving until the damage had had a chance to start knitting together. "Do we have to do something about me?" I asked.

"Oh, yes. We can't have you running about pulling any more idiotic stunts and getting yourself killed. So we're sending you to Chrysopolis."

"Where?"

*

I like it here. Say what you like about Hodda, she has a flair for design. I guess it comes from all those years in the theatre, sets and costumes and lighting and all that. She knows what looks convincing, and Chrysopolis will be that, all right. I might even come to believe it myself, in time.

She's building it on a grid system, which I gather is the next big thing in urban planning. All the streets are straight and equally far apart and they cross at right angles, like the ropes in a net. It's all completely wasted on you at ground level, but suppose you're God, looking down. Chrysopolis is being built that way to look good from His perspective. There'll be a temple on every block, apparently, where you can pray and pay money to have your sins forgiven. The idea is for every single one of the faithful to come to Chrysopolis once a year, on pain of damnation. She's as sharp as a knife, that Hodda.

Suppose there's a plan you can't see on the ground, but which makes sense when viewed from the portals of the sunset. Suppose you've lived inside that plan all your life and never actually twigged. When eventually the penny drops, what are you supposed to think?

I can't begin to imagine how much money Hodda's made out of all this, but she's still pissed at me. How could you do such a thing, she says to me every time we meet. How could you *use* me like that? I point out that thanks to me she's now the richest woman in the world, building her own city. That's beside the point, she says. It was an unintended consequence and therefore you get no credit for it.

When the monastery's finished, I shall live there till I die. Meanwhile, I live in a tent, though it's not so bad. Twice a day I recite from the scriptures in front of a sea of adoring faces, and the rest of the day's my own. The library we're assembling here will be the biggest and best in the world, and when it's finished that's where you'll find me, doing what I do second best; reading, researching, gradually putting things together into orders and patterns, figuring a way out of here, a way home. I shall be wasting my time, because the Great Queen, She Stamps Them Flat, has given strict orders that I'm never to be allowed to leave this place. I'll be safe here, she says.

That's a poor translation, because in Robur it can only mean one thing: here I shall not be in danger. In Apiru it's ambiguous. It can mean either I'll be safe from everything else, or everything else will be safe from me.

I can see her point. Still, a man can read a book, can't he? Jot down a few notes, points of interest, that sort of thing. Maybe write his memoirs, or plan for the future.

Occasionally people bring me reports about the Robur. I don't read them. Fuck the lot of them, I say.

Unintended consequences; unintended by who? Saloninus says that the man who attains his goal by that very act transcends it. All I ever wanted to do, since the day I heard the news about Ogus and the Robur, was to get back what had been stolen from us and take my people home. If it turns out that I'm wrong, and that God exists and I am his prophet, the first thing I'll say to him will be: how could you do such a thing? How could you *use* me like that?

He will most likely answer: stop moaning. You're a translator, nothing more or less. Your words and actions; my ideas. You don't have to believe what you say so long as you translate accurately. To which I reply: I'm an interpreter. My job is to take the real meaning and put it into a form that can be understood and acted on. Real, I shan't add, in the Sashan sense. I use words carefully, and between translation and interpretation there's a sliver of difference, as thin as a knife blade. Very thin, but it's amazing the difference a knife can make. All the intended consequences in my life have turned to shit and all the unintended ones have turned to gold. Everything I've touched I've translated, into one thing or the other.

But this conversation will never take place because he doesn't exist. He's not real (except, just possibly, in the Sashan sense). And when I meet him, I intend to tell him that, to his face.

Translator's Note

The Felix manuscript (Fitzwilliam 3776A:42) is written in three languages; pre-Exilic Robur, Echmen and Old Shasu. Most of the dialogue in the first half of the book is in Echmen. The characters used are pre-reform, with a few very ancient archaic types. The first two-thirds of the narrative are mostly in Robur, though one or two of the monologues and digressions are in Echmen. The last third, both narrative and dialogue, is in Shasu.

Over the years, many theories have been proposed to account for this, ranging from Momigliano's unitary interpretation (the book is the work of one author using different languages) to Becker and Chan's multiple authorship theory, which sees Fitzw 3776A:42 as a compilation of three sources redacted some five hundred years after the events described, probably as a literary hoax.

Regarding its value as a historical text, opinions differ. Very few scholars nowadays are prepared to take it at face value, either alone or as part of the so-called alternative history of the period between the fall of the First Robur Empire and the foundation of Carlomanople and the rise of the Second Empire. As historians, we have long since ceased to view history as a catalogue of the deeds of great men. We look for the underlying social and economic factors that truly shape the sequence of events. Narratives such as those attributed to Orhan, Notker and Felix must, therefore, be inherently suspect, and current opinion prefers to see these strange and discordant works as either the apologist self-justifications of the current elite projected backwards in time or mere fictions, designed only to amuse. The facts, after all, are readily available from reliable sources. A coalition of western nations came together to overthrow the Robur empire; Lysimachus, presumably a military officer of some sort, evacuated the City; and Carloman, a distant relation of the old ruling family, founded Carlomanople shortly afterwards. After a shaky start the new colony prospered, the Second Empire was formed and embarked on three hundred years of disastrous war with the Sashan–Echmen alliance, mainly on religious grounds, but with strong underlying economic factors playing their part.

If, as de Weese so ingeniously proposes, the Felix manuscript is a Second Empire forgery intended to discredit the Sashan–Echmen religious establishment, it has to be said that it is a pretty poor one. We would assume that someone setting out to create such a forgery could easily have made a better job of it. In the absence of any more convincing hypothesis, we really have no other option but to let the Felix author speak for himself, in the hope that what he says may be of some small interest.

extras

orbit

meet the author

K. J. PARKER is a pseudonym for Tom Holt. He was born in London in 1961. At Oxford he studied bar billiards, ancient Greek agriculture and the care and feeding of small, temperamental Japanese motorcycle engines. These interests led him, perhaps inevitably, to qualify as a solicitor and immigrate to Somerset, where he specialised in death and taxes for seven years before going straight in 1995. He lives in Chard, Somerset, with his wife and daughter.

Find out more about K. J. Parker and other Orbit authors by registering for the free monthly newsletter at orbitbooks.net.

if you enjoyed
A PRACTICAL GUIDE TO CONQUERING THE WORLD

look out for

BROTHER RED

by

Adrian Selby

From one of the most exciting voices in dark fantasy comes a sweeping story of a soldier on a brutal quest to preserve her kingdom's future.

She was their hope, their martyr, their brother....

Driwna Marghoster, a soldier for the powerful merchant guild known as the Post, is defending her trade caravan from a vicious bandit attack when she discovers a dead body hidden in one of her wagons. Born of the elusive Oskoro people, the body is a rare and priceless find, the center of a tragic tale, and the key to a larger mystery.

355

As she investigates who the body was meant for, Driwna finds herself on a path paved by deceit and corruption... and it will lead her to an evil more powerful than she can possibly imagine.

Chapter 1

The Magist

She's been more brave, more resistant to the torture than any of the humans.

"I'll say his name again. Lorom Haluim."

Behind her stands one of her own people, an Ososi, a giant of their kind. Some of the slaves here hail him as a brother, proclaiming that they have been changed from ordinary humans to immortal Ososi soldiers. Full of pride they show me their glistening brains and the artless ruin they've become under the knives of these drudhas who removed the tops of their skulls and experimented with flowers and roots, poisons and herbs in that quivering, warm clay.

She watches me as all the elderly Ososi have in the time since I have served the Accord, as I take their hands, transmit this shivering dust and let what I taste evolve their pain. They look at me with all the contempt a mortal lifetime confers. "It is just power" speak their eyes. Between her cries of pain she hums a handful of cracked notes, a childhood song, I think, for it is a song I heard also the Oskoro children put into harmonies, the Ososi's distant kin that once lived far across the Sar sea in the Citadels. She sings one note in a minor key here, and I marvel at the depth of the change it makes to the lullaby, a note that remakes the song as though she's sending it backwards to the girl she once was.

Then I catch a word – the dust has unlocked something in her, the name of a river, and hearing it sends a rare shiver of happiness through me. In her delirium, mumbling, chasing a memory that must have followed her song, she has given me a clue to where the rest of her tribe may live. I look up at the giant Ososi behind her, known to all in these lands as Scar. Many years ago he had been capped, the top of his skull removed to leave the braegnloc ready to receive the Flower of Fates. It would have made him the tribe's chief. The work done on his skull had only just been completed when the elders of his tribe learned he was not worthy of the honour of leading them. He carved the skin from their faces, cut their own skulls to pieces and stitched both to cover his head again. He is my finest hunter. He knows of the river this old woman's pain has revealed. I'll join his crew and we will find the children belonging to her tribe. I will hope too for that wisp of disorientation, that lurch in the belly if it's close, the power of another magist, of Lorom Haluim, the one I have been tasked to find, to lead the Accord to.

"Thank you." She frowns, not realising I'm speaking to Scar, ordering her execution. His hands go to her head and chin, a smooth, fast twist breaking her neck.

Scar drags her body past me and out of the tent. We've had some quiet while the drudhas have been spooning out the droop to the prisoners, stupefying them for a while. Many are in persistent agony as a result of our work, the price of progress on any frontier.

A cold wind enters the tent as Scar leaves. This camp is high in the Sathanti Peaks, away from the scrutiny of all but the wretched tribes that live in these heights. The drudhas make good progress for they are working with living slaves that I have provided them. The soldiers they will soon learn to make from these slaves will be more than a match for any army this world could muster. The Lord Yeismic Marghoster has been as generous in the provision of slaves as his word. It took very little to fix the deformities of his younger daughter and his gratitude has been predictably ample. I recall he wept and kissed my feet as she ran about us for the first time in her life. Who alive, after all, has met a magist such as I? Their myths make us out to be gods, understandable given their limitations. His wife, more sensibly, screamed, a horrified suspicion on her. For some time she thought it must have been a trick, some potion that would wear off. I wish I could feel as these people do; their mortality generates such heat.

As I ate and nodded where required at a feast to celebrate the miracle of her straightened bones, Marghoster shared his fears for the prospects of his oldest daughter, a potential marriage to the heir to the throne of Farlsgrad, young Prince Moryc Hildmir. As I told him how little the Hildmirs would soon matter I felt his wife next to me grow more disturbed by my proximity, shifting in her seat, sweating. Yeismic would not have approved of some of her thoughts. She suffered the memories that come unbidden while in proximity to a magist for two whole courses of our dinner before excusing herself, tears streaming from her eyes. We agreed that the joy of seeing a crippled child cured could be overwhelming to a woman's more sensitive disposition.

Scar returns, giving a short grunt as he forces his huge frame through the flap of the tent. He stands once more, silent, eyes following me as I wipe the Ososi woman's piss off the only chair here.

"I don't like this place. I wish I could return home." I don't expect a reply but I need, sometimes, to say it out loud. I unstopper the wine flask and pour a cup. Taste is the second most interesting thing about taking the form of a human.

"I hope we'll find those escaped Oskoro with that old woman's tribe." Scar remains silent, watches me drink. I see a subtle shift in his eyes, a tenth of a smirk, a mote of annoyance. We had tried to capture or kill the Oskoro that lived across the sea in Citadel

Hillfast. Bigger than the Ososi, an older race, all of their kind are as dangerous as Scar, and their chief, the Master of Flowers, far more so. With Scar's crew we butchered all the Oskoro we could find, for they could not withstand me. They cried out for Lorom Haluim, even his master, Sillindar, one that I dared not hope would appear. Sillindar is the Accord's great enemy and the reason for my search for Haluim, who has made his home on this world. I quelled as many Oskoro as I could, my dust taking their strength so they could be tied up. But a handful of them saw their chance, aided by the Master of Flowers, drawing in and killing two of our mercenaries, wounding even Scar. The Master, a drudha and five others fled. Worse was still to come, for as we threw lime bombs into the houses that remained, one of the women came out holding a great prize in her arm, a baby girl, her skull newly cut, the skin sewn back and a seed in her skull – clearly marking her as their future leader, the next Master of Flowers. Her mother saw us, saw me and raised a knife. I raised my arms up, a supplicating gesture, waving to instruct my men to stay back. In the sudden stillness, all of us focused on the child, I felt it, like a gossamer skin on every particle of air and tree, flower and body. Sillindar. Sillindar was here not many years past, within the life span of the woman before us. Then she brought the knife down. The baby didn't make a sound. I threw forward my arms, the dust of creation from my hands, a moment too late. The air spun savagely, my thought made material, a force to tear the knife from her fingers. But she'd stabbed herself in the gut, the force I'd applied pulling the knife up through her stomach instead of into the air. She fell to her knees gasping, letting her baby fall to the ground. Scar rushed forwards to it, kicking her back. He took the baby up in an arm while the other reached for a pouch, a salve that hissed hot on the tiny body. He hummed and shushed her as he did so. I ran to them, smoothing my dust over the hole in her chest but she was already dead. Reversing death is beyond me. I attempted it nevertheless. I always do.

The wind scuffs and kicks at the tent flap. I stand and take a fur from the desk nearby. Scar remains still. He's elsewhere, eyes vacant.

"You'll leave tomorrow. Tell your soldiers. I will return to Farls-grad's capital, Autumn's Gate. The High Red, Yblas, has returned from the Old Kingdoms. I must be at his administrator's side."

Chapter 2

Driwna

I look over at Cal as we ride at the head of the caravan, my best friend in all the world. He's started singing an old ballad I taught him, "At The Willow", and looks over at me with a wink, for my mun would sing it when I was a child, a song from my homeland that we were cast out of.

"You go well together, Driwna, you and Cal. You're quiet, he's always singing. He's going to sing me to sleep in my furs tonight, in't you Cal?"

Leis this is, on the lead wagon, poking her tongue out of the gap where she used to have front teeth so she can lick her lips.

"He could slide it in there without you moving your jaws, Leis," shouts one of the crew further back.

"Sure he could. Long as he sings me "Away To The Corn" I'll go down easy."

Cal's singing breaks up at this, he's laughing.

A horse canters up behind us, its rider, my captain, clears his throat. "Driwna, it's getting late, ride on with Cal and find us a spot we can pull the wagons around."

Garn this is, Vanguard, as the captain of a caravan's called. He runs the Post's sheds in Lindur as well, the settlement I've called home these last few summers. He's easy to respect, old man been in the field some ten years, lost an arm, but as reds guarding the lots on vans such as this that's far from a steep price for the coin he's made.

"Yes, Vanguard," I say. "I've seen some whitebark up on the slopes; we should do some cutting once we're settled. Laurel might like this earth and all; I'll scout for it." Laurel and whitebark are always welcome in our fieldbelts; they grind well for "scabbard sauce", the poisons our blades soak in.

"Good idea, Driwna. Not seen much but the firs. Head off with Cal while the wagons are rounded off and there's still some light; you're our best sniffers for plant."

"Let's go then, Driw, I'm keen for a few pipes tonight." Cal this is.

Trail's been cut and shored up now we're nearing Lindur, a blessing as we've been making good ground and looking forward to getting back to our sheds there in a few days. Border with the Roan Province has been quiet, must have had a purge on as we heard they were losing vans on Cruck's Road. Did fuck all about our vans getting taken, mind, but it was crossroads coin for this van, meaning we were paid the same purse as those on runs that were a risk to their lives. This run didn't look to be taking us through bandit country, but I couldn't pass that kind of coin up anyway with the shit my pa's been in at the kurch. Long story.

Clouds are coming in, air's got a lick of ice to it as I nudge my horse into the yampa and sedgegrass. I turn to look back at Cal riding after me. He's away in the clouds, humming and taking in the view.

"Beautiful as it all is here," I say, "I need your eyes between the yampa around us and the stands of pine we're heading into. You see any dung or hoof from horses, I need to know."

"Sorry, Driw." He stops his humming.

"Are you going to put her out of her misery and fuck Leis before we tally up at Lindur?" I ask. He smiles, knows I'm fluffing him.

"She's a bit thin for me. It's like she's been chipped out of flint and her colour doesn't help. It's turning us all from whatever colour we've had to this cold grey, this fightbrew they've been training us on. We look like we're dead already. You know I need a bit more than a handful in the furs anyway."

"I do."

I'll say it now, upfront. I wanted a go at his handful, years back at Epny, and he wanted a go at mine, not long after we became friends at the academy there. He's a beautiful man, with a smile that fills his big brown eyes and brings the sun out. I was mad to kiss him first time I saw him. There were a few of us had a bet on getting in his leggings, for along with his look he was the son of a wild and disgraced Rulger, noble blood, while his singing could put a dog in season. Back then, same as now, I had bad blood with my pa, for the Rulgers had fucked my family as immigrants on their land long after the Marghosters had betrayed us out of our own. Well, we got mashed one night, too many cups and kannab, and I fancied I'd do something I knew would upset Pa. So I got into Cal's furs and after some kissing where I bit his tongue and his elbow smacked me good in the nose as he tried to get up on me and collapsed, there came a sort of stillness with the moment when he finally got it in. We looked at each other properly, clearly. You don't look at someone that sort of clearly when you're body's rising to it and we both felt it. I remember we smiled at the same time, shrugged at the same time and laughed all the more for how we matched those gestures. It wasn't what we really wanted from each other. We held each other till we fell asleep, him telling me how lucky he was to have met me. Me the same. We've been on the same crews ever since.

We use sign lingo while scouting, talking with our hands as we nudge the horses through a few rare oaks. Beyond them there's a bit of a rise in the land that'd give us a decent lookout. We dismount to check it a bit more closely, sniff the air.

This looks right, Cal signs.

I shiver then, put my hand up to still his moving about. I flick my head over to our left, roughly in the direction we'd come from. I hear the low whoop of a grey grouse's mating call. I tap my finger in the air in time with the whooping, to single out the sound for him. He nods.

It's not mating season, I sign.

Fuck.

Mount casual, turn, juice eyes in cover of trees.

The juice'd sharpen our eyes fierce, help us to pick out who might be thinking of an ambush. I follow him, try to flatten off my breathing. It's cold, they'll see me blow and know we've cracked them.

As we walk the horses into the oaks we get our bilberry thumb-bags out and squeeze juice into our eyes. I grit my teeth with the pain of it, listening best I can while my eyes burn. Other calls I hear then, the grouse again, brown robins but not sweet or clear enough, mouthpieces not up to the mimicry. They're between us and where the wagons would be.

We kick the horses to a canter.

Dayers, signs Cal, meaning the mix that gives you a touch of the strength and speed a full fightbrew can give without paying the awful price after.

Agree. We take a slug. A sword rings in the distance, at the van. We kick up to a gallop, my heart thumping and I feel sick. Now the juice has got in and the itching's worn itself down a bit I see them, bandits it must be, moving through the pines near the van. Horn blows as they're spotted, but there won't be anyone on a full brew and no time to flatten one and get up on it. I hope to Sillindar that these are bandits too poor to have a real brew. Cal rattles his sword in its scabbard to freshen the sauce before pulling the blade free. I do the same and we ride in. Our vanners have been caught cold really, bandits chose a good time after a long day and no guard or defences set. I can hear Garn, our Vanguard; he's calling in Farlsgrad field lingo for the crew to gather up and push to the trees, towards our coming, for he's rightly assumed we've got wind of the fighting. It's dusk though, and hard to see what's going on. Cal gallops away right to run down two that are trying to put arrows into those of our van who are crouching among the wagons. The wagon-horses are stamping and neighing in fear and two break right, taking their wagon off along the path. One's been hit with an arrow to the gaskin; he's frenzied. Garn's near the head of the van where I'm riding in at. He sees me.

"They're brewed, Driw! Get Cal, get to Lindur, there's no hope! It's over!"

"Get on, Garn!"

"Not the Vanguard's purse, Driw, you know that." He's taking mouthfuls of a full fightbrew. It's a stupid thing to do without being able to prep himself for it, but he's going to die anyway. I can hardly believe what he's saying, the last time I'll see him and it's come now, out of nothing. But now I've closed on the wagons I see the massacre. Garn's horse is dead. The van is fucked. I can't see one of our crew alive. The shouting and screeching is of a victory, not a fight. I see one of the bandits leap high and far from a wagon and run for Garn then; he's hot with his brew, fast and savage as a wolf.

"Garn! To me! Please!" But I know he won't.

"Get Cal, girl, you're not dying here!" He hasn't looked back as he's said it. He's standing ready with his two-hander as the bandit runs at him, frighteningly quick on a brew. I look for Cal. He's off his horse, against a tree. He looks to me for sight as I can see past the tree he's behind. No one. He must have killed one or both of the archers. I ride for him.

Garn dies shortly, as anyone would without being risen on a brew to match the soldier they face.

Cal breaks from the trees and runs towards me. The bandit that's killed Garn comes charging after us. I don't trust I'll get an arrow off so I keep for Cal. Two more bandits burst out of the trees behind him. They're closing. Cal's laughing, the mad fucker. He gets like that when death's about. I can't lose him.

"Drop right!" I shout. He knows. I'm grateful for my horse, Anilly; she's calm as a cow as she heads at him. He leaps out of my way as I whip past him, and the two chasing him, only fifteen yards from him then, see too late what I've done as Anilly hammers into the first of them and my sword's out and I swing at the other as he tries to fall out of my way. I've done enough to buy us time. I lead Anilly about, kick up back to Cal, who's standing, sword out as Garn's killer closes. He won't make it. Cal gets my arm, swings up and behind me and we're away up the trail as horns of triumph sound, the van lost.

if you enjoyed
A PRACTICAL GUIDE TO CONQUERING THE WORLD

look out for

ENGINES OF EMPIRE
Book One of The Age of Uprising

by

R. S. Ford

Engines of Empire *is the unmissable start to a new epic fantasy trilogy—a tale of clashing Guilds, magic-fueled machines, intrigue and revolution, and the one family that stands between an empire's salvation and destruction.*

The nation of Torwyn is run on the power of industry, and industry is run by the Guilds. Chief among them are the Hawkspurs, and their responsibility is to keep the gears of the

*empire turning. It's exactly why matriarch Rosomon Hawkspur
sends each of her heirs to the far reaches of the nation.*

*Conall, the eldest son, is sent to the distant frontier to earn his
stripes in the military. It is here that he faces a threat he never
could have seen coming: the first rumblings of revolution.*

*Tyreta's sorcerous connection to the magical resource of pyrestone,
which fuels the empire's machines, makes her a perfect heir—in
theory. While Tyreta hopes that she might shirk her responsibilities
during her journey to one of Torwyn's most important pyrestone
mines, she instead finds the dark horrors of industry that the
empire would prefer to keep hidden.*

*The youngest, Fulren, is a talented artificer and finds himself
acting as consort to a foreign emissary. Soon after, he is framed for
a crime he never committed. A crime that could start a war.*

*As each of the Hawkspurs grapple with the many threats
that face the nation within and without, they must finally
prove themselves worthy—or their empire will fall apart.*

PROLOGUE

Courage. That ever-elusive virtue. Willet had once been told
a man could never possess true courage without first knowing
true fear. If that was so, he must be the bravest man in all Torwyn, as fear gnawed at him like a starving hound, cracking his
bones and licking at the marrow.

He knew this was not courage. More likely it was madness, but then only the mad would have walked so readily into the Drift. It was a thousand miles of wasteland cut through the midst of an entire continent, leaving a scar from the Dolur Peaks in the north to the Ungulf Sea on the southern coast. A scar that would never heal. The remnant of an ancient war, and a stark reminder that sorcery was the unholiest of sins.

Willet glanced over his shoulder, squinting against the midday sun toward Fort Karvan as it loomed on the distant ridge like a grim sentinel. Had there ever been built a more forbidding bastion of stone and iron?

Five vast fortresses lined the border between Torwyn and the Drift, each one garrisoned by a different Armiger Battalion, the last line of defence against the raiding tribes and twisted beasts of the wasteland. Fort Karvan was home to the grim and proud Mantid Battalion, and though Willet hated it with every fibre, he would have given anything to be safe within its walls right now. Instead he was traipsing through the blasted landscape, and the only things to protect him were a drab grey robe and his faith in the Great Wyrms. Well, perhaps not the only things.

"Pick up your feet, Legate Kinloth," Captain Jarrell hissed from the head of the patrol. "If you fall behind, you'll be left behind." The captain scowled from within the open visor of his mantis helm, greying beard reaching over the gorget of his armour.

Willet quickened his pace, sandals padding along the dusty ground. Captain Jarrell was a man whose bite was most definitely worse than his bark, and Willet wasn't sure whether he was more afraid of him or of the denizens of the Drift. The only person he'd ever known with sharper teeth was his own mother, though it was a close-run thing.

By the time he caught up, Willet was short of breath, but he felt some relief as he continued his trek within the sizeable shadow of Jarrell's lieutenant, Terrick. The big man was the only inhabitant of Fort Karvan who'd ever offered Willet so much as the time of day. He was quick to laugh and generous with his mirth, but not today. Terrick's eyes were fixed on the trail ahead, his expression stern as he gripped tight to sword and shield, wary of any danger.

At the head of their patrol, Lethann scouted the way. In contrast to Terrick she was the very definition of mirthless. She wore the tan leather garb of a Talon scout, travelling cloak rendering her almost invisible against the dusty landscape. A splintbow was strapped to her back, a clip of bolts on her hip alongside the long hunting knife. Every now and then she would kneel, searching for sign, following the trail like a hunting dog.

Three other troopers of the Mantid Battalion marched with them but, to his shame, Willet had no idea what they were called. In fairness, each of their faces was concealed beneath the visor of a mantis helm, but even so they were still part of his brood, and he their stalwart priest. Willet was charged with enforcing their faith in the Great Wyrms, and when would they need that more than now, out here in the deadly wilds? How was he to provide sacrament without even knowing their names? It reminded him once again of the impossibility of the task he'd been given.

Since his first day at Fort Karvan, Willet had been ignored and disrespected. The Draconate Ministry had sent him to instil faith in the fort's stout defenders, and Willet had gone about that role with all the zeal his position demanded. It soon became clear no one was going to take him seriously. Over the days and weeks his sermons had been met with indifference at best. At worst outright derision. The disrespect had worsened, rising to a tumult, until the occasion when he had drunk deeply from a waterskin only to find it had been filled with tepid piss when he wasn't looking.

Had Willet been posted at another fort in another part of the Drift, perhaps he would have been received with more enthusiasm. The Corvus at Ravenscrag or the Ursus Battalion at Fort Arbelus would have provided him a much warmer welcome. For the Mantid Battalion, it seemed faith in the Guilds of Torwyn far outweighed faith in the Ministry. But what had he truly expected? It was not the Draconate Ministry that fuelled the nation's commerce. It was not the legates who built artifice and supplied the military with its arms and armour. It was not Willet Kinloth who had brought about the greatest technological advancements in Torwyn's history.

His sudden despondency provoked a groundswell of guilt. As Saphenodon decreed, those who suffer the greatest hardship are due the highest reward. And who was Willet Kinloth to question the wisdom of the Draconate?

"That lookout can't be much farther ahead," Terrick grumbled, to himself as much as to anyone else. It was enough to shake Willet from his malaise, forcing him to concentrate on the job at hand.

They had first spied their quarry four days ago from the battlements of Fort Karvan. The figure had been distant and indistinct, and at first the lookouts had dismissed it as a wanderer, lost in the Drift. When they spotted the lone figure again a second and third day there was only one conclusion—the fort was being watched, which could herald a raid from one of the many marauding bands that dogged the border of Torwyn.

Raiding parties had been harrying the forts along the Drift for centuries. Mostly they were small warbands grown so hungry and desperate they risked their lives to pillage Torwyn's abundant fields and forests. But some were vast armies, disparate tribes gathered together by a warlord powerful enough to threaten the might of the Armiger Battalions. No such armies had risen for over a decade, the last having been quelled with merciless violence by a united front of Guild, Armiger and Ministry. But it still paid to be cautious. If this scout was part of a larger force, it was imperative they be captured and questioned.

The ground sloped ever downward as they followed the trail, and the grim sight of Fort Karvan was soon lost beyond the ridge behind them. Willet stuck close to Terrick, but the hulking trooper provided less and less reassurance the deeper they ventured into the Drift.

Willet's hand toyed with the medallions about his neck, the five charms bringing him little comfort. The sapphire of Vermitrix imparted no peace, the jade of Saphenodon no keen insight. The jet pendant of Ravenothrax did not grant him solace in the face of imminent death, and neither did the solid steel of Ammenodus Rex give him the strength to face this battle. His hand finally caressed the red ruby pendant of Undometh. The Great Wyrm of Vengeance. That was the most useless of all—for who would avenge Willet if he was slain out here? Would Undometh himself come to take vengeance on behalf of a lowly legate? Not likely.

Lethann waved from up ahead. Her hand flashed in a sequence of swift signals before she gestured ahead into a steep valley. Willet had no idea how to decipher the silent message, but the rest of the patrol adopted a tight formation, Captain Jarrell leading his men with an added sense of urgency.

Their route funnelled into a narrow path, bare red rock rising on both sides as they descended into a shallow valley. Here lay the remnants of a civilisation that had died a thousand years before. Relics from the age of the Archmages, before their war and their magics had blasted the continent apart.

Willet stared at the broken and derelict buildings scattered about the valley floor. Alien architecture clawed its way from the earth, the tops of ancient spires lying alongside the weathered corpses of vast statues. He trod carefully in his sandals, as here and there lay broken and rusted weapons, evidence of the battle fought here centuries before. Cadaverous remnants of plate and mail lay half-reclaimed in the dirt, the remains of their wearers long since rotted to dust.

Up ahead, Lethann paused at the threshold of a ruined archway. It was the entrance to a dead temple, its remaining walls standing askew on the valley floor, blocking the way ahead. She knelt, and her hand traced the outline of something in the dust before she turned to Jarrell and nodded.

Terrick and the three other troopers moved up beside their captain as Willet hung back, listening to Jarrell's whispered orders. As one, the troopers spread out, Jarrell leading the way as they moved toward the arch. Lethann unstrapped her splintbow and checked the breech before slotting a clip of bolts into the stock, and the patrol entered the brooding archway.

Willet followed them across the threshold into what had once been the vast atrium of a temple. Jarrell and his men spread out, swords drawn, shields braced in front of them. Lethann lurked at the periphery, aiming her splintbow across the wide-open space. At first Willet didn't notice what had made them so skittish. Then his eyes fell on the lone figure perched on a broken altar at the opposite end of the temple.

She knelt as though in prayer. Her left hand rested on a sheathed greatsword almost as tall as she was, and the other covered her right eye. The left eye was closed as though she were deep in meditation. She wore no armour, but a tight-fitting leather jerkin and leggings covered her from neck to bare feet. Her arms were exposed, and Willet could make out faint traces of the tattoos that wheeled about her bare flesh.

"There's nowhere to run," Jarrell pronounced, voice echoing across the open ground of the temple. "Surrender to us, and we'll see you're treated fairly."

Willet doubted the truth of that, but he still hoped this would end without violence. This woman stood little chance against six opponents.

Slowly she opened her left eye, hand still pressed over the right, and regarded them without emotion. If she was intimidated by the odds against her, she didn't show it.

"You should turn back to your fort," she answered in a thick Maladoran accent. "And run."

Lethann released the safety catch on his splintbow, sighting across the open ground at the kneeling woman. With a sweep of his hand, Jarrell ordered his men to advance.

Terrick was the first to step forward, the brittle earth crunching beneath his boots. Two of the troopers approached from the flanks, closing on the woman's position. Lethann moved along the side of the atrium, barely visible in the shadow of the temple wall.

"I tried," the woman breathed, slowly lowering the hand that covered her eye.

Willet stifled a gasp as he saw a baleful red light where her right eye should have been. Stories of demons and foul sorceries flooded his memory, and his hand shook as it moved to grasp the pendants about his neck.

Terrick was unperturbed, closing on her position with his sword braced atop his shield. When he advanced to within five feet, the woman moved.

With shocking speed she wrenched the greatsword from its sheath and leapt to her feet, blade sweeping the air faster than the eye could comprehend. Terrick halted his advance before toppling back like a statue and landing on his back in the dirt.

Willet let out a gasp as blood pooled from Terrick's neck, turning the sand black. The other two troopers charged in, the first yelling in rage from within his mantis helm, sword raised high. The woman leapt from atop her rocky perch, sword sweeping that mantis helm from the trooper's shoulders. Her dance continued, bare feet sending clouds of dust into the air as she sidestepped a crushing sweep of the next trooper's blade before thrusting the tip of her greatsword into his stomach beneath the breastplate. Willet saw it sprout from his back in a crimson bloom before she wrenched it free, never slowing her momentum, swift as an eagle in flight.

The clacking report of bolts echoed across the temple as Lethann unleashed a salvo from her splintbow. Willet's lips mouthed a litany to Ammenodus Rex as the woman sprinted around the edge of the temple wall, closing the gap on Lethann. Every bolt missed, ricocheting off the decayed rocks as the woman ate up the distance between them at a frightening rate. Lethann fumbled at her belt for a second clip, desperate to reload, but the woman was on her. A brutal hack of the greatsword, and Lethann's body collapsed to the dirt.

"Ammenodus, grant me salvation that I might be delivered from your enemies," Willet whispered, pressing the steel pendant to his lips as he did so. He found himself backing away, sandals scuffing across the dusty floor, as the woman casually strode toward the centre of the atrium. Captain Jarrell and his one remaining trooper moved to flank her, crouching defensively behind their shields.

They circled as she stood impassively between them. For the first time Willet noted the white jewel glowing at the centre of her greatsword's cross-guard. It throbbed with sickly light, mimicking the pulsing red orb sunk within her right eye socket.

This truly was a demon of the most corrupt kind, and Willet's hand fumbled at the pendants about his neck, fingers closing around the one made of jet. "O great Ravenothrax," he mumbled. "The Unvanquished. Convey me to your lair that I might be spared the evil propagated by mine enemies."

In the centre of the atrium, the three fighters paid little heed to Willet's prayers. The last trooper's patience gave out, and with a grunt he darted to attack. Captain Jarrell bellowed at him to "Hold!" but it was too late. The woman's greatsword seemed to move of its own accord, the white jewel flashing hungrily as the blade skewered the eye socket of the trooper's helmet.

Jarrell took the initiative as his last ally died, charging desperately, hacking at the woman before she ducked, spun, twisted in the air and kicked him full in the chest. Willet held his breath, all thought of prayer forgotten as he saw Jarrell lose his footing and fall on his back.

The woman leapt in the air, impossibly high, that greatsword lancing down to impale the centre of Jarrell's prone body, driving through his breastplate like a hammered nail.

It was only then that Willet's knees gave out. He collapsed to the dirt, feeling a tear roll from his eye. The pendants in his fist felt useless as the woman slowly stood and turned toward him.

"Vermitrix, Great Wyrm of Peace, bring me a painless end," he whispered as she drew closer, leaving her demon sword still skewered through Jarrell's chest. "And may Undometh grant me vengeance against this wicked foe."

She stood over him, hand covering that sinister red eye once more. The jewel that sat in the centre of the greatsword's crossguard had dulled to nothing but clear glass, but Willet could still feel its evil from across the atrium.

"Your dragon gods will not save you, little priest," the woman said. Her voice was calm and gentle, as though she were coaxing a child to sleep.

Willet tried to look at her face but couldn't. He tried to speak, but all that came out was a whimper, a mumbled cry for his mother. He could almost have laughed at the irony. Here he was at the end, and for all his pious observance he was crying for a woman who had made his life a misery with her spiteful and poisonous tongue.

"Your mother is not coming either," the woman said. "But the voice is quiet, for now. So you should run, little priest. Before it speaks again."

Somehow Willet rose to his feet, legs trembling like a newborn foal's. He took a tentative step away from the woman, who kept her hand clamped tight over her eye. The white jewel in her sword, still skewered through Jarrell's chest, shone with sudden malevolence. It was enough to set Willet to flight.

He ran, losing a sandal on the rough ground, ignoring the sudden pain in his foot. He would not stop until he was back at the gates of Fort Karvan. Would not slow no matter the ache in his legs nor lack of breath in his lungs. He could not stop. If he did, there would be nothing left for him but the Five Lairs. And he was not ready for them yet.

orbit

Follow us:

/orbitbooksUS

/orbitbooks

/orbitbooks

Join our mailing list
to receive alerts on our
latest releases and deals.

orbitbooks.net

Enter our monthly
giveaway for the chance
to win some epic prizes.

orbitloot.com